To So Few

Struggle

Books by Cap Parlier:

Anod series

The Phoenix Seduction (1995)
Anod's Seduction (2004) [reprint of The Phoenix Seduction]
Anod's Redemption (2004)

Sacrifice (2000)
The Clarity of Hindsight (2016)
Apocalypse Endeavor (2019)

To So Few series

To So Few – In the Beginning (2014)
To So Few – The Prelude (2014)
To So Few – Explosion (2015)
To So Few – The Trial (2016)
To So Few – The Verdict (2017)
To So Few – Frustration (2018)
To So Few – Deflection (2019)
To So Few – Hunter (2020)
To So Few – Struggle (2021)

and with Kevin E. Ready:

TWA 800 - Accident or Incident? (1998)

Coming soon from Cap Parlier, To So Few – Overlord, the tenth book of the To So Few series novel of flight and a warrior's life.

These and other great books available from Saint Gaudens Press
Post Office Box 405
Solvang, CA 93463-0405
URL: http://www.saintgaudenspress.com
Visit Cap Parlier's Web Site at: http://www.parlier.com

To So Few

Struggle

by

Cap Parlier

SAINT GAUDENS PRESS

Phoenix, Arizona & Santa Barbara, California

Saint Gaudens Press
Post Office Box 405
Solvang, CA 93464-0405

Http://www.SaintGaudensPress.com

Saint Gaudens, Saint Gaudens Press
and the Winged Liberty colophon
are trademarks of Saint Gaudens Press

Print edition ISBN: 978-0-943039-59-6
Ebook edition ISBN: 978-0-943039-60-2
Library of Congress Catalog Number - 2021937576

Printed in the United States of America

The TO SO FEW series books are works of fiction. Any reference to real people, objects, events, organizations, or locales is intended only to give the fiction a sense of reality and authenticity. Other names, characters and incidents are the products of the author's imagination and bear no relationship to past events, or persons living or deceased.

Dedication

—

This volume of the To So Few series is dedicated to all of the patriots from the various Allied nations who served in combat during World War II in defense of freedom.

May God bless the immortal souls of all those who served.

—

Acknowledgement

—

John Richard continues his valiant efforts to challenge me to do better and to tell a more compelling story. His interest in history always stimulates me to dig deeper into the extraordinary details I have tried to capture in this series of historical fiction stories. I owe John a debt of profound gratitude that can never be repaid for his critical and constructive review of the manuscript. Thank you so very much, John.

Jeanne remains my steadfast and irreplaceable partner in life. Her support and care sustain my writing. I cannot imagine life without her.

The editors and staff at Saint Gaudens Press continue to amaze me, offering invaluable support and assistance along with incomparable skill and attention to detail.

—

List of Terms

—

As a consequence of complex, evolving, military operations, a consolidated list of operational code names is provided for the reader's benefit. These are terms used throughout this story, and this is not a comprehensive list for the era.

AEF	Allied Expeditionary Force
AF	Allied Forces
AFHQ	Allied Forces Headquarters
ANTHROPOID	SOE operation to assassinate *SS-Obergruppenführer* Reinhard Heydrich [27. May.1942]
ARCADIA	Allied summit conference in Washington, DC (Roosevelt & Churchill) [22.December.1941 – 14.January.1942]
ARGONAUT	Allied summit conference in Washington, DC (Roosevelt & Churchill) [20/25.June.1942]
ATA	Air Transport Auxiliary – British aircraft ferry service
AVALANCHE	Allied Forces amphibious landing at Salerno, Italy [9.September.1943]
BARBAROSSA	Operation Barbarossa (*Unternehmen Barbarossa*) – Nazi German operations plan for the invasion of the Soviet Union (22.June.1941)
BAS	Bainbridge Air Services, Inc. – Drummond's airline company (fictional)
BAYTOWN	Allied amphibious landing on the mainland of Italy at Reggio [3.September.1943]
BC	Bomber Command, Royal Air Force
BEF	British Expeditionary Force
BIGOT	TS-SCI compartment for Operation OVERLORD planning, documents, photographs, surveys, research, intelligence, and support materials
BODYGUARD	Allied umbrella deception operations plan to coordinate all of the related sub-element deception plans
FORTITUDE	Allied deception operation in support of Operation OVERLORD

MINCEMEAT	Allied deception operation using at corpse dressed as a Royal Marine major and carrying fake documents to deceive the Germans in support of Operation HUSKY
QUICKSILVER	Allied deception operation to convince the Germans the fictional First U.S. Army Group (FUSAG) was poised for a cross-Channel invasion centered at the Pas de Calais
BOLERO	Allied operation to move, collect, train and prepare the combat forces for the OVERLORD invasion
Boniface	code word used predominantly by the British to refer to ULTRA Enigma decrypted messages
BRACELET	Allied summit conference in Moscow, USSR (Churchill, Stalin & Harriman) [12/17. August.1942]
BSC	British Security Coordination Office — special liaison office in New York City tasked with coordinating U.S. & British acquisition, intelligence and other functions
CAT	radio beacon used by RAF BC in association with similar beacon known at MOUSE for precise navigation and blind bombing in Germany
CHASTISE	British bombing raid against the Ruhr hydroelectric dams (AKA Dambusters Raid) [17. May.1943]
CIGS	British Chief of the Imperial General Staff (Army)
CinC	Commander in Chief, pronounced 'sink'
CIRCUS	daytime bomber attacks with fighter escorts against short range targets, to occupy enemy fighters and keep them in the area concerned
COI	Coordinator of Information -- the precursor strategic intelligence service of the Office of Strategic Services (OSS)
COSSAC	Chief of Staff, Supreme Allied Command — earlier OVERLORD planning staff, absorbed by SHAEF
DYNAMO	British operation to evacuate the British Expeditionary Force (BEF) from Northeastern France centered at Dunkirk (*Dunkerque*) [May/June.1940]

ETO	European Theater of Operations
EUREKA	Allied summit conference in Tehran, Iran (Roosevelt, Churchill & Stalin for the first time; immediately after the SEXTANT conference) [28. November – 1.December.1943]
GALVANIC	American amphibious operation to capture Tarawa Atoll, Gilbert Islands [20/23.November.1943]
GC&CS	Government Code and Cypher School (AKA Bletchley Park, Station X) [predecessor of British Government Communications Headquarters (GCHQ)]
Gestapo	*Geheime Staatspolizei* (Secret State Police, AKA Gestapo) under the SD and SS
GUNNERSIDE	SOE sabotage mission to destroy heavy water production at Norsk Hydro (Vemork hydroelectric power plant), Telemark, Occupied Norway (27. February.1943)
HMG	His/Her Majesty's Government
HUSKY	Allied Forces amphibious, airborne and glider landings in Southeast Sicily, Italy (9/10.July.1943)
HYDRA	British RAF BC bombing mission against the German Peenemünde Army Research Center (17/18.August.1943)
HYPO	U.S. Navy communications intercept and decryption service in Hawaii Territory
H2S	RAF BC ground mapping radar
KINGPIN	Allied extraction of French General Henri Giraud from occupied France [5. November.1942]
KZ	German contraction for *KonZentrationslager* (Concentration Camp)
MAGIC	TS-SCI compartment for decrypted messages from the Japanese Purple encryption device
Manhattan Project	Allied nuclear weapons development program
MI5	Security Service – British internal security service, roughly equivalent to the American FBI
MI6	Intelligence Service – British Secret Intelligence Service, responsible to collection, analysis, and distribution of foreign intelligence information

MOUSE	radio beacon used by RAF BC in association with similar beacon known at CAT for precise navigation and blind bombing in Germany
MPAA	Motion Picture Association of America
NKGB	*Narodny Komissariat Gosudarstvennoi Bezopasnosti* ([Soviet] People's Commissariat for State Security) responsible for foreign intelligence operations
NKVD	*Narodny Komissariat Vnutrennikh Del* ([Soviet] People's Commissariat for Internal Affairs) responsible for internal security
NSDAP	*NationalSozialistische Deutsche ArbeiterPartei* – National Socialist German Workers Party (AKA Nazi Party)
OBOE	RAF BC radio navigation system for precision blind bombing over Germany
OSRD	Office of Scientific Research and Development
OSS	Office of Strategic Service [predecessor of the Central Intelligence Agency (CIA)]
OVERLORD	Allied Expeditionary Forces (AEF) amphibious, airborne and glider landings in Normandy, France (6.June.1944)
PARAMOUNT	TS-SCI compartment for all classified material associated with the Manhattan Project (fictitious code name)
PFF	RAF Pathfinder Force – precise target marking service for the main bomber force
POINTBLANK	Allied strategic air forces operations to diminish Nazi German fighter operations
PURPLE	TS-SCI compartment for decrypted messages from the Japanese naval code from the JN-25 device
QUADRANT	Allied summit conference in Québec City, Canada (Roosevelt & Churchill; Stalin invited but declined) [17/24.August.1943]
RAE	Royal Aeronautical Establishment – British aviation research organization, roughly equivalent to the aviation segment of NASA
RAF	Royal Air Force

RHUBARB	fighter or fighter-bomber sections, at times of low cloud and poor visibility
RODEO	fighter sweeps over enemy territory
ROUNDUP	notional early planning effort for the invasion of Continental Europe that eventually became Operation OVERLORD
ROVER	armed reconnaissance flights with attacks on opportunity targets
SA	*SturmAbteilung* (Storm Division) – Nazi Party paramilitary unit (AKA storm troops, storm troopers, or Brown Shirts)
SAS	Special Air Service – British special operations service
SD	*SicherheitsDienst* (Security Service) – Nazi Party organization granted state police powers under Hitler regime and the umbrella of the SS; also served as the intelligence service for the SS
SEALION	Operation Sealion (*Unternehmen Seelöwe*) – German operations plan for a cross-Channel invasion of England (1940)
SEXTANT	Allied summit conference in Cairo, Egypt (Roosevelt, Churchill & Chang Kai-Shek; Stalin refused to participate) [23/26.November.1943]
SHAEF	Supreme Headquarters Allied Expeditionary Force
SIGSALY	sophisticated secure voice encryption telephone system (AKA X System, Project X, Ciphony I, and the Green Hornet)
SIS	Secret Intelligence Service (AKA MI6 and the Intelligence Service)
SLAPSTICK	British landing to secure the Italian Navy port of Taranto (9.September.1943)
SOE	Special Operations Executive – secret espionage agency of the Economic Warfare Ministry
SS	*SchutzStaffeln* (protection squads, AKA Black Shirts) – Nazi Party paramilitary organization under Himmler's command
SYMBOL	Allied summit conference in Casablanca, Liberated Morocco (Roosevelt & Churchill; Stalin invited but declined) [14/24.Jaunary.1943]

TIDAL WAVE	Allied strategic bombing campaign against the oil refinery complex at Ploesti, Romania (initial raid: 1.August.1943)
TORCH	Allied Forces amphibious landings at three sites in French Colonial Morocco and Algeria (9.November.1942)
TRIDENT	Allied summit conference in Washington, DC (Roosevelt & Churchill; Stalin invited but declined) [12/25.May.1943]
TS-SCI	Top Secret – Sensitive Compartmented Information
TUBE ALLOYS	British nuclear weapons development program collateral to the Manhattan Project
TWA	Transcontinental & Western Airlines (predecessor to Trans World Airlines)
UPKEEP	hydrostatically fused, spinning, barrel bomb used during Operation CHASTISE
ULTRA	TS-SCI compartment for decrypted messages from the German Enigma device
USAAF	United States Army Air Forces (predecessor of the U.S. Air Force)
USO	United Service Organizations Inc. – American nonprofit-charitable corporation provides live entertainment to members of the U.S. Armed Forces and their families
U.S.A.	United States of America
USA	United States Army
VENGEANCE	American operation to assassinate *Kaigun-gensui* Isoroku Yamamoto [18.April.1943]
WATCHTOWER	Allied amphibious landing on Guadalcanal, Solomon Islands (7.August.1942)
WINDOW	Allied radar countermeasure, specifically designed aluminum covered glass fiber stripes deployed en masse to saturate enemy radar and confused enemy operators; eventually it became known as chaff

Prologue

—

The year 1942, the first full year with the United States of America as a declared ally in the war, proved to be a difficult beginning with mounting defeats and disappointments—the fall of Singapore, the Channel Dash, the Bataan Death March, the Dieppe Raid, and Rommel's *Afrikakorps* marched across North Africa into Egypt. Yes, 1942 did not start as a good year.

However, there were positive signs—the Red Army and the Russian winter stopped the German advance on Moscow, as well as the Doolittle, Bruneval, and St. Nazaire Raids. Perhaps, the most notable victory of the year was the pivotal naval Battle of Midway in the Pacific region. By joint agreement at the ARCADIA Conference in Washington, DC, Operation BOLERO began the build-up of American forces in the United Kingdom for the ultimate invasion of Europe and Germany's defeat. The land campaign in the Pacific region began with Operation WATCHTOWER and the Battle of Guadalcanal. The British 8th Army stopped and then turned the *Afrikakorps* at the decisive 2nd Battle of El Alamein; Rommel never retook the offensive. The first major Allied combined operation of the war began in November 1942, as the Allied Forces executed Operation TORCH in Northwest Africa under the command of Lieutenant General Dwight David 'Ike' Eisenhower, USA [USMA 1915]. The Axis forces of Germany and Italy in North Africa faced a closing vice with the sea to the north, the barren desert to the south, the British 8th Army to the east, and the Allied Forces to the west. The Red Army surrounded the German 6th Army at Stalingrad. The tide of war was changing but not yet turned.

President Franklin Delano Roosevelt served in his unprecedented third term, although the tolls of war were taking a marked effect on his health. The mid-term elections of 1942 reduced his party's share of seats in Congress, but they still held a commanding majority in both chambers. The president used his influence to pass landmark legislation providing a virtual blank check for vital support to the United Kingdom with the Lend-Lease Act's approval in March 1941, nine months before the United States entered the war. The program sustained the British as they stood alone against the Germans. When the Nazi leader turned his country east and invaded the Soviet Union in June 1941, the United States extended Lend-Lease to the Soviets and the Chinese. The personal relationship between Roosevelt and Churchill proved vital to the developing war effort.

Prime Minister Winston Leonard Spencer Churchill, CH, TD, FRS, Member of Parliament for Epping, was in his third year as the leader of Great

Britain and the nation's coalition wartime government. While Churchill utilized his exceptional rhetorical skills to inspire his countrymen to defy the odds against them, he recognized reality. Great Britain needed American industrial capacity to hold on, but they required American armies to defeat the Nazis, or Nawzees as he preferred to call them. Churchill understood the resistance of isolationism that Roosevelt faced and the political risks the president was taking in helping the British people. The two leaders met in August 1941 and signed the Atlantic Charter that committed the two countries to the defeat of fascism and the independence of all people; the agreement signaled the end of the British Empire. Often overlooked but of pivotal and critical importance, Prime Minister Churchill, with the War Cabinet's support, ordered the unilateral transfer of his country's national defense secrets to the United States in what became known as the Tizard Mission during the summer of 1940 that opened an intimate, technical collaboration that lasted throughout the war and beyond. Included in the Tizard Mission transfer was the accumulated research regarding nuclear fission that would contribute to what became the joint Manhattan Project—the extraordinary physics and engineering program to develop the atomic bomb.

As war approached for the United States, President Roosevelt recognized he was missing a strategic intelligence perspective beyond the military intelligence branches. He was expected to make decisions and felt blind in doing so. Roosevelt recalled to national service and tasked his Columbia Law School classmate and Medal of Honor recipient Brigadier General William Joseph 'Bill' Donovan, USA, to form a national intelligence apparatus that became the Office of Strategic Services (OSS). In cooperation with the British Secret Intelligence Service (MI6) and the Special Operations Executive (SOE), the OSS began joint training with the British and Canadians. They started deploying agents behind enemy lines in both the European and Pacific Theaters. Donovan utilized his extensive international contacts to develop the intelligence President Roosevelt needed.

Numerous American citizens defied federal law and volunteered to serve in the British armed services before the United States entered the war. Among those American volunteers, Brian Arthur Drummond left his childhood home in Kansas when he turned 18 years of age, crossed the border into Canada, and joined the Royal Air Force before the war in Europe began. He acquired the callsign 'Hunter' and became an ace fighter pilot during the epic Battle of Britain during the summer of 1940. Brian transferred from his original squadron to No.71 (Eagle) Squadron, the first of three RAF squadrons with American volunteer pilots. Ten months after the United States entered the war, all three American squadrons were transferred to the U.S. 8th Air Force and became the

4th Fighter Group. As soon as Brian became a captain in the U.S. Army Air Forces, he was ordered to temporary duty back in the states to support the First National War Bonds Drive that just concluded before Christmas.

The widow Charlotte Grace Palmer née Tamerlin had been in the right place at the right time when an unconscious RAF pilot descended under a parachute into the large pond on her farm in Hampshire—Standing Oak Farm. She risked her life and nearly drowned, but she managed to save the pilot. As she would learn, the pilot was an American volunteer fighter pilot stationed at RAF Middle Wallop, just north of her farm. For her courage and heroic, selfless rescue, King George VI awarded her the George Cross. The pilot was Brian Drummond. Brian felt the profound attraction to Charlotte before she felt a similar affinity to him, but their relationship evolved. They married two days after Christmas 1940, and their first child, a son Ian Malcolm, came into the world the following June.

Brian's parents had been tragically killed in an automobile accident, and Brian learned for the first time that he had inherited a small empire his parents had quietly accumulated with no sign of pretense or privilege. His holdings included substantial land, several small businesses, and oil and gas extraction wells along with bank accounts to match. Brian's newly acquired wealth was not sufficient to convince him to leave the cockpit, but the money allowed the Drummonds to expand Standing Oak Farm and begin growing crops to support the war effort. A hybrid U.S. government contract helped rapidly develop Bainbridge Air Services (BAS), a fledgling airline operating as a commercial transportation company but surreptitiously moving OSS personnel around North and South America, with a vision of expanding to international destinations including Europe and Africa.

Brian's mentor and flight instructor, Malcolm Bainbridge, perished in a tragic winter aircraft accident, but not before he engaged his Great War Royal Flying Corps comrade to assist Brian in reaching the cockpit of the premier British fighter aircraft, the Supermarine Spitfire. Malcolm's war buddy was now Air Commodore John Henry Randolph Spencer, CMG, DFC, serving as the Operations Officer of No.11 Group covering Southeast England. John was also a nephew of Winston Churchill. John's wife, Mary Elizabeth Ann Spencer née Armstrong, gave birth to their first child, a son named Malcolm Brian, who was two months older than Ian. The Spencers and Drummonds held considerable common ground, including a strong and growing friendship that transcended their service.

Squadron Leader Jonathan Andrew Xavier 'Harness' Kensington had been best friends and mates with Brian since they were together in training before the war began. They served together in the same fighter squadron, No.609

Squadron, during the Battle of Britain. After his latest promotion, Jonathan took command of No.266 Squadron, flying Hawker Typhoon Mk IB fighter-bombers. Jonathan was also an ace fighter pilot and held the distinction of being one of the RAF's designated operational exploitation pilots, having flown all of the captured German aircraft the British held. The Spencers and Drummonds had been Jonathan's guests at his wedding to Linda Kensington née Mason, a woman and friend Brian had known almost as long as the American had known Jonathan.

Wing Commander Lord Jeremy Robert Kenneth 'Mud' Morrison, Esq., had served as their flight instructor during Brian and Jonathan's operational training and remained a close friend of both younger pilots. Jeremy's older brother, 'Bobby' Morrison, was the 8th Duke of Cottingstone. Mud also served a full tour as the commanding officer of No.32 Squadron before he was promoted and assigned as the base commander at RAF Hamble, where he met Air Transport Auxiliary (ATA) Third Officer Marilyn Powell. Marilyn served as an American volunteer pilot who joined the ATA as part of famed aviator 'Jackie' Cochran's contingent of some 30 American female pilots preparing to establish an ATA equivalent in the United States.

Trevor Thomas 'Diamond' Andersen had been serving in the Royal Navy's Intelligence Division since he graduated from Cambridge University, having been personally recruited by Director of Naval Intelligence Vice Admiral Sir Geoffrey Ian 'Jumper' Pike, KCB, DSC. Of particular interest to Sir Geoffrey was Trevor's degree in European history together with his fluency in German, French, Polish, and of course, English. Trevor was instrumental in working with the Polish Secret Service chief in early 1939 to acquire a current service unit of the vaunted German Enigma encryption device. By mutual agreement, Trevor transferred to the newly established Special Operations Executive (SOE) just after the organization was formed. In his new capacity, he supported several significant operations, including the Special Air Service (SAS) attempt to capture or kill German general Rommel, reconnecting with surviving French intelligence assets, and his most recent operation to support the German student resistance group at the University of Munich known as The White Rose—*Die Weiße Rose*.

And so, here begins our story.

———

Chapter 1

If you can't be
with the one you love,
honey,
love the one you're with.
-- Lyrics by Stephen Stills
Credit to musician Billy Preston

Wednesday, 6.January.1943
Bainbridge Ranch
Rural Route 14
Wichita, Sedgwick County, Kansas
United States of America
13:25 hours

The drive out to Bainbridge Ranch gave Brian some peaceful, quiet, alone time to think. The road conditions were less than optimal with a slippery combination of packed and fresh snow. Brian continued to feel an admixture of emotions regarding his return to England. He had been away from the cockpit and Charlotte for better than three months. Brian needed to get back, but the silence of winter on the Great Plains offered a unique calm that did not exist in England. He wanted to return to his Spitfire Mark V, but he was not eager to get shot at again, but that was the job he needed to do.

As usual, Gertrude Bainbridge stood on her porch in the cold air with only a shawl across her shoulders. She was smiling broadly and appeared to be laughing as Brian exited the truck given to him by Gertrude and the Bainbridge Estate.

"What's so funny?" As he shut the truck's door, Brian asked as he walked across the gravel and up the porch steps.

"You look like the boy that left here nearly four years ago," she answered.

Brian gestured to get inside for the warmth of the interior. Once inside and after he closed the door, Brian followed Gerty to the kitchen. "A lot has happened in my life in the last four years," he said.

Gertrude Bainbridge chuckled softly. "You have a way of understatement, my dear Brian. You are married, have a child between you, and you are still a serving fighter pilot. Yes, I would agree; a lot has changed."

"Yeah, that is life in these strange times."

"I saw a picture in the newspaper a few weeks ago, with you in your uniform with that Hollywood actress, made you look so grown up, so sophisticated, so . . . so . . . so regal. But, the caption said, 'Marlene Dietrich with an Army pilot escort.' I found that very odd. You may not be as famous, but you are far more accomplished, my dear Brian."

"That is sweet of you to think so, Gerty."

"I remember that first day you ventured out here on your bicycle, and you just jumped in and started helping Malcolm without any expectation of return or compensation. Malcolm and I were impressed with your energy and sense of commitment from that very first day. He was so proud of you, Brian. He thought of you as his son, as did I. You have always been very special to us, to me."

"As you are to me, Gerty."

"Are you going back to England?"

"Yes."

"When do you leave?"

"I have to report back to my squadron by the 15th. I have a seat on several aircraft being ferried around for different reasons. I leave Wichita on Friday, the 8th, and I expect to arrive at Standing Oak Farm on the afternoon of the 11th, or thereabouts, depending on how successful these ferry flights are."

Gertrude nodded her head. "You said we were going to have a special guest today."

Brian glanced at his wristwatch. "Yeah, he should be arriving any time now. Where is Bobby?"

"He's out at the hanger with Charlie Rogers, making sure the aircraft are ready for our guest."

Bobby Joe Sales had known Brian since 1939 when he flew with then Group Captain, now Air Commodore John Spencer, to evaluate Brian's flying skills before he headed off to join the Royal Air Force the following month. Bobby had known Brian's mentor, now deceased World War I fighter ace Malcolm Bainbridge, since the mid-30s when they both were struggling to make their aviation businesses profitable during the Great Depression. Brian hired Bobby to be the operating director of Bainbridge Air Service (BAS) two years ago. Charles 'Charlie' Rogers had been hired by Gertrude Bainbridge after Malcolm's death to maintain her husband's aircraft. When Brian formed BAS, he hired Charlie, who was now working for Bobby as the company's chief mechanic.

Brian smiled and nodded. "I'd better get out there to see what's going on."

"Should I make some sandwiches?"

"That would be nice and greatly appreciated, Gerty. Thank you. He will have been flying for six hours, so he will probably be hungry."

"Who is he, Brian?"

Brian looked Gerty in the eyes and then smiled at her. "Howard Hughes."

"Damn, Brian! Howard Hughes, the movie producer?"

"Yes. Hughes makes movies . . . and he builds airplanes, among other things."

At Brian's last meeting with Hughes before Christmas the previous year, they discussed their common business interests and talked about their shared love of flying machines. Howard asked Brian to fly Brian's pristine BAS Sopwith F.1 Camel.   By a telephone call a couple of days ago, this day was that opportunity. None other than Director of the Office of Strategic Services (OSS) Brigadier General Bill Donovan had directly asked Hughes to assist in the dramatic expansion of BAS to support the direct government contract for transportation services. Howard Hughes gladly and eagerly accepted the challenge. He committed his controlling interest in Transcontinental & Western Airlines (TWA) to bring BAS up to operational performance as quickly as possible. He also transferred a portion of TWA's purchase orders for the new, fast, four-engine, tripletail, Lockheed Model 049 Constellation to BAS. Hughes also owned and operated Hughes Aircraft Company, RKO Pictures, in addition to his inherited oil field drilling equipment and services business—Hughes Tool Company. Hughes had met with Brian a few times the previous year and continued working directly with Bobby Sales and his growing staff to plan, train, and operate various transport aircraft. BAS began using small aircraft as a commercial airline as a direct cover for moving OSS personnel to various training and readiness sites in North America. The OSS contracts proved rather sporty to fulfill. However, Howard Hughes and TWA's expertise helped achieve smooth operations as the airline grew in size.

"I'm not prepared for someone that important, Brian."

"Gerty, please, he's just a guy. I think you will like him. A few sandwiches and your famous iced tea will be more than sufficient."

"OK. I'm trusting you. I don't want to be embarrassed."

Brian smiled. "You won't. Trust me. I'm going to go check on Bobby and Charlie."

The walk from the house to the hangar in the warmer than usual but still cold, crisp air of winter on the Great Plains proved refreshing. The Sopwith Camel, one of the Jennys, and one of Bobby's FF-1 surplus fighters were already outside and prepared for flight.

The three men greeted each other. They were ready. Brian informed them of their guest's identity. Charlie was surprised by the information, but Bobby was not, having met with Hughes numerous times as they brought BAS into operational status.

The drone of aircraft engines caught their attention first. They walked outside and turned to the approaching sound. Brian was the first to spot the aircraft, descending toward them from the south. He pointed, and the others nodded. It was a twin-engine, twin-tail aircraft. They lost sight of the airplane behind the tree line to the south. The sound continued to increase until the Lockheed L-10E Electra roared across the treetops, dropped to just above the grass airstrip, and then pulled up as they passed the three observers. The Electra banked, climbed, and reduced power to decelerate. They watched the landing gear extend, and the flaps come down. The airplane landed smoothly without even a little bounce. After the aircraft came to a complete stop, it made a half-turn, taxied back to the parked aircraft, and turned into a parking spot on the far side of the FF-1. The engines and propellers stopped. Hughes Tool was prominently painted on the fuselage in large, black block letters.

Brian walked to the left side of the aircraft, just forward of the H-tail. Bobby and Charlie stood behind Brian a few paces. Brian waited for the hatch to open. When the hatch opened, Howard stepped out, waved to Brian, and turned back to the open hatch. Hughes extended his left hand. A curly blond-haired woman dressed in a blue sweater and beige slacks took his hand. She stepped out of the aircraft and stood up straight.

"Damn!" Brian exclaimed. "I didn't expect to see you, Marlene."

Dietrich embraced Brian and kissed him on the lips. "When I heard Howard was going to make this journey, I insisted on coming along." Her distinct German-accented English identified her as much as her appearance.

"And Marlene is a very persuasive person," Howard added. Everyone laughed.

Marlene Dietrich was a popular actress and fervent anti-Nazi. She also was a knowledgeable consultant and occasional agent for the OSS. Marlene met and became familiar with Brian during his assignment to the 1st National War Bonds Drive at the end of last year. She had been impressed by and attracted to Brian's accomplishments in fighting the Nazis. Marlene was also quite familiar with Howard Hughes and Bill Donovan for different reasons. Marlene and Brian had been photographed together by paparazzi numerous times during the War Bonds Drive in various locations and venues.

Brian introduced Marlene to Bobby and Charlie. Howard and Bobby renewed their acquaintance.

"Welcome to Bainbridge Ranch," Brian said. "I imagine y'all could use a relief break."

"Yeah. Six hours is a bit long," Howard added.

"Gertrude, Malcolm's widow, has sandwiches and drinks in the house."

The group walked together to the house. Brian introduced Howard and Marlene to Gerty. The group enjoyed the ham & cheese sandwiches. They laughed and enjoyed the stories regaling Brian's accomplishments. Brian tried to deflect their collective attention to Howard's and Marlene's fame without success.

Howard was the first to display his impatience. They briefed the requested flight, covering their flying procedures and the initial engagement conditions for the air combat maneuvering they would use. Howard would fly the Camel, Brian the Jenny, and Bobby would fly the FF-1 to observe. Marlene considered flying in the backseat of the FF-1 with Bobby, but eventually, she decided to remain on the ground with Gerty. Charlie arranged three chairs and brought blankets from the hangar storage locker for the three ground observers.

Brian gave Howard a quick cockpit checkout on the Camel as well as the aircraft's peculiarities. He crouched on the left-wing root in case Howard had any questions during the engine start process. Charlie swung the wooden, fixed-pitch propeller to start the engine. Once things stabilized, Brian jumped down and jogged to the Jenny, strapped in, and started quickly. Bobby already had the FF-1 running at idle.

As they had briefed, Brian positioned his aircraft behind the left wing of Hughes in the Camel. Bobby would take off after Howard and Brian. Howard gave the gesture for takeoff. Brian acknowledged. Howard smoothly and evenly advanced his throttle and began to roll. Brian followed as Howard's wingman. They lifted into the air nearly together. They dressed for the cold, but their attire was never enough for open cockpit aircraft. The Camel banked right and climbed. Brian followed, glancing over his right shoulder to see the FF-1 airborne and closing on them. They climbed to 5,000 feet.

Brian flew on the opposite side of a wide circle from Bobby and around Howard as he ran through a series of maneuvers to quickly gain a feel for the Sopwith F.1 Camel. When he was ready, Howard signaled. Brian acknowledged the signal and maneuvered to set up the first briefed engagement—a head-on pass initial condition. Howard and Brian flew a series of initial conditions. The Camel had the speed and maneuverability advantage, but Brian had actual combat experience and the tricks he had learned the hard way. Hughes flew exceptionally well and was certainly not a novice, but he could ultimately not make up the difference in level of experience. Howard rocked his wings, signaling he had enough, and they joined up and descended to land. They shut down and turned the aircraft over to Charlie.

"That was fun to watch," Gertie offered. "Reminds me of you and Malcolm back in the day," she added to Brian.

"Yes," Marlene contributed, "even more special when we know the pilots."

"Let's go inside . . . a little warmth would be appreciated," Howard said.

They all walked inside. Gertrude made a fresh pot of coffee, and Marlene laid out cookies Gertie made just this morning. Howard and Bobby had coffee. Marlene and Brian chose hot chocolate. Brian always enjoyed Gertie's cookies, or biscuits as his British brethren call them.

The conversation focused solely on the aviator exchanges about the Sopwith F.1 Camel. The women tolerated the discussion, adding a brief comment here and there when appropriate. Charlie eventually joined them in the kitchen, also in need of hot coffee to warm up. They laughed and joked about everything aviation, including Howard's epic *Hell's Angels* movie ten years ago and the film's extraordinary aerial combat scenes. Howard and Bobby inevitably inserted questions about Brian's experience with the Supermarine Spitfire fighter.

Shadows deepened as dusk approached. Howard excused himself. He wanted to move the Electra to Wichita Municipal Airport for an early morning departure to return to Culver City. Howard needed to get back to Los Angeles for the first flight of the Lockheed Constellation aircraft prototype, scheduled to occur on Saturday, the 9th, from the company's Burbank facility. Bobby made a couple of telephone calls to arrange for hangar space and servicing of the Hughes Tool aircraft for the night and transportation for their two guests into Wichita. They had already booked rooms at the Hotel Lassen downtown. Marlene and Howard thanked Gertrude, Bobby, and Charlie for their hospitality. Brian walked them outside and to the aircraft. Charlie reported on the servicing he had performed and grabbed the fire extinguisher cart for the engine start. Bobby and Gertrude stood back to observe their guests' takeoff.

As Howard opened the boarding hatch, Marlene turned to face Brian. "You will be able to join us for supper," she said in her most seductive, demur, and yet commanding voice.

"At the hotel?"

"Yes. How about eight?" Marlene looked to Howard and then Brian. Both men nodded their agreement. "Then eight it is. See you then, *mein Liebchen*."

Brian smiled. Marlene only switched to her native German among friends. She had faced but seemed unphased by the anti-German mania she encountered in these troubled times. Brian looked at Howard. "As I recall, the Lassen is at Market Avenue and 1st Street downtown, correct?"

Hughes referred to a small slip of paper in his shirt pocket inside his leather aviator's jacket. "Yes, that's correct. See you in a few hours."

Marlene embraced Brian and kissed him in a more than familiar manner. Howard smiled broadly, and the two men shook hands, although Brian noted

Howard casually wiping his hand with his handkerchief as Marlene boarded the aircraft. Brian joined Gertrude and Bobby as they watched both engines start in sequence. Charlie waited for Hughes's signal to remove the wheel chocks and moved the fire extinguisher cart to clear the path for the aircraft. They all waved as the plane taxied to the strip's downwind end and then again as it roared passed and lifted into the air. The aircraft banked initially to the right and then back around to the left. Howard made a very low pass down the strip as fast as he could make the Electra go. They all waved again. Howard climbed and wagged his wings.

As the sound diminished rapidly, Gertrude turned to Brian with an unusually stern expression. "You and Marlene appear to be very friendly, young man."

Brian smiled modestly. "She is a very friendly person."

"Brian Arthur Drummond! I hope and trust you have not betrayed Charlotte." Bobby looked very nervous and uncomfortable, but he did not move.

"Of course not, Gertie. I love and miss Charlotte and Ian. I eagerly await my return to them, even though I must return to the fighting." *If they only knew . . . She is from a different era and wouldn't understand. There is no point in attempting an explanation.*

—

Saturday, 9. January. 1943
Bureau of Engraving and Printing
14th and C Streets, SW
Washington, District of Columbia
United States of America
22:20 hours

President Roosevelt's traveling wheelchair moved smoothly across the ramp and through the various doors of the special armored railroad car known as U.S. Car One. The Secret Service detail pushed him directly to his sleeping compartment, a comparatively small but plush room. Franklin's trusty and loyal valet Arthur Prettyman assisted the president in preparing for bed.

As he settled into his comfortable bed, Roosevelt said, "Thank you, Chief. I don't know what I would do without you."

Chief Steward Officer's Cook 1st Class Arthur Shelton Prettyman, USN, became Roosevelt's personal valet in 1939, after the president's long-time valet had been fired for drinking on the job instead of attending to his duties. Prettyman would eventually retire from the Navy as a chief petty officer. "Thank you so much, Mister President. Sweet dreams." Prettyman switched off the light and closed the door. He would not be far away through the night transit south. A duty armed Secret Service agent would remain posted outside the president's sleeping compartment all night.

U.S. Car One had been presented to President Roosevelt by the Pullman Company on 18.December.1942. In 1928, the famous railroad car company produced six luxury railroad cars and named each car after a famous explorer from history. One of those six cars known as Ferdinand Magellan had been chosen for further conversion to the president's use and became U.S. Car One.

The 140-ton car had been armored with steel plates and bullet-proof glass. The car had also been specifically modified to accommodate the peculiar requirements of the handicapped president. U.S. Car One was always the last car in the train, as it was this night. The train included other regular Pullman cars for the entourage, a dining car, a baggage and equipment car, and a special secure Army Signal Corps car to handle presidential encrypted communications. U.S. Car One lurched forward and soon joined the railroad network routed south.

President Roosevelt was not particularly fond of flying and preferred the train for his travel, thus his choice for the first leg. U.S. Car One would move south from Washington to Miami. They would arrive circa 01:30 on Monday, at Military Junction, Miami, Florida. The itinerary called for the president to board a majestic, chartered, Pan American Boeing Model 314 flying boat known as Dixie Clipper. Roosevelt accepted Harry Hopkins' recommendation to utilize the flying boat for his transit across the Atlantic Ocean to the next summit conference (codenamed SYMBOL) in Casablanca, in newly liberated Morocco. The Dixie Clipper would carry the president across the Caribbean and Northern South America to Brazil, and then, across the South Atlantic Ocean to the British Colony of Gambia. From there, they would board a chartered, TWA DC-4 transport aircraft for the flight to Casablanca. Premier Stalin had been invited to attend as he had for previous conferences. However, yet again, Stalin had declined to make the effort to attend, citing the urgency of the Soviet military situation. Nonetheless, Roosevelt had important business to tend to with Winston Churchill. They were on their way.

———

Monday, 11.January.1943
Standing Oak Farm
Winchester, Hampshire, England
United Kingdom
10:15 hours

When the taxi driver crested the last ridgeline, and Standing Oak Farm blossomed before him, Brian felt tears well up in his eyes. This is home. This feels like home. This is where Charlotte and Ian wait for me to return. "Would you mind stopping for a moment?" he asked.

"As you wish, Mister Drummond?" the driver responded.

Somewhat surprised by the recognition, Brian diverted his attention to the man's face now smiling at him. "Do I know you?"

"I have driven you both ways several times in the last two and a half years, sir. You have changed uniforms."

Brian smiled. "My apologies for not remembering. What is your name if I may ask?"

"Jurdy, sir," he responded, twisted in his seat, and extended his right hand to Brian. "Mortimer Jurdy. You can call me Morty, if you wish."

"Thank you for remembering me."

Jurdy put his right fist to his mouth and chuckled softly. "You are easy to remember, so handsome and accomplished, I must say, sir. You are perhaps the most famous person in or near Winchester. Everyone knows your name."

"That is somewhat embarrassing, Morty."

"Shouldn't be, Captain, is it? Captain Drummond."

"Yes, they transferred all three of the RAF Eagle squadrons to the U.S. 8th Air Force before I left last autumn. Captain it is."

"Yes sir. I picked you up that morning from the farm and delivered you to the rail station. You were still in your RAF uniform . . . flight lieutenant, as I recall."

"I'm sorry I didn't remember."

"You had so much on your mind, I'm certain."

"Yes, indeed. Please give me a minute to stand outside."

Brian did not wait for consent but heard the acknowledgment as he stepped out. He scanned the idyllic scene spread out before him. Brian filled his lungs with fresh air and the scent of the earth. The diminutive figure of Charlotte and Ian appeared at the front door. They both waved. Brian returned the gesture and jumped in the taxi. "They are waiting for me," he announced.

"Then let's get you to them."

"Thanks, Morty."

Brian noted that Jurdy was driving a little faster than he was used to but trusted Morty's skills. By the time Jurdy stopped the taxi in front of the house, and Brian paid him with an added large gratuity, the whole and larger crew had joined Charlotte and Ian. All of them applauded as Brian got out and pulled his bag with him. Charlotte had lifted Ian and handed him to Edith Hanscom, their nanny. He just had time to drop his bag and catch Charlotte as she leaped into his arms, as the taxi pulled away. They whispered their love for each other and their welcome home greeting. She pulled her head off his shoulder several times to kiss him. Charlotte eventually settled back down on the gravel driveway and released her embrace. Brian stepped toward Edith and extended his arms. Hanscom transferred Ian to Brian's waiting arms. His 18-month-old son stared at him with a mixture of wonderment and confusion. Brian kissed Ian on the forehead several times. He looked up. "Great to see you again, Edith."

"Welcome home, Captain Drummond."

"Thank you, Edith, and I think we are past formalities, aren't we?"

"I was taught by my parents to show respect for my employer."

Brian smiled and nodded his head. He stepped to his left, extended his hand, and greeted Charlotte's old farmhands, Lionel Bridges and Horace Morgan. "Where is Jacob?" Brian asked of their youngest farmhand, Jacob Holden, a local teenage boy not yet to conscription age.

"He's in school today," Charlotte answered, jumping in quickly. "He should join us in a few hours. Are you hungry?"

"No. I had a sandwich on the train from London."

Horace, the older of the two, raised his right hand. "We best be getting back to the chores, mum. And I do believe you two have a lot of catching up to do."

"Yes, yes," Charlotte responded. "Quite right. Thank you, gentlemen. We'll join you for the afternoon milking."

Horace and Lionel strolled back to the barn. Edith took Ian into the house. Charlotte moved Brian's bag to the porch. She took Brian's hand and led him down the path to their oak tree.

"It's a little chilly for this, isn't it?"

Charlotte smiled. "I made a few changes while you were gone."

Brian laughed. "Do tell, woman." Charlotte did not answer and just continued walking slowly. He turned to look to the large mature oak tree that had become a symbol of his resurrection and their eventual union. A circle of stone about a foot above the gravel had been constructed. Brian waited until he could see inside the circle at the partially burnt wood and ash. "A fire pit?"

"Yes, my darling. It gets a trifle chilly here in England at this time of year."

Brian chuckled. "Quite so." Brian gathered up a handful of split logs from a modest supply shelter while Charlotte prepared the kindling, and then she retrieved a flint and striker.

They had a modest fire providing comfortable warmth. Brian turned to Charlotte, hugged, and kissed her. "I've missed you so much, and I'm sure glad to be home."

"I knew I couldn't ask you, but are you going back to your squadron?"

"Yes."

Charlotte nodded her head, but her smile evaporated. "How long do I have you this time?"

"I have to check-in at Debden by midnight Thursday." Charlotte nodded her head in acceptance. Brian stood back and placed both his hands on Charlotte's lower abdomen. She exaggerated a frown and shook her head in the negative. "I'm sorry, sweetheart."

"Not to worry. It gives us more of a reason to try again."

"I'm all for that. We can try as much as you wish."

With the fire burning nicely and the warmth verging upon excessive, Charlotte gestured to the bench. "So, tell me about your tour across America," Charlotte said.

"It was an adventure, but mostly it was boring, monotonous, and far too long. I saw cities I had heard about and read about in the newspaper, but I had never seen up close. There were many us from each of the services, including the Coast Guard, along with several dozen celebrities, mostly movie stars."

"Like whom?"

"James Cagney was perhaps the most well-known, but also Fred Astaire and Ginger Rogers, Walter Pidgeon, Jane Wyman, Basil Rathbone, and many others."

"Did you get to meet them all? Are they as glamorous as they seem on the silver screen?"

"Yes, I suppose so . . . well, at least most of them over the whole tour. They were divided into seven groups of a half dozen stars in each group. All of the military personnel made every stop and every event, but the movie stars rotated with at least one group at each stop. I met and got to talk to the author C.S. Forester."

"Horatio Hornblower?"

"Yes, exactly. I loved those stories." Brian also told her about his discussion with Forester and his meetings with Howard Hughes, including flying together in Wichita. He added, "I also met Marlene Dietrich."

"The actress? The German actress?"

"She is an American now. Marlene left Germany and is very anti-Nazi, anti-Hitler. She's even doing work for the OSS."

"OSS?"

"Office of Strategic Services. It's the American equivalent to the Intelligence Service."

"She's a spy?"

"Not full time, but she has done missions for the OSS and the FBI, mostly with Germans in the States legally. She wants to meet you."

"Me?"

"Yes."

"Why?"

"Well, I didn't ask her, but my guess is, she has listened to me talk about you, and you are someone she wants to know better."

Charlotte shifted her position and looked directly at her husband. "It sounds like you are more than acquaintances."

"Yes."

"Intimate?"

"Yes. She is a very persuasive person, as you will notice when you meet her."

"I'll bet she is." Charlotte stared at Brian for several minutes. Brian held her eyes, allowing her to think through how she wished to respond. "Do you love me?" she asked.

"Yes, absolutely . . . without qualification, doubt, or reservation."

Charlotte nodded her head and held Brian's eyes. "Then, I must confess as well."

What the hell? What does that mean? Brian waited patiently.

"Mary and Malcolm came to stay with us for a week, two different times while you were gone."

"Excellent."

"Yes, well, it was a joy watching Ian and Malcolm toddling around the house. It is quite like two little ones just discovering their uniqueness and mobility. Edith tended to both of them as if they were her children. It was fascinating watching the boys play together every day. You might be interested in what Mary told me." Brian gestured for her to continue. "She told me that your seducer Lady Castlerosse committed suicide with an overdose of sleeping pills last month. Apparently, the war dried up her source of potential lovers, and she got crosswise with the law when she tried to pawn her diamonds and jewelry. Anyway, one night on their first visit, Mary and I had too much to drink . . . and . . . well . . . she introduced me to the pleasures of the female body."

Brian smiled. "Are you teasing me?"

Charlotte did not smile and only shook her head in the negative.

Brian stoked the fire to retain the warmth. He turned to her. "We have plenty to talk about, don't we?"

"Yes, we do, Brian."

"Do you love me?"

Charlotte grinned deviously. "Yes, absolutely, without qualification or reservation," Charlotte repeated Brian's response to the same question. "We have time to discuss all this. There are other things we need to talk about, as well."

"Like what?"

"I suppose we should start with the changes. We bought four beautiful Cleveland Bay horses—three mares and one breeding stallion. One of the mares is already pregnant so that we will be able to expand." Brian smiled and nodded his head, not wanting to interrupt Charlotte's stream of consciousness. "We have been forced to conserve petrol. The rationing is changing everything from how we work to what we eat. We have been encouraged by the government to grow a variety of vegetables to support the war effort. The horses will help us plow and furrow the fields. Our Brownfield property has the perfect field with excellent water access from the creek that runs through the land when irrigation is needed. The elevation of the north boundary gives us an easy diversion aqueduct for the water. We will have to modify the plow for the horses, but Horace thinks it is manageable. I'm talking to several women with experience in gardening that I think can help us scale up. The government has offered us contracts to produce corn, green beans, squash, cucumbers, celery, carrots, potatoes . . . as much as we can produce and at a handsome price. They also declared they would buy other produce if we could grow them, like tomatoes. They also wanted lemons and limes, but none of us are confident we can protect the trees from freezing, and even if we could, we are unlikely to yield any fruit in time for the war effort."

Brian waited for Charlotte to continue. When she did not, he said, "Wow! You've been very busy."

"Yes, we have, and we clearly need to hire workers. The men are not available. I'm reluctant to hire more boys like Jacob, although he has been a good and valuable worker. We need full-time employees. That leaves us, women."

"If they want to and can do the work, I see no problem."

"The main obstacle, at least from my perspective, is I want steady, dependable, full-time employees that can stay longer than the war. But more importantly, I've got to figure out what to do with them during winter, when we can't grow anything."

"What about fences, corrals, and other improvements. I'm sure there are house repairs to maintain the buildings at each site."

"That's true. We are also trying to expand our herd of milk cows. We acquired a productive bull that has proved himself worthy."

Brian laughed heartily. "Well, I guess I have my work cut out for me to achieve productive status." They laughed together at the observation.

"Yes, you do, my virile stud." They continued to laugh and poke at each other. Their frivolity subsided when Brian and then Charlotte saw and heard gravel crunching as Edith walked toward them. Sunset had come and gone without them noticing, and evening twilight was rapidly vanishing.

"Excuse me, ma'am and sir. The crew has completed the afternoon milking, and we have a large pan of Lord Woolton's Pie for supper."

"Thank you so much, Edith," Charlotte responded.

"Go ahead. I'll tend to the fire and be right there," Brian added.

Charlotte and Edith walked to the house.

Brian spread the flaming logs and coals. The flames vanished. Brian spread the glowing coals as much as possible and considered dowsing the remaining coals with water from the lake. He decided they were dispersed enough and left them to extinguish on their own. By the time Brian entered the house, Charlotte was sitting at the table, breast-feeding Ian. The others stood around the table. Brian removed and hung up his uniform tunic and hat.

"Please, please," Brian said, gesturing for everyone to sit. They did so. Sitting at the head of the table opposite Charlotte, Edith held the large serving spoon for Brian. He scooped out healthy servings for Edith and Charlotte and then Horace, Lionel, and Jacob. He served himself last. The magnificent aroma of the brown gravy, along with cauliflower, parsnips, carrots, and potatoes, stimulated his appetite. The entire group joked and laughed about life on a farm without one word about the war surrounding them. Brian was silently grateful for the sense of normalcy embodied in the evening meal. Jacob and Brian had seconds. Ian finished and seemed sound asleep in his mother's arms. When they had all finished eating, the men cleared the table and began washing the dishes. The group had devoured the entire pan of food. Edith lifted Ian from Charlotte's arms and took him upstairs to prepare him for his night's sleep.

As the evening concluded, Horace, Lionel, and Jacob conveyed their gratitude for the delicious meal and their appreciation for Brian's return. Charlotte and Brian sat on the couch in front of the fireplace and the modest fire. Edith returned only to announce, "Young master Ian is fast asleep, ma'am. With your permission, I shall retire for the evening."

"Thank you so much for your assistance this evening, Edith. See you in the morning."

"You are most welcome, ma'am. Again, welcome home, Mister Drummond."

"Thank you very much, Edith. Well done."

Edith went upstairs. They heard a door close, presumably to her room. Charlotte snuggled up to Brian and placed her head on his right shoulder.

"It's great to be home," Brian said softly.

"At least for a few days . . . and then, you must head back to the war."

"Yes, my darling, sad but true. Hopefully, we can enjoy the time we have."

They sat in silence, listening to the infrequent crackle of the fire. Eventually, Charlotte whispered, "What do you think of my confession."

"No less than my confession, sweetheart. The important thing is that we both love each other."

"Yes, we do."

"I didn't expect it to happen," Charlotte added.

"Nor did I. It just did."

"Mary is a wonderful and generous woman."

"Yes, she is." They held each other and listened to the fire.

"The Spencers invited us to dinner with the children."

"When?"

"Mary suggested the 7th of February, a Sunday."

"I haven't even checked in yet. I've no idea whether I can get that time off."

"Even if it's only the evening after your squadron is secured, that should be enough. I can handle Ian."

"That should work."

"Mary also told me that John has been or will be knighted by the King. The King's New Year honors awarded him Knight Commander, The Most Distinguished Order of Saint Michael and Saint George. He is also being promoted to air vice-marshal. But he has orders to deploy abroad to North Africa to be the group commander of a newly formed Three Seven Group—all Spitfire fighter squadrons. He is due to deploy in mid-February. So, we may not see John for a while, and Mary thought it would be good to get together, to congratulate him and offer our *bon voyage*."

"Wow! Good for him. Well deserved. I guess that makes it an imperative."

"That was the point. So, if you are able, once you settle back into your squadron, I think it would be an appropriate gesture for us to celebrate with them."

"Agreed."

Charlotte again lapsed into contemplation. Brian pointed at the dwindling fire. Charlotte nodded and sat up to free her husband. Brian added one more split log and stoked the coals. He wanted to keep the fire going without making it too large. Returning to the couch, the two kissed passionately and intertwined.

"Mary told me she and John want another child fairly soon."

"Excellent. Good for them. So do we."

"Yes, we do. They've been trying without success." Brian looked into Charlotte's eyes. "According to Mary, they are convinced they need your help."

Brian tried very hard not to react to Charlotte's words. He studied her eyes. Charlotte's expression did not change. She's serious. "Are you saying what I think you're saying?"

Charlotte's expression again did not change, not even a blink or twitch. "Yes."

"And you are OK with that?"

"They are close friends, Brian. Mary was very sensitive to my feelings. We talked a lot. I think and feel it is what friends do for each other. John has helped you many times, as you've told me and others. I believe it is the least we can do to help them."

"Am I the last to know?"

Charlotte finally broke into a smile. "Yes, my glorious stud. This was all discussed and agreed upon while you were on your jaunt across America, and I didn't think you would have a problem repeating what you gave them two and a half years ago."

"How about we go get some practice time?"

"You're reading my mind." Charlotte stood, grasped his hand, and started toward their bedroom.

Brian pulled up and pointed to the fireplace. She nodded. While Brian spread the coals from the partially burnt log to extinguish the fire, Charlotte switched off the electric lights. They retired to their marital bed and renewed their physical union.

—

Monday, 11.January.1943
Pan American Airways Dixie Clipper
International Pan American Airport
Dinner Key, Miami, Dade County, Florida
United States of America
06:05 hours

"Welcome aboard, Mister President," the aircraft's pilot greeted his famous passenger at the sponson entry hatch.

Pan American Airways Captain Howard M. Cone, Jr., was a lieutenant in the U.S. Naval Reserve and had been flying for PanAm since February 1934. He was an accomplished long-distance pilot and had flown this route numerous times. Unbenownst to the president, PanAm ordered three times the normal stockage of food, beverages, linens and other supplies. Cone had been temporary returned to active duty for this mission.

"Thank you, Captain Cone, and thank you for your service to the nation. I must tell you I'm not a fan of air travel, so please be careful."

"Yes sir. You're not alone. We shall do our best to make the ride as smooth and enjoyable as possible. The forecast weather en route is good. We are ready for takeoff once you are settled."

Cone went to the flight deck to prepare for takeoff. The aircraft stewards and Mister Prettyman maneuvered the president into his first class seat and ensured he was seatbelted in the plush fixed chair. The flights would record numerous firsts in history, not least of which was the first time a U.S. president had flown on an aircraft and the first president to fly across the Atlantic.

The Dinner Key facility allowed docked boarding rather than the common motor launch to a moored aircraft. They were ready in short order. The aircraft engines started—two, three, one, four. Soon, the engines advanced to full power, and the aircraft accelerated down the Bay of Biscay. The thumps of the small waves against the hull increased in frequency and then vanished. As the Dixie Clipper climbed away from the water, it banked left, turning southeast on their flight across the Caribbean Sea to Trinidad and Belém, Brazil. From Belém, the Dixie Clipper would cross the South Atlantic Ocean to the British Colony of Gambia. They expected to arrive in Casablanca on the 14th.

—

Monday, 11.January.1943
No.10 Downing Street
Whitehall, London, England
United Kingdom
15:45 hours

"The flight crew has advised us the weather along the planned route of flight is not within acceptable constraints," announced Duty Private Secretary John Martin as Prime Minister Churchill gathered the last of his planned reading material for the long flight.

"Well, bollocks," Winston protested. "What about a different route?"

"Over France?"

Churchill smiled and then frowned. "Well, that would not work out so well, would it? What about farther into the Atlantic?"

"I thought of that and asked. The Met Office chaps indicated the frontal system is too big to go around."

"We must get to Casablanca for the SYMBOL Conference."

"Captain Vanderkloot has indicated they have a window on the backside of the storm system tomorrow evening. We will get you to RAF Lyneham tomorrow for a planned takeoff at 21:30."

William J. 'Bill' Vanderkloot, Jr., was a former pilot for Transcontinental & Western Airlines (TWA). In June 1941, he became an American civilian volunteer pilot assigned to RAF Ferry Command, specializing in celestial navigation for long-range flights. He made several trans-Atlantic ferry flights before his reputation came to the attention of Chief of the Air Staff Air Chief Marshal Sir Charles Frederick Algernon Portal, GCB, DSO & Bar, MC, in July 1942. A specially modified, newly delivered, Consolidated Model LB-30 Liberator B Mk II aircraft known and marked as 'Commando' was stationed at RAF Lyneham. After in-person interviews with Portal and Churchill, Vanderkloot became the prime minister's designated pilot, and the same American and Canadian handpicked crew joined as the sole crew for Commando. The Vanderkloot crew did not have an assigned navigator since Bill preferred to do his own navigation, and he was very good at it. All of them had significant experience operating the B-24 Liberator.

"What time will that put us in Casablanca?" asked the prime minister.

"About dawn the following day," Martin responded. "I should also add that General Dill is already in Casablanca, so you can complete your requested preparatory meeting with Sir John before the president arrives."

Field Marshal Sir John Greer 'Jack' Dill, GCB, CMG, DSO, had been the chief of the Imperial General Staff before Prime Minister Churchill felt he needed Sir John's acknowledged inter-personal and diplomatic skills as head of the British Staff Mission to the United States in Washington, DC, a newly created position to ensure the utmost coordination and cooperation between the two nations. He was the principal military liaison with the Americans, thus the prime minister's need to confer in advance with Dill for the pending summit conference.

"Where is the president?"

"Our last report indicated he is on schedule and due to arrive Thursday afternoon."

"Very well. Please affirm the schedule change and notify the staff and Sir John."

"I will do so immediately, Mister Prime Minister. I will also notify the household staff that you will be remaining here this evening."

"Thank you, John."

—

Tuesday, 12.January.1943
RAF Lyneham
Lyneham, Wiltshire, England
United Kingdom
21:15 hours

Commando had been modified for long-range VIP transport. The bomb racks had been removed, the bomb bay doors sealed and locked, and a small bed with a mattress installed. Plush seats had been installed beside the sleeping compartment, and the aircraft had a galley for food preparation. The aircraft had typical green and brown mottled camouflage on the sides and top with flat black on the underside surfaces. The airplane also had only RAF roundels and no tail designator letters—only the aircraft number, AL504.

The prime minister had taken the train on the Great Western Railway Line from London-Paddington to Swindon. A limousine was waiting at the rail station and took him directly to the aircraft.

Bill Vanderkloot stood at the after boarding hatch. "Welcome back to Commando, Prime Minister. We are ready to take off as soon as you are safely and securely aboard."

"Tell me about the weather, Bill."

"The Met lads tell us there is a break in the frontal systems. We will have some rough spots just off the coast, but we should have an easy flight once we are through that, although we will have to go a little farther west to avoid the storm's trailing edge before turning south. Unless we encounter some unexpected problems or unforecast weather, we should arrive at Anfa Airport around dawn tomorrow. We expect a squadron of Spitfires to escort us for the last hundred miles into Morocco."

"Take good care of us, Bill. Let's get this caravan on the road."

"Very well, sir. Let's get you settled, and get the motors turning and be on our way."

Churchill went directly to his compartment, took the forward-facing seat at the table, and buckled his seat belt. He stared out the adjacent window to the darkness and paucity of lights as he heard and felt the engines start up and stabilize one by one—all four of them. Soon after all four engines were running smoothly, the aircraft began to taxi. Winston could feel the joints in the pavement as they moved. He continued to gaze out the portal but could only see the passing of concrete underneath them by the diffuse reflected light from the landing lights. The aircraft stopped to complete the run-up and pre-takeoff checks and then turned onto the runway. The engines advanced to takeoff power. A minor jolt marked the release of the wheel brakes and the beginning of their takeoff roll. The aircraft accelerated smoothly and was soon airborne. Churchill watched the main wheels retract. The whirring and gushing sounds delineated the airplane's changing configuration. Within minutes, the sound stabilized to a nice steady moan as they climbed away from RAF Lyneham.

Winston glanced out of the window one last time and saw nothing but the ink-black of night. The entirety of the night would be spent in the air.

He decided to wait for several hours until they were well into the flight plan and probably heading south before visiting the cockpit and the crew. In the meantime, Churchill turned his attention to John Martin and the dispatch box of endless communications. He had his glass of brandy, and someone had turned on the special exhaust fan in his compartment to extract the smoke from his Cuban cigar. The two men jumped into the plethora of correspondence marked for the prime minister's attention.

—

Wednesday, 13.January.1943
59 Königinstraße
München
Deutsches Reich
16:30 hours

Trevor held considerable trepidation as his appointed meeting approached with two principal members of the White Rose, sibling students Hans and Sophie Scholl. Both siblings attended the University of Munich. Agent Diamond was on his fourth penetration of Germany in the SOE effort to connect with and nurture the White Rose resistance group. MI6 and SOE analysts had briefed Trevor before his first mission in October 1941, before the White Rose group solidified. The information was updated with the best available data before every penetration. Diamond's most troubling fact was Hans Scholl's membership and service in the Hitler Youth before entering the university. He had not expected to affect physical, face-to-face contact, but the situation presented two days ago and necessitated the meeting. He believed the risk was worth the potential benefit.

They had agreed to meet at the Scholl's apartment not far from the university campus. Trevor also acknowledged that the risk to them was equally as significant. Diamond held the utmost respect for the Gestapo's effectiveness— *die Geheime Staatspolizei*, the Nazi Secret State Police. The outcome of discovery for them or him was the same—a painful and tortured death. On the other side of the balance equation, the White Rose represented significant potential benefits to the Allied war effort, the Nazis' defeat, and perhaps even a useful intelligence source.

Diamond walked casually but with purpose, using his best tradecraft to appear normal while he continuously evaluated his surroundings and what lay ahead. He walked through the university campus and down *Schackstaße. So far, so good.* He turned the last corner to see the apartment building he had scouted twice since Monday. He looked first left and then right, rather than the other way as he was accustomed to in England, checking for traffic, and then Trevor crossed the street. He carefully assessed the exterior situation. *Still nothing out of place or remotely threatening.* Trevor entered the building as if he lived there and ascended the stairway to the second floor. Standing in front of the door with brass numerals 59, he knocked twice, paused, and knocked twice again, as they had agreed. He heard movement inside but nothing unusual. The door unlocked and opened a crack. The left side of Hans' face appeared. The door opened wider, and Hans gestured for him to enter.

They spoke in the standard High German, although Trevor knew Sophie Scholl was fluent in English and her brother spoke passable English, but heavily accented. Trevor chose to avoid English to maintain his cover with them. "Welcome, Mister Weber."

"Thank you, Hans, and thank you for meeting with me."

Trevor greeted Sophie in the European manner. Sophie offered a chicory-based pseudo-coffee due to the wartime shortages, but Trevor declined. They sat on three chairs around a low rectangular table in front of a coal heater.

"You said you want to talk," Hans said.

"Yes. First, I must acknowledge to both of you that I recognize and respect the risk you face. I face exactly the same risk from a different perspective." Both of them tried to retain a severe and suspicious expression, but a twinge of confusion could be seen in their eyes. "We have discussed the White Rose and some of the extraordinary work the group is doing. I know and acknowledge that you are deeply committed German citizens who care a great deal about the country. Lastly, I shall trust you with my life and place my life in your hands." More confusion appeared on their faces. "Tobias Weber is a cover name. My real name is Robert Johnston. I am a Swiss intelligence officer." Trevor Andersen had used his Johnston alias numerous times in Germany and Poland for earlier missions going back years before the war began. He just could not use his real name. If he was captured and tortured, he was committed to die anonymously. "You are probably asking yourself what is going on here. The answer is, my government wants to help you."

"How can you possibly help us? This is a German problem, not a Swiss issue," Hans responded with a touch of anger.

Trevor held up his left hand, palm out. "I . . . we have no interest in interfering in German politics. Yet, to think National Socialism is only a German problem must be considered rather myopic, it seems to me."

"Why are you here?" Sophie pressed.

"We have watched the passive resistance of the White Rose since your organization coalesced last year. We have been impressed with the content of your leaflets and the passion you convey in your writing. We also note that your efforts are becoming progressively more strident. We would like to help."

"I will repeat my brother's question. How can you possibly help us?"

"We have resources you do not have."

"Like what?" Sophie challenged.

"Before I answer your understandable and appropriate question, I offer a couple of observations for your consideration. We cannot claim to have seen and read all of your leaflets. However, for those we have studied, the words and the image they create are clearly your words and experiences. We encourage you to retain that flavor. If information begins to appear in your writing that a university student group could not possibly have access to without outside sources, you will attract the progressively more intense attention and focus of the Gestapo, and none of us want that kind of attraction. That said, we are prepared to give you whatever you believe best serves your purposes from information to money, to weapons should your movement go that far."

"No weapons!" Hans protested. "We are working against violence, against fighting. We will not add to the violence."

"We understand. I can assure you that we do not want to compromise your position or path. I was only trying to answer Sophie's question."

"As you may well know, we are not alone, and we do not decide such things. We need time to discuss your offer with our colleagues."

Trevor agreed and told them to take the time they needed. He also gave them just enough clandestine tradecraft to signal him without direct contact when they were ready to talk. The potential back-up for possible compromise was also discussed. The Scholl siblings asked questions and repeated back the procedure they would use for the next contact.

Diamond had prepared for this potential. He could remain in Munich indefinitely. Other intelligence collection tasks did not risk exposure or compromise. Trevor could stay productive while he waited, but he would also minimize his public exposure to the best of his ability.

"Thank you for the courtesy of meeting with me. I hope your group will receive our offer with the generosity it was extended. I shall wait for your signal." They shook hands, and Trevor departed with the same care and attention to detail as he arrived. *It would have been better to have a clear answer this evening so that I can leave, but I must deal with what comes.*

—

Friday, 15. January. 1943
Idou Anfa Hotel
85 Boulevard d'Anfa
Anfa, Casablanca
Protectorat français au Maroc
10:00 hours

The combined British and American leadership and joint chiefs of staff gathered and were assembled in the conference room without the associated staff members. General Eisenhower stood next to the large map of the Mediterranean region. President Roosevelt and Prime Minister Churchill sat together directly opposite from the map. The respective chiefs of staff sat opposite each other. The president nodded for Eisenhower to proceed with his briefing.

"Thank you, Mister President, Mister Prime Minister, for the opportunity to brief you on our situation." The general covered the disposition of Allied forces within his sphere of responsibility. He also covered the latest intelligence on the deployment of enemy forces facing them. Questions came from the leaders and the generals. They discussed the communications with the British 8th Army, in the eastern Sahara, as both Allied groups tightened the noose around the vaunted but seriously diminished *Afrikakorps*.

"Thank you for your briefing, General Eisenhower," Roosevelt said. "As you know, this summit conference's primary purpose is the progressive assessment of our strategy to which we jointly agreed a year ago at the ARCADIA Conference in Washington. We further agreed at our ARGONAUT Conference that our first major joint action would be North Africa and Operation TORCH. I will also add on behalf of myself and Prime Minister Churchill that Premier Stalin has been and continues to apply considerable pressure on us to open a second front in Europe." Roosevelt nodded to Churchill.

Churchill added, "The president is quite correct. With Averell Harriman as the president's representative, I met with Premier Stalin at our BRACELET Conference at the Kremlin in Moscow last August. He declared TORCH to be a minimal, almost irrelevant, campaign that would not satisfy their requirement for a second front, to draw off many German divisions in front of them. He wants us to invade Europe yesterday."

Roosevelt again nodded, "Soviet requirements will not drive our strategy. That said, I do believe we all agree that the second front would help the Soviets. However, we also agreed that we would not attempt a cross-Channel invasion until we had assembled overwhelming forces and softened the German defenses in France. Operation BOLERO is proceeding as fast as we can stand up combat forces and transport them to England."

"So far, we are staying ahead of BOLERO in quartering American forces."

"Yes, I believe we would agree."

"We must secure the Mediterranean to free up and transfer our forces from North Africa for ROUNDUP or its equivalent." The code name referred to the cross-Channel, full-on invasion of the European continent. "The key, as we agreed at ARGONAUT, is finishing off the Axis in North Africa." Churchill paused to think for a moment. "If we are to attempt ROUNDUP this year, we must execute the invasion no later than September before the weather window closes, which in turn means we must consolidate North Africa this month or February at the latest. We need a goodly portion of our North Africa forces for ROUNDUP." Churchill looked directly at Eisenhower. "What is your current conclusion estimate?"

"I wish it was clearer or more certain. We would like to conclude our operations by February, but April or May is more realistic based on our present situation."

"That would give us insufficient time to move forces," interjected U.S. Army Chief of Staff General George Catlett Marshall, Jr., USA [VMI 1901]. "What do you need to conclude sooner, to make the February mark?"

Eisenhower did not hesitate. "Ten full-strength armor divisions."

"We don't have them, and neither do the British," Marshall responded. "It would take us the better part of a year to raise, equip, train, and transport ten armored divisions."

"We want to conclude this campaign as soon as possible, but our available forces constrain us," said Ike. "I think the outcome is inevitable, although there is still plenty of bite in the dog. The relevant questions are when and at what cost? I have offered my estimate of when. Our air and naval forces have been quite effective with the supply interdiction task. The *Afrikakorps* has repeatedly notified their higher headquarters that they have been short of fuel and ammunition since November. They have conducted an admirable retreat. Yet, as long as their supplies are choked off, the end is inevitable. We are in close coordination with General Montgomery and the 8th Army. We're likely to link up in South Tunisia next month based on our rate of progress. We still must penetrate the Aurès Mountains—the last geographic obstacle before reaching the coastal plain of Tunisia. The 1st Army is advancing nicely along the coast road toward Bizerte and Tunis. The Second Corps has had slow going through the mountainous terrain of the Tunesian Dorsal. The addition of 37 Group next month will give us more close air support. As the Germans get more desperate, I expect our casualty rate to increase, unless we can bleed them dry for lack of supplies."

The military chiefs erupted into active debate whether sufficient forces and aggressiveness were being applied to the interdiction process. They also debated the options of adding additional naval forces—surface, aviation, and submarine—to the interdiction mission. President Roosevelt and Prime Minister Churchill listened with occasional whispered comments to each other. The aviation chiefs were challenged on the deployment of bombers and fighters to the North African Theater. The intelligence services provided to the operational forces valuable target lists in fairly precise terms. However, the chiefs all agreed there was not enough intelligence. Patrols picked up some Axis logistics ships and aircraft that the intelligence services had not illuminated. They all agreed some supplies were still successfully running the gauntlet.

President Roosevelt raised his right hand, palm out. "This debate has been informative. We can continue, but I'm afraid we are all faced with restrictive constraints. There is a very tangible reason Premier Stalin is clamoring for the second front. He does not have unlimited forces, either. As much as we," Roosevelt looked at and gestured to Churchill, "would like to provide our front-line commanders all the forces they want and need, there are limits we all face. The home forces and industry are working overtime to deliver. As Commander-in-Chief," again, Franklin looked at Winston, "I recognize and acknowledge that you must do the best you can with all that we can provide you. Reality is unavoidable. Now, with the prime minister's consent," Roosevelt glanced at Churchill and received a confirming nod, "before we conclude this session and mindful that General Eisenhower must return to his command, I would like to hear his counsel and recommendation on what should be next." All heads turned back to Eisenhower.

Again, Ike did not hesitate. "When the leadership sanctioned Operation TORCH, we set course through the Mediterranean Theater. The next step or two are logical and perhaps even obvious."

"They are?" Churchill interrupted with impatience in his voice.

"Sicily and Italy."

"Rather than southern or even western France," interjected Marshall.

"Yes. While our strategy remains Germany first, eliminating Italy as a threat in the Mediterranean would essentially secure the region and free up forces for continental operations. Further, the OSS suggests we may be able to not only eliminate Italy from the Axis but possibly turn them to assist us with the Germans."

"Do you really believe that?" asked Chief of Naval Operations Admiral Ernest Joseph 'Ernie' King, USN [USNA 1901].

"I must say," interjected Churchill, "General Donovan is not alone in that assessment. Colonel Menzies at MI6 has reported similar analyses of source material from inside the Italian military."

"Won't that distract us from ROUNDUP?" the president asked.

"If I may," began Chief of the Imperial General Staff (CIGS) General Sir Alan Francis 'Brookie' Brooke, GCB, DSO & Bar. He waited for a head nod from Churchill and Roosevelt. "We just heard from General Eisenhower that given our available resources, we are not likely to secure North Africa until well after our defined window for ROUNDUP preparations."

"Which in turn means we cannot execute ROUNDUP before the winter weather makes such operations too risky," Churchill added.

"Correct," Eisenhower affirmed.

"We are caught between a rock and a hard spot," added King.

"True," the prime minister replied, "but we can put our available forces to good use. To a certain extent, the geography of Sicily restricts the field of maneuver and reinforcement. We can take Italy out of the Axis camp and potentially bring them, or some of them, to our side . . . at least not be available to the Germans. BOLERO is barely marginal for 1943, better for 1944, but still not what we ultimately need for continental operations. We are the carnival artist balancing a dozen spinning plates."

"It seems we have what we need from General Eisenhower," the president pronounced. "Noting the time, I suggest we adjourn for lunch, get Ike fed, so we can get him back to fighting the enemy."

—

Friday, 15.January.1943
USAAF Station F-356
Saffron Walden, Essex, England
United Kingdom
11:30 hours

Brian had checked in at 23:10 last night. He had only been able to reconnect with Captain Paul James 'Dusty' Langford, USAAF, his former right wingman. Dusty brought him up to speed on the changes in the 334th Fighter Squadron (334FS)—the former RAF No.71 Squadron—since Brian's departure last September. Major Chesley Gordon 'Pete' Peterson, USAAF, was now their commanding officer. The squadron had been removed from operational status for their transition from the Supermarine Spitfire Mark VBs to new Republic P-47D Thunderbolts. Since he had not flown in military aircraft in more than three months, Pete wanted him to take a currency flight in his familiar Spitfire. Brian would take a refresher flight in the Spitfire, and then later in the afternoon, he would make his first flight in the Thunderbolt.

With his British flight gear, Brian walked to the aircraft. The British roundel had been over-painted with an American star. The No.71 Squadron 'XR' tail designator was replaced with their new 'QP' designator for the 334FS. The 'G' aircraft tail designator had not been changed. The squadron callsign has been changed to 'Pectin.' To Brian's surprise, his old RAF ground crew stood at his old aircraft.

"Welcome back, sir," said Corporal Henry Jacobs, his previous crew chief.

"Thanks, Henry. Great to be back, although I must confess, I'm surprised to see all three of you here." Brian shook hands with all three men.

"We will leave when the Spits are returned to the RAF."

"Major Petersen granted me one last flight in your Spitfire before I begin the transition to the Thunderbolt this afternoon. You lads did a magnificent job keeping me in the air."

"The honor has been ours, sir. We have been and remain very proud of what you have been able to do with our fighters."

Jacobs assisted Brian as he strapped into and connected with the Spitfire fighter. "Enjoy her one last time, Captain Drummond. We'll be here when you've had your way with her." They all laughed. Henry jumped down off the wing and joined his comrades in front of the propeller.

In another sense, he felt home, again. Brian quickly scanned the entire cockpit to ensure nothing had changed in three and a half months. He promptly stepped through his start procedures and had the powerful Rolls Royce Merlin 45 engine purring at fast idle. When he was ready and cleared to taxi, Brian stuck his left hand out of the cockpit with his thumb up. All three men came to a sharp position of attention and saluted together. Brian returned the salute and signaled for the wheel chocks to be removed. They stood back outside the left wingtip and held up the chocks. Brian taxied to the runway, completed his engine run-up and pre-takeoff checks. *Everything is perfect.*

The flight took just over an hour. Brian put the machine through her paces from stalls to red line dives, aerobatics of all types not involving zero or negative 'g' flight. The terrain was familiar. Off and on, Brian spotted aircraft—fighters, bombers, transports, and even a Coastal Command seaplane. He had a full load of ammunition but there would probably be nothing to shoot at on this flight. They were not operational at the moment and could not be assigned; however, things happened unexpectedly in war.

Brian landed smoothly and perfectly, without the slightest hint of a bounce. Jacobs was waiting for him as he taxied into his parking spot, switched everything off, and shut down the Merlin engine. Brian removed his leather helmet and oxygen mask.

"You still have your gunport tapes," Jacobs declared.

They both laughed. "Nothing to shoot at, I'm afraid. She was perfect. I regret that may be my last Spit flight for a while."

"Good luck, Captain Drummond. We will miss you, sir."

"Please, Henry, let's stay in touch. You all have been very good to me, and I will not forget." Brian shook hands with Henry Jacobs. "I'll find Hawking and Easton to thank them as well." Jacobs saluted. Brian returned the salute.

Brian returned to the squadron building that was earlier their dispersal hut when they were RAF No.71 Squadron four months ago. Just in time for lunch, Brian walked with the fellows he had served with before and met the pilots that flushed the unit out to full strength under the Air Corps organization. Instead of four three-plane sections, they now had four four-plane flights, two two-plane sections each. Brian remained listed as an assigned spare pilot and would use 'Pectin 99' as his flight callsign at least through their transition and re-training period.

15:10 hours

Brian had introduced himself to his new crew chief Sergeant Larson Tomlinson from Wichita, Kansas, earlier in the morning. The two men shared stories of the Wichita aviation culture from their youth. Larson was actually older than Brian but had been serving two years less than Brian. Larson had been with P-47s from the beginning.

Brian completed his walkaround inspection, as he had been shown in the morning. The P-47 was a monster compared to the sleek, curvaceous lines of the Spitfire, and the "Jug" was three times the maximum gross weight of the Spitfire. The large, twin-row, super-charged, air-cooled, 18-cylinder, Pratt & Whitney R-2800-59 Double Wasp radial engine delivered 2,000 horsepower at full power and made for a very wide nose. Brian used the concealed, pocket handhold to pull himself up onto the left-wing root. He had done his cockpit checkout in the morning. Using another covered, pocket footstep, Brian climbed up and entered the comparatively large cockpit. He strapped into his parachute harness and then secured his seat straps. Larson hand-pulled the 13-foot diameter propeller through eight blades while Brian tended to his cockpit checks. Brian connected his new American flight gear—a heavy cloth helmet with headphones, goggles, and oxygen mask. Tomlinson stood ahead of the propeller and off the left wing with the large fire extinguisher cart next to him. Larson gave Brian a thumb's up.

Brian stepped through the start procedures:
-- Throttle cracked OPEN ¼ inch
-- Propeller lever FULL FORWARD
-- Mixture control IDLE CUT-OFF
-- Fuel boost pump control to START and ALTITUDE
-- Primer five strokes – it's cold
-- Magneto switch BOTH

Brian made a quick scan to make sure everything was correct. He leaned his head as far out the left side of the open canopy and shouted, "Clear!" to ensure the propeller arc was clear of any obstructions.
-- Starter switch ENGAGE

The big engine turned through two blades. The first cylinder fired off, followed by a second cylinder.
-- Mixture lever AUTO RICH

The engine rumbled to life. Brian opened the throttle more until the engine was running smoothly. He checked to make sure the oil pressure was rising, and then he pulled the throttle back to stabilize at 900 RPM. Brian switched on the generator, his radio, checked his oxygen flow, uncaged his attitude gyro, and noted the temperatures were rising. Brian called the tower and was cleared to taxi. He depressed the brake pedals, released the parking brake, and signaled Tomlinson to remove the chocks. Larson disappeared beneath the wing and then reappeared. He stood clear of the left wing, held up the chocks in his left hand, and saluted with his right hand. Brian returned the salute. He released the parking brake and opened the throttle to begin his taxi to the run-up area. Temperatures and pressures were all in the green. With his engine run-up and magneto checks complete, Brian called for takeoff.

Brian checked to make sure the approach line was clear, checked his flight controls were free and clear one last time, taxied onto the active runway, aligned on the centerline, and locked his tail wheel. One more check of the cockpit ensured the engine was running well and warm. *I'm ready.* Brian released the brakes, dropped his feet on the pedals to ensure he did not inadvertently tap the brakes, and slowly pushed the throttle about halfway to 25 inches of Manifold Air Pressure (MAP) and added rudder to compensate for the engine torque. The aircraft accelerated nicely. The airspeed needle bounced a couple of times and began to rise. The tail rose off the runway, the rudder was effective, and Brian adjusted his pedals to keep the aircraft on centerline. Brian slowly advanced the throttle to 52 inches MAP. The aircraft lifted off the runway smoothly. Brian retracted the landing gear. With the gear up and locked, climbing swiftly, Brian pulled the throttle back to 35 inches MAP and the prop lever back for 2500 RPM—the climb power setting.

The much larger aircraft handled nicely. Brian ran through the same flight maneuvers he had used in the morning. *The aircraft feels heavy, but I'll probably get used to it as we go.* Comfortable with his first feel out flight, Brian returned to Debden, as he knew the airbase, for a handful of touch-and-go landings. When he was done, Brian taxied back to his parking spot. Tomlinson met him, inserted the wheel chocks, and signaled chocks in place to Brian. He secured his electrical equipment, caged his attitude gyro, secured the oxygen, and moved the mixture lever to CUTOFF. The engine clanked to a stop. Brian disconnected and unstrapped. Larson waited for him at the aft wing root.

"Any squawks, sir?" Tomlinson asked.

"Not a one, Larson. She is a brute of a machine."

"So they tell me. Do you need a quick turn, sir?"

"Nope. I'm done. Give her a drink and put her to bed."

A good first day.

—

Monday, 18.January.1943
Villa Mirador
Allée des Mûriers
Anfa, Casablanca
Protectorat Français au Maroc
20:15 hours

"**W**elcome to Mirador, General," Prime Minister Churchill greeted Major General George Smith Patton Jr. [USMA 1909]. Commanding General I Armored Corps and Commander Western Task Force.

The villa served as the prime minister's residence for the SYMBOL Conference and was not quite a mile from the hotel. The location and accommodations were perfect for Churchill.

Winston had always been impressed by Patton's sense of pomp. The general wore his favored, modified pink & green service uniform with the riding britches, boots, and crop of a cavalry officer, and polished leather waist belt, gold buckle, and double holsters—a Colt Model 1873 45-caliber Single Action Revolver on his right hip and a Smith & Wesson .357 Magnum Revolver on his left hip. Both pistols had custom ivory grips etched with his GSP monogram. He had two silver stars on his jacket epaulets, both shirt collar points, and prominently displayed his polished helmet.

"Thank you, Prime Minister."

"No need to be armed, General. No one will disturb us this evening. Mirador is well guarded, I assure you."

"This is a war zone, Prime Minister. Anything can happen at any moment. I do not intend to go down without a fight, and the Peacemaker," Patton said, patting the pistol on his right hip, "packs a helluva wallop." Patton rested his hands on the ivory pistol grips as if he was going to draw them.

"Your firearms are impressive."

"All part of the image, Prime Minister."

They were both served flutes of chilled champagne without asking. They toasted each other, their countries, and the success of the on-going campaign.

"Is it to be just us, this evening?" Patton asked.

"Yes. I will confess to my protracted desire for a personal conversation with an accomplished armor general."

"You have your own, Prime Minister. Monty is doing a masterful job chasing Rommel across the desert, although I prefer a more aggressive offense. Unfortunately, I sit here in Morocco cleaning up after the Vichy French."

"You will get your time, General. Patience. I have discussed your service with General Eisenhower. While I cannot know your service record, I certainly understand and appreciate the fine balance Ike must find among two distinct heads of state, groups of military chiefs, and of course, a disparate joint staff. I hold considerable empathy for General Eisenhower's predicament. Further, if you will permit me, he is doing a smashing good job. You are a direct part of these accomplishments, General." Churchill paused, slowly sipped his champagne, to give Patton a chance to say something. Patton matched Churchill's movements—waiting. Churchill smiled broadly. "Well done, General. You did not take the bait. We have hard fighting ahead, and I remain confident we shall prevail. The only question is how long? Can we get this done in time for the big show—the invasion of Continental Europe—Operation ROUNDUP?"

Patton raised his eyebrows. "As much as I would love to dish out a good healthy dose of *Blitzkrieg* to the Nazi bastards for starting all this, we have insufficient forces in theater. Central Europe is not the same as North Africa."

"In time, George. The question I wanted to discuss this evening is what is next? I wanted to ask a renowned armor general what he would recommend as the next step, once North Africa is secure."

"I am just an armor corps commander, Prime Minister. I am not the chief of staff, sir."

"Is that your answer, George?"

Churchill stared directly at Patton with a cold, stern, serious expression. Patton held Churchill's eyes for a score of seconds. "Are you testing me, Prime Minister?"

"Of course, I am, George." Churchill waited. "I seek your professional opinion . . . in confidence and in private. I appreciate your sensitivity for the chain of command, and I have no intention of compromising your status. Your answer, General?"

Patton considered exactly how to respond to this unique opportunity. "I am not much for politics. I am a ground general. We had a hard time gathering the lift capacity for TORCH. We hardly have the transport and supplies sufficient for ROUNDUP."

"So, you would wait to gather up the necessary forces for ROUNDUP?"

"No sir. Sitting around for another year or so is not acceptable. My inclination is to land 50 divisions in Northern France and race to Berlin and Warsaw . . . vanquish Germany and save as much of Europe from the Commie bastards as possible."

"That's ROUNDUP or something bigger," Churchill responded. "I appreciate your vision of Berlin and Warsaw. This war will not end like the last one. There will be no armistice, no ceasefire. The despicable corporal must be resoundingly defeated. Germany must be defeated in total . . . see it to the end. Germany must be totally subjugated and rebuilt from the ashes, so we do not repeat the Great War. Further, I am seriously concerned about Uncle Joe and his ambitions. With the massive forces he has gathered and is continuing to collect, I fear he has broader long-range objectives."

"Replacing Hitler in dominating Europe?"

"Yes."

Patton shook his head almost in disbelief. "A few steppingstones are needed on that path."

"That is my point precisely. What is the next stone?"

"Once we link up with the British 8th Army, we will have adequate forces in North Africa. Southern France is the logical step, but the exposure to greater forces would be too much. Given our shipping lift constraints, the Germans can redeploy forces much faster than we could accomplish by sea. The logical step is Sicily. Their reinforcement constraints would be roughly the same as ours. With a good deception campaign, we might gain the necessary positive margin. Once we have Sicily, we will have a perfect base for Mainland Italy."

"We can't get to Berlin through Italy," added Churchill, "practically speaking."

"No sir. The Alps are not armor country."

Churchill held Patton's eyes in contemplation for a few seconds. "You do know, General, the Army staff favors ROUNDUP sooner rather than later."

"Yes sir. I have heard the arguments."

"But you do not agree?"

Patton smiled and said, "Why do I feel an ambush?"

"No, no, General. That is not my intent. I only reflect the current debate in which we are immersed. My query and our privacy reflect the esteem with which I hold your accomplishments."

"That was quite some flattery, Prime Minister," Patton said and grinned.

"Not flattery, George, just the truth." Churchill held his face devoid of expression. "You've done well deflecting from my interrogative."

"I will give you the exact same answer I have given Generals Marshall and Eisenhower, and the War Plans Department. I want nothing more than to have a substantial armor force for the run across France to Berlin and beyond. However, I am also a pragmatic soldier. The issue from my perspective is the rapidity of reinforcement or massing of forces. As long as the ratio remains negative, ROUNDUP is not advisable."

"So, BOLERO is the key?"

"Yes, absolutely. Sicily and the Italian boot, for that matter, are channelized battlefields. France, the Low Countries, and Northern Germany are not. We will need 50 to 80 combat divisions for Berlin; about a third need to be armor divisions. More importantly, we need to land two or more divisions a day after the initial assault landing of something 10 or more divisions."

"That's a lot to move."

"Indeed, it is, Prime Minister."

"I like your thinking, George. I think that is the direction we are headed. The president and I believe we will have that agreement by the end of the week. Now, the clock continues to turn, General. We need to get you fed."

"I will follow your lead, Prime Minister."

"Yet, before we adjourn to what I expect will be a sumptuous meal in these troubled times, I have one more pointed query. I've voiced my apprehension regarding Stalin's intentions in the post-war world. I shall utilize this moment and your expertise to float the notion and seek your opinion that potential for using Italy as a base of operations for a major continental effort through the Balkans into Eastern Europe to the Baltic Sea."

"To cut off the Red Army advance," Patton observed.

"Precisely. I fear for the future of Poland and other nations the Red Army will occupy before we meet them."

"An interesting strategic objective, I must say. I have a couple of relevant thoughts. One, the Balkans are not armor country either. Our accumulation of combat forces in England is progressing well to support ROUNDUP. Such a strike through the Balkans would require a major redeployment of BOLERO from England to Italy, which, in turn, means sufficient geography on the Italian boot must be firmly held to protect those forces. Second, presuming we are successful in heading off the Red Army, we would be faced with the Germans on our left flank and the Russians on our right flank, and further, the Russians might well become hostile. Third, by cutting off the Russians, the defeat of Germany would be left to the Western Allies alone. We would essentially replace the Russian army with ourselves without their support. I can see the political motives for such an action, but militarily, the risk appears to be too great to be considered practical."

Churchill withdrew into his thoughts. "Well said, General. Thank you for your candid perspective. Now, let's go enjoy our meal."

The two leaders ate their supper comparatively late for both of them. Their conversation during the meal and after-dinner turned more social than the earlier business. They remained actively engaged until well after midnight—normal for the prime minister, not so much for the general. Both men declared the evening a success as they parted. The prime minister retired, reading his preparatory material for the late morning's next plenary session of the conference. General Patton returned to his quarters for the night. The consolidation operations of his armored corps were not yet complete.

—

Monday, 25.January.1943
Flower Villa [AKA Villa Taylor]
Route d'ourika
Marrakesh, Marrakesh-Safi
Protectorat Français au Maroc
07:45 hours

"**T**hank you so much for inviting me, Winston," President Roosevelt pronounced. "You were precisely correct. That sunset last night was truly magnificent."

The villa was owned by a friend of Churchill's and had acquired its name from the lush, floral gardens in and around the property. The colorful flowers added an enchanting quality to the retreat.

"I have found this place to be magical," Churchill responded. "Glorious sunrises and sunsets are the norm here. I have enjoyed every minute in Marrakesh since I discovered this city a decade ago."

"I must confess to my doubts, Winston, but you are always so convincing. I'm so glad I gave into your persuasive powers and stayed an extra day for this," Roosevelt said, waving his arm around the courtyard. "Regrettably, I've a very long journey ahead of me, and I really must be on my way."

"Quite understandable. My travel back to London is long, but certainly not as long as yours. *Je souhaite un bon voyage, mon ami.*"

"*À toi aussi.*"   The president glanced over his shoulder and nodded to the chief of his Secret Service detail.

With the president's consent, Churchill chose to ride with him to Marrakesh Menara Airport. The prime minister was not particularly bashful or self-conscious dressed in his robe and slippers. Their joyful and humorous banter about the events of the last two weeks kept their parting upbeat and positive. They waited in the limousine until Admiral Leahy signaled they were ready for takeoff. Getting the president aboard the aircraft and secured in his seat would be the last action prior to closing the hatch and starting the engines.

"Until the 'morrow, my friend, please take care. My very best wishes to Clemmie and the family. Thank you for everything you do so well."

"Thank you, Franklin. We shall see you soon."

Churchill stood outside by the limousine and waved as the president disappeared into the aircraft. He waited on the tarmac until the president's aircraft was in the air and the landing gear began to retract. The long journey home had begun, as the president and his party would retrace the outbound itinerary for the return home. Churchill returned to his villa.

Winston Churchill had learned the pleasures and satisfaction of painting in 1915. The president's visit offered needed inspiration for a distraction. For the first time since the second war in Europe began, Churchill decided to pick up his brushes and face his easel with his paint tray to complete a painting. The prime minister decided to spend an extra week himself to paint and relax. He chose for his subject the famous Koutoubia Mosque of Marrakesh with the snow-capped Atlas Mountains in the background.

Churchill finished the painting and gifted it to President Roosevelt the next time they saw each other during the TRIDENT Conference in Washington, DC, the following May. "The Tower of Koutoubia Mosque" was the only painting Churchill completed during the Second World War. Roosevelt proudly displayed the painting at Hyde Park. After the war and Franklin's passing, the painting was sold.

In 2011, the actor William Bradley 'Brad' Pitt purchased the painting as a gift to his then girlfriend and future wife, actress Angelina Jolie, née Voight. On 1.March.2021, Jolie sold "The Tower of Koutoubia Mosque" for a record £8.3 million (US$11.5 million).

———

Monday, 25. January. 1943
Allied Forces Headquarters Forward
Hôtel Saint George
24 Avenue Souidani Boudjemââ
Algiers
Algérie Coloniale Française
13:30 hours

"**W**elcome to Headquarters Allied Forces Forward," General Eisenhower greeted his guests—General Marshall and Admiral King. The three men shook hands but did not speak until they were in Ike's office with the door closed. The office had been a luxury suite in the luxury hotel.

"Quite the headquarters," King observed, scanning the light blue walls and desert scene paintings, or rather prints, on the walls. They all laughed lightly.

"We appropriated the entire facility. It was the best we could find here in Algiers and easier for security."

"Well done, Ike," Marshall said. "Admiral King and I thought we would check your accommodations on our way home. Well done indeed."

"Thank you, sir."

"You did a masterful job, as always, Ike. The prime minister, the president, and the combined joint chiefs were appreciative of your direct and candid briefing. We wanted to give you our firsthand views of the decisions made during the Casablanca Conference. The leaders endorsed your recommendation. Your next objective beyond Tunisia and finishing the *Afrikakorps* is Sicily and HUSKY, and as soon as you are able after HUSKY, you are to proceed with AVALANCHE." Operation AVALANCHE was a broad combat plan for landing a substantial force on the Italian mainland. "Your planning staff should draw upon the War and Navy Departments planning staffs as you are able."

"Understood," Eisenhower responded.

"We also affirmed the Germany first strategy established at the ARCADIA Conference a year ago," added King. "Our leaders decided to focus ROUNDUP planning on a quasi-independent staff we have identified as Chief of Staff to the Supreme Allied Commander." The staff would be commonly referred to by the acronym of the title—COSSAC. "The staff will initially be under British leadership. The British chiefs have provisionally selected General Morgan to lead the planning staff." Major General Frederick Edgworth Morgan would take up his new assignment in March. "We are unanimous that ROUNDUP in some form is essential to achieving our agreed strategy. The only question is when."

"Well, Ernie, there are other subsidiary questions like where and at what risk," Marshall added. "We," he gestured to King, "have been tasked to thoroughly assess what we can do to accelerate the BOLERO build-up to support ROUNDUP for this year.   That means, as I said in Casablanca, you are unlikely to receive the ten armored divisions you need. I think you recognize that reality."

"Yes sir, I do."

"We'd love to give you those divisions to finish off Rommel earlier, but we simply don't have them," the Army chief of staff said. Eisenhower nodded his head. "While we agree with your assessment of our North Africa operations, we cannot emphasize enough that we need to secure North Africa and Sicily as quickly as possible and at least fully engage on the Italian mainland to prepare for ROUNDUP. While we discussed the potential for autumn execution, none of the chief, including me, are eager to add inclement weather to our list of obstacles. That said, the combined joint chiefs do not advocate for excessive risk in the interest of time. We all feel Stalin's need, but that simply cannot be a controlling factor. This should be the most pressure applied. Ernie and I wanted you to hear from us directly that we support your prosecution of the North Africa campaign, as I believe the whole of the combined joint chiefs do. Keep doing the best you can with the forces you have."

"Thank you, sir. We'll get this done, but I do caution that we are not over the hump, yet."

"We understand, Ike."

"Agreed completely," King contributed.

"We have not decided who will be assigned as Morgan's deputy," continued Marshall. "Ernie and I have some work to do on that assignment. We will notify you immediately once the assignment has been made. It is important for you to keep an eye on Morgan's planning development when you are in London."

"I will do that," Eisenhower acknowledged.

"Lastly, it is also important for you to be aware that we also sanctioned a new strategic bombing campaign. Operation POINTBLANK has been approved and sanctioned by the political leaders and the combined joint chiefs. As soon as Bomber Command and the 8th Air Force are ready, they will conduct concerted, day and night, strategic bombing operations of German fighter production and supply facilities, sites, and infrastructure. We agreed the effort to be an essential ROUNDUP preparation action."

"That is not going to be easy," Eisenhower observed.

"No, no, it's not going to be easy," said Marshall. "General Arnold and Air Chief Marshal Portal indicated at Casablanca that the air forces are capable and will be ready to begin POINTBLANK operations in a few months. The effort will occupy the attention of the German Air Force, which makes it less likely they will divert air superiority resources elsewhere."

"Every little bit of assistance is appreciated," Ike said.

"We're trying to help. Just get this done, so we can move on."

"Yes sir. We will."

Admiral King added, "We've seen what happens when commanders sit down and wait for the enemy to attack. Keep slugging!"

"Will do, sir."

They adjourned their private meeting. Eisenhower gave the two senior military leaders a quick tour of the developing headquarters facility along with introductions to keep staff officers. They enjoyed an earlier dinner than usual in the hotel dining room with the senior Allied Forces staff officers before they boarded a flight to Gibraltar on the journey back to Washington.

—

Chapter 2

Sic transit gloria
(So passes glory,
or more popularly,
all glory is fleeting)

Tuesday, 2.February.1943
British Embassy
7 Ahmed Ragheb
Qasr Ad Dobarah, Qasr El Nil
Cairo Governorate
Kingdom of Egypt
14:15 hours

Prime Minister Churchill arrived without incident in Cairo aboard his B-24 Liberator known as Commando. The ambassador's limousine transported him from the airfield to the embassy.

Commander-in-Chief Middle East Command General Sir Harold Rupert Leofric George Alexander, GCB, CSI, DSO, MC, stood alone under the embassy awning, as the prime minister's vehicle came to a stop in front of him. He came to a position of attention and saluted crisply. "Welcome to Cairo, Prime Minister," Sir Harold said confidently as the prime minister exited the car.

Churchill, attired in his RAF air commodore uniform, returned Alexander's salute. "Thank you, Sir Harold." The general gestured for them to proceed inside.

In the embassy's foyer anteroom, Ambassador Sir Miles Wedderburn Lampson, GCMG, CB, MVO, PC, waited for his guest. "Welcome back to the Cairo Embassy, Mister Prime Minister."

"Thank you, Sir Miles. Let us go to your secure conference room, so we can speak frankly."

Lampson nodded and led the two men to the interior and stairway. They descended to the basement and the embassy's secure and guarded conference room.

They sat at a square table with maps of the Mediterranean, North Africa, and the Middle East covering the walls. "Your status report, General Alexander," the prime minister requested.

"Yes sir. Leading elements of the 8th Army are currently 100 miles west of Tripoli, just crossing the Tunisian frontier. The city of Tripoli was secured a week ago. The Germans destroyed the port facilities and military structures. Our engineers have jumped into clearing the harbor and restoring the port facilities. We might recover partial use in a week or two. The Axis forces have withdrawn to fortifications at Mareth inside Southeast Tunisia. General Montgomery intends to draw up, rest, and resupply his troops before engaging the Mareth Line."

"When do you expect to link up with the Americans?" asked Churchill.

"It depends upon how long it takes for the 8th Army to penetrate the Mareth Line, and what other surprises Rommel has in store for us. Based on Montgomery's rate of advance, I would estimate three to six weeks. That link up will complete the encirclement of the *Afrikakorps*. If the Germans decide to fight to the end, it could be another couple of months. But, at least in North Africa, the end is in sight."

"That will alter our timetable," Churchill observed.

"Yes sir. I know both General Eisenhower and I recognize the consequences. If we could induce their surrender, we would do so. In the interest of time and with your sanction, perhaps after the encirclement is complete and solidified, we could offer Rommel surrender rather than a fight to the end."

"To that end, I must remind you that we affirmed our unconditional surrender position. Securing North Africa is essential for our offensive plans this year. I would agree such an offer is appropriate, but Rommel's choices are surrender in total or take it to the end."

"Understood, sir. Do you have any other questions on the status of our campaign?"

"No. That should suffice for the moment."

"I am not sure what intelligence information you have had access to for the last few days, so I thought I would cover a few of those items. We can call in the necessary experts as you may wish."

"Proceed."

"First," Alexander continued, "it is my duty to inform you that the deaths of both Brigadiers Dykes and Stewart three days ago have now been confirmed."

"The Liberator crash?"

"Yes sir."

"Tragic. Dykes has been on the Secretariat staff for some years. I will write to their families."

"We also confirmed that a flight of Mosquitos struck a specific radio station in Wilhelmshaven during Goebbels' broadcast two nights ago and knocked him off the air, mid-speech. Bomber Command did a magnificent job and sent a very clear message."

"Excellent. I'll send a congratulatory message to Sir Arthur."

Air Chief Marshal Sir Arthur Travers 'Bomber' Harris, KCB, OBE, AFC, has been the Air Officer Commanding-in-Chief, RAF Bomber Command, for one year. He was already developing a reputation for an unswerving and ruthless application of strategic bombing of Germany.

"One last item, for now, reliable sources have confirmed that the German 6th Army has surrendered to the Red Army at Stalingrad."

"When?" Churchill asked excitedly.

"It took our sources several days to confirm the initial indications, but it was confirmed to have occurred two days ago, on the 31st." Churchill recognized that the reliable sources General Alexander was referring to in this statement was ULTRA, and Ambassador Lampson was not on the access list for ULTRA products. "He had repeatedly informed Berlin that they were out of ammunition and food. I should also add a touch of irony in the intelligence findings that Hitler promoted Paulus to field marshal earlier that morning, presumably under the assumption that he would commit suicide at a minimum since no German field marshal had ever been captured."

Generalfeldmarschall Friedrich Wilhelm Ernst Paulus became commander of the German 6th Army in January 1942, having commanded nothing larger than a battalion. Paulus and the 6th Army led the advance on Stalingrad later that summer. For three months, they fought the Red Army in brutal and merciless urban warfare. The Red Army successfully encircled Stalingrad and beat off repeated counterattacks by the Germans in their attempt to relieve the encirclement.

"Their fate will not be a pleasant one," observed Churchill.

"No sir. Hitler's fight-to-the-last-man admonition is likely to be what Rommel will face before we are done."

"Yes, well, then he shall bear the same fate—unconditional surrender or die."

"As you command, sir."

"Now, if there is nothing else . . . ," Churchill said and paused for both men to shake their heads in the negative, "it is nap time for me. I assume I shall see you both for dinner as your guests." Churchill held the eyes of Ambassador Lampson.

"My pleasure, Mister Prime Minister. We are scheduled for eight this evening."

"General," Winston said to Alexander, "is that time acceptable to you?"

"Yes sir."

"Then, we have a date. I will see you both then."

They left the basement secure room. The ambassador showed Churchill to the specially prepared, second-floor suite. Winston's duty private secretary Anthony Bevir was waiting for him. They all knew the routine. Churchill retired for his afternoon nap.

———

Sunday, 7.February.1943
No.417 Sudbury Hill
Harrow, London, England
18:25 hours

As Brian had done more than a few times, he met Charlotte with Ian at Waterloo Station. Their date at the Spencers' residence was the first since their last visit in September 1941. Brian kissed Charlotte and took Ian from her arms. He gladly carried Ian. Father and son entertained each other as they navigated the journey to Harrow. The reunited Drummond family boarded the Underground Jubilee Line, switching to the westbound Piccadilly Line at Green Park Station, to arrive at Sudbury Hill Station. It was a short walk from the above-ground Underground station to the Spencers' home, but the damp, chilly air of winter convinced them a taxi was a better choice.

Brian used the door knocker below the shiny 417 numerals, and it was answered promptly by John Spencer. "Welcome back to Harrow," he said cheerfully and stepped aside to allow the Drummonds to enter.

Ian began squirming immediately when he saw his alter-ego Malcolm toddling up to them. Brian set their son down, and two small boys trundled off in their little world. They all laughed. Mary joined them at the entryway. John remained in his uniform without his tunic. Mary wore a simple, well-tailored, medium blue dress. She kissed Charlotte and Brian on their cheeks, and she added her greetings.

John took their overcoats, scarfs, and gloves, hanging them on the coat rack.

"This is the first time we have seen you in your new uniform," John announced.

Brian held his arms out and did a crude pirouette.

"Where are your ribbons?" John asked.

"Too much attention . . . more attention than I prefer, so I choose not to wear them in everyday attire."

"Well, at least you wear your RAF wings along with your American wings."

Per U.S. Army regulation, Brian wore his USAAF pilot wings above the left breast pocket on his tunic and his RAF pilot's wings above the right pocket.

Following his mentor's lead, Brian removed his tunic and hung it up. They assembled in the living room and watched the toddler excitement of the two boys. John poured the champagne for all four of them.

"I understand congratulations are in order, sir," said Brian.

"Yes," Mary jumped in, "John was recognized in the King's New Year's Honors List. He was made Knight Commander of The Most Distinguished Order of Saint Michael and Saint George."

"So, it is now, Sir John," Charlotte commented.

John chuckled modestly. "No. John is sufficient. We are friends."

"Congratulations indeed. Well deserved," added Charlotte.

"Thank you very much," John responded.

"But this occasion," Mary continued, "is also a going-away party."

"Charlotte told me of your promotion to air vice marshal," Brian said.

"It's true. The promotion was effective a week ago. The honors list was published on New Year's Day. Along with those goodies came orders to deploy to North Africa and stand up the new 37 Group, part of the Northwest Africa Air Force. I will be the inaugural air officer commanding-in-chief for an all-Spitfire fighter group, and with that, I can return to the cockpit. Yet, all of that comes at a price. I am not eager to be leaving Mary and Malcolm."

"Well," Mary interjected, "it's not like you have been home that much . . . more in the last year, but still . . ."

"We all miss our men in this damnable war," Charlotte contributed.

"And you, young Brian, are home from the States," said Mary.

"Yes, just last month . . . and I'm so glad to be home."

"And back to your old squadron," John added.

Brian chuckled softly. "Well, my new old squadron. Most of the guys are still there, but we're also a larger squadron, so new guys as well. We're transitioning from Spits to the P-47 Thunderbolt. They call it the Jug for a reason. The airplane is three times the gross weight of the Spitfire."

"Enough aeroplane talk," scolded Mary.

"When do you leave?" Charlotte asked John.

"My investiture at Buckingham Palace is two weeks from Tuesday, and I am scheduled to depart by Liberator in the evening of the following day."

"So soon?"

"'Afraid so. The war waits for no man."

Harriett Peterman, the Spencers' long time chef and cook, appeared. "Excuse me, Ma'am. Supper is ready."

"Thank you, Harriett." Mary looked at Charlotte. "Shall we?" she said, gesturing to the dining room.

"Before we enjoy dinner," Brian said, "I would like to toast, Air Vice Marshal Sir John Spencer, good luck on your new assignment."

"Hear, hear," they all said. They held up their flutes and clinked glasses.

Malcolm's nanny, Grace Perkins, had already collected up the two boys and was tending to their feeding. She would prepare and put the boys to bed.

Laughter frequently punctuated their dinner conversation that focused solely on the antics of their boys. They reveled in the boys' evolving personalities and strengthening of the connection between them. The four of them enjoyed the meal, the laughter, and the light-hearted conversation among friends.

Sir John served up brandy. The ladies, in some collaborative move, excused themselves to go upstairs and check on the boys.

John looked at Brian. "Are you OK with these changes?"

What changes? The puzzled expression gave his thoughts away.

"A lot has happened in the last four months. You are no longer in the R-A-F. I think to all we have been through together."

"Yes, we have, sir. I am immensely grateful for everything you and Malcolm have done for me. I doubt I would be where I am without your assistance."

"Nonsense, Brian. We don't get to see skills like yours, my boy. Malcolm saw them long before I did. But I saw it myself for the first time that day in St. Louis in May of 1939. This nation has benefited from your skills, Brian, and we are immeasurably grateful for your service to the King, the kingdom, and freedom itself."

"Thank you, sir."

"It is I who should be thanking you. I cannot bestow a knighthood or barony upon you, but you certainly deserve such accolades. How do you like your new squadron?"

"It's mostly the same lads we had in 71 Squadron. The Jug feels heavier in flight, but it's got more armor than the Spit. The 50 cals are not the 20mm cannons we had of the Five Bs, but they should be better than the 30 cals we had."

"Maybe someday I'll get to fly one."

"I don't know how to make that happen, but where there's a will, there's a way."

"That would be great, Brian, but you cannot stick your neck out on my behalf." Sir John smiled affectionately at Brian. "You have given Mary and me a far more cherished creation."

Brian smiled. *Oh-oh! Where is he going with this?*

"I have been led to believe that Mary and Charlotte have colluded to press you into service again." John paused to allow Brian to respond. When he only noted a meek, almost undetectable, head nod from Brian, John continued. "We are most grateful, Brian. I hope and trust that you will be successful again."

"I don't know what to say, sir."

"Nothing to say, my boy. I will only add that now is the time, since I may be away for an indeterminant amount of time."

Mary and Charlotte made sufficient sounds to announce their approach before they appeared.

"The boys are soundly asleep," Mary stated. "What time do you need to be back?"

Brian glanced at his watch. "I need to be back at Debden by midnight, which means I should be leaving."

Charlotte and Ian planned to spend the night with the Spencers and return to Standing Oak Farm tomorrow morning. Brian had a little slack to make it back to Debden in time, but he did not want to use up that slack. He went upstairs to kiss their son on the forehead. After conveying his gratitude to Mary and Sir John for the delightful meal and evening, Brian wished Sir John good luck on his new assignment. He donned his tunic, overcoat, and cap. Charlotte took a proffered shawl from Mary and stepped outside to say good-bye to her husband. Brian waved to Charlotte as he turned down the street and again as he turned the corner to the elevated Sudbury Hill Underground Station.

—

Tuesday, 9.February.1943
Oval Office
The White House
Washington, District of Columbia
United States of America
10:10 hours

"**W**hat's happening to the German 6th Army?" Roosevelt asked.

Chief of Staff Admiral Bill Leahy smiled across the desk and took a moment to consider the commander-in-chief's query. "I'll ask Bill Donovan to keep from distracting the G-2. I imagine whatever is happening is not good. The Red Army is most likely going to exact their revenge, and it's still winter in Russia. I suspect those Germans who survived the battle will probably not survive captivity. When the history is eventually told, the aftermath of Stalingrad may pale the Bataan Death March."

Admiral William Daniel 'Bill' Leahy, USN [USNA 1897], had served as chief of naval operations, governor of Puerto Rico, and U.S. ambassador to Vichy France before being hand-picked by Roosevelt to be his chief of staff in July 1942.

"War is so terrible."

"Yes, it is and has been throughout recorded history."

"General Eisenhower met with Churchill on Friday. Have we heard anything from Eisenhower?"

"No, not to my knowledge."

"Winston returned to London on Sunday, so we should get his summary soon. Eisenhower has been pretty good about keeping us informed."

"Yes, he is," Bill added. "I'm not sure we should poke him with operations approaching a critical phase in North Africa. The Germans are surrounded in Tunisia. Cunningham has them sealed off to seaward. They are cornered, and we know that cornered animals can react very aggressively. The general assessment is that there is much more fight in that dog."

"Agreed. But we're only a couple of weeks past Casablanca, and we both know Winston can be very persuasive."

Leahy chuckled softly. "That is perhaps an understatement, Mister President." They both laughed. "I'll give Ike another couple of days, and if we've not heard anything by the end of the week, I'll send a personal and private to the general."

"That should work. Where is the four-star promotion list with the Senate?"

"The list passed committee last week. We expect the Senate to confirm the list this week."

"Excellent, and Eisenhower in on the list?"

"Yes sir," Leahy answered. "He should have his promotion by the weekend."

"We agreed at Casablanca that we would knock Italy out before attempting ROUNDUP, and we can't execute HUSKY and AVALANCHE until we secure North Africa for those operations."

"It doesn't look like they're going to finish off Rommel this month. A month or two delay would push ROUNDUP past the weather window for cross-Channel operations and into 1944 for the next opening in the spring."

"Uncle Joe will not be happy," Roosevelt said softly, almost mumbling.

"No, but the lives of those men who will make the assault across the Channel are far more important than Stalin's feelings. Churchill has clearly articulated the requirement for an overwhelming force to avoid being bogged down in a stagnant battle of attrition. We all understand why Stalin wants a strong western front, to reduce the resistance the Red Army faces on the eastern front."

"Exactly," the president affirmed. "While the political motives are strong and the generals have not been unanimous, I do subscribe to Churchill's caution."

The knock on the large, conformal door preceded Harry Hopkins. "This just came in from Frank Knox," Harry said, holding a folder, and then handed it to the president.

Roosevelt opened the folder and read the message.

SECRET

```
MMKJD TQR NR 0709
S 091511Z FEB 43
FM SECNAV
TO WHITE HOUSE
S E C R E T
SUBJ RETRANS
BT
S 082332Z FEB 43
FROM CG 14CORPS
TO CINCSPA
INFO CINCPOA CINCPAC CINCSWPA SECNAV SECWAR
S E C R E T
SUBJ OPERATION WATCHTOWER
TOKYO EXPRESS NO LONGER HAS A TERMINUS ON
GUADALCANAL
BT
NNNN
```

SECRET

Roosevelt handed the folder to Leahy. Bill quickly read the message. "It appears we finally have our first land victory in the Pacific," Roosevelt observed with a broad grin.

"It was a nip and tuck affair for far too long," Leahy added and returned the folder to Hopkins.

"And we came dreadfully close to losing the Marines on that island."

"Yes, we were, but Halsey had to protect the few remaining carriers we have in the Pacific . . . at least until we can deliver more."

"Yes, yes. Ernie King explained all that, but the image of that Marine division being abandoned on the island was not a pleasant one to hold in our thoughts. Waking up and seeing all of their support ships gone had to be quite disconcerting."

"Yes, but those are the exigencies of war."

"Perhaps . . . but we must avoid those necessities."

Leahy nodded his head several times. "What happened on and around Guadalcanal has been discussed and debated at length from the secretary on down. I think it is safe to say the operational admirals know exactly how close they came to tragedy. Fortunately, the Marines are a feisty bunch."

Roosevelt chuckled softly. "Yes, they are. Thank goodness."

The three men returned to the affairs of state. They had a long way still to go before this dreadful episode in human history was done, but this was another step upward on the journey to the 'sunlit uplands' of which Churchill so eloquently spoke.

—

Friday, 12.February.1943
USAAF Station 356
Saffron Walden, Essex, England
United Kingdom
11:30 hours

The transition and training of the 334FS continued at what Brian considered was a plodding pace. The majority of the squadron were experienced fighter pilots, but the leaders felt more effort was needed to adapt them to the 'American way' of conducting fighter operations.

As the squadron's spare pilot, Brian was added as a tag-along with Pete Petersen's Blue Flight. They had flown their training flights with loaded guns, but this was their first gunnery flight since they had begun their transition to the Thunderbolt.

The flight plan called for basic stationary ground gunnery, followed by moving targets—first a surface target at two speeds, and then a towed banner target at flight speed. Each of them would take two passes at each target. An old, Great War, beat-up, British Mark VIII Liberty tank hull with its odd full-body, wide tracks had been used for years by the Royal Air Force, and now by the U.S. Army Air Forces. The old tank hull sat in a dirt circle devoid of vegetation from all the impacts around the target. Brian's positional callsign was Blue Five. On signal, they peeled off in sequence in a wide orbit around the target. The sun was near its local zenith, so they had no definitive sun line other than the comparatively low winter track across the scattered clouds.

"Pectin Blue, the range is hot. Pectin Blue One rolling in," radioed Pete.

Brian watched Petersen's aircraft rolled over onto his back, and the nose pull through into a modest dive. As he kept track of the other airplanes, Brian rechecked his armament switches were set, and the gunsight illuminated and set. The flashes on the target, the dirt clouds kicked up, and the red tracer elements of the ricochet rounds made quite a show. Pete pulled up smoothly, adjusting his flight path to take his position in the circle.

"Pectin Blue Two in hot," broadcast Pete's wingman, Second Lieutenant Bradley Thomas 'Hick' Hickerson. Hick's first impact hit short in the existing grass, walked across the dirt circle, and the last few of his burst hit the target.

"Pectin Blue Three in hot," announced second section leader, First Lieutenant James Edward 'Jimmy' Stonestreet. Both Hick and Jimmy had been with Brian in No.71 Squadron. Jimmy hit the target and beyond.

Brian throttled back a little to avoid getting too close to Jimmy's wingman, Second Lieutenant Gregory Bradford 'Jerk' Harrison from Butte, Montana, and then he widened his orbit a little more.

"Pectin Blue Four in hot."

Brian watched Jerk kick up dust short of the target. He could not see any on target flashes. *Bad sight setting or fired too early. That may have been his first actual firing run.* Brian watched the nose of the QP-F Thunderbolt come up and climb. Brian depressed his radio button. "Pectin Blue Five in hot." He rolled over, pulled the nose down to a good run-in line, and rolled his wings level. The aerodynamic sound grew as the aircraft accelerated in a 30-degree dive. Brian retarded his throttle to give himself a little more time. He held the sight reticle pipper on the target. When the tank grew to the desired span in his sight, Brian squeezed the trigger for a two-second burst from all eight 50-caliber machineguns and then pulled back on the stick, feeling the g-load build up on his body. He reduced the back, stick pressure for a 20-degree climb, and pushed his throttle forward to the stop to hold his speed. Adjusting his flight path, Brian took his position in the orbit and glanced over his left shoulder. The dust cloud around the target suggested he had hit the target, although he had not been able to see the impacts.

Blue Flight repeated the process with another pass for each of them with a diving delivery. When Brian finished his second run, Pete took the flight down to just above treetop level. They each took one low-level pass at the target. The Thunderbolt handled well. The bullets from the aircraft's guns had a flatter trajectory that gave him a great range window for both ground attack and aerial combat. The Spitfire's 20 mm cannons had more bite, but the Thunderbolt's 50-caliber machine guns gave him more engagement latitude.

As soon as Brian pulled up from his low-level pass, Pete radioed, "Pectin Blue Flight join up."

Brian was the last to complete the rendezvous. Pete had already taken up the planned heading out over the North Sea for the moving, surface, and aerial targets. Their assigned area was beyond the coastal shipping lanes. A Royal Navy Motor Torpedo Boat (MTB) with a towed sled on a long cable was easy to spot on the water with no white caps and heading north.

"Sled Four, Pectin Blue, we have you in sight."

"Pectin Blue, Sled Four, likewise. Give us a few minutes. We need to come about and increase speed to give you the 20-knot target speed you need."

"No problem, Sled Four. We'll be orbiting you. We're ready when you are."

"Roger, Pectin Blue. Stand by."

Pete held the flight together in a 'V' formation and entered a wide orbit around the target sled. *He's going to peel off from here.* The MTB was heading south, and the frothing wake signified its increasing speed.

With the target sled in the MTB's wake and stable, they heard, "Pectin Blue, Sled Four, on speed, ready for your gunnery runs."

"Sled Four, Pectin Blue, roger. Pectin Blue Flight peel off in sequence. Pectin Blue One in hot." Pete pulled and rolled into his dive on the target. The remainder of the flight did not broadcast their roll-in as they each took their turn following their leader. Hick duplicated Pete's roll-in, followed by Jimmy and Jerk. Brian remained in his shallow left bank until his turn came. He could easily see each pilot's burst at the target. Again, only Jerk failed to lead the target properly, as the bullet geysers sprang up behind the target.

"Sled Four, Pectin Blue, next speed." The plan called for the highest speed the MTB could reach while pulling a target sled. The MTB was capable of 40-knot maximum speed without a sled, so it would be the best speed they could reach at full power.

"Roger, Pectin Blue. We need a few minutes more heading south and then a turn to the north to remain within our designated area."

"Understood. We're ready when you are. Break. Pectin Blue, throttle back to max endurance. Take up in trail orbit."

Brian complied with Pete's instructions as the other pilots did as well. The process of the MTB repositioning for the next target condition took ten minutes. They watched the boat turn north and boil the wake behind them as the target sled added resistance.

"Pectin Blue, Sled Four, on speed."

"Roger, Sled Four. Pectin Blue One in hot."

Brian watched Pete make his run on the target. He throttled up as the others did. Being more spread out enabled him to clearly see the effectiveness of each pilot's pass on the full speed surface target sled, probably at 35 knots or so. *Much better. Even Jerk got the target that time. He's learning. My turn.* Brian rolled into a good intercept line. He displaced his pipper ahead of the sled and closed rapidly with the target. The sled grew in his gunsight reticle. Brian adjusted his lead as his range decreased. He squeezed the trigger. Again, all eight machineguns erupted for the two-second burst. Brian pulled his nose up and rolled hard left. He saw the sea explode around the sled along with what he thought were bits of the sled.

As Brian scanned the sky to reacquire the flight, he heard the broadcast. "Pectin Blue, Sled Four, good shooting. We'll have to repair the sled before the next flight arrives. Well done, mate." Brian was the last to join up off Hick's right wing.

"Thanks, Sled Four. Pectin Blue out. Break. Pectin Blue, switch to Button Dog."

Brian glanced down to his right console to his SCR522A VHF radio control head with its red, OFF, and four preset radio channel buttons. He pushed 'D' and waited. He heard two, three, four. Brian depressed his radio transmit button and said into his oxygen mask microphone, "Five."

"Sleeve Seven, Pectin Blue Flight."

"Pectin Blue Flight, Sleeve Seven. We are in position, in a racetrack, at Angels Eight."

"Roger, Sleeve Seven. We are climbing and about ten minutes out." Pete adjusted their heading to remain clear of the scattered cumulus clouds and headed toward the expected rendezvous point with the tow aircraft and target sleeve. The flight climbed above the cloud tops at 6,600 feet. The locating of the tow aircraft did not take long.

"Sleeve Seven, Pectin Blue Flight, tally ho. We're climbing at your five o'clock."

"I've got you, Pectin Blue. I'll hold the northerly track until you're in position, then we will need to head south."

A diminutive RAF Miles M.9 Master airplane towed a 7 x 40 white canvas banner at the end of a 1,000-yard cable. The banner had a bright orange border and a bright, two-foot diameter, orange circle, aim-point in the middle. The flight leveled off at 10,000 feet. Pete signaled for the formation to disperse in trail, in a wide orbit around the Master. As they had planned and briefed, they took a longer spacing than they used on the ground attack segment. The tow pilot recognized the initial conditions and made a 180-degree turn heading to the south.

"Pectin Blue Flight, Sleeve Seven is on condition and ready. You are cleared for the banner."

Petersen continued to lead them around the orbit until he reached his planned perch position off the right side of the banner. "Pectin Blue One in hot."

Brian watched as Major Petersen rolled into his dive on the target banner. Pete's tracers appear to pass through or near the banner. Brian thought he saw the banner wiggled a little several times that appeared to be hits. As Pete's QP-A Jug climbed back to their orbit altitude, Hick took his pass at the banner. They went in sequence with what appeared to be similar results. Even Jerk seemed to hit the banner. *He's improving.*

Brian made his call and rolled in on the banner target. The tow aircraft was probably doing about 180 knots or so, but the banner was not maneuvering.

He set up a good intercept track and adjusted to hold the lead angle for the estimated speed. Brian squeezed off a two-second burst. The tracers intersected with the banner nicely. He climbed and returned to his place in the orbit. The tow pilot announced his course reversal. Blue Flight maintained its counterclockwise orbit. The plan called for them to make another pass on the opposite side of the banner and to oppose the tow aircraft's track. Each of the firing runs went well. Jerk was the first to radio that he was 'Winchester,' meaning he was out of ammunition.

"Pectin Blue Flight join up. Break. Sleeve Seven, Pectin Blue, we are complete. We're bingo with what we have left."

"Roger, Pectin Blue. Glad to be of service."

"Pectin Blue out. Break. Pectin Blue Flight, switch to Button Baker."

Each pilot reported on frequency in sequence. Pete adjusted their heading for the return to Debden. The transit back to base was uneventful, and their landings in sequence after the break were equally routine. Green and Red Flights were already airborne for their gunnery runs. Yellow Flight were at their aircraft and preparing for takeoff. The pilots reported their aircraft status and debriefed as a flight. Jerk Harrison accepted the coaching from the other, more experienced pilots. Pete was happy with their progress. He also informed them that they would be spending more time in the ground attack training role.

—

Saturday, 13. February. 1943
Allied Forces Headquarters Forward
Hôtel Saint George
24 Avenue Souidani Boudjemaâ
Algiers
Algérie Coloniale Française
15:30 hours

General Eisenhower stared at the latest intelligence wall map that displayed both Allied and Axis field dispositions as of noon. He continued to be dissatisfied with the II Corps slow advance and vulnerable deployment. Ike sensed the Desert Fox was not far away and probably saw the weak spots in the Allied line.

The knock at the door preceded the appearance of Ike's Chief of Staff Major General Walter Bedell 'Beetle' Smith, USA. His broad, toothy grin caused Eisenhower to pause.

"OK, Beetle, what's got you fired up this afternoon?" Eisenhower queried.

Smith held out his right hand, holding four, connected, silver epaulet stars, the rank insignia for a full general. Beetle retained his grin and stared at his boss, waiting for recognition. Ike shook his head.

"A message from the War Department 30 minutes ago. The Senate confirmed your promotion yesterday evening. Congratulations, General."

"Well, now, that was fast."

"Please allow me to do the honors," Beetle said and produced the smaller collar stars. Ike nodded his consent. Smith removed Ike's three-star insignia and pinned on the new four-star device on each collar point. When finished, Smith stepped back and saluted the full general.

"Thank you, Beetle."

"A strong vote of confidence, I'd say."

"I'd like to think so, but we are not out of the woods. I'm quite concerned about Lloyd's exposed right flank and the proximity of the *Afrikakorps*. I called Lowell. He should be here shortly. I don't like the looks of this," Eisenhower said, pointing to the Central Task Force area of responsibility. This," he said, again circling the II Corps area, "feels like an ambush. The Germans have been probing the II Corps line for several days now. Something's brewing out there, and Fredendall is not taking the potential seriously."

Major General Lloyd Ralston Fredendall, USA [USMA 1905] had been Commander-in-Chief, Central Task Force, since his selection by Eisenhower in August 1942 and the beginning of Operation TORCH—the Allied forces invasion of Northwest Africa. As such, he commanded the U.S. II Corps composed of the 1st Armored Division, the 1st Infantry Division (1ID), and two activated National Guard units, the 27th and 44th Infantry Divisions.

"What do you want to do?" Beetle asked.

Eisenhower started to pace as he alternated between looking at the wall map and the floor in front of him. "Lloyd is a good man, well-trained, accomplished, but too damn cautious. We have him spread out too damn thin, and he appears to be unwilling to take the associated risk to focus the forces he has at the point intelligence tells us the enemy is likely to attack."

"Intelligence is not always correct," Smith mumbled.

"True, but some intelligence is better than others." Eisenhower did not share with his chief of staff that ULTRA gave him confirmatory information of the aerial reconnaissance photographic evidence. The knock at the door broke Ike's thinking.

Assistant Chief of Staff G-3 (Operations) AFHQ Brigadier General Lowell Ward Rooks entered the map room. "Yes sir. You wanted me?" he said to Eisenhower and then noted the new rank insignia. "Congratulations on your promotion, General. Justly deserved, I must say."

"Thank you, Lowell. What is the latest from Anderson and Fredendall?"

"General Anderson's 1st Army remains in a slugfest and continues to make progress, but understandably, he is quite reluctant to give up combat forces that will expose the 1st Army or slow down their advance. We have been working with General Fredendall to help with the redeployment as you suggested."

"So, the map board is correct?"

Rooks studied the various grease pencil markings locating Allied and Axis units on the map to the best of their knowledge. "Yes sir, I think it is."

"Which means they have not reinforced the right flank."

"Correct, sir."

"Do I need to issue direct orders to generals here?"

"No sir. I know they are working on the reinforcement process, but they're stretched thin, General. They are fighting a determined enemy without normal reserves. None of them wants to fail."

"What about drawing from Patton's Western Task Force?" Smith offered.

"We've discussed that potential a number of times over the last week. The capacity of the roads and rail lines are the choke point. It would take us weeks to move a division from Morocco to Tunisia."

"Then, we must gamble."

"Yes sir." Rooks stared at Eisenhower, expecting more guidance.

Eisenhower looked over his left shoulder at Beetle Smith. "Arrange transport, Beetle. I need to go sit down with Fredendall, eye-to-eye. I want General Ferryman to go with me."

Assistant Chief of Staff G-2 (Intelligence) AFHQ Brigadier Eric Edward Mockler-Ferryman had served as Eisenhower's chief of intelligence since August of last year.

"I'll set it up," Smith responded.

Eisenhower nodded, and then he looked at Rooks. "Thanks, Lowell. Keep at it."

"Yes sir." Rooks departed.

Eisenhower waited for the door to close after Rooks left. "Lloyd is just too damn cautious," Ike mumbled more to himself than to Smith. Ike stared at the map. Beetle knew the signs and left his boss to his contemplation.

Tuesday, 16.February.1943
No.10 Annexe
New Public Offices
Whitehall, London, England
United Kingdom
16:25 hours

Sir Charles McMoran Wilson, Kt, MC, MD, had been Churchill's personal physician since Winston ascended to the premiership. He had also been elevated in the King's New Year Honours List to be 1ˢᵗ Baron Moran with his investiture by the King scheduled to take place at Buckingham Palace in two weeks.

Lord Moran completed the medical examination of his charge. "Your lungs are heavily congested, Winston. I'm afraid you have a bad case of double pneumonia. I will prescribe a course of penicillin that you must take exactly as prescribed. Worse for you . . . my friend . . . you are confined to bed for one to two weeks."

"Impossible, Charles. I have a war to fight."

"If you do not follow my instructions, you will soon be unable to fight anything, set aside this war. My task here is to get you healthy and keep you healthy."

Churchill coughed hard. "I received a personal from Franklin this morning, or at least from Harry Hopkins. Apparently, he is quite ill and confined to bed as well."

"As you are, Winston. Casablanca was not kind to either one of you."

"It was a very positive conference."

Wilson chuckled softly. "Nothing could be so important to cost you your life."

Churchill joined him in laughing that stimulated more coughing. "Perhaps, but it came damn close."

"I will trust you to comply. I will also properly instruct your private secretariat staff to enforce the rules should you feel the urge to deviate. This is very serious, Winston. You are not the spring chicken you once were, and you must respect your aging. We need you healthy. Let me do my job. I'm also going to instruct Mister Martin and his colleagues to minimize your correspondence to only the essential."

"It's all essential, Charles. We're in a war, in case you hadn't heard."

"Essential, Winston. You must trust me."

Churchill huffed and puffed for a minute in his frustration. "Against my better inclinations, I shall remain in bed for now." Winston reached to the nightstand and raised a book. "I'll try to confine my reading for pleasure rather than work."

"Excellent. The closer you follow my instructions precisely, the sooner you will be rid of this pneumonia and return to good health. By the way, if I may ask, what have you chosen to read."

"Daniel Defoe's *The Fortunes and Misfortunes of the Famous Moll Flanders*, published in 1722."

"That is a rather bawdy novel, as I recall," observed Lord Moran.

"Yes, Charles, it is. The book was considered quite radical back in the day. I read the book many years ago, out of curiosity. Now, it is just for pleasure."

"I don't think I've ever read it. Perhaps, I should."

"Of course, you should, Charles. It is quite entertaining. If you are so inclined, I would also recommend other tomes of a similar vein. John Cleland's *Memoirs of a Woman of Pleasure*, also known as Fanny Hill, was published in 1748, and Henry Fielding's *The History of Tom Jones, a Foundling*, was published the following year. Then, there is always D.H. Lawrence's *Lady Chatterley's Lover* published in 1928, and the subject of so many obscenity cases in England, the dominions, and the United States."

"I've read that one," Lord Moran said. "Intriguing writing style. I can understand why the moralists object to the writing and the story."

"I've not been particularly partial to a small group of cads and rascals deciding what books I can read."

"Quite so."

"But all of those are tame in contrast to *Justine, ou les Malheurs de la vertu*, published in 1791, or *L'Histoire de Juliette ou les Prospérités du vice*, published in 1797."

"The Marquis de Sade?"

"*Qui. L'avocat libertin extraordinaire, ou peut-être plus approprié les défenseurs de la pratique libertine.*"

"My, my . . . my dear Winston, what has returned you to this carnal genre?"

"I suppose if I had to blame someone or something, it is my illness. I do not feel well. This affair stimulates the imagination."

"Just what the doctor ordered, so read away, my friend."

"One last request, Lord Moran. This place is rather dreary. What do you say about moving my convalescence to Chequers or Ditchley?" asked Churchill.

The 16th Century manor house known as Chequers Court had been transferred to the nation in 1917 and configured as the country retreat for the serving prime minister. As The Blitz reached its full ferocity, Chequers was considered too close to London, too easily identified from the air, and too much of a target. Ditchley Park in Oxfordshire was lent to the prime minister as a more secure country manor house for the prime minister's relaxation.

"We can entertain such a move once you are on the mend. However, you have not yet turned the corner, and such a move is simply too risky. I need you close by to the best medical facilities and treatment as humanly possible. The countryside offers neither."

Churchill frowned demonstrably and glared at the doctor. "That is not the response I sought."

"I'm sure it's not, but that is the best response for you."

The prime minister held his bulldog glare. "Very well, then . . . for now. We will revisit my request soon."

"Quite so. We can, and I'm sure will do so, once the worst is behind you."

Churchill was not happy with the last exchange, but he conceded the moment. He picked up and opened his book, signaling the conversation was over. Doctor Wilson smiled modestly, nodded his head, and departed the Annexe bedroom. He stopped to provide instructions and guidance to the prime minister's Duty Private Secretary John Martin.

—

Thursday, 18 February 1943
59 Königinstraße
München
Deutsches Reich
16:10 hours

Trevor Andersen walked briskly with his overcoat collar up, wrapped around his neck and head, and had his fedora pulled down as far as it would go, as he braced himself against the cold but dry north wind. Fortunately, the sidewalks had been swiftly swept and shoveled clear from the snow last week. Snow filled the street gutters and some of the building cracks and crevasses. Packed snow and ice covered the streets, except where the sun was able to reach the asphalt.

His eyes moved constantly as he persistently checked the windows, doorways, and small side streets for any warning signs. Trevor saw none. As he turned the last corner, the experienced agent instantly saw the black Mercedes and Opel staff cars along with several uniformed SD and SS soldiers parked in front of his destination. Gestapo officers were undoubtedly inside the building. He kept his head down, his hands in his coat pockets, and he did not alter his pace or movement. Trevor tried to glance nonchalantly at the gathered men in front of the Scholl's apartment building, as a curious or concerned citizen might do. He did not look back. His tongue transferred the small glass capsule from his cheek to between his left side molar teeth— just in case.

At the first cross-street, he turned back north and out of sight. The urge to run as fast as his legs would take him verged upon overwhelming, but he resisted the urge with all his will. His best chance for escape depended upon his appearing normal and routine. Trevor made it back to Ludwig Street at the university's edge and the well-scouted café near the campus. *Herbstcafé* had an unobstructed rear exit should he need it. He took a table toward the back and ordered a chicory pseudo-coffee. The warmth felt good. Trevor tried as hard as he could to appear casual, calm, and unaffected as possible.

Do I wait and see if the Scholl's are OK? The Gestapo might have been at the building for someone else. Maybe the Scholl's are safe. If the Gestapo has the Scholls, they will undoubtedly be tortured. The risk is too great. They will give me up before their friends and comrades. Fortunately, my escape plan has been tested several times. No, not worth the risk. Way too close. I've got to get out of the city. I'll send my abort and evacuation signal as soon as I get some distance. Best get on my way. Nothing unusual or out of the ordinary outside. Clear so far.

Trevor paid his bill, made sure he smiled and offered a cheery salutation, and then went to his apartment. He approached carefully to ensure the Gestapo was not already waiting for him. As was his practice, his bag had been packed before he left for the meeting. Trevor recovered his preferred Walther PPK 32-caliber semi-automatic pistol with silencer installed and donned his shoulder holster with four loaded spare clips. He checked to make sure he had a full clip in the pistol and a live round in the chamber. The safety was engaged. He checked and wiped down the apartment to ensure not a trace of his presence was left. The last thing he did was check his travel papers one last time. They appeared proper and reasonably well worn before stepping out and closing the door behind him.

Trevor stopped at the landlord's ground floor apartment. He knocked. "Good morning, Mrs. Schmidt. I regret to inform you that my company has recalled me. I must leave for Zürich immediately."

"I'm so sorry to lose you, Mister Weber, but I understand. These are troubled times." Trevor made a point of extracting his business card and giving it to Mrs. Schmidt. Would you be so kind to forward any mail that comes here to my office address," he said, pointing to the postal address on his business card.

"Of course. Thank you very much, Tobias. You were a perfect tenant."

"Thank you. I try to be good and respectful. Thank you again for taking care of me. Perhaps we shall see each other on a future date." He tipped his fedora and lifted his bag. Mrs. Schmidt leaned forward and kissed him on the cheek. Trevor smiled, nodded his head, and tipped his hat one last time before he departed.

Trevor Anderson, alias Tobias Weber, walked to the *Marienplatz* tram station, checked the destination sign, and boarded the waiting tram. Sitting in an open seat gave him a good opportunity to scan the other passengers and the rail car area. It was a short ride to *München Hauptbahnhof*—Munich Central Rail Station.

Uniformed police patrolled the facility inside and outside. None of them appeared to be agitated or unusually attentive. Trevor presented his travel documents and purchased a ticket to Stuttgart. He had 35 minutes to wait before boarding time. Trevor bought a newspaper, went to a small coffee shop, and ordered another chicory pseudo-coffee. He carefully examined everyone moving through the facility. The public address system announced train departures to Zürich, Nürnberg, and Berlin. He feigned attention to the newspaper while he scanned every person in or moving through the station.

"Der zug nach Stuttgart einsteigen am Gleis Sechs."

Trevor finished his drink, folded his newspaper under his left arm over the concealed pistol, and paid the bill with a modest gratuity. A railroad employee with a uniformed SD policeman watching closely checked Trevor's travel documents and cleared him to board the train. Thank goodness for the skill of the forgery office. He found his compartment, took his seat, and unfolded his newspaper. Twenty minutes later, the train lurched forward, and the next leg of his egress plan began.

—

Saturday, 20.February.1943
No.10 Annexe
New Public Offices
Whitehall, London, England
United Kingdom
08:55 hours

Churchill remained in bed with his heavy robe on for extra warmth and propped himself up sitting against the headboard. The frequency and harshness of his cough and congested lungs seemed to be diminishing. His fever had broken. All of the medical signs of his recovery remained positive, except for his persistent cough. Winston felt better sitting up, but he still tired quickly. He pushed the bedside buzzer.

Duty Private Secretary John Peck knocked and entered. "You rang, sir."

"I'm ready for breakfast."

"Very well, sir." Peck left the bedroom to call the galley and returned in a few minutes. "Your breakfast should be here shortly, Mister Prime Minister."

"Thank you, John. When you get a moment, would you be so kind to knock up Lord Moran? I have had enough of the Annexe. I want to complete my recuperation at Chequers."

"I will call Doctor Wilson. However, I am compelled to remind you that the doctor wanted to keep you close to the hospitals should you develop complications."

"Yes, yes, he has been very insistent, but I am feeling bet . . ." A hard, deep, wet cough interrupted the prime minister.

Peck shook his head. "I'm afraid your body betrays you, Prime Minister."

"Nonetheless, I would be far more comfortable at Chequers."

"As you wish, sir. I will call Doctor Wilson and asked him to attend to you."

"Thank you, John."

"With your consent, I would like to constrain your workload to en . . ." A knock at the door interrupted Peck. "That is likely your breakfast." John went to the door. Churchill's valet, Frank Sawyers, held a bed tray with the prime minister's breakfast. John opened the door wider for Sawyers, who went directly to the prime minister and placed the tray across his lap. Sawyers departed.

The prime minister managed a couple of bites of his fried eggs on toast before he spoke. "Yes, I consent. I'm certain you've been managing the dispatch box admirably, and I'm extraordinarily grateful for the respite from the tumult of the war."

"It is my honor to serve, sir. I'll leave you to eat your breakfast in peace."

"Thank you, John."

Before Peck reached the door, another knock preceded the door opening. Sawyers poked his head in past the door. "Please excuse me, Prime Minister." He looked at John. "If you will, Mister Peck."

The prime minister's duty private secretary stepped out and closed the door. He returned a minute later. "Brigadier Menzies just arrived with an urgent matter."

Brigadier Sir Stewart Graham 'C' Menzies, KCMG, CB, DSO, MC, had been director-general of the Secret Intelligence Service (MI6) since 1939 and the passing of Admiral Sinclair. As director-general, Sir Stewart acquired the moniker 'C' in honor of the original director Captain Sir George Mansfield Smith-Cumming, as his predecessors had maintained the tradition.

"Please show him in," Churchill responded and took another bite of his breakfast.

"Good morning, Prime Minister. Please pardon my intrusion. I trust your recovery is progressing nicely."

"Yes, I am feeling better every day, although I'm not done with this pneumonia just yet. Thank you for your beneficent wishes. Now, what is so urgent?"

"Reports from North Africa indicate Allied Forces suffered a significant defeat just inside Tunisia at Kasserine Pass. The Germans achieved a significant victory, and the prevailing opinion among our analysts is the only thing stopping Rommel from thrusting deep into Algeria is their strained supply lines."

"Who is that?"

"The American 1st Infantry Division of the II Corps."

"What is Eisenhower doing?"

"He's ordered the immediate redeployment of front-line forces, which will weaken other areas of the line. Eisenhower is meeting with General Anderson as we speak. My guess is, he's discussing the slowdown of the northern axis of advance and at least the temporary transfer of 1st Army units to help plug the gap at Kasserine."

"Bad news, indeed. This is quite likely a setback for our plans."

"If I may ask, sir, how so?"

"We have not discussed the SYMBOL Conference. However, the short version is, we needed North Africa secure by this month so that we can move onto Sicily and at least landing major forces on the Italian mainland in order to consolidate the Mediterranean. We have deemed that objective necessary to free land, sea, and air forces to execute Operation ROUNDUP."

"The cross-Channel invasion?"

"Exactly . . . and the final push to Berlin." Churchill lapsed into contemplation. He eventually pushed his bed tray and half-eaten breakfast away. Winston looked back at Menzies. "I'm certain the War Office will pick it up from here. Do we have anything from Boniface on Rommel?"

Boniface was the double code name given to ULTRA, the product of deciphering the vaunted German encryption device – Enigma. The British led the German decryption activities, while the United States led the Japanese decryption effort under the code name MAGIC. Since the ARCADIA Conference in Washington, immediately after the U.S. joined the war, both programs were now truly joint projects.

"No sir, but we keep looking. Our productivity continues to improve, so if he talks, we should eventually read his mail."

"Good. The field commanders need all the help they can get. What else do you have?"

"Hitler's chief propagandist spoke at a party rally day before yesterday and demanded total war to win the war for The Leader."

"Total war? What does he think they have been doing for the last three and a half years?"

"Our analysts have studied the transcript of Goebbels' speech, well a partial transcript . . . the best we could obtain in a couple of days, and our opinion is the speech was intended to remove whatever restraints might have existed within the party apparatus, namely the various elements of the SS, SD, Gestapo, and their various sub-elements."

"I shudder to think about what that may look like given the brutality of those NSDAP enforcement arms."

"Agreed. We will be watching and documenting."

"Excellent. We reaffirmed the Germany-first strategy at SYMBOL, along with our insistence upon unconditional surrender. There will be no armistice in this affair. Given your information, we are likely to witness even more fanatical actions by the Nawzees. We also decided that we will conduct public trials for the perpetrators, those who committed war crimes, crimes against humanity, and violated the rules of war established by the Geneva Conventions."

"Understandable. We will help gather the evidence. To that end, I have established a war crimes section tasked with gleaning from our intelligence collection activities and collecting the evidence for such future tribunals."

"Good. Quite appropriate.

Menzies nodded his head. "There is obviously a lot more going on in the world, but those were the top items I thought appropriate to inform you of quickly, even though you are still on your sickbed."

"Thank you, Sir Stewart. I should also offer my sincere and genuine congratulations for your well-deserved knighthood on the King's New Year's Honours List."

"Thank you, sir, and please allow me to express my gratitude for your recommendation to the King."

"As I said, well deserved. Keep up the great work you are doing."

"Certainly. My apologies for interrupting your breakfast, sir. I wish you a speedy recovery."

"Thank you, Sir Stewart." Menzies departed.

John Peck returned. "Are you finished with your breakfast, sir?"

"Yes."

"I'll ask Sawyers to clear your tray. Is there anything else I can do for you?"

"No, John. Thank you. I need some thinking time. Please inform Sawyers I'll take my bath, in say, an hour."

"I will do so, Prime Minister." Peck left Churchill with his thoughts.

—

Chapter 3

There is no kind of life,
whether public or private, at home or abroad —
that is free of obligations.
In their due discharge is all of life.
-- Cicero

Thursday, 4.March.1943
Chequers Court
Ellesborough, Buckinghamshire, England
United Kingdom
16:10 hours

Churchill's convalescence progressed well under Lord Moran's medical supervision, and the doctor finally allowed the prime minister to relocate to Chequers at the beginning of this week. Winston's mood instantly improved, as noted by his family, friends, and staff. He took his afternoon nap a little earlier than usual. Winston found Clementine in the library reading a book in one of the sizeable, overstuffed leather chairs by the modest fire in the large fireplace. He started to sit in the other chair when he noticed their third child and second daughter Sarah in the garden. She was smiling and laughing, which in itself was not unusual even in these troubled times, but then, Winston saw U.S. Ambassador John Gilbert 'Gil' Winant, who was one of their planned guests at the country estate this coming weekend. Winant had arrived while Churchill was napping. Churchill watched his middle daughter frolic with Winant.

"Clemmie?" Churchill called without taking his eyes off the couple in the garden. She did not answer. "Clemmie?" he said a little louder. He saw them kiss, and then Sarah stepped back and looked guilty of some unseen offense.

"Yes, dear," Clementine finally answered.

The couple held hands and walked back toward the mansion. "Oh, nothing . . . never mind." There was no longer anything for her to see. "I need to talk to Sarah," he muttered.

"What was that you said, Winnie?"

"Nothing, darling. I was just talking to myself."

"Oh, very well, then. How was your nap?"

"Excellent. Thank you very much." Churchill walked across the extensive library, intent upon finding Sarah, when Lieutenant General Sir Hastings Lionel 'Pug' Ismay, KCB, DSO, appeared in the open doorway.

Ismay held numerous titles and positions, including principal assistant to the Minister of Defence, secretary of the Imperial Defence Chiefs of Staff

Committee, and the War Cabinet's deputy secretary. Churchill saw Ismay as his primary military liaison to the joint chiefs and the military services.

Ismay did not speak and only nodded toward the prime minister's private and secure study. Churchill followed Ismay into the study. Ismay closed the door behind them. The prime minister took one of four comfortable chairs around a low, round table and gestured for Ismay to proceed.

"I have several items for your interest, Prime Minister." Ismay received only a head nod. "First . . ." Ismay opened his folder and extracted another folder with a red border, handing it to the prime minister without words.

MOST SECRET - ULTRA

```
MOST SECRET ULTRA

DATE 1152 4 MAR 1943

SECRET

DATE 30 DEC 1942

TO OKW OKM

FROM CHANCELLOR

COPY OKH OKL

COMMAND

BREAK I HEREBY NOTIFY ALL COMMANDS GRAND

ADMIRAL RAEDER HAS RESIGNED AS COMMANDER IN

CHIEF NAVY AND IS REASSIGNED TO THE POST OF

ADMIRAL INSPECTOR EFFECTIVE IMMEDIATELY BREAK

I THANK ADMIRAL RAEDER FOR HIS SERVICE TO THE

EMPIRE BREAK ADMIRAL DONITZ IS HEREBY PROMOTED

TO GRAND ADMIRAL AND ASSUMED POST AS COMMANDER

IN CHIEF NAVY BREAK THE LEADER END

SECRET

DECYPHERED 0757 4 MAR 1943
```

MOST SECRET - ULTRA

"This one took three months to decipher," Churchill noted.

"Yes sir. A note inside the secure case indicated their primary techniques did not work. They had to use a more laborious process to break it. Station X believed the message had relevance, although not timely."

"Indeed. This is from that scoundrel corporal himself, or at least in his name. Do we know what this admiral inspector position is?"

"No sir. I'll ask Admiral Pike to see what Naval Intelligence knows."

"So, Raeder is out, and Dönitz has the whole kit and caboodle."

"That is the way I read the message."

"If you would, please ask the Admiralty and Jumper Pike if they anticipate any changes in enemy naval operations. Also, I would like to know if Jumper knows why they removed Raeder?"

"I'll get on it as soon as we finish here."

"What's next?"

"I have the personal message you sent to Field Marshal Dill."

MOST SECRET
FOR YOUR EYES ALONE

```
ZZZZ/8471AEK7845/PM-MILUS/466753/LWMM/637/ZZZZ
DATE 04 03 43 1445 HOURS
FROM PM UK
TO CHIEF MIL LIAISON USA FOR YOUR EYES ALONE
NO COPIES ALLOWED
SUBJECT OPERATION HUSKY
BREAK
ON NO ACCOUNT ARE YOU TO GIVE ANY ENCOURAGEMENT
TO THE POSTPONEMENT OF THE JUNE DATE FOR HUSKY
OR FOR THE SAKE OF BOLERO
END
ZZZZ/8471AEK7845/PM-MILUS/466753/LWMM/637/ZZZZ
```

MOST SECRET
FOR YOUR EYES ALONE

"We received confirmation from Sir John 30 minutes later," Ismay said.

"We must push hard to move along the next two steps if we are to have any hope of landing our main forces on the Continent. I think Sir John appreciates the significance of my message."

"Yes sir, he does. He is as sharp as they come. Sir John knows from this message that any effort by our comrades to push back the execution date will precipitate immediate notice to you. If I may, sir . . ." Ismay waited for Winston's gesture to proceed. "Isn't North Africa a greater obstacle to holding the line on HUSKY?"

"Yes, it is, Pug. The Americans are still working to stop the bleeding after the smashing they took at Kasserine Pass. I have it on good authority that the supreme commander is going to replace Fredendall with Patton."

Pug let out a louder laugh that sounded more like a cough. "That will be quite the switch. Fredendall is a competent, successful commander, but Patton is a hungry, angry, Staffordshire Terrier that packs one helluva bite. You had dinner with the general in Casablanca, did you not? What was your assessment, if I may ask?"

"I like your description, Pug . . . quite apropos. What else do you have?"

"Just after lunch, I took a call from Lord Selborne on your behalf. Operation GUNNERSIDE, the SOE raid on the Norsk Hydro heavy water production facility, was executed last Saturday night through early Sunday morning."

In February 1942, the prime minister and War Cabinet had appointed Roundell Cecil Palmer, 3rd Earl of Selborne, to the minister of Economic Warfare, replacing Hugh Dalton. The Special Operations Executive (SOE) had been created under the ministry in July 1940.

"I was informed of the raid. Does Lord Selborne have results yet?"

"Yes sir. The raid was more successful than the initial reports suggested. They destroyed the entire electrolysis array as well as 500 kilos of heavy water supply, their entire stock. Even better, the entire team appears to have made good their egress. Half the team has been accounted for, and the other half are making their way to Oslo or Sweden, so we are not out of the woods just yet. However, Lord Selborne spoke in very positive terms."

"Does TUBE ALLOYS know any of this?" asked Churchill, referring to the code name for the British atomic weapons development program in parallel and contributing to the joint Manhattan Project in the United States.

"No sir, not to my knowledge."

"Please ask Lord Selborne to do so and ensure he briefs Bill Donovan and the OSS of these results. This is a major setback for Werner Heisenberg and the Nawzee effort. The scientists have fretted to the point of distraction about the perceived advantage the Germans have enjoyed. Hopefully, this success will settle the team down a little so that they can focus on the task at hand. I will send a congratulatory letter to Lord Selborne, Gubbins, and the GUNNERSIDE field team. Well done to all."

Major General Colin McVean Gubbins, DSO, MC, had an exceptional reputation in special operations. He had been the director of operations and training from the inception of SOE. Gubbins remained one of the most passionate voices espousing the benefits of irregular warfare.

"Lastly, on my list, the *Luftwaffe* attacked the city last night. During the attack, a tragic event occurred at Bethnal Green Underground Station. The Fire Brigade is working to rescue any survivors, but it appears well more than a hundred men, women, and children may have been killed. The Commissioner of the London Fire Brigade used the term 'charnel house' in describing the incident at the tube station last night."

"A death chamber."

"Yes, precisely. They are focused on rescue at the moment, and they have not been able to conduct a proper investigation to determine what happened. According to the commissioner, the Bethnal Green incident appears to have been induced by panic rather than bomb damage."

"Dear God!" Churchill lapsed into thought for a few seconds. "We need to handle this carefully. We may have gotten out of practice with our sheltering process since the last of The Blitz."

Churchill went to his desk and depressed the signaling buzzer. The prime minister's duty private secretary appeared. Churchill instructed John Martin on the new actions from Ismay's briefing. Ismay and Martin left the prime minister with his thoughts, warming his hands in front of the modest fire.

—

Friday, 5.March.1943
II Corps Headquarters
Djebel Kouif
Algérie Coloniale Française
09:00 hours

"Welcome to my headquarters, General, although I suspect this is not an auspicious visit," announced Major General Lloyd Fredendall. "And congratulations on your promotion."

Eisenhower smiled briefly, then pointed to the stairs, implying they should retire to Fredendall's office. Once perhaps the small hotel's only quasi-suite, the modest sized room had been converted to a functional commander's office complete with wall maps and map board with the unit's current disposition of forces. Eisenhower gestured as he entered it would be a private closed meeting.

When the door closed, Eisenhower did not waste time with salutations and turned to Fredendall without making any move to sit. "The time has come, Lloyd. We need your experience back in the States training our combat troops rapidly."

Fredendall shook his head, perhaps in resignation, maybe in disagreement or disappointment. "We've recovered from Kasserine, Ike."

"Yes, we have. Thank you for that."

"Then, why are you relieving me?"

"I urge you not to think of this move that way. I certainly am not doing so. I meant what I said. We need your combat experience in the monumental training task ahead of us as we build our forces for victory."

"It sure feels like I am being relieved."

"That is your choice, Lloyd. I can only say that is not the way I am thinking of this, and that is not how your record will reflect."

"When will this change take place?"

"Now. There is a staff car out front and a plane waiting upon your arrival in Algiers for your flight home."

Fredendall deflated. The general stared at his commander for several seconds. "Can I say good-bye to the staff?"

"There is no time, Lloyd. Your transportation is on a tight schedule. Thank you for your hard work. Safe journey. Do good work getting us the troops we need." Eisenhower did not wait for a response, turned, opened the door, and gestured for Fredendall to precede him back out of the hotel headquarters. Eisenhower followed Fredendall out. The transferred commander did not look at anyone or say anything. Before he entered the staff car's passenger compartment, General Fredendall turned, came to sharp attention, and saluted General Eisenhower. Ike returned Lloyd's salute.

The staff car departed promptly, followed by an armed half-track escort. Eisenhower watched the two vehicles depart on the road to Algiers. He waited for the dust to settle, then returned to the office.

13:50 hours

General Eisenhower stood from the desk, opened the French doors, and stepped out onto the small balcony. He knew what was coming, what to expect, and wanted to watch. Ike saw the dust trail growing before he could see the source. A few minutes later, a WC51 ¾-ton weapons carrier approached Djebel, followed by an M3 half-track with an M16, quad, 50-caliber, anti-aircraft gun mount, and a second M3 half-track with a squad of infantry troops. Ike considered grabbing the binoculars on the desk but quickly abandoned the thought. Several minutes passed before Eisenhower could see that Patton was standing in the truck like a triumphant Caesar returning to Rome. Ike smiled. No one could claim Patton was not audacious and flamboyant.

Eisenhower could not resist the spectacle of Patton's arrival. He remained on the balcony as the three-vehicle convoy came to a dusty stop in the courtyard at the front of the hotel. A half dozen headquarters staff troops sat around the central fountain smoking.

Patton dismounted, came around the front of the truck, stopped, and grasped the pistol handles on each hip. The slovenly troops got the message of the imagery before them, came to attention, and saluted their new commanding officer. *Yes, George would set a different tone.* Patton never looked up to the balcony.

Eisenhower returned to the office interior to await the arriving general. Several minutes past, Aide-de-Camp Captain Calhoun knocked on the door, opened it partially, and announced, "General Patton, sir." Eisenhower gestured for Calhoun to show the general into the office, then checked his wristwatch—yep, spot on time. He was dependable.

Patton entered, came to attention, and saluted. Eisenhower returned the salute. "Major General Patton reporting as ordered, sir."

Eisenhower walked around the desk and extended his hand to Patton. The two men shook hands. "You do arrive in style, George."

"You saw that did you?"

"Yes, I did."

"I must play the part, Ike."

"Indeed."

"So, how may I be of service?" Patton asked.

"I relieved Lloyd this morning and sent him home. I want you to take command of Two Corps."

Patton smiled briefly, then it disappeared. "Rommel . . . finally."

"Yes, George. The *Afrikakorps* is just over the eastern ridgeline," Eisenhower said, gesturing to the east. The two generals conferred on the disposition of forces in the II Corps area of operations and adjacent regions. II Corps was the right flank of the Allied Forces front line. There were no friendlies to the south. "You'll likely be the next to face Rommel as well as the first to link up with Montgomery's Eighth Army. This is your début moment, George. Do not fail me here."

"I will make you proud, Ike. Thank you for this opportunity."

"I know you will, George. Also, one last item, the president has nominated you for promotion to lieutenant general. We are waiting on confirmation by the Senate, and we will make it official. Congratulations in advance. Now, I'll take your escort and return to Algiers. We have the next step to finish planning out for all of us."

"Thank you, Ike. We'll get this done and get ready for that next step."

"Carry on, George."

The two generals shook hands. General Eisenhower departed promptly and left General Patton with his new frontline combat command.

Friday, 5.March.1943
Krupp Werks, Essen, Nordrhein-Westfalen
Deutsches Reich
23:10 hours

The first major raid on the massive steel and armaments factory complex owned and operated by Friedrich Krupp AG at Essen began just before midnight British time, after midnight German time. Bomber Command had not attacked Essen since March 1942. However, this particular raid marked the beginning of what became known as the Battle of the Ruhr—the industrial heartland of Germany. This was also the first combined advanced technology attack by Bomber Command to improve night bombing accuracy.

In the summer of 1941, Prime Minister Churchill became seriously concerned about the after-action bombing accuracy reports submitted by aircrews. After conferring with his chief science advisor, Baron Cherwell, Professor Frederick Alexander Lindemann, often referred to as The Prof, Churchill commissioned a detailed statistical analysis of bomb damage assessment reports over three months. The report became known as the Butt Report in recognition of the analysis team leader David Miles Bensusan-Butt. The report findings indicated only five percent of the bombs dropped impacted within a five-mile radius of the intended target. Bomber Command, the Royal Air Force, and the War Cabinet decided the Butt Report findings were not acceptable for the war effort. The shocking results instigated a six-month suspension of the night bombing campaign to absorb the analysis and develop corrective actions. The night bombing campaign resumed in February of 1942. Bomber Command worked hard and continuously on its night and inclement weather navigation techniques to improve their bombing accuracy.

This night's Essen mission on the Krupp Works was the first time the whole package came together—a large formation of heavy bombers, the Pathfinder Force, the OBOE navigation system, the H2S ground-mapping radar, and the WINDOW radar countermeasures.

A total of 442 heavy and medium bomber aircraft from Bomber Command participated in the Essen raid through the middle of the night. Lancaster, Wellington, Halifax, and Stirling bomber squadrons proceeded by different routes with specific timing to converge on the target, which was the entire 116-acre Krupp Essen factory complex.

The RAF Pathfinder Force (PFF) this night was a squadron of Mosquito medium bombers that dropped flairs and incendiary bombs to mark the target for the main bomber force. The fast, wooden aircraft offered a very low radar cross-section target to German radar systems, making them difficult to engage with anti-aircraft defense systems, both ground-based and airborne. The Pathfinder aircraft were equipped with the OBOE and H2S systems to determine the target's precise location at night and in inclement weather.

The British OBOE navigation and blind bombing system installed initially on the Pathfinder aircraft utilized two coded, Very High Frequency (VHF) radio signals to locate the proper bomb release point to get bombs on the intended target. Two high powered radio stations were located at Trimingham, Norfolk, and Walmer, Kent. On any given night, one of the stations was designated as CAT and the other MOUSE. Using on-board electronic equipment, the pilot intercepted and flew at a prescribed altitude and speed on a constant range arc from the CAT transmitter. When the crew intersected the MOUSE station beam, the bombardier released his payload. All of the geographical and mathematical calculations to put bombs on the desired target were done on the ground prior to the mission. The system was similar to the German *Knickebein* system used during The Blitz over England.

The H2S radar had been a specific derivative radio direction and ranging device designed for ground mapping. The radio signals reflected back to the aircraft transceiver antenna and displayed on a cathode ray tube enabled the skilled operator to see key features like rivers, bridges, roads, piers, and other distinctive features. The bombardier did not need to "see" the actual target; he only needed to know the target's specific location from any radar identifiable feature.

The last of the new tools used by Bomber Command on the Essen raid was the WINDOW radar countermeasure. The system allowed aircraft to disperse precisely cut, lightweight fiberglass or plastic strips covered with an aluminum coating designed to be highly reflective of specific frequency radar signals. The metalized ribbons fluttered and descended slowly to the ground. The bloom on the enemy radar screen made tracking of aircraft nearly impossible.

The Essen raid was successful, but there was room for improvement. The aircrews improved with experience in combat, and the engineers and scientists were in perpetual development to enhance the performance of their equipment as they incorporated the operators' feedback. This night's raid was just the beginning of the destruction to be wrought by the Royal Air Force and, eventually, the U.S. Army 8th Air Force.

In contrast to the British insistence on night bombing to minimized losses, the Army Air Forces decided to use daylight bombing and the American vaunted Norden bombsight—a precision visual aiming device.

—

Saturday, 6.March.1943
Standing Oak Farm
Winchester, Hampshire, England
United Kingdom
04:30 hours

Fire, fire, the fire is getting so close. So hot! Rubble everywhere, blocking the door, my only way out. I can't get out. The door won't move. Oh God, so hot! The paint and wood are bursting into flame. Is this how it all ends? My skin . . . OH GAAAWWWDDD . . .

Brian woke in a startled jump, sitting bolt upright in bed, staring into the darkness of the room, and panting against his fear.

"It's all right, Brian," Charlotte whispered to him. "You're safe. You're home."

Brian was shaking in fear. Charlotte's soothing hand on his damp shoulder helped him take deeper, more controlled breaths to regain control. Charlotte sat up and moved next to her husband. She put her right arm around his shoulders and stroked his chest with her left hand. She waited patiently for him to calm.

As his breathing began to return to normal, she whispered, "The same nightmare you've had before?"

Brian nodded his head in confirmation.

"What have they done to you?" Charlotte continued to soothe her husband.

"They didn't do anything to me, Charlotte. It's a consequence of what I do."

"Then maybe you should find something else to do."

"Charlotte, please . . ." Brian turned his head and kissed her forehead. "I know these damn nightmares scare you."

"Yes, they do, darling. I worry about you and . . . I am scared that your violent reaction might hurt me."

Brian put his arms around Charlotte and held her forehead to his lips. "I'm so sorry I scared you. I wish I could just make these damn nightmares go away, but I can't."

"I know." They held each other for several minutes in the silent darkness. "And I have also been around you long enough to know what they mean."

"Really? Do tell."

"You are done with your transition training, and your squadron is headed back to combat."

Brian chose not to answer or react. *But she's right. That is precisely what they mean, but I had no idea she perceived that reality.* He gently guided her back to lying down with her back toward him. Brian wrapped his arms around her, drew her close, and felt her warmth and the smooth, softness of her flesh. They laid together like two spoons in a silver case.

14:15 hours

The morning chores had been completed, the crew fed, and the afternoon product delivery to market sent off. Charlotte grasped Brian's left hand and led him to the oak tree. *She wants to talk.* The overcast sky, low clouds, and damp, chilly air did not make for a comfortable chat in the open air, even under their large oak tree. Brian and Charlotte managed to get a modest fire going in the fire pit. They sat together, holding hands and staring at the flickering flames. *This is nice. There's no need to talk.* The modest fire's warmth was just the correct balance with the not cold but chilly, damp air.

Charlotte turned on the bench to look directly at Brian. "I've been through three of your nightmares."

"There have been more than that."

"Oh great! Is that supposed to assuage my worry?"

Brian chuckled nervously. "That was not my intent. They are what they are. I don't control them. I wish there was a switch that allowed me just to turn them off."

"I wish they would go away for your peace of mind . . . and for my fear . . . my fear for your safety."

"They don't affect my flying. They're just something I . . ."

"We."

"Yes, of course . . . we must deal with from time to time."

Charlotte held Brian's eyes and touched his cheeks. "You're going back to combat, aren't you?"

Brian turned to face Charlotte, held both her hands, and focused on her glorious blue-gray eyes. "Yes. They gave us a four-day leave to rest up before we return to operational status."

"So, you come home, and I put you to work with manual labor." They both laughed heartily. "Are you resting?"

"Well, I'm not being shot at for now." They laughed again.

"At least we are together. I appreciate every day and every hour."

"As do I, my sweetheart."

Charlotte stood and put another split log on the fire.

I guess we're going to be here a while. We have time before the evening milking.

"Do you want to be involved in the hiring I'm proposing to do?"

"For farming?"

"Yes."

"I will be involved as much as you need me to be, and I am able."

"We've talked about my plan."

"Yes, we have, and I absolutely agree. I like your idea of transforming the adaptable land from pasture we don't need for the dairy into large scale gardening as you are able. I still think that would be a great way for us to use our land to support the war effort. You know what to do, and you know the people you need to make this transformation work."

"Very well. I'm looking for experienced women and non-conscription age men."

"It doesn't matter as long as they can do the job."

"I'm glad you feel that way. From my assessment, we need a master grower, a supervisor if you will, and probably four to six full-time employees, a couple for our garden and the rest for the Brownfield property."

"We need a better term of reference. The land no longer belongs to the Brownfields; it belongs to us, to Standing Oak Farm. And, that sounds reasonable. We need employees to expand, and you need people you can trust."

"The Brownfields have vacated and moved to Blackpool. I have thought about converting the house to a dormitory of sorts. I always have a degree of guilt that Horace, Lionel, and now Jacob must commute to work here." Charlotte paused and stared toward the distant ridgeline on the far side of the pond. "Mister Harris passed away last year, shortly after the sale was complete. Mrs. Harris is in failing health. Their daughter is tending to her. I've told them they could stay as long as they need."

"Very wise."

"So, you are OK with all of these changes?"

"Charlotte, my darling, you do not need my approval. At best, during these years of war, I'm an absentee partner, a missing husband. You've done a magnificent job of managing three farms. I see no reason to doubt your capabilities now."

"Thank you for that vote of confidence," Charlotte responded and kissed her husband. "I also got a call from Mary this morning. She wanted us to be the first to know. She's pregnant."

"So soon?"

"Yes, my magnificent, productive stallion. Mary was over the moon."

"You still think this was the right thing to do?" Brian asked, looking directly at Charlotte.

"If you had heard Mary . . . yes, I do. It was a generous gift we gave Mary and John."

"Uh-ha."

"I didn't want to know ahead of time, but now is a good time for you to tell me the tale."

Brian took in a deep breath and exhaled. He offered a summary description. Charlotte asked questions and offered comments, but she again thanked Brian at the end of the discussion, and she chose to reassure him of her support and confidence in him.

Charlotte glanced at the barn. The truck had returned without her being aware. The cows were moving to the barn. "Perhaps, we can continue this discussion later," Charlotte announced. "I think we should contribute." Brian looked over and noticed what she had seen. He nodded his head and stood to douse the remains of the fire. They held hands as they walked in silence toward the barn for their afternoon chores.

—

Monday, 8.March.1943
Chequers Court
Ellesborough, Buckinghamshire, England
United Kingdom
11:45 hours

Prime Minister Churchill stood outside in the chilly mist of late winter. The King's Rolls Royce limousine rolled to a stop at the entrance. King George VI leaped out before his aide could open the door.

"My precious prime minister," the King proclaimed, "why are you outside in this damp air?"

"To welcome you to Chequers, my Regent."

King George VI grasped the prime minister's arm and led him to the interior. "I came to you because you have been ill, and I missed our weekly luncheons." The King knew the way to the library and what he expected to be a warm room. "I would not have come here if I had known I was putting you at risk."

"Nonsense, your Majesty. Lord Moran informed me yesterday that I am on the mend. You are due the respect of your station."

They entered the library as they sat in the chairs before the fire. The prime minister's duty private secretary and the King's aide closed the door to leave the two men alone.

"Before we start," the King said, "I wish to offer my apology to you for risking your recovery."

"You did not, sir."

"I shall take you at your word, Winston, but I would never forgive myself if I endangered your health or capacity to bring us through this terrible trial."

"You are most generous, your Majesty."

"Have you managed to stay current on our affairs of state?"

Churchill chuckled inaudibly. "I can't say I'm back to my usual self; however, I have a few items we can discuss. First, as your Majesty may recall, Lord Cherwell guided an Admiralty statistician, David Bensusan-Butt, in a study of our night bombing accuracy."

"I remember."

"We suspended bombing missions for the next six months until we developed a more accurate means of nighttime bombing. We resumed bombing the following February, as we continued our scientific development efforts."

"I recall that, as well."

"On the night of the fifth, three days ago, Bomber Command executed our first large scale raid using the new equipment and techniques on the Krupp Works in Essen. We received the bomb damage assessment from the Analysis Branch this morning. I can inform your Majesty that it was a very successful mission . . . better than 50 percent of the bombs were on target. Aerial photography confirms serious damage to Krupp Works and associated support facilities. The analysts believe they will be out of operations for at least three months, more like six, depending upon how much that foul corporal can give Speers to throw at the repair task."

"Would it be appropriate for me to send a letter of congratulations to Air Marshal Harris and the crews involved?"

"Yes sir. If I may, I would urge caution in overplaying this success. The accomplishment of the aircrews, scientists, engineers, and support personnel is certainly noteworthy. However, we have a long way to go."

"Very well. I shall be sensitive to your observations."

"Another positive news item arrived over the weekend. While we have not yet closed the encirclement of the *Afrikakorps*, Hitler apparently didn't want one of his favorite field generals to face capture. We have confirmed that he has personally recalled Rommel to Germany. Rommel was promoted to field marshal in June of last year, and we surmise the prospect of having another field marshal being captured alive, after Paulus at Stalingrad, was too much for him. Field Marshal Rommel has transferred command of the *Afrikakorps* to Colonel General von Arnim."

"If I understood you correctly, Eisenhower's Allied Forces have not yet linked up with Montgomery's 8th Army to complete the encirclement of the Germans and Italians."

"Correct, sir. We experienced a serious setback two weeks ago, a product of our forces being stretched far too thin in facing a determined and experienced enemy."

"Was that Kasserine Pass?"

"Yes sir. General Eisenhower has recovered quickly and plugged the gap. He relieved the American II Corps' commanding general and replaced him with General Patton, whom I've watched, met, and discussed his generalcy. I have high expectations for Patton, and we should soon see the results. I must also say we have done our best to choke the Germans, but they are a very determined force. As we discussed last month, the knock-on effects of the fight left in the Germans appear likely to push back our timetable for the final assault on the Continent until the spring of 1944."

"Is President Roosevelt in agreement?"

"Yes sir. We regularly converse, if not daily, it is nearly so. The earlier point I failed to make was Rommel's removal from North Africa is another positive sign that our domination of North Africa is a month or two away. Premier Stalin will not be happy, but these are the realities of modern warfare."

"The second front in the west?"

"Yes sir. Although I would say the signs on the eastern front are comparably positive, he has been very insistent. The Red Army has found its footing, and its battlefield successes are mounting. Certainly, the jeopardy they faced in the winter of 1941 has eased substantially."

"We are still supplying them?"

"Yes sir. The Americans have extended the Lend-Lease provisioning to China and the Soviet Union, so we are no longer carving out portions of our supply line to support the Soviets as we were compelled to do in '41 and '42. I must say here; the Soviets are never satisfied. They always want more of everything. We are planning several joint operations that are necessary until we can land our final assault force on the Continent."

"And you think that final offensive to defeat Germany will be moved to 1944?"

"In part, yes, but in total, no. As you may recall, we agreed with our comrades at Casablanca that our next two steps after we secure North Africa and the Southern Mediterranean Sea are Sicily followed by mainland Italy. Our joint intelligence indicates that the Italian military has a substantial restive element that we believe we can exploit once they are presented with the reality of their situation. Eliminating Italy is the logical next objective. The weather window for a large-scale cross-Channel assault is May to September. At Casablanca, we agreed to that strategic plan, and we also agreed that we had to secure North Africa by February to allow for Sicily in April and landing a sustainable force on the Italian boot so that we could transfer, prepare, train, and deploy the necessary resources for the cross-Channel operations by September. Although we have not jointly conceded the time shift, the facts are quite apparent."

"Why not skip Sicily?" the King asked.

"We considered that potential, but the collective military opinion in doing so would place an even greater and more protracted demand on our available landing craft."

"Then, what is your current estimate for the liberation of North Africa?"

"Both generals Eisenhower and Alexander agree that it looks like April or May."

"With that, when is the earliest we can cross the Channel?"

"May 1944."

"Does Stalin have that date?'

"No sir. We will not inform him until we have a clear conclusion to the North Africa campaign."

"Well, that gives a good . . . ," the knock at the door interrupted the King's sentence.

Duty Private Secretary John Martin opened the door just enough to stand halfway into the room. "Lunch is ready, sir."

"Thank you, John." Martin closed the door. Churchill looked back at the King. "Would you like to freshen up before lunch, your Majesty?"

"Not necessary, Winston. Let us go see what Mrs. Landemare has conjured up for us with the exigencies of wartime sacrifice."

Churchill chuckled. "She will be ecstatic that you remembered her skills."

The King stood, and Churchill joined him. "Oh, my dear Winston, please tell her I would steal her away if she worked for anyone else but you."

"We are all your servants, your Majesty." The two men walked casually to the dining room, laughing and speculating on the potential of the approaching spring.

—

Tuesday, 9.March.1943
No.10 Downing Street
Whitehall, London, England
United Kingdom
14:30 hours

It had been two months since the prime minister had been in the traditional London residence. Churchill had departed for the SYMBOL Conference in Casablanca from No.10. The closest he got upon his return to London was the Annexe, mainly due to his serious illness and Lord Moran's strict convalescence restraints. The PM took a quick tour of the on-going repairs and improvements being carried out since the end of The Blitz. The progress was slow but steady, and the War Cabinet concurred that the priority for war materials must remain with the combat services.

Churchill had barely settled into his refurbished office/study when Duty Private Secretary John Peck announced the unscheduled arrival of Director-General, Secret Intelligence Service (MI6), Brigadier Sir Stewart 'C' Menzies.

"Welcome back to Number 10, Prime Minister," said Menzies. "I trust you are fully recovered from your illness."

"Thank you, Sir Stewart. Not fully, but sufficiently to return to harness."

"Great to have you back. Please allow me to jump right into the purpose of my unannounced visit. As soon as I was notified of your return, we received a critical Boniface message." Menzies placed the manacled, locked case on the prime minister's desk.

Churchill retrieved his key, always carried on his person, and unlocked the case. He removed a single piece of paper from the red-striped folder.

MOST SECRET - ULTRA

```
MOST SECRET ULTRA
SECRET
DATE 0717 9 MAR 1943
TO OKW OKH
FROM CMDR DAK
COPY SUPREME COMMANDER NORTH AFRICA XX CORPS
ARMORED AFRICA GROUP
BREAK
TOO MANY NEGATIVE COINCIDENCES BREAK SERIOUS
CONCERNS WITH SECURITY OF OUR COMMUNICATIONS
BREAK REQUEST INTERNAL SECURITY ASSESSMENT BY
INDEPENDENT SPECIALISTS BREAK FM ER CONCURS
BREAK HAIL VICTORY BREAK HAIL HITLER END
SECRET
DECYPHERED 0946 9 MAR 1943
MOST SECRET ULTRA
```

MOST SECRET - ULTRA

"Oh, dear God above," exclaimed Churchill. "Have we made a dreadful mistake and inadvertently cut down our golden apple tree?"

"Let us not overreact, sir. They have faced a string of serious defeats since we plugged the inadvertent vulnerability exposed by the unwitting American Colonel Fellers in Cairo last June. The Germans knew their intelligence source dried up, and we've seen no evidence they knew or even suspected why. The 8th Army stopped the German advance the next month and turned them onto the defensive three months later."

"Yes, yes, but they are now suspicious that their communications have been compromised."

"Again, please don't be so quick to jump to that conclusion. This message," Sir Stewart said and pointed at the paper still in Churchill's hand, "was not conclusive. It was suspicious. Please remember that Hitler himself just recalled Rommel. Von Arnim inherited a beleaguered army group that has been on the defensive and pushed around the desert since October of last year. He knows, and I imagine he appreciates Rommel's reputation. We believe 'FM ER' in the message is, in fact, Field Marshal Erwin Rommel. Our preliminary assessment of that message is a natural consequence of the situation in which von Arnim is now faced."

"Who do you think are the independent specialists the message refers to in the message?"

"That could be interpreted in many ways. The German Army and Military Intelligence have noteworthy counterintelligence and communications skills. However, our analysts believe the use of the word 'independent' probably means engagement of the SD's considerable capability beyond the military."

"Their Security Service?"

"Yes sir, the *Sicherheitsdienst des Reichsführers-SS*, the Party and State security apparatus."

"Are there any preventative actions we should take? We simply cannot lose the ULTRA intelligence source, especially with ROUNDUP approaching."

"We must be careful to not raise suspicions with our intelligence services, just in case we may have a mole. I do not believe we do since we do not see any other signs. I might suggest a minimal and restricted pause in our use of ULTRA products, and by restricted, I mean you, me, and I think we must engage Jumbo Travis, and perhaps even David Petrie."

Commander Edward Wilfrid Harry 'Jumbo' Travis, RN, CMG, CBE, had replaced Commander Denniston as the director of Bletchley Park, the Government Code and Cypher School (GC&CS), also known as Station X. Bletchley remained the sole source of codebreaking of Germany's vaunted Enigma encryption device.

David Petrie became the director-general, Security Service (MI5) nearly two years ago. His agency was responsible for counterintelligence operations. MI5 had watchers embedded in GC&CS since the war began, and the importance of codebreaking effort reached paramount status.

"How would you suggest that work?" asked the prime minister.

"I can have Travis restrict distribution of ULTRA products to just you and me, so it would only be the three of us. I would be comfortable with you making the immediate decision on further distribution based on the immediate content and situation. It will place an extra burden on us, but we could watch and redirect any actions during the suspension period, at least until we regain confidence in our security procedures."

"What about MI5?'

"As you know, MI5 has been assisting us in protecting the security of Station X. I do not think David needs to know what has precipitated this moment; however, sensitizing him to our concerns here may be beneficial. I propose that you confer with David, rather than me, as you will give us a little more distance from ULTRA. You might have several reasons for concern."

Churchill stood and went to the window. He stared at nothing in particular beyond the still disheveled garden that would be the last element of the prime minister's residence to be repaired from the repeated bomb damage of The Blitz. Eventually, after several minutes of quiet contemplation, Churchill turned back to face Sir Stewart. "Very well. You will engage Travis at Station X. I will talk with Petrie at MI5. I will have to inform the War Cabinet."

"Excuse me, Prime Minister. I know why you feel that responsibility, but for this hiatus, I would ask you to postpone further exposure if we are to have our best shot at this assessment. There are a variety of reasons we might have a gap in the availability of ULTRA products. As you know, we have been and continue to struggle with the changes the Germans have implemented in their use of the naval codes. We do not have to disclose why the gap occurred. The three of us—you, Travis, and me—are sufficient to open that gap for a week or two. The three of us will have to screen the ULTRA traffic during the pause. With something this important, we should see prompt action. If we see no indicators within a week or two at the outside, then I think we can relax a little and return to our normal distribution processes. The message may well have been an effort to deflect from their failure rather than a serious evidentiary warning. It should not take long to know which it is."

"I pray you are correct, Sir Stewart. If you are not, the loss of our golden apple tree will extend the war and the extraordinary sacrifices of our people." Menzies nodded his agreement. "Very well, we shall proceed as you propose. May God help us."

Churchill returned the message to Menzies, who returned it to the case and locked it. The two men shook hands, and C departed.

While His Majesty's Government (HMG) had been rightfully focused on the security of ULTRA to preserve their access to German sensitive communications, they remained unaware that ULTRA had been compromised with the Soviet Union by a small group of double agents that became known as the Cambridge Five.

The *de facto* leader of the Cambridge Five was Harold Adrian Russell 'Kim' Philby, who had been carefully recruited by the NKVD in 1934. Through Philby, the NKVD went on to recruit the other members of the Cambridge Five—all of them Cambridge University graduates. The other members of the spy ring were: Donald Duart Maclean, Guy Francis de Moncy Burgess, Anthony Frederick Blunt, and John Cairncross. They held various important positions within HMG prior to and throughout the war and fed extraordinarily sensitive information including ULTRA decryptions to their Soviet NKGB and NKVD handlers.

Philby remained the most prominent and productive of the Cambridge Five spies as he worked his way up in the British Secret Intelligence Service (MI6). The ring was not detected, exposed, and broken until well after the war, with Philby defecting to the Soviet Union in 1963.

—

Wednesday, 10.March.1943
Villefranche-sur-Saône, Département Rhône
France Occupée
01:25 hours

The waxing quarter moon did offer adequate illumination for sufficient confidence. The three weeks since his escape from Münich had been nothing short of harrowing, but Trevor Anderson had arrived at his secondary extraction point two days earlier. The primary site had too many police in the area, clearly searching for something—probably him. Trevor had not waited to find out and left the area, disappearing into the night without informing the local agent. His movement to the secondary extraction point had taken another nine days and gave them a waxing quarter moon. The coded confirmation message for his pickup mission had arrived yesterday morning. The local *Maquis* unit with their two SOE and OSS advisers had taken excellent care of Diamond, including feeding him a surprisingly sumptuous meal for a clandestine field unit, before they made the two-hour hike to the farm field pickup site. They arrived an hour early and searched the area to make sure the site was clear, then they waited.

The aircraft was 25 minutes late to plan when they first heard the distinctive, single, radial engine sound. The sound increased in volume, and then the unique dark silhouette appeared in the moonlight over the western tree line. Trevor recognized the shape of the Westland Lysander Mark IIIA aircraft with its high wing, booted fixed landing gear, and torpedo-like, centerline, equipment/baggage pod before he could see any details. The black paint made the details difficult to see, and he really could not tell the color. It was dark. He had seen the aircraft in the daylight and knew most of the Special Duty Lysanders were painted black. As the pilot spun the aircraft's tail around for immediate takeoff, Trevor noted the large, rusty-red, tail designation letters in the existing moonlight—MA-D. The pilot and aircraft belonged to No.161 (Special Duties) Squadron out of RAF Tempsford—one of the most experienced special operations aviation units in the RAF.

Trevor quickly shook hands with his hosts and jogged to the aircraft. The engine remained at idle. Trevor had been through this routine more than a few times and was well rehearsed in the process. He climbed the fixed footholds, slid back the canopy transparency, and jumped into the rear passenger compartment. Trevor quickly fastened his seat lap belt and shoulder harness, then donned the headset and boom microphone.

"Ready," Trevor said over the intercom as he slid the canopy closed and locked it.

The pilot smoothly advanced the throttle and began his takeoff roll. The pilot remained as low as he could, given that he was relying on moonlight and his memory of the area map study he had performed for this mission. Several turns and tracks of different duration were part of his evasive maneuvers to make interception or anti-aircraft tracking more difficult. They were generally heading west.

Forty-five minutes after they had taken off, the pilot finally said, "Welcome aboard, Diamond."

"Thank you for the lift. It is great to be on my way home."

"We'll get you there, but first, we must stop for petrol. That pickup site was near our maximum range. I had to top off my petrol outbound, and we need to do the same on the way back. We have a clandestine, remote site in Central France that has a fuel bowser for missions like this one."

Trevor was not familiar with such a site, but there was no reason he should be, other than he was an experienced special operations agent. "No long-range tanks on this bird?" Trevor asked.

"Nope. Not yet."

"Whatever you need to do is fine by me."

The pilot did not respond. Twenty minutes later, the pilot reduced power and maneuvered for landing. Once on the ground and having slowed the Lizzie, he spun around and fast taxied to the downwind tree line. As before, the pilot kept the engine at idle in case they needed to make a quick getaway, even with partial fuel. A dozen men in dark clothing appeared from the trees. Four of them pulled a two-wheeled, fuel tank cart from the trees. Two men worked the hand pump as the ground crew made quick work of the refueling.

A thumb's up hand signal preceded the disappearance of the ground crew. The pilot took off quickly and smoothly. Again, the pilot repeated his anti-aircraft countermeasures.

Trevor felt a sense of relief when the few lights of France disappeared behind them as they crossed the English Channel. It took another 45 minutes for them to reach RAF Tempsford and land. Morning twilight had begun to illuminate the eastern horizon. Before the pilot shut down the aircraft's engine, he said, "Let me be the first to say, welcome home to Mother England, Diamond."

Trevor responded to himself as the pilot switched off the electrical power and shut down the engine. A small welcoming party approached the aircraft. He made sure to shake the pilot's hand before being led away by the SOE recovery team. The next few days would be consumed with various debriefing sessions to assess his mission and what happened.

———

Wednesday, 10.March.1943
USAAF Station F-356
Saffron Walden, Essex, England
United Kingdom
09:25 hours

The pilots of 334FS waited not so patiently for their commander's return. They instinctively knew something was afoot, although some were more vociferous than others. Brian was now the flight leader of Red Flight as they shifted assignments and integrated the last of their replacement pilots.

Major Peterson entered the squadron's humble operations building. The pilots stood. "At ease," he said before he turned to face them. "Well, the day has arrived. Our transition is complete, and Group has declared us operational." Cheers and applause interrupted Pete's briefing. He indulged the exuberance as long as his patience would allow. Pete raised his hands to stop. "We have our first combat mission." More cheers. The veterans remained silent. They knew what this meant. Again, Peterson raised his hands. "Now, if you rookies will restrain yourselves," he paused for effect, "I will brief this mission, and we'll get on our way."

The Skipper began briefing what the RAF called a RODEO mission—a ground attack operation. They were going back to the German fighter base at Calais-Coquelles they had attacked in September 1941, when the veterans were still part of No.71 Squadron. Pete rolled open a large map of the airfield with the latest aerial reconnaissance and photographic information annotated on the map. They would use a novel approach to the attack. Sweet's Yellow Flight would provide high cover just in case fighters from other German bases in Northeast Occupied France were scrambled against them. The other three flights would split before crossing the coastline and taking different routes to the target. The leg distances were planned so that their intended target would not be discernible until they made their final approach run-in. They would arrive at the target from three different directions, five minutes apart, to provide maximum confusion for the enemy. Each flight had its specific attack objectives. Pete's Blue Flight had the German flight line and runway, trying to catch as many enemy aircraft on the ground. Dusty's Green Flight had the hangars and ammunition dump. Hunter's Red Flight had the fuel storage tanks at the eastern edge of the airfield. Pete produced the only aerial photograph they had to show the camouflage the Germans had installed for the fuel tanks. The ammunition loads for each flight had been tailored for the intended targets. Brian's ammo load was mostly armor-piercing and incendiary rounds. The Skipper covered the use of their four preset VHF radio channels, their control procedures, the ingress and egress risks and procedures, and especially the timing of their attack. Group enabled them to take any targets of opportunity they found on the way out, not before. All questions were answered. Lastly, Pete instructed everyone to relieve themselves for the full duration mission.

Brian's Red Flight was composed of two veterans from No.71 Squadron and one new guy, or newbie as they called such men. Second Lieutenant Henry Carl 'Buddy' Courtland, a veteran, flew as Hunter's wingman. First Lieutenant Arnold Samuel 'Salt' Morton had the 2nd Section with Second Lieutenant Jackson 'Horn' Lee of Richmond, Virginia as Salt's wingman. They walked together to their aircraft. Before they split, Brian stopped and faced them.

"As the Skipper said, we've been to Calais before. It was well defended the first time. It is likely to be defended better this time around, and I imagine we were not the last to hit that place. We are also the last flight into the target, so the Gerries are going to be really pissed off by the time we get there. Keep your heads on a swivel, concentrate on your assigned target, but do not get target fixation; it will kill you. Remember what the Skipper said, our first priority is to defend ourselves, so don't be some kind of hero. This place isn't going anywhere, and we can come back. Let's get the job done, lads. Mount up."

"Yeah," they shouted exuberantly in unison and then split to their aircraft. Others looked around to see what the commotion was.

They were all strapped in and connected. When Pete signaled, they started their engines, stepped through their pre-flight checks, taxied, completed their run-up checks, and took off heading south. As they approached their designated split point, Yellow Flight remained at Angels Five, while the other three flights took up their respective first leg headings and descended to their penetration altitude—treetop height plus a little for margin of error. Brian gave his flight the combat spread signal that opened the spacing between them before crossing the beach. He stayed on his map to ensure they made their milestones on time. The sky remained surprisingly clear, and their route had been chosen to avoid known air defense locations. Red Flight's ingress proceeded exactly as planned without opposition. As their last waypoint passed underneath them spot on time, Brian turned the flight south-southwest, directly at their target. A massive, brilliant explosion sent shockwaves out, condensing the air into a rapidly expanding dome. *Green Flight hit the ammo dump.* Brian rechecked his armament switches to make sure his guns were armed. *Ready.* Smaller fires burned all over the airfield. The last of the Green Flight Thunderbolts made it away from the field. The fuel storage tanks were not easily seen, but Hunter knew they could not move. Tracers shot up at the retreating Green Flight, enabling Red Flight to cross the airfield boundary without opposition.

Brian's sight pipper remained steady on the base of his target, the largest of the fuel storage tanks on the far side of the tank farm until it reached the desired size. He depressed his trigger. All eight 50-caliber machine guns opened up. The tank exploded in a brilliant, yellow fireball with deep black smoke. Brian banked 90-degrees to the left and pulled hard, straining against the g's he was pulling. He could not avoid the edge of the smoke plume. His engine coughed when it ingested the smoke but quickly refired on the other side of the plume. As Brian shallowed his turn, he looked back over his shoulder to see two burning 109s on the runway and perhaps another handful burning. He also noticed that two other tanks were burning, and then he witnessed the billowing explosion of the fourth and maybe a fifth tank. *Got 'em.* Tracers began to dance around them as they made the quickest egress possible.

"Pectin, Pectin Yellow, bandits approaching from east."

"Pectin Yellow, Pectin, if we can't outrun them, we'll engage. Break. Pectin, we'll pass on the targets of opportunity. Bingo. Let's get home."

Hunter checked his engine temperatures. *All good.* He kept the throttle up, cowl flaps wide open, checked his map, and tried to keep track of Yellow Flight, now paralleling the Red Flight course. He saw what looked like canopy glint to the east about ten miles out from Yellow Flight. Brian worked hard to keep up with their progress and track what he thought were the enemy fighters. He finally saw the blue of the sea on the horizon. *The coastline is approaching.* A couple of minutes later, they crossed the beach—*feet wet.*

"Pectin Yellow, report feet wet."

"Wilco," came the broadcast acknowledgment from Sweet. "They are not closing fast."

Blue Flight had slowed significantly in a gradual climb. Green flight had already joined up. Brian adjusted his heading and climb angle, and slowly throttled back, as he signaled for Red Flight to close up for the merge.

"Pectin Yellow, feet wet. We're a couple of miles behind you and closing."

"Roger Yellow."

As they neared the squadron, Brian looked over his right shoulder to see Yellow Flight closing rapidly.

"Pectin, Pectin Yellow, bandits just bingo'd. We're clear."

"Roger, Yellow."

Minutes later, as Hunter continued to scan the sky, all four flights were back in their transit formation and level at Angels Eight. Hunter checked his fuel. They had ample remaining to make Debden.

Pete led the squadron around a few cumulus clouds passing through the area, but other than that, the return to base was uneventful and easy. The Skipper signaled for right echelon, flights in trail for the break. Pete worked his way up to full throttle for the squadron to roar into the break—a very stylish squadron break left for landing in sequence.

Brian taxied into his spot, completed his shutdown, and unstrapped.

Sergeant Tomlinson waited for him at the aft left wing root. "How'd it go, Captain?"

"We won't know until we get the aerial photos in a day or so, but from what I saw, we got the job done. All guns functioned, no jams. No holes, only petrol, and ammo."

"You mean gas?" Both men laughed.

"Yeah," Brian answered and chuckled. "Holdover from those years in the RAF. So, yes, gas, if you will, and give her a good look-see. I didn't hear or feel any hits, but we got shot at, and I flew through a dense, black, smoke cloud. The engine coughed but immediately refired."

"You got it, sir."

The chilly spring air drove them inside. Once all the pilots were present, Pete said, "OK, guys, good job today. We're barely going to make lunch. We'll assemble back here after lunch for our debriefing." Petersen nodded his head to Squadron Operations Clerk Sergeant Julius Roman 'Juli' Ellison, who knew he had to call Group Operations with their return and status, and Group Intelligence to postpone the debriefing until 13:00 hours. "OK, let's get out of our flight gear and skedaddle. The Mess closes in 20 minutes. Let's hop to it."

———

Friday, 12.March.1943
Headquarters, Special Operations Executive
No.64 Baker Street
Marylebone, London, England
United Kingdom
09:30 hours

Trevor sat alone in the small conference room that SOE used as one of a half dozen briefing and debriefing rooms for agents going to and returning from the field. Two large maps covered the long side walls—Europe & North Africa, and the World. He stared at the spot on the Europe map that was annotated as Münich. *That was a helluva run, and I'm so glad I'm home.*

Lord Selborne entered first, followed by Brigadier Gubbins, and six other men he did not recognize. Trevor stood. Selborne and Gubbins took seats across the table from Trevor, who sat after the two senior men. The six other men stood along the wall behind Selborne and Gubbins.

"Welcome back, Trevor," Selborne opened.

"Thank you, sir."

"We are grateful you made it out safely," added Gubbins. Trevor just nodded his head.

"We wanted to hear your story directly," Selborne said, "which is why we are here in addition to the usual debriefers. Four of these men are SOE analysts. The other two are from MI6. Any questions so far?"

"No sir."

Lord Selborne nodded his head. "We will confine ourselves for the time being to what you learned on your latest mission and especially the events that precipitated your aborting the mission." Trevor nodded his agreement. "We will update you on what we know as of this morning once your briefing is complete." Again, Trevor nodded his head. "Very well. Please proceed."

Trevor knew precisely where to begin and did not hesitate. "My transport to Zürich was uneventful and without challenge. Using my Tobias Weber documents, I crossed the border checkpoint at Lindau in a chauffeured limousine belonging to a German company. The SD Border Police were skeptical and inquisitive as usual, but nothing out of the ordinary. Once again, my compliments to the Documents Branch. None of my papers attracted the slightest observable attention. My work purpose drew the most questions, but my cover alias worked like a charm. We did have a tail for the leg to Memmingen, probably SD or Gestapo. They apparently lost interest or had something more important to do, since they dropped off just before reaching the village. We made Münich just before noon. I completed my usual pass through the Hotel Siegestor and went on to the apartment I've used on earlier missions—all without incident or tail. That was on Friday, the 8th of January. I didn't connect with Sophie Scholl until the following Monday. She seemed calm, collected, and rather grounded when she invited me to the apartment near the university that she shared with her older brother. That meeting occurred on Wednesday, the 13th."

"Were you at all suspicious of an ambush or setup?" Gubbins asked.

"Yes sir. I was prepared with my usual weapons. Winter clothing makes whatever bulges remain to disappear. I must also note my compliments to the Germans for keeping their sidewalks cleared and dry in winter, most impressive, actually." Trevor smiled and shook his head as if bothered by a fly. "I met with the Scholl's at their apartment after classes on the afternoon of the 13th. I offered what they believed was Swiss-German assistance of general, unspecified, and unlimited form. I conveyed our admiration for their passive resistance."

"Were they ever going to do more than distribute pamphlets?" asked one of the unknown analysts. "Their writing had become progressively more strident and even a tinge more aggressive."

"It is my opinion and assessment that the group was struggling internally with that very question. I offered a full range of support up to and including weapons and explosives. Hans reacted rather strongly against violent means, but I did notice that Sophie did not blink or twitch at the topic. My response to your query is I am doubtful. Their experience in medical units on the Eastern Front has been clearly and markedly dramatic, more so on the males who had to serve directly, like Hans. I detected a definite sense of mounting frustration, verging upon anger at what they had to deal with in Russia. Hans was not at the frontlines, but he was keenly aware of what was happening at Stalingrad and the siege of Leningrad. At the conclusion of the 13th meeting, they asked for time to consider my offer and confer with their colleagues in the White Rose. I wanted to lay back and not offer any pressure. I told them to take whatever time they needed. We also agreed on the precise signaling technique when they were ready. As I waited, I exercised my cover at the university library.

"I finally detected the 'ready to meet' sign a month later on the 17th. We had agreed I'd meet them after their classes the following day, on the 18th, and we would meet at their apartment that afternoon. It was a bright, clear day with a cold north wind, so I was bundled up against the cold, as was every other person outside that morning. As I turned the last corner, I immediately noticed four Mercedes and Opel staff cars along with two SD and two SS uniformed soldiers fully armed by the entry door. I could only surmise there were a half dozen more were inside. I offered no reaction or hesitation, and I continued walking at the same pace down *Königinstrasse*. I was not challenged or followed. I stopped at a café used by the students and faculty across Ludwigstrasse from the campus. When neither of them showed in the allotted time, I considered the mission compromised and executed my escape plan immediately, not knowing how long they would be able to hold out under Gestapo torture, if they had been arrested. I still had no direct evidence or sign the security services were at the Scholls' apartment, but the risk of waiting longer was too great.

"I immediately and carefully returned to my apartment, cleansed it thoroughly, and boarded the train for Stuttgart. I chose to cross the Rhine just south of Karlsruhe and below the old French border intersection. It took me a couple of days before I found a small boat, not in the best condition and probably abandoned. That night I made it successfully across the Rhine without being noticed. My primary extract point, northeast of Dijon, I had to deem compromised."

"How so?" Gubbins asked.

"Too many police and some military were looking for something, not particularly vigorously and aggressively, but definitely searching. It had been eight days since leaving München, so I had to assume they were following leads. Once I reconnoitered my route beyond, I sent my flash message with my water bottle transmitter. It took me another week to reach my secondary extraction point at Villefranche-sur-Saône, including a couple of days to surveil and clear our designated local *Maquis* agent. They took surprisingly good care of me. I was pretty hungry by then. I must say it was a genuine blessing to hear the familiar accents of the SOE and OSS agents embedded with the local *Maquis* group. They were the ones who sent the extract message. My pickup occurred just after midnight on the 10th. The 161 Special Duty Lizzie and pilot were perfect, and here I am."

"Thank you for that, Trevor," Selborne said. "Several things happened while you were in your egress phase. Regretfully, I must inform you that Hans and Sophie Scholl were indeed arrested by the Gestapo on the 18th. They were tortured and executed four days later at Stadelheim Prison after a Freisler sham trial. The execution of the Scholl siblings was announced in the newspapers. Reliable sources informed us their last days were not pleasant. They were executed by guillotine." Trevor lowered and shook his head in genuine remorse. "It will take some time to ascertain exactly what happened, how they were compromised, and how extensively the White Rose group has been compromised. We know other arrests were made, but we do not know who just yet. Our brethren at MI6 are listening, but we do not want to probe for fear of making matters worse for whatever survivors may exist. Also, while you were making your way out of Germany, the Red Army surrounded and destroyed the remnants of the German 6th Army at Stalingrad. They were out of ammunition and starving at the end. Our 8th Army and Eisenhower's Allied

Forces are moving toward completing the encirclement of the *Afrikakorps* in Tunisia. The end for the Axis in North Africa appears to be only a matter of when. Any questions?"

"No sir. Hans and Sophie were exceptional human beings who cared deeply for their country. They had become progressively more disgusted with what the Nazis had done to their beloved country. I shall mourn their passing. I don't know if any of my actions contributed to their compromise, but that potential shall haunt me. They were really good young Germans."

Lord Selborne nodded and smiled. "I think your mind and conscience can rest easy, Trevor. Neither SOE nor MI6 have seen even the slightest suggestion that the Nazis were aware of your presence or your assignment regarding the White Rose. The students had already done plenty to attract the attention of the Gestapo. We're simply extraordinarily lucky their arrest didn't come a few minutes later than it did. As I understand the aviators like to say, better lucky than good. So it is here. We're exceptionally grateful to have you home, safe and sound. Thank you for indulging our curiosity." Selborne looked at Gubbins. "Do you have any questions for Agent Diamond?"

"No sir."

"Very well, then. The brigadier and I shall leave you with the debriefing team, who will cover the details with you over the next few days. Once they have what they need, please take a week to decompress and visit your family. We will discuss another mission once you return bright-eyed and bushy-tailed."

Lord Selborne and Brigadier Gubbins left the room and closed the door. The six debriefers sat for the first time and jumped into their task. Trevor was quite accustomed to the process. It still felt great to be back home.

As Allied investigators learned in the post-war analysis, the Scholl siblings departed their apartment in the morning of 18.February.1943, with a small suitcase full of new resistance leaflets, their sixth edition, for distribution that day. As they had agreed, they left their lecture room classes early, allowing them to deposit small quantities of their leaflets in the empty corridors near the various lecture rooms for the students to pick up as they left the rooms. Circa 11:15, as their distribution window closure approached, the Scholls noticed that they had some left-over copies in the suitcase and decided to distribute them. Sophie grabbed the remaining leaflets and tossed them from the top floor into the atrium of the university main building to flutter down to the ground floor. As fate would have it, a university maintenance man, Jakob Schmid, happened to be in the atrium and observed Sophie's spontaneous action. Unfortunately for the Scholls, Schmid was an active member of the NSDAP and the SA, and he immediately reported the event to the Gestapo.

The Scholls were promptly arrested. Hans attempted to destroy the draft of the seventh leaflet, written by Christoph Probst, by tearing it apart and trying to swallow the pieces. However, the Gestapo recovered enough of it and were able to match the handwriting with other writings by Probst, which they found when they searched the Scholl's apartment. Probst was arrested that afternoon. The main Gestapo interrogator initially thought Sophie was innocent. But, after Hans had confessed, Sophie assumed full responsibility in an attempt to protect other members of the White Rose. The Gestapo moved swiftly to wrap up the network. Over the following months, the Gestapo connected the dots and arrested the other White Rose members, with most of them receiving the same consequence.

—

14.March.1943
Kraków
German Occupied Poland

SS-*Untersturmführer* Amon Leopold Göth led a team of *SS-Totenkopfverbände* troopers to complete the final liquidation of the Jewish ghetto at Kraków. They sorted the last of the Jews from the enclave as they were removed. Those still fit for work were sent to the newly constructed, *Konzentrationslager* (KZ) *Kraków-Płaszów* for forced slave labor—a slower version of death. Several thousand who did not meet the labor filter threshold were sent to *Konzentrationslager Auschwitz-Birkenau* to be murdered as swiftly as possible. Hundreds unable or unwilling to move were shot or beaten to death during the final liquidation. For his accomplishments, Göth was promoted two ranks to *SS-Hauptsturmführer* and appointed to be the inaugural commandant of Kraków-Płaszów KZ.

Of historic note beyond the obvious, one of the factories in Kraków that was served by the labor camp was an enamelware plant belonging to German industrialist Oskar Schindler. He witnessed the brutal liquidation of the Kraków ghetto and became disgusted with what he saw. Schindler used his connections and skills to save his laborers. The efforts of Oskar Schindler were dramatized in Steven Spielberg's movie *Schindler's List* that won seven Academy Awards. Schindler was also honored for his efforts by Israel's Yad Vashem official memorial to the victims of the Holocaust.

Göth was captured, tried and executed in 1947 for his crimes.

—

Chapter 4

Like a gold ring in a pig's snout
is a beautiful woman who shows no discretion.
-- Proverbs 11:22

Sunday, 14.March.1943
Chequers Court
Ellesborough, Buckinghamshire, England
United Kingdom
17:25 hours

"**M**ister Prime Minister, Brigadier Menzies has arrived," announced Duty Private Secretary Anthony Bevir. The request for the unscheduled visit came while the prime minister was taking his afternoon nap. Tony accepted the offer knowing his principal would want to meet with the MI6 director-general as soon as possible, especially with the director-general's unsolicited request.

"Show him in." The prime minister's study at the country retreat served as the security space when the prime minister was present.

Menzies entered, dressed in a modest business suit. "My apologies for disturbing your Sunday evening peace, Prime Minister."

Churchill waved his right hand dismissively and gestured to 'C' to take the other overstuffed chair by the modest fire in the stone fireplace.

Menzies began, "I have several follow-up items from earlier discussions." Winston nodded slightly. "First, as you may recall, we were aware of the plot by general officers to assassinate Hitler. We provided the Composition C plastic explosive they sought and some technical assistance. This particular plot centered upon Captain von Schlabrendorff, aide-de-camp to Major General von Tresckow, Chief of Operations, Army Group Center. We helped them fashion the explosive in two bottles of Cointreau cognac. We received word this morning from our agents in Smolensk that the bottles were loaded on Hitler's Focke-Wulf Fw200 Condor. We also received word from Rastenburg that Hitler's Condor arrived safely and that von Schlabrendorff retrieved the two bottles from Colonel Brandt before they could be delivered or discovered for their designed intent. Schlabrendorff suspects the timer mechanism froze in the cold of the Condor's baggage compartment during transit. So, the plot failed, and the conspirators were not discovered."

"Nor our contributions?"

"Correct. We'll have to watch things closely for a few weeks, but it appears no-harm-no-foul."

"So that damn corporal's luck has saved him again."

"Yes sir. We haven't yet been able to determine whether Captain von Schlabrendorff will make another attempt. The fact that he managed to retrieve the bombs without suspicion is miraculous. Theoretically, the plan is still valid, although the problem with the detonators must be resolved." 'C' paused, perhaps to give the prime minister the opportunity for comments or questions. None came. "I am also happy to report we've nothing further on the issue we were concerned with last week. We've seen no changes in the Army or Air Force encryption, traffic, or content other than the daily Enigma setting changes. Our productivity on the naval codes has improved, but we are still a long way from what productivity we enjoyed last year."

"Have you been able to reconstruct what happened?"

"No. We're working on it. Until we can reliably break the naval code in a timely manner, we won't know what or why the change occurred last December."

"I know Station X is working over . . ."

"Yes, they are, Prime Minister. Commander Travis has expressed serious concern for the durability and effectiveness of his personnel in this situation. They know and feel the importance, but we're burning them up."

"Sir Stewart, I beg your pardon. The commander is entrusted with the entire process including his personnel. He must use his best judgment to balance the conflicting elements. The people of Bletchley Park are not consumables that can be replaced like petrol, wood, or water. He must protect them as the cherished resource they are. Their knowledge and skills are not easily replaced."

"Yes sir. I shall ensure that Commander Travis understands those realities."

"Please do. As I was going to say, the latest Admiralty shipping report clearly states that they lost more ships and crews to the North Atlantic's nasty winter weather than they did to the U-boat menace. We're not faced with those tragic days of '40 and '41 when the U-boats were so successful, and we're so close to the edge of the abyss. Let us all keep things in the proper perspective."

"Yes sir."

"Our golden apple tree is far too important to take unnecessary risks. Is there a reason or evidence that we should return to our normal distribution?"

Menzies considered Churchill's interrogative. "We've seen no reason not to do so."

This time Winston considered 'C's reply. "I'm not comfortable, or perhaps I'm just an old worry-wart." He lapsed into further contemplation. "I think we should extend the moratorium if you and Travis agree, for another week or two, just to be safe. Until further notice from me, ULTRA will be used only on great occasions, or when thoroughly and heavily camouflaged. Do you wish to query Travis?"

"I don't think that is necessary. Jumbo knows the criticality, and he has not resisted the restrictive process we have temporarily implemented. I think it safe to speak for both of us. We agree."

"Very well, then. Make it so. Do you have anything else we need to discuss?"

"No sir."

"Will you stay for dinner?"

"Thank you ever so much, Prime Minister, but I'm afraid I must decline. I need to get back to London and Broadway House. We have several sensitive operations at a critical stage."

"Quite understandable. I'm sure Mrs. Landemare can whip up a sandwich or two for you and your driver for the journey back."

"Thank you so much, Prime Minister, but that will not be necessary."

"Safe journey."

"Thank you, sir."

Menzies departed, and Winston went to the large window to peer out at the dreary, late winter garden and forest beyond. Even the hint or suggestion of a threat to ULTRA sent shivers through his body and his mind. Churchill sighed deeply, shook his head, and then he turned to return to his weekend guests.

—

Sunday, 14.March.1943
96-311 Park Lane
Mayfair, London
United Kingdom
18:45 hours

The distinctive triple raps of the brass doorknocker announced her expected arrival. Sarah Oliver, the middle daughter of Clementine and Winston Churchill, went to the door. Without opening the door, Sarah said in a firm, feminine voice, "Yes. Who is it?"

"It's me," came the familiar male voice.

Sarah opened the door, smiled at Gil, and stepped back, holding the door open wider for U.S. Ambassador Gil Winant to enter. He passed without touching her. Sarah closed the door and turned to Gil. The two lovers embraced, kissed, looked longingly into each other's eyes, and kissed again.

"I have missed you," Winant proclaimed, as they declutched.

"It's only been a couple of days, silly."

"Yes, but I still missed you."

Sarah changed the subject. "How's the weather outside?"

Gil smiled and nodded his head. "It's partly cloudy, still a little chilly even for late winter, but the five-block walk from the embassy was actually refreshing."

Sarah gently touched Gil's cheek. "You are on the cool side."

"I will warm quickly with you."

"Oh, you naughty boy." Sarah handed a pre-poured glass of burgundy wine to Winant. She held up her glass, clinked glasses, and they said cheers simultaneously. Sarah sat on the couch, and Gil Winant sat next to her. "Supper is in the oven and should be ready for consumption in 30 minutes."

"What are we having?" Gil asked.

"I managed to collect up a small roast from number ten, thanks to Mum."

"Very good. I suppose you saw the papers?"

"In the *Mirror*?"

"Yes."

"Pamela has not been particularly discreet."

Pamela Beryl Churchill, née Digby, had married Sarah's older brother Randolph in October 1939, just after the war began in Europe. She was six years younger than Sarah and just as free-spirited as her sister-in-law. Her husband deployed to North Africa as an Army staff officer, and Pamela soon became restless and attracted to William Averell Harriman.

Harriman had been President Roosevelt's special envoy to Europe and served as a high-level coordinator for the vital Lend-Lease Program in England since spring 1941. He was a frequent visitor to No.10 Downing Street and Chequers, which was the venue of his first introduction to Pamela. Averell was 29 years older than Pamela and remained married to his second wife, Marie, since 1930.

Sarah Millicent Hermione Oliver, née Spencer-Churchill, had married popular comedian and musician Vic Oliver, born Victor Oliver von Samek, against her parent's wishes and had been estranged from Oliver for years, but she was still married. Sarah considered herself an actor with several bit parts to her credit so far. Winant contracted for the apartment on stylish Park Lane, overlooking Hyde Park, just as Harriman had done for Pamela on Grosvenor Square, for Sarah and him to share.

Gil Winant was 25 years older than Sarah and remained married to his second wife, Constance, since 1919.

"Averell bears a fair portion of the blame there," Gill added. "He has been rather bold and flamboyant in his enjoyment of the night-life returning to London after The Blitz. He is almost flaunting his relationship with Pamela . . . in public."

"True, and she seems quite accepting of the exposure. I saw the photograph of them in the *Mirror*. I love Pamela as a sister, but it just seems so unfair. Randolph is not the easiest man to be around, so I empathize with her need for attention, and Averell is certainly giving her what she craves."

"It sure did look like they were having fun in these difficult times. Do you wish we could have fun too?"

Sarah took a sip of her wine and then smiled. "We have our fun in private."

"Yes, we do, but do you wish we could celebrate more like them?"

"Oh, sure, but I cannot do that to Papa . . . or your wife. I'm afraid, Gil, we must enjoy our relationship in private. I simply refuse to complicate Papa's life and premiership with his daughter displayed in public and excoriated by the press for a scandalous affair with a married man."

"Is that how you think of me – an adulterous husband?"

"No, Gil, I think of you as a gentle, attentive, gracious man . . . a handsome man, I must add, and an exquisite lover. But the fact remains you are married. You have a wife and family. For that fact alone, I feel some guilt . . . just not enough to turn away from a gorgeous man and a good friend—an intimate friend."

"Thank goodness for that. I'll say it, again, Sarah, you and I have far more in common than I do with Constance."

"She is the mother of your three children, Gil," Sarah said more sternly than she intended.

Winant frowned noticeably and shook his head. "As you remind me oh so often. I'm grateful for her motherhood. She's a good woman, but I love you."

Sarah smiled coyly. "And I love you, Gil. I accept that you cannot divorce Constance in your position. I cannot ask you to do so. I'm far more driven by my respect for and loyalty to my father. As I said, I can't make his position as prime minister more difficult. I wish I was as bold as Pamela, but I'm not. We shall just have to be content to love each other in private. Pamela knows about our relationship, but Diana and Mary don't, and we're not going to tell them."

"Do you think either of your parents know or suspect?"

"I have flashes where I suspect that at least Papa might. I felt that twinge when we were last together at Chequers ten days ago. I know Mum doesn't. She'd have confronted me directly if she even suspected. She is very protective of Papa, as I am, and I know she would see our affair as a threat to Papa. So, you will have to love me alone."

"Do you think Pamela might have confided in Averell in a moment of passion?" Winant asked.

"No. She knows better. I don't gossip about her, and I know she doesn't talk about me, at least in that context. We protect each other. Now, I notice the time. I need to check on the roast. Would you be so kind to set the table for us?"

Sarah went to the kitchen, while Winant tended to the plates and utensils. He refreshed their wine glasses and then went to the kitchen to hug Sarah from behind as she checked the roast, potatoes, and carrots.

"It's ready. Would you get the plates? Let's get this carved up and served in here. It'll be easier than lugging this awkward pan to the dining table."

They worked together, sat down at the table, and ate their meal with chit-chat about their daily routine odds & ends. Gil discounted and deflected from his duties as the U.S. ambassador. Sarah avoided pressing him on issues that he was cognizant of in their daily lives. He never pried into her family life. Gil was very respectful of his relationship with Sarah's father. He did not hide his marriage, just as Sarah did not conceal her marriage, but they felt a kindred spirit and agreed to live in the moment since they both knew and acknowledged the reality as they understood it—this too shall pass.

—

Tuesday, 16.March.1943
Royal Aeronautical Establishment Farnborough
Farnborough, Hampshire, England
United Kingdom
08:50 hours

The Hawker Typhoon Mark IA with a tail designator UO-A landed smoothly. Jonathan 'Harness' Kensington knew exactly which hangar he needed to taxi to for this assignment. He had been here several times before. Jonathan taxied his Typhoon to the large, separate, solo hangar set, turned his tail to the hangar, and shut down the aircraft.

An RAF flight lieutenant he did not recognize appeared from the hangar's interior and walked slowly to the aircraft's left, trailing edge, wing root. Jonathan unstrapped, removed his headgear with oxygen mask attached on one side, and kept it in his left hand since he knew he would likely need it. "Welcome back, Squadron Leader Kensington," the man said, as Jonathan jumped down from the wing. He saluted. Jonathan returned the salute. "I'm Flight Lieutenant

Henry Jewell, and I'm the engineering pilot assigned to this project. Follow me, please."

Jewell walked to the two-story office section between the two massive hangars, and then to the briefing room they had used before. Henry went directly to the lectern. Harness sat at the same school desk in the front row as he had for each of the other exploitation flights he had flown—the Bf109E-3 primary German fighter aircraft on the 4th of July 1940, and the Me110C-4 twin-engine fighter three weeks later, along with the He111 and Do17 medium bombers on the same day.

"Today's event is the Focke-Wulf Fw190A-4 frontline fighter."

"I'll be damned!" Jonathan exclaimed.

"The aircraft was captured four months ago. The government completed its detailed evaluation last month. We began the familiarization campaign last week. You will be the third line pilot to fly the German fighter. We will brief the flights after I complete the background briefing."

Jewell covered all of the features that distinguished the Fw190 from the air-cooled, 14-cylinder, BMW 801D-2 radial engine delivering nearly 1,700 horsepower to the impressive armament—two, nose-mounted, synchronized, MG 131 13-millimeter machine guns with 475 rounds per gun plus four, wing-mounted, MG 151 20-millimeter cannons with 250 rounds per gun. The radios and oxygen equipment had been changed out to the British standard. The aircraft markings had been changed from the black crosses to British roundels. Jewell also covered the performance differences with the Bf109E-3 as the baseline. He went through checklist procedures for pre-start, start, run-up, takeoff, and landing, using large photographs of the instrument panel, and left and right consoles. Jonathan and his brethren had learned about the Fw190's capabilities the hard way. Some of the details Jewell briefed were new information for Jonathan. Jewell answered every single one of Jonathan's questions.

"Let's move onto the next phase," Jewell announced. He went to the telephone, lifted the handset, and simply said, "We're ready."

A refined, distinguished-looking man with light, curly brown hair and brilliant emerald green eyes entered the briefing room dressed in an olive green, overall flight suit. He walked directly to Jonathan, saluted, and extended his right hand. "Flight Lieutenant Ellison . . . an honor to meet you, sir."

They shook hands. "Thank you."

"I'll be your adversary for today's evaluation flights. If I've been informed correctly, you've flown all of our exploitation aircraft."

"I've no idea. I don't know what you hold. I've flown the 109, 110, Heinkel 111, and Dornier 17."

"You flew with Flight Lieutenant Kiernan on the 4th of July 1940 and Flight Lieutenant Logan on the 25th of that month?

"Yes. I flew here on those dates, but I was never introduced to the pilots I flew with on those dates. An unnamed wing commander briefed me on the aircraft the first day. The only officer who introduced himself was Flight Lieutenant Stemple, my liaison or coordination officer for both dates."

Ellison ignored the earlier lack of introductions. "As you know from Flight Lieutenant Jewell's briefing, we've got a new one for you today—the Focke-Wulf 190. I surmise you've already run into the Shrike."

"Shrike?"

"The German name for the 190 is *Würger*, which translates as Shrike, Kurt Tank's latest *wunderkind* and a rather diminutive but resourceful bird of prey."

"Yes, we have . . . an impressive machine."

"That it is, and I suspect you will learn more today. I have been and still serve as the principal test pilot assigned to the Exploitation Branch for the 190. I've lived with this machine since we acquired her."

"How did you acquire the aircraft, if I may ask?"

"A defector, actually. The young man became disillusioned with *Der Führer* and made a run for it. Got a bit sporty approaching England, from what I've been told, but the lads that intercepted him chose not to shoot the fellow down. Their restraint and that young lad's courage brought us the machine you will fly today."

"Better lucky than good."

"So they say. We will use the same process as your prior events. For the first sortie, you'll be in the 190. I'll be in a Mark Nine Spit. The second sortie, we'll switch seats. On the third sortie, we'll fly engagements with you in your Typhoon. Any questions so far?"

"Nope. I know the routine."

"From a throttle jockey perspective, you will notice a few distinct traits. The 190 has the best power-to-weight ratio of any German fighter, and truth be told, between us, better than any of our fighters, so the Shrike has excellent acceleration. It gives them the advantage in breakaways. It has slightly higher wing loading than the 109, so not quite the turn rate. The aircraft has slightly less climb rate and lower service ceiling. She has a helluva bite. The roll performance is noteworthy, as you will soon feel. She's very agile. I'll show you some of the tricks we've documented that the Germans use to take advantage of the Shrike's capabilities. You may have already seen some of their tricks, but we'll step through them. There are other advantages like the armored seat and the lack of liquid coolant for the engine that distinguish the aircraft. This is a machine to be respected. In the hands of an accomplished and skilled pilot, the Shrike is a formidable aircraft."

George 'Sprinkle' Ellison did not re-address the checklist items, but he did discuss the known idiosyncrasies of the Fw190 from a procedural standpoint.

With the briefings complete, George led Jonathan to the closed hangar. Harness recognized the Fw190 instantly as they stepped into the hangar. The widely spread landing gear, streamlined shape, and bulbous nose surrounding the twin-bank, radial engine marked the Shrike. The British roundel replaced the black crosses on the empennage and wings. Sprinkle walked through the pre-flight inspection. *He clearly admires this aircraft*, Jonathan thought.

George had Jonathan jump into the cockpit, and he helped Harness with his connections and strapping into the parachute and seat. He reinforced the instrument layout, markings, controls, settings, and switches.

"Any questions?" Sprinkle asked.

"No. I think I've got it."

"Very well, then. Let us get started. We don't leave the bird outside any more than we have to for events like these. I'll leave you to it. They'll open the doors and tow you outside. I'll jump in the Spit that is already out there. Start when you're ready. We'll do a radio check to make sure we can talk. Give me a thumb's up when you're ready to taxi."

"Wilco."

Just as George stated, the tractor pulled the Shrike outside. The ground crew chocked the main wheels, disconnected the tow bar, and prepared for the start. Jonathan rechecked his switches. The crew chief gave him a thumb's up. Harness returned the hand signal. He flipped the battery switch ON. Switch the fuel boost pump ON, checked the mixture RICH, cracked the throttle a quarter of an inch, and pushed the starter button. The propeller turned, and the engine fired off in less than one full turn of the three-bladed propeller. The engine coughed and sputtered but stabilized at fast idle. It had a chunky, throaty sound and a strong vibration. The engine sounded and felt powerful, but more rough and rugged than Jonathan was used to with the Merlin engines.

They took off smoothly as a section and headed north to some dedicated airspace that allowed them to focus on their flight tasks. As they had briefed, the two pilots stepped through the familiarization. *My gosh, this is indeed a sporty machine, nimble and robust.* As he continued to fly, Jonathan gained new and added respect for the Fw190.

The two pilots stepped through the briefing elements of all three flights. It was mid-afternoon when Jonathan landed at Farnborough in his Typhoon, followed by George in the Shrike. Ellison did not even have time to extricate himself from the 190 cockpit when the ground crew towed the aircraft into the hangar and closed the doors.

Harness met Sprinkle in the briefing room along with Flight Lieutenant Jewell. They debriefed all three flights. Ellison emphasized several points regarding the Shrike's performance, its capabilities, and more importantly, its vulnerabilities. The German fighter was not some invincible super-machine. It was a formidable aircraft in the hands of an experienced pilot but still not invulnerable.

Flight Lieutenant Jewell concluded the day's events. "As with the other exploitation flights with which you were involved, you will be expected to visit other fighter squadrons to brief the pilots on what you've learned today. What is different now is the mutual agreement between the Air Ministry and the 8th Air Force; you will be expected to visit American fighter units as well. Do you have any questions?"

"The former American volunteers are at Debden, I do believe. I'd like to have them on my assignment posting."

Jewell opened his binder to the correct page and ran his finger down the page. "Easy as pie, Mister Kensington. Debden, although the Americans refer to the base as F-356 now, is on your assignment list. As always, we remain an active resource for you, or anyone else, as the need arises."

"Excellent."

"Thank you for joining us and thank you very much for your insights and contributions. You are free to return to your base."

Jonathan shook hands with both Jewell and Ellison, and then he grabbed his flight gear and headed back to his aircraft. He sat in the seat of his single-place fighter-bomber with his parachute buckled and cinched up tight, along with the shoulder and lap belts locked and tight. The crew chief waited for his signal to start, but Jonathan sat staring out beyond the aircraft's nose at nothing. *That is one impressive little scooter with big teeth. But we know it can be beaten. Every single one of our pilots must know how to fight this bird of prey.* Jonathan finally diverted his attention from his thoughts to the task at hand. The crew chief continued to wait patiently without expression. Harness gave the start hand signal and received an acknowledgment. Jonathan switched on the battery and the boost pump, primed the engine, and depressed the starter button. The 2,180 horsepower Napier Sabre engine started smoothly and robustly. With all 24 cylinders firing nicely and the coolant and oil temperatures rising off the peg, Jonathan signaled chocks out and called to taxi for takeoff. His mind focused solely on following the procedures and returning to his base without incident. *A good day was nearly done.*

—

Friday, 19.March.1943
No.10 Downing Street
Whitehall, London, England
United Kingdom
18:05 hours

It had been a long, complicated day already, and he was late leaving London for Chequers. Winston always felt a degree of frustration, but the telephone call from 'C' told him they had a message from Boniface. The prime minister instinctively knew that whatever it was, it had to be important. Churchill's frustration level crossed his threshold of tolerance. He pushed his desk buzzer.

Duty Private Secretary John Martin entered the prime minister's office and closed the door behind him, just in case. "Yes sir?"

"Where is the courier?"

"He has not arrived, sir."

"I know that John, or he would be in here. Why is it taking him so long to get here from Broadway House?"

"I will call the director-general's office to make sure nothing nefarious has happened."

"Thank you, John. I am already going to be late for supper."

"I'll see what happened." Martin stepped out and closed the door. No sooner had he closed the door, he opened it again to announce, "The courier has arrived, sir."

Churchill waved his hand impatiently. "Please show him in. Let's get this done, so we can be on our way."

An armed army sergeant with the hardened case manacled to his left wrist entered and saluted.

The prime minister pointed at the desk and retrieved his access key. The sergeant turned away from Churchill. Opening the case, he found only one red-striped folder in the active section. He extracted three pieces of paper.

MOST SECRET - ULTRA

```
MOST SECRET ULTRA
DATE 1552 19 MAR 1943
SECRET
DATE 13 MAR 1943
TO CHIEF OKW
FROM CHIEF OKL GS
COMMUNICATIONS SECURITY
```

```
BREAK
REF 9 MAR 1943 MSG DAK BREAK CONCUR WITH
CMDR DAK BREAK TOO MANY INTERCEPTS OF SUPPLY
AIRCRAFT TO BE COINCIDENCE OR GOOD LUCK BREAK
RECOMMEND ALTERNATIVE ACTION BREAK HAIL VICTORY
HAIL HITLER END
SECRET
DECYPHERED 0411 19 MAR 1943
MOST SECRET ULTRA
```

MOST SECRET - ULTRA

Churchill shook his head and stared at the blackout curtains drawn over the window overlooking what used to be the garden of No.10. His mind ran through potential explanations and consequences of this latest message. This one was written five days after the original. The Germans knew it had to be more than just good luck that had enabled the interception and destruction of so many resupply flights head to Tunisia in a desperate attempt to sustain the *Afrikakorps* against the closing noose around their neck. He felt the monumental burden and squeeze of the proverbial rock and a hard spot. Winston wanted to use every means possible to choke the *Afrikakorps* to death. Yet he could not ignore the consequences of stimulating the Germans to change their communication encryption techniques. The golden apple tree was too bloody essential to the overall conduct of the war. His thoughts went to those fateful days before the enemy's devastating bombing raid on Coventry and the second Great Fire of London during The Blitz. Churchill sucked in a deep breath and exhaled audibly. The restrictions agreed to with 'C' five days ago would have to remain for a while longer.

The prime minister thought about recalling Eisenhower and Alexander to London to inform them of the intelligence situation and enjoining them to do the best they could without ULTRA for the time being. He shook his head again. *They would just have to cinch up the belt on their britches.* If or when they might question why the flow of valuable intelligence had slowed substantially or stopped, that would be the time for the conversation. Until then, the restriction of ULTRA products would have to hold.

Churchill shuffled the message to the back and read the next one.

MOST SECRET - ULTRA

```
MOST SECRET ULTRA
```

```
DATE 1202 19 MAR 1943
SECRET
DATE 14 MAR 1943
TO RHSA
FROM SSPF KRAKOW
BREAK
KRAKOW GHETTO LIQUIDATED BREAK HAIL VICTORY
HAIL HITLER END
SECRET
DECYPHERED 0952 19 MAR 1943
MOST SECRET ULTRA
```

MOST SECRET - ULTRA

"That cannot be good," Winston mumbled to himself. *RHSA is Himmler, so SSPF must be the local commander of the SS in Krakow, Poland.*

"Excuse me, sir?"

"Sorry, Sergeant. I was just yammering to myself . . . aloud, I guess. He shuffled the second message to the back and turned to the third one.

MOST SECRET - ULTRA

```
MOST SECRET ULTRA
DATE 1610 19 MAR 1943
TO PM
FROM C
BONIFACE
BREAK
STATION X BELIEVES THEY HAVE RECONCILED THE GAP
IN NAVAL CODE PRODUCTS BREAK NAVAL DEVICE HAS
ADDED FOURTH ROTOR BREAK NEXT FEW WEEKS SHOULD
CONFIRM ANALYSIS BREAK DEPLOYMENT NOT YET
COMPLETE END
MOST SECRET ULTRA
```

MOST SECRET - ULTRA

"I'll be damned!" Churchill exclaimed aloud.

"Sir?" the sergeant interjected.

The prime minister smiled and waved his hand dismissively. He reread each message again and then returned the three messages to the folder inside the case. Winston locked the case himself and checked to make sure it was fully secure.

"Thank you, Sergeant. Please convey my gratitude to the director-general. No action is required. I'll talk to him on Monday."

"Yes sir. I will inform the director-general, as you indicated."

The sergeant departed, and Martin returned. Churchill said, "I assume Sergeant Carrick is waiting."

Sergeant Stanley 'Stan' Carrick, a former race car driver, and now Royal Army Service Corps driver, had been assigned as the prime minister's driver for several years now.

"No sir. He had a death in the family and is on bereavement leave. It is Corporal Kaye this weekend, and yes, she is ready when you are, along with Detective Thompson."

Women's Auxiliary Air Force Corporal Irene Kaye, an attractive young woman with demonstrated exceptional driving skills, had been Carrick's designated alternate for all of those years.

Detective-Inspector Walter Henry Thompson had been assigned as Churchill's bodyguard since August 1939. He was a long-serving officer of the Special Branch of the Metropolitan Police (Scotland Yard). Churchill was rarely without Detective Thompson close by.

"Please send a quick message to Chequers to inform them we are leaving now, so we shall be a little bit late for supper."

"Already done, sir."

"Excellent, John. Then, gather up the dispatch box and let us be on our way."

Within a couple of minutes, the 1939 black Rolls-Royce Phantom III limousine moved smoothly and deftly through London's streets, heading to the northwest and Chequers Court.

—

Tuesday, 23.March.1943
Cabinet War Rooms
New Public Offices
Whitehall, London, England
United Kingdom
08:30 hours

"Good morning, Fred," General Ismay said, as he entered the small, secure, underground conference room.

Lieutenant General Frederick Edgworth Morgan had been the commanding general of the British I Corps before he was hand-picked to lead the planning staff for the invasion of Continental Europe.

"Good morning to you as well, Pug."

"Let's jump right to it." Both sat across from each other at the small, four-chair table without papers or maps. "As a consequence of the summit conference in Casablanca two months ago, you were jointly selected by both heads of state to lead a planning staff designated as Chief of Staff to the Supreme Allied Commander or COSSAC for short."

"Who is the supreme allied commander, if I may ask?"

Ismay smiled. "He has not yet been selected or assigned."

"Then, who am I to report to in my assignment?"

"For the time being, let us just assume you will be a quasi-independent group. You will loosely report to the joint chiefs, but I shall coordinate your support. I'm certain you recognize that the PM will be deeply and directly involved as the planning evolves."

"That is his nature."

"Yes, it is."

"And what are we planning?"

"Are you familiar with Operation ROUNDUP?"

"No."

"Then, that is your first step. Review what has been done so far on ROUNDUP. That is the basis or foundation of the objective. Your staff will be planning the final invasion to end the war. This is not a half-step, a diversion, or some other intermediate operation. The Allies intend to land an ultimate force of 50 plus combat divisions for the final push to Berlin."

"That is no small task."

"No, it is not. As I am certain you are aware, the prime minister and American president agreed more than a year ago in Washington to what is known as Operation BOLERO, the movement, build-up, training, and preparation of troops for ROUNDUP. The build-up of American forces has been well underway for a year now. The chiefs do not want to preempt or channel your assessments and planning, so you will operate largely independently for the time being. For planning purposes, you should assume the execution of the plan by September of this year to avoid the dreadful autumnal and winter weather."

"That is not much time for an operation this large."

"No, it is not. Give us the best you can within the time you have. You should anticipate the first comprehensive review in June."

"A very tall order."

"Yes, Fred, and that is why you were selected for this assignment."

"Where are my staff and offices?"

Ismay smiled. "In work. You shall retain your aide, two orderlies, and a driver with a commandeered vehicle from First Corps, not an auspicious starting point, but that is where we must begin. We expect to have your principal staff in place by the end of the week. Everyone should already be in England. It will take another week or two to flesh out your immediate personnel. Allied Forces have vacated Norfolk House. You will headquarter there until you need more space. The combined joint chiefs are all working on transferring your staff and planning specialists. You will lead a comparable combined joint staff. For now, the chiefs have decided to keep COSSAC highly classified and restricted. For now, your planning work will be compartmented and code-word protection with a restricted access list as approved by the chiefs alone. All of your work will be classified MOST SECRET – BIGOT. Eventually, you can anticipate having other allied specialists assigned, but not until both heads of state agree to open it up. You will operate under stringent security."

"Are there other pre-conditions like landing sites?"

"No. You will see what has been done so far in the Operation ROUNDUP plan. That should be your starting point. You should look at options quickly to achieve the objective—land 50 combat divisions plus their support divisions and logistics for the drive to Berlin. As you know, you must balance our operational objectives with the best intelligence of the German order of battle to achieve the objective. This is not much guidance, but it is the best we can offer at present. The chiefs want to get your initial thoughts and concepts one week from today. Do you have any questions?"

"I don't know enough to ask questions. Let me jump into this, and let's talk at the end of the week."

"Very well. Good luck, Fred. Keep me posted as you are able. I shall try to run interference for you until you get your feet on the ground."

"Thanks, Pug. This should be quite the challenge."

"That, my dear Fred, may well be a serious understatement."

Morgan nodded his head with a broad smile. The two men shook hands. Morgan departed the underground War Rooms and headed directly to Norfolk House. Ismay decided to walk to No.10 to brief the prime minister on the conversation.

—

Tuesday, 23.March.1943
USAAF Station F-356
Saffron Walden, Essex, England
United Kingdom
09:20 hours

The Skipper informed the squadron they would stand down for the morning. A briefer was inbound to cover his experience with the exploitation of a captured Focke-Wulf Fw190A-4 fighter. For the newbies, this was their first exploitation briefing, so their uncontained excitement was understandable. Even the veterans wanted to hear and learn what an experienced pilot thought about the 190.

Brian joined several other pilots sitting outside in the warmer than usual air with a spot of sunlight shining brightly through a hole in the broken clouds passing over them. They detected and called out the single aircraft on approach. They saw it before they could hear it. A Hawker Typhoon Mark IA with a tail designator UO-A landed nicely and taxied toward them. The aircraft was bigger than the Spitfire, about the size of the P-47, but not as hulky as the Thunderbolt. Brian continued to watch as several others stood to take a closer look at the new aircraft type. The engine stopped, the pilot unstrapped, and then he jumped out of the cockpit. Brian recognized him as soon as he stood up straight—Squadron Leader Jonathan Kensington. Brian jumped up and walked briskly toward Jonathan. Brian and Jonathan embraced each other. The RAF pilot told the Americans who approached behind Brian that they were welcome to examine his aircraft.

"So, you've been at it again, I suppose," Brian observed.

"Yes, indeed, and I requested I be assigned to Debden, so at least I could stop and say hello."

"I'm glad you did. How long are you going to be here?"

"I'm supposed to brief the three squadrons of the 4th Fighter Group, of which I believe the 334th Fighter Squadron is one of those units."

"Then, you will have lunch with us at the Mess."

"Yes."

"Good. Perhaps, we can have an early supper for a little private time before you have to head back." Major Peterson walked toward them. "Skipper, please allow me to introduce Squadron Leader Jonathan 'Harness' Kensington, a squadron mate from my days with 6-0-9 Squadron. Jonathan, this is Major Chesley 'Pete' Peterson, our Skipper. He joined us in 71 Squadron." The two men shook hands.

"I take it you are our guest of honor," Pete said.

"I don't know about honor, but yes, I am your guest to brief your pilots on my experience with exploitation of the Focke-Wulf Fw190 at Farnborough."

"Excellent. Are you ready to begin?"

"Whenever you say go."

"All right guys," shouted Pete, "gather in the ops shack now." As the pilots made their way to the building, Pete looked directly at Brian, "Since you two know each other, why don't you do the introduction, Brian."

"No problem." Brian patted Jonathan on the back, and they walked with Pete to the operations building. Pete raised both hands for quiet and then gestured for everyone to take their seats. Once he was satisfied, Pete gestured to Brian. "Our guest speaker today is an old . . ."

"Who are you calling old?" Harness interrupted. All of the pilots laughed.

Brian nodded his head as he smiled. "OK, OK. A young mate of mine from my old squadron is our guest speaker. Squadron Leader Jonathan 'Harness' Kensington is an ace and commanding officer of 2-6-6 Squadron, flying Hawker Typhoon fighter-bombers like the one outside. He is here to convey his experience flying a captured Focke-Wulf Fw190 at RAE Farnborough." They all applauded. Brian weaved his way to the back of the room to the chair that had become known as Hunter's chair.

Jonathan began with his description of how the subject aircraft came into the Royal Air Force's possession. Next, he described the day's flight plan for the exploitation flights. Once he had set the stage, Harness described the maneuvering features the Royal Aeronautical Establishment Exploitation Branch sought to display, and then he added his thoughts on the strengths and weaknesses of the 190. When Jonathan finished his intended talk, he opened it up to questions. What ensued was an energetic question and answer session that transitioned to a more free-ranging discussion of fighter operations, including quite a few questions to Harness about his Typhoon.

The schedule called for lunch at the Mess, and then sessions with the 335FS and 336FS in the afternoon. Lunch turned out to be slightly more raucous than usual, with the joking and jabs between Jonathan and Brian providing the catalyst.

"Thank you for the entertainment and sustenance, gentlemen," Jonathan announced. "I had better be on my way to avoid being tardy."

The squadron was supposed to remain on standby for air defense back up for the RAF. The pilots made their way back to the operations building. Brian and Jonathan reaffirmed their dinner date before they went their separate ways for their afternoon duties.

The 334FS pilots spent the afternoon in sporadic discussions about what they heard in the morning and what those facts meant to their operations. While they remained on alert status, they had a comparatively lazy afternoon. Brian listened to the observations, opinions, and debates on the broader state of fighter operations. He rarely chose to participate, and occasionally, he had to take breaks to refresh in the outside air. They were still on duty as the afternoon waned, and Jonathan reappeared at the 334FS operations building. Jonathan and Brian waved at each other, but several newbies jumped him with more questions and discussion. Fortunately, the squadron was released early.

Although the weather remained unusually mild, allowing a pleasant stroll, Jonathan and Brian walked to the front gate and grabbed a taxi to save time. The Fighting Cock Public House would serve their purposes well. They were comparatively early, so the pub's dining room was lightly attended. They took a table at the back corner and ordered two pints along with two servings of Shepherd's Pie.

As they waited, Jonathan started the conversation, "The last time I was here was in July of last year when you blokes were headed to Russia."

"Yep. Then our fighters were sunk by the Germans."

"War is like that."

"Indeed. So, tell me, my friend, how is Linda?"

Jonathan smiled broadly. The waitress delivered their pints. "Perfect is the word I would use. Her small flat in Knightsbridge makes it much easier for me to see her when we get a rest break, and she absolutely loves her job at the Air Ministry."

"So, I take it that her relationship with Virginia North and Anne Booth did not hurt her employment."

"No more than it did you, my friend. How's Charlotte and Ian?"

"Excellent. Ian is growing like a bad weed, and Charlotte is deep into expanding the farm. Looks like we're getting into farming and growing produce for the war effort."

"How about that! Good for you. I look forward to seeing your growing farm."

"We really need to have you and Linda down for a weekend when we're both off. I know Charlotte would love it.

"As would Linda and me." They had not yet drained their pints when their meals arrived. Both men took several bites of the simple but delicious meals. "By the way, I saw Mud last week at Shepherd's Pub. He's not the same Mud, the Mud we have known since he met Marilyn."

"I heard Jackie Cochran and the female American pilots returned to the States to set up an American version of the ATA."

"Yes, they did . . . at year-end. But apparently, Marilyn decided she found true love and chose to stay, kind of like you did. Mud is much less wild and more domesticated. He is enjoying himself as base commander at RAF Hamble, which is conveniently the home base of the ATA."

"Well, I'll be . . ."

"She is still flying for the ATA. The real shocker is, according to Mud, they are talking about getting married later this year."

"We've heard nothing."

"They've not told many folks."

"How is your sister?" Brian asked.

Jonathan smiled broadly. "You dog. She still talks about you. She misses you. Rose completed her medical education, took her certification exams, and is now a doctor in residence at Watlington Hospital in Oxford."

"Congratulations to her. I'm so glad she is doing well."

"I will pass along your well wishes. Now, my first mate, I really must be on my way. I'd like to get back to Duxford before the end of twilight."

"Afraid of the dark?" Jonathan gave his buddy a shot in the shoulder. "Ouch!" Brian stood. "I'll pay the bill, and . . ."

"No, Brian. We can split it."

"You are my guest. End of discussion. I'll pay the bill, and we'll get you on your way shortly." Brian found their waitress, paid the bill with a handsome gratuity. "Let's get you to your noble steed my oh-so-gallant knight of the realm." Jonathan gave Brian another shot on the other shoulder.

The proprietor called them a taxi, which arrived promptly. The driver dropped them off at the front gate. The two pilots walked directly to Jonathan's Typhoon. Brian acted as the crew chief. Jonathan started smoothly and efficiently. Harness gave the hand signal for chocks out. Brian pulled both wheel chocks, moved outside the left wingtip, held up the chocks, dropped them, and then saluted. Jonathan saluted back and started his taxi for takeoff. Brian remained where he stood, listened to the distinctive scream of the powerful Napier Sabre engine, and watched his friend lift off into the setting sun. The Typhoon sucked up its landing gear, banked left, and climbed away. Brian waited until the Typhoon was out of sight and beyond sound, and then he walked back to the Mess.

—

Friday, 26.March.1943
Law Offices of Donovan Leisure Newton & Irvine
2 Wall Street
Manhattan, New York City, New York
United States of America
09:30 hours

Bill Donovan entered the reception lobby to see his three other founding partners—George Stanley Leisure, Carl Elbridge Newton, and Ralstone R. Irvine. Donovan wore the uniform of an army brigadier general while the three other lawyers were dressed in conservative business suits. The two attractive female receptionists behind the partners stood but did not react.

"Welcome back to the fold," announced Leisure.

"Thanks, Stan," Bill said. Donovan shook hands with all three of his friends and partners. He waved to the receptionists, and then he looked back at the partners and gestured to the interior of what everyone presumed was the senior partners' modest conference room.

"What do we owe the honor?" asked Newton. "I think I was the last one to see you at the football game in December of '41."

Donovan nodded. "The assignment from the president has saturated my capacity. Standing up a new organization, especially in the political quagmire of Washington, has added substantially to the challenge."

"Do you expect to return to the practice when this war is done?" asked Irvine.

Bill smiled. "I appreciate your concern, Ralstone. My intentions and plan have not changed since I gave all of you notice of my call-up by the president in the spring of '41. The OSS has a monumental task to support the war effort. What happens when the war is done remains anyone's guess?"

"How is it to work for a Democrat and especially Roosevelt?" Newton asked.

Donovan knew the basis of the question. All of the senior partners were long-term, committed Republicans. "As you may recall, I'm not the only Republican working for Roosevelt. Heck, Frank Knox was our vice-presidential candidate in the '36 election. I tell you without equivocation, he is a leader of exceptional capacity, and from my perspective, he is a helluva man to work for—very commanding personality."

"I'm sure you did not make the journey to New York," interjected Leisure, "for some chit-chat with your partners."

"It is always a pleasure to be back with friends on familiar turf, but no, that is not the purpose of my visit. I'm here to ask for your assistance." None of them reacted or spoke. "What we are about to discuss is sensitive, so I must ask that these details are confined to the four of us." Donovan did not wait for consent, or did he ask for it. "The OSS, as it is today, came into existence by executive order a year ago June. Some of the work we are asked to do in support of the president's intelligence needs occurs within the military structure of the Navy and War Departments. However, there is an element that is covert beyond the governmental establishment. To that end, we contracted with and supported an off-the-books transportation company. I enlisted the services and contributions of Howard Hughes in assisting the stand up of that company through his ownership of Hughes Aircraft, Hughes Tool, and his majority ownership of Transcontinental & Western Airlines. We decided it was safer to build-up a private company with a commercial façade rather than attempt the reverse process with an established commercial company. Further, we learned quite early that we needed transportation means beyond the military structure and governmental travel priority constraints. The company at issue here is known as Bainbridge Air Services. It is solely and privately owned by a rather wealthy army aviator—Captain Brian Drummond."

"I've seen and heard that name," observed Leisure. "He was one of the military heroes involved in the War Bonds Drive last year, I do believe."

"One and the same. I could expound at some length about his accomplishments and virtues."

"Wait just a minute," interrupted Irvine. "I also saw more than a few newspaper photographs and articles of Drummond in the company of that German actress, Marlene Dietrich."

"I'm not particularly interested in gossip column nonsense, Ralstone. I'll only say here that Miss Dietrich has been and remains a valuable asset of the OSS. Now, back to my explanation, Mister Drummond, Captain Drummond, has entrusted his airline company's management to another accomplished aviator by the name of Bobby Joe Sales. The company is based in Wichita, Kansas, and it is operating nationally and internationally. They have engaged the local law firm Bender, Braddock & Sloan for legal services."

"Don't know 'em," added Leisure.

"Me either," Irvine contributed.

"There is no reason you should," Donovan continued. "Nonetheless, they have run into a few sticky legal points that are squarely in our bailiwick. It is in this context I'm here to request your off-the-books, *pro bono* assistance to Bainbridge Air Services and Bender, Braddock & Sloan. I've not had the time to dig into what exactly the problem is, but I certainly trust you," he said, looking at each of his partners, "to sort it out quickly and quietly. I don't want any of this to reach the public domain and especially the press, which is precisely why I want no financial transaction record associated with my request. If you find any obstacles you cannot help them resolve promptly, please come talk to me. I assure you there will be adequate opportunity to reimburse the firm, as appropriate, but off the open ledger."

"What is the problem?" Newton asked.

"My understanding, it is a contractual nuance between BAS, TWA, and Lockheed for aircraft and logistical support. The BAS lead attorney Jonas Braddock requested expert contract and trust legal counsel."

"I think we can handle that, Bill, if there are no objections," Newton said and looked at Leisure and Irvine. Both shook their heads in the negative. "Will Braddock expect our call?"

"Yes, but I would urge one of you to travel to Wichita for at least a get-acquainted meeting with Braddock and Sales. Several other people might be involved, but I would start there." Donovan pushed a single typewritten paper across to Carl Newton. "Here is all of the contact information for both Braddock and Sales. Again, if you have any problems whatsoever, please contact me any way you wish. If I am unavailable for any reason, my deputy Ned Buxton is fully up to speed and able to assist. Ned generally manages the headquarters. I am quite often on the road, in clandestine meetings of one form or another, or just simply unreachable."

The four men agreed. They spent a few minutes talking about the law firm's business and continuing success, given the flood of business associated with corporate growth, international law, and a plethora of legal services work. The firm had nearly tripled in size and breadth since Bill Donovan joined the government. Bill had to draw the conversation to a close as he had an important meeting with Bill Stephenson scheduled in 30 minutes. He bid his partners and friends a warm *adieu*. He left the building and headed uptown.

William Samuel 'Bill' Stephenson, MC, DFC, AKA 'Little Bill' in deference to his relationship with Big Bill Donovan, had been Churchill's handpicked special agent in the United States since June 1940. Within intelligence circles, he was referred by his codename 'Intrepid.' Stephenson's cover operation was as the head of the British Security Coordination Office (BSC) within the British Passport Control Office and occupied the 35th and 36th floors of the International Building, Rockefeller Center, Manhattan, New York City. His unit serviced a wide variety of special, extra-governmental purposes ranging from intelligence collaboration to special material acquisitions. Stephenson had a long friendship with Churchill and deep roots in England and North America, not least of which was his wife, American tobacco heiress Mary French Simmons.

—

Tuesday, 30.March.1943
Cabinet War Rooms
New Public Offices
Whitehall, London, England
United Kingdom
15:40 hours

Generals Ismay and Morgan sat alone, waiting in silence for the service chiefs to arrive for the scheduled meeting already 10 minutes overdue. Neither of them displayed any signs of irritation, as they sat together, midway on the left arm of the U-shaped conference table.

First Sea Lord Admiral of the Fleet Sir Alfred Dudley Pickman Rogers 'Dudley' Pound, GCB, GCVO, was the first of the service chiefs to arrive. He quickly gestured for the two generals to sit and took a seat on the far side of the prime minister's well-cushioned, high back, leather-covered chair. No staffers would attend this particular meeting.

Chief of the Air Staff Air Chief Marshal Sir Charles Portal entered a few minutes later, followed by Chief of the Imperial General Staff General Sir Alan Brooke. One of the two Army guards closed the door. Portal and Brooke took seats on the other side of the prime minister's chair from Pound. None of the senior military officers spoke. Brooke twirled his hand for the presenters to begin.

"As decided at the SYMBOL Conference and directed by the Chiefs Committee," meaning the three service chiefs, "I briefed General Morgan a week ago regarding his assignment as the head of the COSSAC planning group. The Committee requested a quick-look assessment of the operation. This is that requested briefing."

General Morgan cleared his throat, but before he could speak, General Brooke interjected. "This is a joint planning assignment with the Americans, and only the supreme commander, when he is appointed, along with the combined joint chiefs of staff, will recommend the plan to the heads of state for execution. Where are the Americans?"

"Brigadier General Ray Barker joined us at Norfolk House late last week as my deputy. My apologies, Sir Alan. I assumed this was a briefing to the British chiefs, and General Barker did not need to attend."

Deputy Chief of Staff, European Theater of Operations, Brigadier General Ray Wehnes Barker, USA GS, picked up the additional assignment as the senior American officer on the COSSAC staff.

Brooke shook his head. "Never mind. For the time being, we will leave it as is. I've not discussed this with General Marshall. I will only say here, we must be mindful of our position *in situ* to avoid offending our comrades. Please proceed."

"Yes sir. General Barker is reviewing our current library of direct, associated, and affiliated documents. This briefing is classified MOST SECRET – BIGOT. I have initiated a comprehensive hydrological and geographical survey of potential landing beaches on the Channel and Atlantic coasts of France. I expect to have the first general assessment in two weeks. Along with the beach studies, I've asked the Intelligence Branch to give us the current and anticipated German order of battle for Northern and Western France. We expect to have that report later this week. I've read through all of the Operation ROUNDUP documents generated so far, so I feel pretty good about the state of planning to date. Lastly, as my preface and from General Ismay's initial briefing, I have assumed an initial landing date of mid-September of this year and an ultimate deployed force of 50 combat divisions. With that, here is how I see things at the moment.

"Our primary chokepoint is and most likely will remain the quantity of amphibious capable shipping and landing craft. The quantity we have available today, assuming we strip the Mediterranean of all of their landing craft, would enable us to land roughly eight divisions, ten at the outside. Given our cycle time, that would mean it would take us more than a month or two to move 50 divisions across the selected beaches. The farther our selected landing site is from the South Coast of England, the longer that the logistics tail and cycle time become.

"One of many lessons learned for the Dieppe Raid in August of 1942 was that a hard harbor was necessary to avoid the susceptibility to weather at the landing beaches and was required for logistics sustainment. We have assumed, so far, that capturing an existing harbor is not feasible given the current known deployment of German forces and defenses. As such, we strongly endorse the planning and construction of the so-called Mulberry Harbor structures to provide a robust temporary harbor to avoid any interruption of reinforcement and logistical support.

"Lastly, as part of my initial assessment, I cannot emphasize enough the importance of Operation BODYGUARD to not only protect our actual plans under ROUNDUP, but also to tie up or at least disperse German forces in France. We must keep them guessing until we have sufficient forces on the ground in France. According to current intelligence, the Germans appear to have a predisposition to Calais, apparently because that was their assessment in support of the intended invasion of England under their Operation SEALION in 1940. It would appear our best approach is to subtly reinforce that predisposition."

The Western Allies established Operation BODYGUARD as a broad, cover, deception program composed of many sub-elements to support their combat operations. The title evolved from an observation by Prime Minister Churchill, "In wartime, truth is so precious that she should always be attended by a bodyguard of lies." That was Operation BODYGUARD.

"For a first impression," began Sir Alan, "I'd say you have a good handle on the task."

"We will need an inventory of all naval support craft from escort and bombardment to landing craft," added Admiral Pound.

"Yes sir. We are compiling the list from ROUNDUP work to date along with our working assessment."

"The same for air support," added Sir Charles.

"A key metric for both the American and British chiefs," said Sir Alan, "as well as the heads of state will be the size of the initial landing force. If our operations are to be regulated by the quantity of landing craft, then we must consider the employment of airborne divisions in the initial assault."

"Yes sir. We have assumed that potential. Our initial listing from BOLERO suggests we may have two American and one British airborne divisions available."

"We'll have to do better than that, but that is a reasonable assumption for now." No one else spoke. Sir Alan continued, "We need to know the decision threshold for assembly and deployment of Allied forces to support ROUNDUP by mid-September. To that end, what is your initial milestone?"

"I am reluctant to answer the question since there are so many variables we do not yet understand. However, if you will allow me some latitude, I will say four months is a minimum, more preferably six months."

"So mid-May," Sir Alan responded.

"Yes sir . . . at the very latest."

"We are not likely to achieve that as events are unfolding in Tunisia and the decision taken at SYMBOL," said Sir Charles.

"Agreed," Sir Dudley added.

"For now, I think we are agreed," Sir Alan said and looked at both Sir Dudley and Sir Charles to receive a head nod of agreement, "to use those control dates, namely mid-May for a commit decision and mid-September for the landing on Continental Europe. Good job so far, Fred. I'm certain you recognize that you do not have much time to support those milestones, so do the best you can in the time you have. Lastly, I think you should anticipate that the prime minister will take a very keen interest in your work, and if his interest is adding to your burden, you must inform us. We shall do our best to protect your work."

"Yes sir. Thank you, sir."

Brooke looked directly at Ismay. "Pug, when you inform the prime minister of today's meeting, please ask him for as much latitude as he is able to provide for the planning to proceed unimpeded." Sir Hastings nodded his head in agreement.

The service chiefs thanked Morgan and Ismay for their work and quickly dispersed to attend other priority tasks.

—

Chapter 5

War is barbarism . . . Its glory is all moonshine.
It is only those who have neither fired a shot
nor heard the shrieks and groans of the wounded
who cry aloud for blood, more vengeance, more desolation.
War is hell.

-- William Tecumseh Sherman

Thursday, 8.April.1943
USAAF Station F-356
Saffron Walden, Essex, England
United Kingdom
09:20 hours

The RODEO 280 mission plan, as briefed by Pete, impressed Brian as one of the more complex fighter sweep plans he had yet seen in the war. Three entire fighter groups—the 56th and 78[th,] in addition to their own 4th Fighter Group—were to conduct a coordinated swarm sweep of Northeast France. Nine Thunderbolt squadrons crisscrossing the region to confuse the enemy were perplexing enough when viewed on the mission's full, broad depiction. Brian worried about so many moving pieces and its timing, but they had to trust everyone would do their part in hitting their targets and milestones on time. Adding time for a ground target strike always added a dimension of uncertainty.

The plan called for the 334FS to execute hit-and-run attacks in the vicinity of three towns—Dunkirk, St. Omer, and Boulogne. Their assigned targets were a general pass on the port town, a railroad, switching yard at St. Omer, and the German E-boat docks in the port of Boulogne on their way out and toward home base.

The 334FS took off first and entered a wide orbit around the airfield to allow the rest of the group to take off and join up. Once the group was assembled at 5,000 feet, they turned south and headed across the Channel.

Ten miles from the beach, they spread into a box of four flights with each flight in a line abreast. Next to Pete's Blue Flight at the front left corner, Brian's Red Flight had the right front corner. Sweet's Yellow Flight, the second flight of Brian's 'B' Division, had the right rear corner. They descended to wave top height. "OK, Pectin. We're hot. Any target that moves." They slowed slightly. They were just ahead of the plan.

The squadron box's lead flights crossed the shoreline and hit any moving or German military vehicle of any type in and around Dunkirk. A German staff car. Hunter quickly adjusted his sight pipper on the target and squeezed the trigger. All of the guns erupted. Flashes on the vehicle's metal skin preceded by an instant the explosion of the car's gas tank. *A grey-green truck . . . outside my cone of action.* Brian pressed on, correcting to maintain his track. Tracers probably from 'Horn' Lee's Thunderbolt on the outside of the flight went directly to a half-track heading into town. The explosion marked his success.

As they passed the city heading due south over the farm fields south of the town, they began to see evidence of the squadrons that preceded them—plumes of black smoke rising into the clear spring air. *Where are the German fighters?* Five miles south of Dunkirk, they wheeled left heading south-southeast toward their next checkpoint of Cassel. Tracers angled down fired from various, unseen, members of 334FS. A few resulted in new explosions and fires. At Cassel, slightly ahead of their crossing-time, Pete turned the squadron south-southwest toward Aire-sur-la Lys. They crossed Aire within seconds of their crossing time. *Pete's doing a helluva job keeping us on the plan.* Another Thunderbolt squadron passed a couple of miles to the west, headed in the opposite direction. At Aire, the squadron turned sharply to the northwest.

Approaching St. Omer, Pete adjusted their heading, so the box's left side, Pete's 'A' Division, lined up on the railyard. Brian's 'B' Division would continue to pick up targets of opportunity. Explosions, fireballs, black smoke, even large blossoms of white smoke burst out to their left, even before they reached the city. Brian was aware of successes to his left, but he focused on the streets and plazas before them. Tracers erupted from the rest of Red Flight to his right as Brian squeezed his trigger.

Trucks and cars were moving through the city. St. Omer was far busier than Dunkirk. A dozen grey and grey-green cars parked nicely in a row beside a large building. *Perfect!* Brian sharply adjusted his track slightly to the left and put his sight pipper short of the first car and squeezed the trigger, holding it down. Tracers hit the paving stones short of the first car and walked perfectly along the line of vehicles. Each one burst into flame, and a couple of cars exploded lifting them off the ground. Tracers danced everywhere around them—*more targets than expected.*

Brian continued at rooftop height. He saw a canvas-covered truck ahead. Troops were bailing out as fast as they could move. Brian centered up his pipper, let it rise to the truck and scrambling troops, and squeezed the trigger. Flashes all over the truck marked his hits. His 50-caliber rounds were not kind to the German troops who had not yet made it out of the truck bed. Then, one of the truck's fuel tanks exploded. Brian had to jink sharply left to avoid the fireball and smoke. They were out of town into farmland again. *We're late to the turn.* Brian turned left. He glanced over his right shoulder. A bright flash. *Canopy glint.* Then, Brian saw them. A squadron of 109s diving on them.

"Bandits! East and closing. Pectin Baker, break right and engage." Brian pulled up sharply, jammed his throttle to the combat stop, and rolled right.

The rest of his division followed him. They were maneuvering as best they could with no thrust margin to their aerial combat spread. The big radial engine was giving him all the power it could provide. Brian adjusted his flight path, placing his pipper on the lead 109. The bad guy was growing fast in his sight. The disadvantage position convinced Brian to take the first shot early. He moved his pipper a little higher on his target and squeezed the trigger. The tracers arced above and descended to the German. Several flashes marked impacts. The lead German pulled up abruptly with no signs of firing. Tracers streaked in both directions. A flash occurred behind his right wing. The two opposing flights passed through each other.

"Sweet, I'm hit. Engine running rough."

That sounds like Dog. Brian rolled left, pulling hard as the aerodynamic noise decreased rapidly. *Running out of airspeed.* His nose came down through the horizon. Brian strained his neck against the g's, looking high over his left shoulder. He expected to see the Germans in climbing turns to reengage, but they were not. *Where the hell are they?*

"Pectin Yellow, disengage. RTB. Do the best you can to keep her running, Dog. We'll cover you."

Yellow Flight Leader First Lieutenant Robert Charles 'Sweet' Sweeny, Jr., took the remainder of his flight to cover his wingman Second Lieutenant Donald Stephen 'Dog' Gaines from Santa Fe, New Mexico—the next to newest of the newbies.

"Pectin, Pectin Baker. Bandits through us . . . may be running to you." Brian rolled to a westerly heading in a shallow dive. He quickly scanned the sky around him. *Clear.* He checked his instruments.

"Roger, Hunter. We're running to target three. Catch up as you can."

"Wilco."

Brian quickly scanned his instrument panel, again. Everything still green. The other three aircraft of Red Flight were in position. Brian could see the distinctive harbor of Boulogne and the coastline ahead. *Not descending fast enough.* Brian slowly pulled his throttle back a quarter and increased his dive angle. Everyone adjusted properly. *Where are the German fighters? They must've gotten another assignment against one of the other RODEO squadrons. The sky is clear . . . for now.*

A couple of smoke plumes began to rise from the harbor. *Able Division has some success.* Brian adjusted their heading slightly for a good line up on their target. He signaled for a line abreast attack formation. Buddy took his left wing this time. Salt was on the right wing with Horn outside of him. Red Flight moved fast above the trees. Then they saw the docks. Two E-boats were moving. Brian lined up on the last moving torpedo boat. All four Thunderbolts opened up at virtually the same time. Streams of red tracers reached out to various spot targets—the flashes all over Brian's target. A fire erupted on the boat, and then a massive explosion startled Brian. He pulled up hard. The shock wave briefly jolted his aircraft. Thuds all over the belly of his aircraft meant that shrapnel from an exploding torpedo warhead had probably hit him. *Wings are still smooth.* In clear air, tracers streaked up from the ground. He dove for the water, continuing straight to get out of range of coastline air defenses. Brian checked his gauges. *Nothing wrong.* He glanced over his right shoulder and estimated they were out of range. Brian rolled smoothly to a northerly heading but kept them at wave top height.

With the French coast vanishing quickly behind them, Brian throttled back an inch and began a shallow climb. He noticed what appeared to be a frothy white wake heading north a couple of miles to their east. An E-boat at speed. Brian signaled toward the German torpedo boat, and then for trail formation. Tracers began to rise from the boat. Brian put his pipper above the target and squeezed off a two-second burst to hopefully distract the German gunner. Impact geysers astern of the speeding boat. He squeezed off another burst. At least a couple of impact flashes stopped the German guns. Brian closed rapidly. In range, Brian squeezed the trigger and held it down. Flashes and geysers appeared all around and on the boat. Brian pulled up to give the rest of his flight a clear shot at the target. He saw the reflection of a bright explosion in his cockpit. Rolling to the right, Brian looked back to see a large white circle of what had been a German E-boat.

"Pectin Red, Pectin, was that you?"

"Affirmative, Pectin. I think Salt may get the credit."

"Affirmative, Pectin Baker. Smacked that bastard."

"Good. They were probably after Dog, who is in the water."

Oh shit. That's not good. The water is still cold.

"Pectin Red, how far back are you?"

"Pectin, Pectin Red. Looks like we're about ten miles behind you."

"Roger, press on. Sweet is staying overhead for rescue. We picked up Sloppy and Rolo."

Sloppy was First Lieutenant Michael Raines 'Sloppy' Butterfield, who had transferred with No.71 Squadron and now led the second Yellow Flight section. Sloppy's wingman was Second Lieutenant Ronald Carl 'Rolo' Stanfield from Houston, Texas.

Brian followed Pete and kept the rest of the squadron just above the horizon. Pete called Sector Control to inform them of the separate transit as well as Dog's bail out and Sweet remaining overhead for the rescue team.

They landed at Debden without incident. Sweet would be 30 minutes behind them at most, or he would have to divert to a closer base for fuel. Brian taxied to his spot, caged his attitude gyro, switched off his electrical equipment, and shut down the engine. Sergeant Tomlinson waited for him at the left, trailing edge, wing root.

"Must've been a rough one," announced Larson. "Lots of holes in your belly panels."

"Exploded a torpedo at Boulogne. I don't think anything vital was hit."

Brian and Larson went around the wing, and they squatted down to examine the damage. "I think you're done for the day, Captain . . . at least until we can get the bird in the hangar and give her a thorough check."

"OK. Thanks, Larson. Sorry about the damage."

"Forget it, Captain. We'll get her checked out and patched up lickety-split." Brian nodded and left.

The debriefings took a little longer than usual, but fortunately, they had more intelligence personnel to debrief them. The processing of the gun camera film would take a few days.

"What's wrong?" Brian asked when he saw the long faces.

"Dog didn't make it," announced Captain Paul James 'Dusty' Langford, Green Flight Leader. "By the time the rescue boat arrived, hypothermia had taken him."

"May God rest his immortal soul," pronounced First Lieutenant Joshua David 'Frog' Forcier, Dusty's second section leader.

"Where's Sweet?" Brian asked.

"He landed short at RAF Hawkinge," answered Dusty, "on fumes. He stayed overhead Dog until the rescue boat arrived, but they were too late. Dog got into his life raft, but the cold still got him. Sweet should be able to get back here in an hour or so. He may have more."

Silence enveloped them for several minutes. A couple of the guys rose and went outside.

"Damn! Did you see all those rusting wrecks littering the beach at Dunkirk?" asked Horn.

"Yes. I saw them live during DYNAMO," Brian muttered.

"What was dynamo?" Horn pressed.

"The evacuation of the BEF from Dunkirk in June 1940," said Frog, jumping into the conversation. "A third of a million Allied men were saved."

"No shit! All of those trucks, cars, tanks, and cannons have been there since 1940?"

"Yes," Brian answered matter-of-factly. "They wanted to save the soldiers. The equipment was sacrificed to save the men."

A half dozen other aircraft sustained sufficient battle damage, including Brian's Thunderbolt, for the squadron to be reported temporarily inoperable. The squadron was done for the day. They were released for the rest of the day.

A bunch of the guys decided to make a run into London for a hamburger at the Eagle Club, and then they would have a few beers at Shepherd's Pub and mix it up with other fighter pilots before returning to Debden.

—

Thursday, 8.April.1943
Allied Forces Headquarters
Hôtel Saint George
24 Avenue Souidani Boudjemaâ
Algiers
Algérie Coloniale Française
15:40 hours

Chief of Staff General Beetle Smith knocked and entered the supreme commander's picturesque office overlooking the blue Mediterranean Sea. "George just sent a message confirming that the Germans evaporated in front of him at El Guettar. What intelligence we have indicates the Germans are withdrawing north. Monty also reported the same before him at the Mareth Line. The Germans abandoned their defensive line. Both messages indicate the 8th Army and II Corps linked up near Gafsa, Tunisia."

"So, the encirclement is finally complete."

"It appears so. The G-2 doesn't think von Arnim is inclined to surrender even though his situation is hopeless."

"No, it's not going to be easy. Have we seen another stand or die order from Hitler?"

"Not that I'm aware of, but I'll ask Kenneth."

Kenneth was Assistant Chief of Staff for Intelligence (G-2) Brigadier General Kenneth William Dobson Strong, who had joined the Allied Forces general staff last month and was a career military intelligence officer.

"Where is Alexander?" asked Eisenhower.

"At the 18th AG HQ at Constantine."

The 18th Army Group stood up in January under General Sir Harold Alexander as the overall ground commander of American, British, and Free French forces. The rudimentary field headquarters grew around an airfield under construction near the scenic city of Constantine and served the British 1st Army initially, then Allied Forces Forward, when Eisenhower assumed command of the ground forces to deal with the recalcitrant French, and currently serving as Alexander's 18AG headquarters. Constantine is roughly halfway between Algiers and Tunis, 40 miles inland from the coast.

"I guess we made the correct choice installing Patton," Ike added.

"You, Ike. You did what had to be done." Eisenhower nodded his head but did not answer. "Knowing George, I imagine his victory is somewhat bittersweet in that he was denied a battlefield victory over Rommel."

Eisenhower smiled and looked up from the papers on his desk. "He'll get over it. Rommel's not done. I suspect George will have future opportunities before this affair is over. Given the events of the last few days, I need to have a sit-down with Harold."

"Do you want me to call him here?"

"No. I want to go to Constantine. I want to talk to him in his element. I need to see what he sees. Now that we have the Germans and Italians hemmed in, I want to go through his plans to consolidate and finish off the Africa Corps."

"How about informing Marshall and Washington?"

"I'd prefer to send them a complete summary after I meet with Harold."

"Very well. Are you thinking tomorrow?"

"Yes, if you can get it set up with Constantine. Let's fly out to give us the most time on the ground."

"You'll need an escort."

"Sure."

"They'll probably assign a flight of Spitfires from 37 Group, Air Vice Marshal Spencer's new group."

"Whatever aviators think is necessary."

"Do you want anyone to go with you?"

"Depends on what you've got the staff working on now. I think either the G-3 or the G-2."

"They both have active projects, but I think Kenneth has the most margin."

"That should work," Eisenhower stated. "See if you can set it up for first thing in the morning to meet with Harold, just the two of us, upon arrival, and then we can sit down with the staff, lunch, and whatever Harold would like to discuss."

"I'd better hop to it. I should be able to confirm within the hour."

"This is not life or death, Beetle. Just do the best you can. You can get started on the draft summary report to Washington and London."

"Sure. I'll get back to you as soon as I have everything lined up."

"Thanks, Beetle. Please send a personal to George and thank him for his masterful work."

"Will do." Smith departed and left the supreme commander with his paperwork.

—

Saturday, 10.April.1943
Maragon Manor
Lamport, Northamptonshire, England
United Kingdom
14:30 hours

The invitation to Marilyn and Jeremy Morrison's wedding had arrived at Standing Oak Farm three weeks ago. The drive to the country manor house proved comparably scenic to the drive Charlotte and Brian enjoyed in July of 1941 to Carlingon Castle for the wedding of Linda and Jonathan Kensington. Fortunately, that had been enough time to make arrangements with Pete's consent and two other pilots to have three days leave. He had arrived home yesterday afternoon, and they took the morning train north. The weather had luckily cleared into a crystal clear, blue sky with only a few widely spread fair-weather cumulus clouds spotting the blue. The air temperature was not warm, but it was warmer than typical for mid-spring in England.

Brian wore his pinks and greens service uniform, this time with his RAF wings above his right breast pocket, his USAAF wings above his left pocket, and all of his formal medals. Charlotte wore a light blue knee-length skirt, matching blue, below the hips jacket, and a lighter blue ruffled blouse.

"Beautiful," Charlotte said softly, as they both peered out the windows at the passing scenery.

"Yes, that it is . . . but not as beautiful as you, my sweet."

Charlotte scoffed at Brian's flattery. "Have you been here before?"

"Nope," Brian answered. Jeremy never really talked about his brother or his family much."

"Why not?"

"I asked him that very question several times years ago. He always deflected the conversation. My guess has been that he did not like the trappings of nobility."

"His older brother?"

"Yeah, the 8th Duke of Cottingstone, as I understand it."

Robert James Harlan 'Bobby' Morrison, Jeremy's older brother by two years, became the duke on the passing of their father eight years ago, and his wife Judy became the duchess. Jeremy and Bobby had two younger sisters, Ladies Elizabeth and Kellin, who were both married to commoners.

They entered a forest with tall trees on both sides of the two-lane roadway. Not quite a mile into the forest, they turned off the paved asphalt road onto a two-lane wide gravel road through a brick wall with two columns and open, ornate, iron gates. The gravel road twisted through the trees, over a small creek, and into a clearing with trimmed grass and scattered trees. The brick and stone manor house stood on a slight rise. The two-story house was modest by what Brian understood as British standards. The house was impressive nonetheless.

Other automobiles, some high-end limousines, occupied a portion of the driveway. Two footmen stood at attention as the taxi stopped in front of them. Brian paid the driver. One of the footmen opened the door for Charlotte. Brian followed her out of the cab.

"Captain and Mrs. Drummond," the footman announced. "Welcome to Maragon Manor."

How the hell could he possibly know who we are? "Yes," Brian said simply.

One of the footmen motioned toward the large, open, double door entrance, and then he led Charlotte and Brian to the door. At the door, he stopped, faced the interior, and announced in a commanding voice. "Captain and Mrs. Drummond."

Inside the spacious foyer, Brian recognized Jeremy, who stepped out of the third spot of the reception line. Mud was attired in his RAF uniform with wing commander sleeve stripes along with his wings and medals. Jeremy stepped boldly to and hugged Charlotte, kissing her on both cheeks. "Thank you for coming, Charlotte." He released Charlotte, turned to Brian, and punched him in the right shoulder, jingling his medals. "This rogue does not deserve such a caring and sophisticated woman," he said. Jeremy did not wait for a response. He turned to a man dressed in a black-tie tuxedo and an elegant woman in a peach-colored, blossomy, floor-length dress. "Charlotte, Brian, please allow me to introduce you to my brother Bobby and his wife, Judy."

Charlotte took Bobby Morrison's proffered right hand and curtsied. "It's an honor to meet you, Your Grace,"

Morrison raised Charlotte's right hand to his lips and kissed the back of her hand. "To a holder of the George Cross, it's Bobby, please." He kissed the back of her hand again. "My brother has regaled us with your exploits and accomplishments as well as those of your husband." Charlotte smiled and nodded somewhat in shock. Bobby released her hand and reached for Brian. "Thank you so much for your contributions to the defense of the realm. It is our honor to have you both here with us for Jeremy's marriage to a kinswoman of yours."

"I never thought I would witness Mud getting married, but Marilyn seems to have done the trick."

"Wonders shall never cease."

Charlotte and Brian completed their introductions. They were escorted to a large study or library that had been cleared as a reception room. Brian gave his uniform hat to a coat check woman. He looked around the room with perhaps 40-50 people, none of whom he recognized. Brian was the only person in an American uniform. There were other RAF, Royal Navy, and British Army officers all in uniform, and all of them were senior to Brian. Waiters passed through the group with trays of filled champagne flutes and *canapés*. Brian retrieved two glasses for Charlotte and himself. They both availed themselves of the *hors d'œuvres*.

"Do you recognize anyone?" Charlotte asked.

"Not a soul. I guess we shall just stand here and look pretty."

"You are handsome, my darling, not pretty."

"OK. Then I'll stand here and protect the pretty one."

"Thank you."

An attractive woman with short light brown hair and a seafoam green dress stared directly at Brian and Charlotte. She had a broad smile on her face and walked smoothly toward them. *Who the hell is this? Am I supposed to know her?* As she neared, she extended her right hand. "Hello," she said, "I'm Elizabeth Julian, Jeremy's sister. My friends call me Lizzie." She shook hands with Charlotte and Brian. "If Jeremy informs me properly," she said, looking directly at Charlotte, "you are, or rather were," she glanced at Brian, "a widow. I lost my husband in the Battle of France nearly three years ago."

"Yes, I was. My husband died when his ship was sunk."

"HMS *Glorious*," added Brian, "in June of '40."

Lizzie looked back at and held Charlotte's eyes. "My Michael was killed near St. Valery sur Somme before they could be evacuated. Damn German bastards!"

"I am so sorry for your loss."

"As I am for yours, Charlotte. How did you manage? How did you cope?"

"Excuse me, ladies. I'll give you some space to speak frankly." Brian kissed the back of Charlotte's left hand and left her with Lizzie.

Brian noticed scenery out the windows at the far end of the room. He weaved through the clumps of people, stopping several times as men and women offered their congratulatory words for the medals above his right breast pocket. Some of them knew him, but he did not know them and kept that fact to himself. He stood alone at the window absorbing the magnificent array of spring colors in an immaculately kept garden and evergreen forest beyond. A slap on his back broke his appreciation of the scene. Brian spun quickly.

"Charlotte said you were back here," Jonathan said. He was also attired in his uniform with medals.

"Yeah, they were talking about widowhood, so I figured they did not need me. Where's Linda?"

"With Charlotte and Lizzie. They are gabbing away like fast friends."

"Lizzie is Jeremy's younger sister."

"Ah yes, that explains it."

"Explains what?"

"Lizzie is a very effervescent woman, very much in command of the scene . . . like she belongs here."

"Do you know anyone else?" Brian asked.

"I recognize a few of the senior officers, but I'm sure they don't know me."

"I don't know anyone other than you and Linda, and Jeremy . . . and Marilyn when she app . . ."

A bell rang, interrupting Brian. A man, perhaps the family butler, held a bell high and continued to rap on the bell until he achieved quiet and all eyes on him. "Ladies and gentlemen, the ceremony is about to begin. If you would be so kind to make your way to the Great Room, we will get Lord Jeremy and Miss Powell married."

"Great Room?" Brian said. "As if this room is not large enough." They both laughed. The ladies waited near the doorway, at least Charlotte and Linda, since Lizzie served Marilyn as a bride's maid. Brian kissed Linda on each cheek. They followed the group down a wide hallway and into another ornately decorated room that was indeed larger than the reception room. They sat at the back on the groom's side. A string quartet played music Brian did not recognize.

The quartet stopped, paused, and then began playing Felix Mendelssohn's "Wedding March" in C major. Everyone in the room stood. Marilyn Powell appeared in an exquisite, white, floor-length, lace veiled dress. The duke escorted her down the aisle to the waiting Jeremy Morrison. The traditional Anglican ceremony stepped through each segment until the minister pronounced, "Ladies and gentlemen, it is my honor to present Wing Commander and Mrs. Jeremy Morrison."

Interesting. He still refuses to use his courtesy noble title.

Two long tables managed to seat the whole group for supper, a plump Cod fillet stuffed with shrimp, sliced scallions, and diced gherkins with a cheesy cream sauce. It was a delicious meal despite the constraints of wartime rationing. The table conversation remained light and full of humor, joy, and celebration. The toasts to the bride and groom remained in the same tone—light and humorous.

After dessert and the last of the toasts, they moved from the dining room back to the reception hall that had been slightly rearranged to accommodate a small band playing contemporary music at a lower volume level. Linda and Jonathan reconnected with Charlotte and Brian as far away from the band as they could get. Advancing dusk darkened the exterior. There was less and less to see. Two of the staff pulled the blackout curtains to comply with wartime restrictions. All four of them saw Marilyn wave to them and work her way through the guests toward them. She eventually made it back to the Drummonds and Kensingtons.

"So great to see y'all again," Marilyn announced when she reached the four. "Thank you so much for attending our wedding." They all greeted the bride and congratulated her.

"We've not seen you since The Fighting Cocks Pub last July," Jonathan observed.

"Yeah, and an awful lot has happened in your life," added Brian.

Marilyn giggled softly. "That was it, and you are quite correct. Jeremy and I connected."

"I guess so, huh," Brian responded, inducing laughter in all.

"Mud is a changed man since he met you, Marilyn. Are you going to continue to fly?"

"Absolutely! Jeremy insisted as well. I love flying. We both debated whether I should wear my uniform for the ceremony, but it was Judy who convinced me to take the feminine approach."

"You are so lovely, Marilyn. Wise choice and good counsel," Charlotte contributed.

"So, you don't miss going back to the States with the rest of the American women?" asked Brian.

"No. Do you?"

Brian put his arm around Charlotte's shoulders. "Nope. I found the love of my life . . . and this is where the flying is."

Marilyn giggled again. "My thoughts precisely."

"We look forward to getting to know you better," Linda said.

"Thank you, and the feeling is mutual." Marilyn looked over her shoulder. "Now, if you will excuse me, I am told I must circulate."

They all congratulated the bride again. They tried dancing, but Brian felt incredibly awkward. They also stayed until they noticed the crowd thinning. Both couples had hotels in Northampton for the night. They agreed to meet for breakfast and had tickets on the same train into London where they would split. Both couples paid their respects to their hosts—the duke and duchess—and to Marilyn and Jeremy. A line of taxis and hired cars had been ordered up and stood in readiness. The four of them loaded into the same cab for the drive into Northampton. Linda and Jonathan dropped off the Drummonds and said goodnight. It had been a long day.

—

Wednesday, 14.April.1943
Station HYPO
Administration Building, Naval Station Pearl Harbor
Russell Avenue and Port Royal Street
Pearl City, Honolulu County, Oahu, Hawaiian Islands
Territory of the United States of America
15:15 hours

"**H**ey, boss," Senior Chief Petty Officer Bradley Robertson said, as he stopped in front of Commander Joseph John 'Joe' Rochefort's desk, "the guys just translated this MAGIC decrypt.

"It took us six hours to decipher and another day to translate and analyze the message."

Rochefort gestured for the message. He read it carefully several times.

TOP SECRET - MAGIC

```
T O P   S E C R E T
DATE 19430413 0807 HOME
FROM SUPREME COMMANDER TOKYO
TO BASE UNIT NO 1 11TH AIR FLOTILLA 26TH AIR
FLOTILLA
OPERATION I GO INSPECTION
AMY ITINERARY CONFIRMED INSPECTION TOUR YOUR
COMMANDS
ARR RR 19430417 1530 RON HONORS RENDERED
SERVICES PROVIDED
DEP RR 19430418 0600 BY G4M1 TO RXZ
ARR RXZ 0800 PROCEED BY 13 CLASS TO RXE
ARR RXE 0840 DEP 0945 PROCEED BY 13 CLASS TO
RXZ
ARR RXZ 1030 DEP 1100 BY G4M1 TO RXP
ARR RXP 1110 DEP 1400 BY G4M1 TO RR
```

```
ARR RR 1540 RON NO HONORS SERVICES REQUIRED
DEP RR YOUR COMMANDS 19430419 0830
T O P   S E C R E T
DECIPHERED HYPO 132135Z APRIL 1943
```

TOP SECRET - MAGIC

"This is intriguing and an awful lot to digest," Rochefort observed. "I will need the details of your analysis, but this looks like a detailed itinerary for someone important."

"That it is, sir. It took us hours to identify AMY."

"And?"

"AMY is Admiral-Marshall Yamamoto – Isoroku Yamamoto. The code letters are actually location designators. Confirmation came from Army Intelligence. They have been gathering a list for more than a decade. RR is Rabaul, New Britain. They had been working on code letters for several years. They have validated the designators, like airport designators used by airlines, and they have remained consistent."

"Well, well, well! He's making a command inspection tour."

"Exactly."

"We need to get this decrypt to the sink and DC." Rochefort used the shorthand reference to the commander-in-chief (CinC, pronounced 'sink'), in this instance, Admiral Chester Nimitz.

"Yes. The itinerary got even more interesting when we found out that 'RXZ' is Balalae Airfield, Balalae Island, Shortland Islands Group, Solomon Islands."

"Just north of Guadalcanal?"

"Yes. Exactly."

"Within fighter range?"

"Yes."

"My God!" Rochefort exclaimed. "Wait! I'm not familiar with Balalae Airfield."

"It is a small island in the middle of the Shortland Islands Group, off the south end of Bouganville, at the Solomon Islands Archipelago's north end. The airfield is the island and vice versa. The Japanese constructed the airfield there after they seized control in early 1942. They have since stationed both Army and Navy aviation units at the base."

"Do you think it is possible?"

"Yes," Chief Robertson answered quickly, succinctly, and confidently. "Balalae Island is roughly 400 miles northwest of Guadalcanal, not an easy intercept but possible. One word of caution with this one, Commander . . . It took us a while to figure out that all the times are Tokyo time, time zone India. Balalae and Guadalcanal are in time zone Kilo. The times are one hour different from local and Guadalcanal time. Timing will be crucial for a mission like this, should they decide to attempt it, but on the plus side beyond our acquisition of Yamamoto's schedule is the admiral's reputation for punctuality. He is obsessive about being on time, so much so, that there are multiple independent reports of him chastising pilots, ship's captains, and even simple drivers for making him late to plan."

"So I've heard as well, but others will have to judge that," Rochefort said. "Let's get this transmitted to OP-20G ASAP. I'll take this one to Commander Layton and the sink."

"As you command, sir."

Robertson went to his desk, retrieved a second file copy of the MAGIC message, and weaved his way through the rows of desks to the communications group.

Rochefort took the MAGIC intercept, left the secure HYPO basement cave, and climbed the stairs to the office of the director of naval intelligence for the Pacific fleet.

The message set in motion a series of fast-paced events that would alter the path of history.

—

Thursday, 15.April.1943
No.10 Downing Street
Whitehall, London, England
United Kingdom
16:30 hours

Prime Minister Churchill studied several rather laborious shipping and logistics reports until his patience and tolerance threshold overwhelmed him. He depressed the buzzer button on his desk.

Duty Private Secretary John Martin appeared in the doorway. "Yes sir."

Winston closed the reports and pushed them across the desk toward Martin. "Please send these reports back to the Admiralty with an instruction to correlate tonnage of specific supply categories off-loaded at which port into the distribution system with the convoy shipping en route. I need to know the effectiveness of our selection process. I am concerned we are not adequately watching our delivery yield. Also, ask them to separate and annotate military supplies for American forces that cross our docks. I need to see the correlation between what we decide to load out in North America with what actually arrives to account for battle losses and what our needs are, both civil and military. I am concerned we are not adjusting properly to our demands and losses."

Martin completed his notetaking to ensure he had the prime minister's instructions. He quickly read his notes to make sure he captured the request. "I think I have it, sir. I suspect we shall need more than the Admiralty to satisfy your request."

"Sure, sure, but Admiralty can supervise and manage the coordination with the other ministries."

"I shall so inform them." Martin took the reports from the desk and left the office. Churchill turned to the next report in his pending stack. He had barely read the summary of the latest Allied Forces status report when Martin returned. "Excuse me, Prime Minister. General Ismay has asked for a few minutes to quickly brief you on a few new items."

Churchill impatiently waved his hand. "Yes, yes, please send him in."

Ismay must have been waiting outside the prime minister's office. He entered and closed the door behind him.

"What have you, Pug?"

"Thank you for allowing me to intrude." Churchill waved his hand dismissively. Ismay sat across the desk from the prime minister. "The chiefs agreed and ordered all available landing craft of various types to be moved to Algiers and eventually to Tunis, once it is secured. Allied Forces remain quite concerned they will not have sufficient amphibious resources to land adequate forces given the German and Italian order of battle."

"When you say chiefs, I assume you mean the combined joint chiefs."

"Yes sir. That is exactly what I mean."

"Are they asking for my concurrence?"

"No sir. Just offering you the opportunity to object, if you wish, before the orders are executed."

"Not necessary. I concur. I think Eisenhower is correct, but we must do the best we can with the resources we have available."

"Next, I have been tracking a rather curious situation. We have received several messages from separate sources about the discovery of what may be more than one mass grave, or perhaps more properly, a burial site, in the Katyn Forest near and to the west of Smolensk, just inside Russia from the border with Belarus. The Germans first reported discovering the mass burial site of what appears to be Polish officers—hundreds of them. I contacted the Polish government in exile. Oddly, the Poles agree with the Germans. They both accuse the Soviets, either the Red Army or NKVD, most likely the latter, of slaughtering the captured officers sometime after the Soviet invasion of Eastern Poland in 1939."

"You mean like the Germans have been massacring Jews, gypsies, and others the Nazis deem as sub-human?"

"Yes sir. It would appear so. The Soviets accused the Germans, citing the mounting evidence of the special commando units of the SS in Eastern Europe."

"The killing continues and is not done, and I'm afraid we are a long way from being done with this mindless killing. Please request a full report from the Poles. It is in their best interest to collect the information. Please ensure the Americans have this information, and we make certain the war crimes branch at MI6 has this too."

"Yes sir. Lastly, you asked me to look quietly into the evidence of the German rocket program. I met with the Air Ministry's Intelligence and Research Branches yesterday afternoon. As you may recall, the first inkling of a rocket program in Germany was the Oslo Report. Not everyone embraced the contents, believing that it might be part of a disinformation campaign to distract us. The photographic reconnaissance evidence is mounting. A young Air Ministry physicist by the name of Jones, R.V. Jones . . ."

"I know him."

"Yes sir. He has gone back to the Oslo Report with the latest photographs, and he believes the Oslo Report addresses several specific technologies that support the photographic evidence and reflects at least two forms of rocket weapons. One, an aeroplane-like, pilotless flying bomb, and two, a much larger device Jones believes is a long-range missile guided or directed by a gyroscopically controlled system of some sort."

"So, you think this program and these devices are real, and not just some elaborate hoax?"

"Yes, I do. While the evidence is not yet irrefutably conclusive beyond a shadow of a doubt, it is very compelling information."

"If I understand your independent assessment, you believe there is sufficient evidence to pursue the matter for potential targeting data."

"I'm convinced."

"The Prof has been a consistent believer. When you get a moment, please give him your evaluation."

"I'll contact Lord Cherwell as soon as we are done here."

"I presume the Air Ministry is developing their target list."

"Yes, they are."

"I've decided to focus attention on this rocket program matter at the ministerial level by appointing Duncan Sandys to draw all of this together for the War Cabinet."

Edwin Duncan Sandys had been Financial Secretary to the War Cabinet since 1941 and was married to the Churchills' oldest child and first daughter

Diana since 1935. He was the Member of Parliament for Norwood from six months before he married Diana. Duncan possessed a keen mind for detail, and Winston trusted his judgment.

"Has his appointment been implemented?"

"Not yet, but I would appreciate it if you sit down with him at your earliest convenience to give him your assessment and contacts."

"It shall be done, Prime Minister."

"Anything else on your list?"

"No sir. Please let me know as soon as the actions are completed," commanded Churchill.

"I will, sir. Thank you for your time."

"Thank you, Pug." Winston turned his attention back to his papers. Pug Ismay departed and closed the door behind him.

—

Thursday, 15.April.1943
Little White House
401 Little White House Road
Warm Springs, Meriwether County, Georgia
United States of America
18:15 hours

The president's inspection tour had begun the previous Tuesday as he crisscrossed the country by train en route to meeting President Manuel Ávila Camacho of Mexico on the coming Tuesday. The two leaders planned to discuss Mexico's continuing contributions to the war effort after joining the Allies in May 1942. They also expected to discuss sensitive intelligence matters of mutual interest. President Roosevelt planned on a formal dinner before departing for a night transit by train back to the United States.

President Roosevelt had witnessed a training parachute jump at Fort Benning, Georgia, earlier in the afternoon and returned to his favorite Warm Springs bungalow for supper. The president took one more refreshing dip in the therapeutic warm water before he and his entourage would board the presidential train for the overnight transit to his estate in New York and then onto Chicago.

Secretaries Stimson and Knox, and General Marshall and Admiral King waited on the porch as the president's limousine came to a stop on the gravel driveway in front of what they all euphemistically called the Little White House.

"Well now, this must be serious for all four of you to show up here in rural Georgia," noted the president.

"I'm afraid it is, Mister President," Henry Stimson responded. "We will need some privacy."

"I'm sure the staff is finishing their dinner preparation," Leahy interjected. "We can use my cottage."

"Your residence is clear and empty," added the chief of the president's Secret Service detail. They kept a very close eye on two or up to seven cottages arranged in a semi-circle arc on either side of the president's holiday residence.

The six men entered. Leahy switched on the lights and waited for the others to enter before closing the door. Two Secret Service agents each stood guard in the front and back of the small cottage. The five men settled into the chairs around the dining table with an open space for the president's wheelchair.

"Station HYPO," began Admiral King, "on Oahu intercepted and deciphered a Japanese Navy message under MAGIC that yielded the detailed timetable of Admiral Yamamoto for an intended inspection tour of front-line units in the South Pacific."

"OK?"

"The tour places him about 400 miles northwest of Guadalcanal on the morning of the 18th—three days from now . . . within range of P-38 fighters using extended range fuel tanks."

"You are suggesting we assassinate him?"

"That is a political decision, Mister President," answered Henry Stimson.

"That is not how we do business," Bill Leahy protested.

"There is that aspect, Admiral," replied Stimson, "but it is not without precedent. I will remind everyone of the British Operation ANTHROPOID a year ago."

"But, where does it end?"

"It ends when the war ends," Ernie King answered.

President Roosevelt held up his left-hand palm out. "While the ethics and morality of war are fascinating to me, I remind you all that we are in a mortal engagement with two ruthless enemies. We have documented evidence of genocide . . . literal genocide. We also have strong suspicions that most, if not all, of the Axis nations are carrying out similar crimes against humanity. Our task is to win this war as soon as possible, and return peace and tranquility to this precious planet. We've far more serious ethical decision challenges ahead of us," Roosevelt paused. He did not state the facts, but his thoughts flashed to what lay ahead with the Manhattan Project's expected product. He shook his head and placed both hands flat on the table. "Now, tell me about this MAGIC message."

Admiral King cleared his throat to punctuate the president's statement. "Yamamoto is notoriously punctual. He insists on it and has been that way since he studied at Harvard after the Great War. Admiral Yamamoto will be transiting via a small island off the south end of Bouganville. He is scheduled to arrive at Balalae Airfield at 09:00, local time, on the morning of Sunday, the 18th. The whole island is a large airbase for both Navy and Army squadrons that operate over the Solomons and routinely attack Guadalcanal."

"You think we can do it?" the president asked.

"It's not without risk, but yes, Mister President," responded King, who then looked to George Marshall.

"I had 'Hap' Arnold and his boys look at performance feasibility without discussing why. The P-38 Lightnings," George said, "stationed on Guadalcanal can carry two external fuel tanks, fly low level over the sea to avoid detection by radar or observers, and still give them about 30 to 40 minutes on target. That will leave them sufficient fuel plus a little reserve to return to Guadalcanal. We also have sufficient fighter assets on Guadalcanal to have a couple of Marine Corsair squadrons airborne in case the intercept squadron gets chased."

"So, you all are here to seek my sanction?"

"Yes, Mister President," Stimson said. "We all believe this is a presidential-level decision of considerable import."

"And, you are here because you recommend this mission."

Each of the service leaders responded with the head nod and a verbal yes sir, except Bill Leahy, who held his position against the mission. Roosevelt lapsed into contemplation, staring down at the table as if answers might be written there. The president nodded his head several times, and then he looked at each man in the eyes before he settled on Admiral Leahy. "With all respect, Bill, these are the exigencies of war. You have presidential approval. What are we calling this mission?"

"Operation VENGEANCE, Mister President," answered General Marshall.

Roosevelt smiled. "An apt descriptor, it seems to me."

"Vengeance is mine, sayeth the Lord," Bill Leahy added softly.

President Roosevelt smiled in a rather mischievous manner. "Romans 12:19. This is an earthly decision, and I have made it. Now, supper is probably ready. Can you stay for dinner, gentlemen?"

"No sir," Stimson responded quickly. "Thank you for the offer. We have an aircraft waiting at the airport. We don't have much time, and we need to get back to Washington to issue the appropriate orders. The 339th Fighter Squadron on Guadalcanal appears to be the preferred unit, and they have just a few days to gather the appropriate equipment, check that their aircraft are mission-ready and complete their detailed planning."

"Very well, gentlemen." The five leaders stood. The president extended his right hand to each man and shook it vigorously. "Thank you for making the journey and briefing me. Good luck. Godspeed and following winds to the aircrews."

The secretaries and chiefs departed in two staff cars. Admiral Leahy did not speak and pushed the president's wheelchair across the planked walkway from his cottage to the Little White House. History had been set in motion.

—

Sunday, 18.April.1943
Camp Joseph T. Robinson
North Little Rock, Pulaski County, Arkansas
United States of America
08:10 hours

The visit to Camp Robinson involved various facility tours and a review of troops at the National Guard base, well into mobilization for the upcoming invasion of Europe. Once they returned from Mexico, the tour would press on across the West to California and just a fraction of the state's war effort activities. The plan would not return the president to the White House until Thursday, the 29th of April.

An Army support staff captain excused himself and interrupted the end of the president's breakfast to signal for Admiral Leahy to step out of the small private dining room. He returned with a noticeably stern expression and handed the single page to the president.

CONFIDENTIAL

```
TUTSB AAX NR 0917
C 180628Z APR 43
FM WHITE HOUSE
TO MOBILE STATION 37
SUBJ RETRANS
C O N F I D E N T I A L
C 180519Z APR 43
FM SECWAR
TO WHITE HOUSE
SUBJ RETRANS
BT
C O N F I D E N T I A L
C 180431Z APR 43
FROM 339FS
TO SCSWPA PACOM COSA SECWAR
C O N F I D E N T I A L
```

```
SUBJ OPERATION VENGEANCE
POP GOES THE WEASEL
BT
NNNN
```

CONFIDENTIAL

"So, they did it," Roosevelt observed.

"Yes sir. This message," Leahy said, pointing at the paper in the president's left hand, "simply reports that the intercept squadron shot down the two Betty bombers, one of which was presumed to be carrying Yamamoto. The message also implies the attack squadron has landed safely back on Guadalcanal. We will not have the mission details until we receive the after-action report in several days, presumably. We are also listening intently to MAGIC for some form of confirmation regarding the fate of the passengers on those bombers."

"Who knows?"

"Of the results?"

"Yes."

"The original message from the squadron upon landing notified MacArthur, Nimitz, Marshall, and Stimson. Secretary Stimson retransmitted the original message to us. The squadron is sworn to secrecy until the results are publicly known."

"Casualties?"

"We do not know yet, but the after-action report will contain that information."

"I should have asked earlier when I approved this mission . . . who will know the target?"

"Only those involved in the decision. The pilots and operational staff only knew about their target aircraft and escorts. The mission plan designated four P-38 Lightning fighters to engage two Betty bombers, and the remainder of the squadron, 14 fighters, to engage the expected fighter escort. They did not know who or what was on the bombers."

"Get with Harry to lay the groundwork for our public statement. Of course, we will have to wait for the Japanese to announce publicly the death of Yamamoto. Surely, there will be a state funeral. Once we get that confirmation, we can connect the happenstance fighter engagement with the downing of Yamamoto's aircraft."

"Yes sir. We expect to see Mister and Mrs. Hopkins this evening before we head south."

"Again, I acknowledge that you were not in favor of this assassination."

"No, I am not, Mister President . . . bad precedent."

"The precedent was set with last year's assassination of Heydrich by the British . . . well actually, by the Czechs working for the British."

"Yes sir, but these missions give the Secret Service the jitters, and I share their apprehension. Where do the boundaries lay?"

"Historians will decide on the morality of such missions. There are more difficult such decisions ahead."

"Yes sir. Now, I am mindful of the time. We have a busy itinerary today," Leahy said.

"Very well, Bill. Let's get on with it."

Admiral Leahy pushed the president's wheelchair out of the dining room, and their day's planned events began.

—

Friday, 30.April.1943
HMS Seraph
37° 10' North – 6° 59' West
Offshore near Huelva, Spain
04:30 hours

"**H**ere we go, Chief," commanded the captain. "Bring the boat to periscope depth. All stop. Rudder amidships." The chief of the boat repeated the commands back to the captain.

Royal Navy Lieutenant Norman Limbury Auchinleck 'Bill' Jewell, MBE had been the commanding officer—the captain of HMS *Seraph* [P219, a British S-Class submarine, equivalent to the German Type VIIC submarine] since May 1942. Last November, King George VI made Jewell a Member of the Military Division, Most Excellent Order of the British Empire, for his leadership in the extraction of General Henri Giraud during Operation KINGPIN.

"Search periscope to broach," Jewell ordered. As the scope rose, Jewell lowered the periscope's handlebars. He duck-walked through two 360° searches, and then said, "Up periscope." When the sight reached the full extension, Jewell made two more full circle searches. "We are clear. Thank goodness Spain is not blacked out," Jewell said, as he carefully searched for the first navigation light he wanted. "Faro Light. Mark!"

"Two five seven point four," responded the chief.

Jewell swung around roughly a quarter turn clockwise. When he was satisfied, he said, "Huelva cathedral spire. Mark!"

"Zero two one point two."

Several seconds later, the navigator, working at the plotting table, announced, "We're in the circle, Skipper."

"Excellent. Sea state two. Deck party to execution station. No guns. Chief, surface the boat."

"Surface the boat, aye," the chief answered.

The captain transferred control of the boat to his executive officer, went forward to his stateroom, retrieved his Bible, and joined the deck party below the forward hatch.

"Hatches clear," came the announcement over the submarines loudspeaker system from the executive officer. "Execute the plan. The con is shifting to the tower."

As they had rehearsed, the four-man team moved swiftly, precisely, and silently to open the hatch, and then they lifted the coffin-sized casing up through the hatch to the deck. Jewell was the last to reach the deck. Small swells lapped against the hull and gently swayed the submarine. They opened the case and removed the corpse of a man dressed in a Royal Marine major's service uniform. They manacled the black attaché case to the man's left wrist. All of the man's identification and mission papers had been checked multiple times in London, Portsmouth, and twice more during the transit from Gibraltar, as they warmed the body from its chilled state. The Royal Marine sergeant leading the deck team nodded to Lieutenant Jewell.

The captain opened his Bible to the bookmarked page and switched on a small, shielded, red penlight. He had chosen a passage from Psalm 39 for the occasion. He read aloud, "Hear my prayer, O Lord, and give ear unto my cry; hold not thy peace at my tears: for I am a stranger with thee, and a sojourner, as all my fathers were.

"O spare me, that I may recover strength, before I go hence, and be no more.

"We commit this man's body to the deep." Jewell nodded his conclusion of the brief ceremony. The four Marines lifted the corpse and tossed it into the water clear of the hull, to simulate falling or being washed overboard.

The deck party did not wait for instructions and followed the remainder of their plan. They secured the case, lowered it down the hatch, and then descended themselves into the submarine. Jewell gestured to the executive officer watching from atop the conning tower to dive. Jewell descended through and secured the hatch.

The *Seraph* submerged and slowly moved away from the coastline for the return to Gibraltar. The operative phase of Operation MINCEMEAT began.

Operation MINCEMEAT was just one subset element of the greater Operation FORTITUDE, which in turn was only one part of the umbrella deception effort under Operation BODYGUARD, intended to complement Allied combat operations against Nazi Germany. Conceived by British Intelligence, the deception mission entailed feeding erroneous information to German Intelligence to convince them the Western Allies intended to attack Greece and Sardinia next; and more importantly, Allied activity with respect to Sicily was a feint.

For MINCEMEAT, they needed a corpse and not just any corpse. After considerable effort, they found a homeless Welshman who died at St. Pancras Hospital in London, on 24.January.1943. His body remained unclaimed with no identifiable family or relatives. The body had belonged to Glyndwr Michael. Medical professionals helped the agents prepare and preserve the body; the operation required the body to appear to have died of hypothermia. He would be disguised and identified as Royal Marine Major William Martin assigned to Allied Forces Headquarters.

When the British government was notified the corpse had been found on the beach near Huelva, Spain, the British exerted extraordinary pressure to reclaim the case . . . oh, and the body. The ruckus generated by the British government had been part of the plan to convey the importance of Major Martin's case implicitly. The body and case were released to the British government a week after discovery and confirmed by very special trace marks to be the originals. One month later, Boniface (ULTRA) confirmed that the Germans had taken the bait and ordered the redeployment of combat forces from Italy and specifically Sicily to Greece. Operation MINCEMEAT had been a complete and extraordinary success.

———

Thursday, 8.April.1943
Office of the Director, Office of Strategic Services
National Institutes of Health Building
2430 E Street Northwest
Washington, District of Columbia
United States of America
09:20 hours

Bill Donovan was well into his day when OSS First Assistant Director Colonel Gonzalo Edward 'Ned' Buxton, Jr., arrived early for their 9:30 meeting regarding Bainbridge Air Services. "You're early. You must have something on your mind."

"Sure do, Bill. I just got word via the grapevine, however accurate this is, I don't know, that Dick Groves ordered the formation of an exploitation slant intelligence group he has called Alsos Mission. My understanding is he wants to assign very specialized physicists and engineers to scour Italian and German university and research facilities as they are liberated in Italy, France, Denmark, and Germany to capture all available intelligence on their nuclear energy and weapons work."

"I guess he doesn't trust us with that job."

"That is one way to look at it, but it could be that he thinks the group should be solely focused on nuclear technology and not distracted with other intelligence objectives."

"Is there some meaning to the team's name?"

"They tell me alsos means grove in Greek."

"Clever."

"What do you want to do?" asked Buxton.

"Nothing directly, but I will have a private chat with Dick Groves as soon as I am able to do so. *Prima facie*, such a singularly focused team, might be very useful. I have a meeting with the Military Policy Committee for the Manhattan Project on Wednesday morning at the Pentagon. I'll see if I can get a moment with Groves before or after that meeting."

"OK. I'll let it sit until you say otherwise." Silence filled Donovan's corner office for a moment. Buxton glanced at his wristwatch. "I'll go check on Warner. He should be here by now, or he's late." Buxton opened the office but did not step out. "Do come in, Major Warner."

Major Chester Hugh 'Chip' Warner, USAR, has been assigned as the Bainbridge Air Services Project Officer, or in other terms, the contract administrator, since early February. Chip was an odd combination of degreed aeronautical engineer with a law degree from the University of Michigan.

"Top of the mornin' to ya, General," Warner said, as he entered Donovan's office.

"And the rest of the day to you, Major."

All three men sat at the small conference table in the director's office.

Warner began, "You asked for a status report on the Bainbridge contract. I'm happy to report that the contract issue with Lockheed has been satisfactorily resolved, thanks in full measure to your request for assistance from Mister Newton. I attended a meeting at the office of Mister Braddock, Mister Newton, and Mister Sales. Lockheed will deliver the last four Constellations allocated from the TWA contract. I must say, General, Mister Hughes was instrumental with the last one."

"Yeah, I heard the same from Howard," Bill announced. "I had lunch with him yesterday."

Warner nodded but did not pursue the thread with Donovan. "Bainbridge already has two Constellations, and part of the agreement pushes their final delivery to February of next year to avoid impacting TWA's deployment plan. This contract resolution will flesh out Bainbridge. They already possess and are operating all six Beech Model 18s as well as all 12 of their Lockheed Model 18s. As indicated earlier, they will take delivery of three of the four remaining Constellations before the end of the year. They are meeting our scheduled transportation requirements at a current 94% rate. Our unscheduled spot requirements are running at about 62%; they just don't have enough aircraft to meet their scheduled demands and necessary maintenance."

"That is not a particularly encouraging fulfillment rate," Donovan observed.

"No, it's not, sir."

"What do we need to do to improve the unscheduled fulfillment rate?"

Warner thought for a moment. "One of two options . . . from my perspective and understanding. One, reduce or eliminate unscheduled demands on our transportation system. Two, increase the number of aircraft in service with Bainbridge Air Services, Incorporated."

This time, it was Wild Bill Donovan's turn for contemplation. "The very nature of our business demands spur of the moment decisions and arrangements." Donovan paused to consider his words. "I cannot imagine how to change our unscheduled demands and still address the constantly changing intelligence and special operations situations. I suppose option two is viable; however, this war will not last forever. I am not so bold or naïve to venture a prediction, but Allied Forces are actively planning the final assault for Europe and Germany. The Red Army has finally turned the tide and is on the offensive. The Germans are not finished. There is still plenty of bite in that dog. But, the end is near. The German Army knows it. A plot, the latest plot, to assassinate Hitler failed just last month. The plotters, all in the Army, were not discovered, to the best of our knowledge. They will not stop. They know that Hitler will lead them to the total destruction of their country. The destruction has already begun as Bomber Command and the Eighth Air Force visit them by day and by night." Again, Donovan lapsed into thought. "I'm not comfortable adding more aircraft. Is there anything else?"

"We could ask them to trim their maintenance work, but I can't imagine that suggestion being well-received."

"No, that would be counter-productive. That is not an option either. What about their commercial façade?"

"You mean cut down on the commercial schedule?" asked Warner for clarification.

"Yes."

"That's their cover."

"We could take them completely black."

"Yes, we could," Warner answered. "But that is likely a one-way path that has no return."

"You're probably correct in that assessment. For now, we shall do what we can with the resources we have at hand. In the meantime, think about any other options we might have, please let Ned or me know. Thank you for your time and excellent status report, Major Warner. That will be all for now."

"Thank you, General." Chip looked at Buxton. "Colonel." Warner departed and closed the door behind him.

"So, Ned, anything big on your plate at the moment?"

"Just the usual. The Alsos Mission was my excitement."

Donovan nodded his head and smiled. "I need to go visit our hero the next time I'm in London."

"He might have some ideas," Ned offered.

"I doubt I would ask him. He has his hands full with the Germans." Bill shook his head. "I got a call from Marlene last night."

"Oh my, do tell."

"She's agreed to a USO tour in mid-May."

"The Germans aren't finished yet."

"No, they aren't, but they are in a small and shrinking corner of Tunisia. I guess they figure the fighting will be done so that they can entertain the troops as a thank you for their victory. Anyway, she also informed me that she has a date to visit our hero and his family."

"Including the Mrs.?"

"Yes, so I am informed."

"Are you sure that is a good idea? Marlene is a resource for us."

"As is Brian, Ned."

"True. I just worry about such an event. Jealousy can be a very dangerous and volatile medium."

"True enough, but according to Marlene, Charlotte Drummond agreed to the meeting. And Marlene is a very persuasive, headstrong person. She's going to visit them at their farm in Hampshire on her way back from North Africa."

"I hope everything goes well."

"As do I. It is a complication I do not welcome, since such a meeting, given the intimacy between Marlene and Brian, could go sideways for any one or combination of the three of them."

"I guess we shall just hope for the best. Now, if you will excuse me, Bill, I've got a growing stack of messages on my desk. I'll keep an eye on things, as I always do."

"Thanks, Ned."

Buxton left Donovan's office. Bill stared out the windows to a better than average, early spring day, and then he turned his attention to the inbox.

—

Chapter 6

Though jealousy be produced by love,
as ashes are by fire, yet
jealousy extinguishes love as ashes smother the flame.
-- Margaret of Navarre

Wednesday, 5.May.1943
USAAF Station F-356
Saffron Walden, Essex, England
United Kingdom
08:05 hours

The mission briefing intrigued all of the 334FS pilots. The CIRCUS 47 mission called for 334FS to be one of two fighter squadrons escorting the 128th Bombardment Squadron and the first combined bombing raid for the 8th Air Force inside Germany. The bombers would attack Wilhelmshaven's docks, and the fighters were expected to protect the bombers from enemy fighters. The P-47s would be running at the limit of their combat range.

To give the fighters the most fuel over the target, they picked up the bombers off the east coast of England, and they were assigned to the left side of the bomber formation. The combined formation would stay over the North Sea, turned hard right, and the bombers would run into the target. Once turned off the target, they would run for home.

Every time Brian saw a formation of Boeing B-17 Flying Fortresses, whether a squadron, group or wing, his sense of awe overwhelmed him. He often wondered what it would be like piloting a crew-served bomber like a B-17 as part of a large formation, but that wonderment was never enough to stimulate an effort to experience bomber operations. *The fighter cockpit is enough for me.*

The bomber formation was above and ahead of the 334FS as they climbed for position, now over the North Sea. Brian noticed their companion fighter squadron—62nd Fighter Squadron (62FS) of the 56th Fighter Group, callsign: Spike. The 62FS was behind and slightly below them. In a few more miles, both fighter squadrons were in position above and to their assigned side of the bomber formation. The navigator on the lead bomber provided navigation for the entire formation. The fighters simply maintained position on the bombers, even as the Fortresses climbed to their intended bombing altitude of 18,000 feet. The formation turned to the south-southeast for the planned approach to Wilhelmshaven. They had the coast and the target in sight. *Where are the fighters?*

No sooner had Brian asked himself the question, "Bandits, two o'clock high."

The squadron watched the 62FS roll right into the approaching enemy fighters and climb to engage. Brian knew what was coming. The squadron entered a shallow climb and shifted position, higher overhead the bombers. The boiling furball of fighters twisting and turning above and to the bomber's right kept the attention of the squadron as they continued to scan the skies around them.

Some of the German fighters broke through Spike and dove for the bombers. "Pectin Able engage. Pectin Baker, you have the heavies."

"Pectin, Pectin Baker, roger. Wilco." Brian gave the hand signal for his division to take divisions abreast and combat spread. Pete's Able Division engaged the breakaway Germans. Black pocks of air bursts from the German anti-aircraft guns dotted the sky just ahead of, and among the bombers, they did not deviate. The heavy bombers approached the target, and the bombardiers were busy peering into their Norden bombsight eyepieces.

"Bandits, 11 o'clock high."

Brian instantly looked up and left. A squadron of 109s was not that high above his division. "Pectin Baker, tally ho. Engage."

Brian pushed his throttle full forward. The big radial engine responded. He rolled left and climbed to meet the Germans head-on. The 'B' division faced double their number from a disadvantage position. As he had done in other similar situations, Brian adjusted his stick to place his sight pipper just above the lead German and squeezed off a short, one-second burst. The German was not so easily distracted. He pressed on. As the range closed rapidly, Brian put his pipper on the target, and gave the German a longer, in range burst. The German opened up at the same time. They passed in a flash. *No hits.* Brian pulled up more, rolled left, and instinctively pushed on his throttle already against the forward stop. Airspeed dissipated. He pulled back on the stick to get his nose down. Bran strained his neck against the g's to pick up the Germans. They were all climbing to re-engage. *These guys aren't interested in getting among the bombers with the flak shells going off.*

Brian felt the aircraft shudder near stall as the nose came down below the horizon and accelerated. He let the airspeed build rapidly before he rolled to pick up his next target. Aircraft filled the sky around him. He checked his mirror and quickly glanced over both shoulders. Clear. Brian promptly moved his fighter to get his sight pipper on the target as the enemy aircraft grew rapidly in his sight. Brian depressed the trigger. The guns erupted. Both aircraft, hunter and prey, turned into each other. Brian quickly tried to arc his bullet stream at the closing enemy fighter without any observed impacts. They passed almost canopy to canopy. Another German passed across his sight. Brian rolled sharply left, almost inverted, and pulled hard to bring his nose down and guns to bear.

The German was chasing another Thunderbolt. Hunter got his pipper where he wanted it and squeezed the trigger. The tracers arced to his target. He observed half a dozen impact flashes. The German rolled hard right and inverted, diving away. Brian matched the German's maneuver. A bright burst shook his entire aircraft along with uncountable tinny impacts. *A flak burst.* Brian gently pulled out of his dive. He quickly scanned the sky around him. Buddy was exactly where he should be behind and below Brian's right wing. The damage to the right wing was more dramatic than he expected. Multiple holes of various sizes pocked the top of his right wing. *The engine sounds right. What the hell is that whistle?* Brian shifted his sight attention to his cockpit. The holes in his canopy scared him. A piece of shrapnel from the flak burst had passed through his cockpit inches in front of his face. *Damn, it doesn't get much closer than that.* Several small holes passed through the right side of his cockpit. Brian promptly checked himself. No wounds. Several pieces were stuck on the right side of his armored seat. His radio had numerous deep bulges on the left side.

Blessedly, the Germans abandoned their attack. The bombers had turned away. Brian began to climb back to position. He signaled for Buddy to close up, and then he gestured for Buddy to check out his aircraft's underside. Courtland maneuvered as they climbed. When he returned to his close formation position, Buddy gestured that Brian's QP-G Thunderbolt was not leaking. Hunter hand signaled to Buddy that his radio was shot, and then he gestured for Buddy to spread out for Brian to do a control check. The right aileron had serious damage, and pieces were flapping around wildly. *They won't last long.* Brian checked each control axis. *Rudder OK. Elevator OK. Damn!* The damage to his right aileron caused any roll input to generate as much yaw as roll. *I can't fight like this.* Hunter signaled to Buddy that he had too much damage to lead. Buddy acknowledged and presumably radioed to the squadron that Hunter was flying but seriously damaged.

Thankfully, the CIRCUS formation did not encounter additional fighters as they crossed the coastline out over the North Sea for their return to England. Brian tried his radio again, but it was dead. The squadron had practiced such events. Sweet took over the lead of 'B' Division, and Salt assumed the lead of Red Flight. Buddy remained in his wing position to keep an eye on Hunter's machine.

Brian used the peaceful, quiet transit to assess the formation. They lost two bombers. Spike lost one Thunderbolt, and Pectin had lost none. He could not tell whether other Pectin Thunderbolts has suffered damage. His damage was bad enough.

At the English coastline, the CIRCUS formation split. Each squadron headed to their respective bases. Brian saw the squadron begin to adjust position for landing by sections in trail. Hunter switched positions to fly on Buddy's left wing. Brian tried, but his damaged controls made the task too difficult. He gestured to Buddy that he was dropping back to land solo.

Hunter configured his fighter for landing and managed to slide his canopy back with some difficulty. *Here goes.* He selected his landing gear down. *Whew!* The gear came down and locked. For reasons he could not appreciate, his flaps would not move. With seriously impaired roll control, Brian awkwardly touched down with his right main wheel first, causing the aircraft to bounce precariously several times between the two main wheels. He fought with the aircraft, cut his throttle, and finally planted the aircraft rather hard on the runway. *Damn, that was a bit hairy.*

Taxing back to his spot was easy without any difficulty. Several of the pilots were standing by his spot. Brian completed his shutdown. Tomlinson gestured to Brian like 'what have you done to my machine'? Brian unstrapped and jumped out. They were all examining the damage. It was bad on top, but it was worse on the underside.

Tomlinson asked, "What the hell happened, Captain?"

"Flak shell. Lucky beyond description. One tough bird."

"I suspect this one may be a strike, sir." The cumulative damage might result in the aircraft being striken from the registry of operational aircraft, if a detailed inspection proved the damage was not economically reparable.

"Give her a good examination."

"Will do, sir."

Everyone seemed to be amazed and surprised that the aircraft would still fly with all the damage.

They jumped into their mission debriefings with the intelligence folks. By the time Brian finished his debriefing, word had been sent to the ops shack that Brian's aircraft was indeed a strike. They had considered replacing the right wing but ultimately decided the effort to repair the damage was not worth the effort. A spare Thunderbolt on the airfield would be prepared that night to be ready for a check flight in late afternoon or more likely tomorrow morning. Brian was done for the day.

—

Wednesday, 5.May.1943
RMS Queen Mary
55° 58' 22" North – 4° 44' 49" West
River Clyde Anchorage
Greenock, Renfrewshire, Scotland
United Kingdom
15:05 hours

"**W**elcome aboard, Prime Minister," greeted Royal Navy Volunteer Reserve Captain Richard Pike Pim, standing just forward of the door to the presidential suite. Pim had been the chief of Churchill's Map Room since he became the first lord the second time.

"Thank you, Captain Pim." Churchill trusted Pim.

Duty Private Secretary John Martin inserted the stateroom key and opened the door.

Churchill gestured for everyone to enter. Winston went to one of the two large circular portals and looked out at the green mountains north of the estuary.

"We came aboard this morning," announced Pim, "and we have the Map Room set up and ready in the suite just aft of your suite."

"Excellent. We are underway," Churchill said, as he observed out the portal.

"The captain has invited you to the bridge to observe our departure."

"We've done this before, Pim."

"Yes sir . . . a year and a half ago aboard *Duke of York*."

Churchill turned and faced Pim. "Quite so. These accommodations are a bit fancier than the flag stateroom aboard *Duke of York*."

"Yes sir."

"Let's go take a look at your Map Room, shall we?"

"Should I notify the bridge that you will not observe our departure?" Martin asked.

"No, no, I will go to the bridge after I christen the Map Room."

"I must inform you, Prime Minister," Martin continued, "the Admiralty had not informed us, and I just learned that we have five thousand German and Italian prisoners of war confined below deck. They are being transported to the United States for their further incarceration. With all the POWs captured in North Africa, Trent Park and the other specialty interrogation centers need to free up space to accept the surge."

"Quite understandable," Churchill commented. "Is anyone concerned?"

"Detective Thompson is quite concerned."

"He always is and bless him for his extra attention."

"The Army has provided an armed platoon for security. Detective Thompson met with the platoon's lieutenant in charge to make sure the security provisions were adequate."

"Thank you, John. I'm sure if Detective Thompson has any worries he thinks I should be aware of, he will let me know."

"Certainly, sir."

"Now, if you would be so kind to check with Detective Thompson, again, I will christen Captain Pim's Map Room, and then make my way to the bridge to join the ship's captain."

"Very well, sir," John Martin responded.

Churchill gestured for Pim to lead the way. Martin went forward. Pim and Churchill went aft one stateroom. Pim opened the door. They stepped in, and Pim closed and locked the door. The stateroom bulkheads were covered with large maps covering the Home Islands, the North Sea countries, North Africa, the North Atlantic from the United States and Canada to the United Kingdom, France, Germany, and Eastern Europe to the Ural Mountains. Pim utilized the latest intelligence to brief the prime minister on the status of various areas of operations.

The prime minister took the abridged version in deference to the captain's invitation. Operations in North Africa were progressing quite well. The British 1st and 8th Armies, along with the American II Corps, had encircled the *Afrikakorps* entirely in Northeast Tunisia, and the noose was tightening nicely. The Allied Forces were four months behind where he wanted to be, but at least the end was near. Churchill was eager and perhaps even a bit antsy to move onto the next stage. The Soviets persisted in applying relentless pressure on the Western Allies to open the second front in France. The Red Army continued to make good progress after the bloody victory at Stalingrad, but they still had a very long way to go. The Battle of the Atlantic finally saw positive nets for strings of months. It was still a frantic battle, but the *Untersee Kriegsmarine* was still a lethal service and a threat to Britain's lifeline. The combined American and British bombing campaign of the German heartland was finally yielding results on the battlefield. The Germans were demonstrably struggling to adapt to the onslaught, but there was still a lot of bite in the dog.

Pim's briefing lasted just over 30 minutes. When it was complete, Churchill excused himself and headed to the bridge.

The armed guard at the hatch to the bridge came to attention when he first sited the prime minister approaching and presented arms with his rifle. Churchill returned the salute. The guard opened the hatch, stepped inside, and announced in a booming voice, "The Prime Minister."

The ship's captain jumped down off his plush, raised chair, turned to Churchill, saluted, and extended his right hand. "Captain Illingworth, sir. Welcome aboard and to the bridge of the *Queen Mary*."

Cunard Line Commodore Sir Cyril Gordon Illingworth had assumed command of the *Queen Mary* in August of last year. Like many of the merchant captains, Illingworth also served as a member of the Royal Navy Reserve and felt his responsibility to the war effort.

"Thank you, Sir Cyril."

Illingworth gestured for the prime minister to take the captain's chair. Churchill stepped up and sat heavily in the chair. Illingworth stood next to the chair. His head and eyes were constantly scanning the water, and the specific channel markers, as the officer of the deck ordered the proper commands to transit out of port and obey the anti-submarine countermeasures.

"We are carefully working our way through the anti-submarine safeguards," Illingworth stated.

"I am familiar, Captain. I made this exact departure aboard *Duke of York* a year and a half ago."

"Ah, well then, I do not need to narrate our departure."

"Tell me about your passengers below decks," Churchill said.

"Yes sir. We have 5,000 German and Italian prisoners of war under armed guard for delivery to the United States and the continuation of their internment until war's end. This has become fairly typical for the *Queen*. The ship's staterooms were converted last year, removing our normal passenger accommodations and replacing them with 12, high density, raise-able bunks. For more than a year now, we have been operating under American orders and Operation BOLERO. Eastbound, we carry a full load of American troops as assigned by American commanders. Westbound, we often carry prisoners of war. We have had near full loads going west in our last few transits, as I understand as a consequence of large captures in North Africa."

"Quite so, Sir Cyril. We may well get a message in transit from General Alexander or General Eisenhower that Rommel's vaunted *Afrikakorps* has surrendered, leaving all of North Africa, from the Suez to the Atlantic, securely in Allied hands."

"Excellent. Congratulations, sir."

"You and your crew are doing your part, I must say. Those American troops you transport are crucial to turning the tide in our favor."

"Thank you, Prime Minister. If I may, I would like to inform the crew of your words."

"By all means, Sir Cyril. I do believe you understand and appreciate proper operational security."

"Yes sir, I do."

As they passed Little Cumbrae Island, the officer of the deck commanded an increase in speed. They had cleared the last of the anti-submarine defenses. Speed was now their best defense.

"We will be increasing speed for the transit," announced Illingworth. "This is our vulnerable segment as we head out into the Atlantic. The Navy does a great job keeping the approaches clear of those damnable U-boats. Once we reach the Atlantic, we will be at full speed." Churchill just nodded his head in acknowledgment. "The weather for our transit remains forecast to be favorable for us to maintain full speed, and thus we will not need an escort."

"Excellent, Sir Cyril," the prime minister said, as he returned the chair to the *Queen's* captain. Churchill returned to his stateroom for a good session of paperwork and message traffic that John Martin had prepared for him.

—

Wednesday, 5.May.1943
Room 5E766
Pentagon Building
Arlington, Virginia
United States of America
09:30 hours

The Military Policy Committee of the Manhattan Project had been established by Secretary of War Stimson in September 1942 to specifically address military usage policy matters associated with the project's intended product objective. The committee members had remained the same from the outset, and they were:
-- Committee Chairman, Director Office of Scientific Research and Development (OSRD) Vannevar 'Van' Bush, PhD (Electrical Engineering),
-- Deputy Chief of Naval Operations for Materiel, Rear Admiral William Reynolds 'Bill' Purnell, USN [USNA 1908],
-- Chief of Staff, Army Service Forces, Major General Wilhelm Delp 'Wil' Styer, USA CE [USMA 1916].

For this particular meeting, the committee had three guests:
-- Committee Founder and Secretary of War Henry Stimson
-- Director, Office of Strategic Services, Brigadier General Bill Donovan
-- Director, Manhattan Project, Brigadier General Leslie Richard 'Dick' Groves Jr., USA CE [USMA 1918].

"Let's jump right in," Van Bush announced. "To remain consistent with governmental policy, this meeting and all its words and contents are classified TOP SECRET – PARAMOUNT. Discussion or disclosure of the contents of this meeting to anyone without access clearance and a need to know is strictly prohibited.

"The task at hand is the question of is the focus of engineering resources on specifically the military usage. The civil application is not within the scope of this committee. I'll also add as background that the assumption at the foundation of the project was a counter to the German research and development program. In essence, we seek to beat the Germans to attainment of a military device. To my knowledge, we've seen no evidence that the Japanese are pursuing a fissile weapon."

"The difference between Germany and Japan is substantial and not trivial," added Bill Purnell.

"How so?" Van asked.

"Water . . . to put it succinctly," answered Bill. "The logistics associated with the two theaters of operations are dramatically different because of water, the intervening ocean—the long distances over water."

"True, but as I understand this question, the engineering necessary to utilize the device is similar but sufficiently different with each theater to warrant specificity. While we don't have a viable design, as yet . . . correct General Groves?"

"Correct," Groves responded, choosing not to add more.

"The delivery to Germany is significantly different from delivery to Japan. Today, Germany is doable, while Japan is not." Everyone nodded their heads in agreement. "The basic assumptions that have driven our decision-making to date have been, one, Germany was actively working on the technology. Two, our intelligence assessment at the outset was that Germany was believed to be ahead of us in that development. And three, Germany was the most likely to use such technology if they were successful." Again, everyone nodded their heads in agreement. "At this juncture, I think it appropriate for General Donovan to give us his latest evaluation of German progress."

"Yes, sure," Wild Bill spoke up. "I must first preface my remarks. The OSS has worked aggressively with MI6 to clarify the German status regarding nuclear development. The best we can do collectively at this stage is to offer an educated guess. So, to Doctor Bush's inquiry, the Germans have suffered some notable setbacks, not least of which is the loss of their heavy water supply and the sabotage of the Czech uranium mines. The Germans are working on a functional reactor that we believe is located in the small village of Haigerloch in Baden-Württemberg, Southwest Germany. We don't have evidence that it's operational as yet, but looking from outside, rather closely outside, I might add, it's the OSS opinion that the Germans aren't progressing as fast as we once believed they were. We've seen no construction on the scale of Oak Ridge and Hanford, which leads us to the opinion that they remain in the early research phase, and thus, we don't believe they've yet attained the production phase."

"What is the relationship between their war-making capacity and their nuclear development timeline?" asked Bush.

"Without diverting this meeting to the details of the war's progress, the Axis forces in North Africa are in the death throes. The Germans are on the run in Russia. The U-boat menace in the Atlantic is a mere fraction of what it once was. The difference between German fighter capacity is dramatically different from Northern France to even Russia, and what they can bring up in Germany, which means their resources are shrinking in experienced pilots, machines, and fuel. They're contracting rapidly to the defense of the fatherland.

These facts lead us to the opinion that the Germans are not likely to achieve a functional device before they're compelled to surrender."

"If true, doesn't that negate the basis for the project?" Wil Styer asked.

"Allow me to jump in here," Stimson interjected. "At the conclusion of the ARCADIA Conference last year, we, the British and us, agreed to a Germany First strategy. We witness the result. If I may be so bold, I think Military and Naval Intelligence agree with General Donovan's assessment to the extent they're each involved, respectively. I must remind this committee that the Allied nations are fighting a war in two major theaters of operations against three primary Axis enemies."

"Understood, Mister Secretary. If I may ask General Donovan, what is your summary statement regarding the state of Imperial Japan?"

"To be blunt, Japanese society and the government are more problematic to penetrate; thus, our analyses and impressions are sketchier. Guadalcanal was just the first sampling of Japanese defense intentions. We can expect the Japanese to contest every island with fanatical, if not suicidal, determination. Islands that can't be bypassed or that we need for our offensive operations are going to be very costly to subdue. Further, the closer we get to the Home Islands, the more fanatical and costly those campaigns will be for us. When we add in the complexities Admiral Purnell illuminated, we should expect the Pacific Theater to be more difficult, more costly, and ultimately longer. Dissatisfaction within the German military and society is palpable. The same isn't true for Japanese society."

"Thank you, General," Bush said. "Before we move to the policy questions, at our last meeting, we asked you," he continued, looking directly at General Styer, "to articulate the logistical aspect of this matter."

"I think perhaps the most graphic example to that point is just the aircraft choice to deliver a weapon to the target, whether German or Japanese. The two most capable Allied heavy bombers currently in use are the B-17 that can carry a 4,500-pound payload to a service range of about 800 miles, and the British Lancaster that can deliver a 14,000-pound payload to a target also at 800 miles. All of Germany is within range of both bombers. However, Japan is well beyond any land base site for the Fortress or the Lancaster heavy bombers. The next generation, the B-29, made its first flight in September of last year, and at least by design, it is expected to deliver a 20,000-pound payload to a range roughly double the other two. Available air bases in the Pacific remain beyond the range of even the B-29. Further, if the bomb bay space is to be modified, the extent of that engineering and rework will be the most for the B-17 and the least for the B-29, depending upon the dimensions, mass, and interface requirements for a special weapon."

"We don't have a design yet," stated Groves. "We don't even have general parameters."

"How far away are we, General Groves?" asked Stimson.

"Without getting into the technical obstacles before the scientific and engineering teams, I would say 12 to 18 months, but I must caution that there are serious challenges. There is a genuine potential we may never solve the ultimate design problem."

Silence occupied the secure conference room. "It would seem," Bush spoke, "and I'd propose we shift our focus from Germany to Japan. Solutions that address the difficulties of use against Japan would likewise envelop Germany should the fortunes of war change. Can anyone see a reason that might preclude a Japan focus for the Manhattan Project?"

"I'll only note here," observed Groves, "that some of our scientists possess a rather singular, unique, and emotional motivation due to their refugee status at the hands of the Nazis."

"And," interjected Stimson, "we look to you and Oppenheimer to manage those personnel issues. The shift in project focus seems quite appropriate, given the exigencies of this war. Before we proceed, is the committee in agreement with the adjustment of direction from Germany to Japan for design consideration?" All three committee members nodded their heads. "Very well, then. I'll inform the president. We must provide more precise guidance to Nimitz and MacArthur to get us an appropriate land airbase within range of the Home Islands. We must also get the B-29 into operational status as soon as possible." Stimson looked directly at General Donovan. "We need to collect the necessary intelligence for the eventual selection of Japanese targets."

"That process is already in work," Donovan replied. "Having any of the target requirements would be helpful. What do you want in a target?"

"The committee will work with the project to develop a target requirements list." Bush wrote down some notes on the yellow pad in front of him. "It'll certainly be a living list as the capabilities of the special weapon evolve. The committee will take that task. General Styer, please take the action to emphasize to Headquarters Army Air Forces the need for the B-29." Styer nodded his head. "Since there are knock-on effects, Mister Secretary, should we assume the Japan focus is approved?"

"No, not yet. Let me gain the president's concurrence first. I've a scheduled meeting with him tomorrow. I'll notify you directly regarding his consent and endorsement."

"Very well." The meeting concluded, and the attendees dispersed, except for Donovan and Groves.

"If I may have a word, Dick," Bill said.

"Sure, Bill, what can I do for you?"

"If I've been informed properly, you intend to create a specific intelligence and exploitation team under the Manhattan Project banner."

"Is there a problem?"

"No, no, not at all. I just wanted to coordinate our activities. The OSS fully supports your initiative. A focused technical team on German technology is quite appropriate . . . no distractions."

"Exactly," Groves responded. "I've called it the Alsos Mission if the term appears in any of your work. I would prefer to keep Alsos at the top-secret level. In fact, now that I think of it, we should probably create a specific TS compartment for the work and yield."

"Agreed. Shall we say TOP SECRET – ALSOS?"

"Works for me. I'll get it set up. I still have some hurdles to cross with the chief for approval, and then we face the staffing challenge."

"If I can be of any assistance, just let me know. I'll do what I can to assist. To that end, I'd like to assign one or a few of my agents with your team."

"Agreed. That would be most helpful. Thanks, Bill. I'd like to have the team formed, trained, and ready for deployment before Allied Forces land on mainland Italy—our objective is July. We've no known targets on Sicily. I must say, Doctor Fermi has been most helpful in helping us identify sites of interest, primarily the Universities of Rome and Pisa. The team has to be with the combat forces to maximize the yield."

"Seems quite reasonable, Dick."

The two men shook hands and went their separate ways.

———

Sunday, 9.May.1943
Standing Oak Farm
Winchester, Hampshire, England
United Kingdom
18:30 hours

The journey from Debden to Winchester proved far more torturous and frustrating than expected due to a combination of priority seating and some unspecified equipment malfunction that added more than eight hours to the transit.

No one was outside when he arrived. After paying the cabby he did not recognize, Brian entered the house. Charlotte and the crew had finished supper and were in the clean-up phase. The whole crew plus a new face offered their greeting. Edith placed Ian on the floor and seemed to support him a little as their son waddled toward him. Brian threw his bag and hat toward the front door and dropped to his knees, holding his arms out to his approaching son. Edith released him several yards away, and Ian traversed the remaining distance without support. Father and son embraced. Brian felt tears of joy descending his cheeks as he kissed the top of Ian's head. When Brian looked up, he saw a toddler, perhaps a year older than Ian, walking more confidently toward him with his arms outstretched. He held Ian in his left arm and extended his right arm to the new child.

"Todd, no," shouted the new woman. Brian embraced the child. "I am so sorry, Captain Drummond."

"Nonsense," Brian responded. After holding both boys for a dozen seconds, he released them and stood.

Charlotte kissed her husband and then turned to the new woman. "My dearest, allow me to introduce the newest member of our merry little band – Mrs. Bloodworth."

Mabel Jane Bloodworth had been pregnant with their first child when her husband was killed in action near Dunkirk in 1940. Charlotte hired Mabel for her gardening skills or farming on a larger scale, and her preserving knowledge, including pickling, canning, drying and salting. She had provided samples of each of the preservation techniques she used for vegetables and fruits. Mabel had also offered samples of marinated dried meats she had learned to produce during a family holiday in Spain before the war. It was not until an American serviceman visited her small market stand that she learned the dried meats were called jerky in America.

"It is an honor to meet finally, Captain Drummond," Mabel said. "Your wife is so proud of you."

"As I am of her," Brian offered.

"Mrs. Drummond and Miss Hanscom have been most gracious in tending to my son during the day so that I can work for you."

"I am glad we can help, and I know we both look forward to your contributions."

Charlotte prepared a plate for her husband, placed it on the table, and said, "Brian, come eat your supper so we can finish cleaning up."

Horace, Lionel, and Jacob excused themselves to head home back in town. Brian removed and hung up his uniform jacket along with his necktie, often called a field scarf. He sat at the table. Edith and Mabel occupied the boys with some kind of game. Charlotte finally sat with Brian as he ate his meal.

"What happened today?" Charlotte asked.

In between bites, Brian answered, "I got bumped off one train due to higher priority traffic at Waterloo Station, and then, when I finally boarded a train, we were moving normally until we got stalled somewhere near Basingstoke. The conductor was not exactly sure what caused the problem. All he said was some kind of equipment malfunction. I never did find out whether it was our train, or some problem with the tracks, or a switching issue."

"At least you made it home safely."

"It's great to be home." Brian smiled and took another bite. "I need to keep up with you. Things are changing fast."

Charlotte gave him a break to finish his meal. Then, she whispered, "Mary called a few days ago," she paused to ensure she had his attention, "to tell me, to tell us, the rabbit died."

What the hell does that mean? His confused expression induced Charlotte's mischievous giggle.

"It is medical confirmation that she is pregnant."

"Congratulations to the Spencers."

Charlotte chose not to dwell on the topic. "I received a telegram from Mister Sales last Wednesday and his letter on Friday, which is why I called you. The telegram clarifies a point in his letter sent a couple of weeks earlier. If I am going to continue to act in your stead, I need to understand all this airplane stuff." Charlotte handed both papers to Brian, and then she cleared his plate to finish cleaning up.

TELEGRAM

MAY 3 1943

```
TO CHARLOTTE DRUMMOND
   STANDING OAK FARM
   WINCHESTER ENGLAND

SEE LETTER SENT APR 15 43 STOP LAST ACQUISITION
HURDLE RESOLVED STOP ALL AIRCRAFT DELIVERED
EXCEPT FOUR CONNIES STOP LAST DELIVERIES AGREED
THREE THIS YEAR LAST FEB 44 STOP PLEASE INFORM
BAD END

            BJ SALES
```

Charlotte heard the papers shuffle and added with her back to Brian, "I received the letter in Friday's Post delivery."

Bainbridge Air Services, Inc.
Wichita, Kansas

April 15, 1943

Dear Mrs. Drummond,

Please excuse the typewriter for a personal letter, but I'm afraid you might not be able to read my handwriting. I hope and trust all is well with you and your family.

I'm overdue for a status report to you regarding BAS operations. Our primary customer has agreed to help resolve the last allocation issue between us, TWA, and Lockheed. We have a meeting scheduled in two weeks to complete the resolution. I expect to have confirmation by early May.

We remain net positive regarding funding despite the rapid acquisition of assets. We have no reason to doubt further net positive funding status, at least through the current conflict.

The necessary personnel hiring to support scheduled and unscheduled operations remains the greatest operational challenge. The government's decision to stand up the Women Airforce Service Pilots (WASP) has added difficulty to recruitment. Female crew members are essential as male aviators, service crew, and maintenance personnel become progressively scarcer with war demands.

Our primary customer is concerned about the unscheduled fulfillment rate. Current scheduled fulfillment rate = 94%; unscheduled rate = 62%. We are working to improve the unscheduled rate but limited due to required maintenance hours and the number of aircraft.

Hangars and offices at Wichita Muni were completed last month. BAS has a new home! We are feeling like a real airline. Operations are running smoothly, not without problems, but smoothly.

My very best wishes to you and your family. Please give our hero my regards.

Respectfully yours,

Bobby Joe Sales
General Manager

Brian put both papers on the table. "Have you replied to Bobby yet?"

"No. When you said you would be home today, I decided to wait in case you had something to add. As I read the messages, I surmise it is good news."

"That is my reading, as well. I'm not sure of the detailed reasons for the unscheduled fulfillment rate, but my guess is they are struggling with achieving the necessary capacity given the number of aircraft, positioning, and required maintenance to ensure safe operations."

"Can he resolve the issue?"

"If there is a solution, I am confident Bobby will find it. He was not asking for any assistance from us, so I think all that needs to be said is gratitude for the status report. Have we heard anything from Donovan, Buxton, or Wagner?"

"No. Not a word."

"Then, they are happy and simply stimulating us to do better. I trust Bobby will do his best, and I know the OSS will inform us if our performance is not adequate. I think Bobby's messages were clear enough."

"Excuse me, ma'am," Edith said. Both Charlotte and Brian looked at her. "It is bedtime for the boys."

"Thank you, Edith."

Brian stood, went to Ian, and knelt to embrace their son. "I love you, little man." Ian babbled in what sounded more like gurgling water than speech." Brian chuckled and kissed his forehead.

Charlotte scooped up their son, held him tightly, and kissed him several times before transferring Ian to Edith.

"I shall bid you good night as well," Mabel added, holding young Todd on her left hip.

"Good night, Mabel," Charlotte said for both of them. She waited for the women and boys to retire upstairs. Charlotte said softly, "I have very high hopes for Mabel's contributions to our growth, and I cannot emphasize enough how much Edith has grown and accepted her role as our childcare, allowing us to work. I like how things are progressing."

"Good, and it sounds like our holdings in the States are doing well also."

"That is how I understand things, as well. Now, if we can just end this war . . ."

"We're doing the best we can."

"I'm sure you are, but if I asked you to explain, it would probably spoil the moment," Charlotte suggested. "So, I think it is time to close up so you can take me to bed and perform your husbandly duties."

Brian laughed hard as he stood and began to switch off the lights. "You don't have to ask me twice."

The two lovers quickly fell into their task with vigor. *Yes, it's great to be home.*

———

Tuesday, 11.May.1943
RMS Queen Mary
40° 40' North – 74° 3' West
Upper Bay, New York Harbor
United States of America
11:20 hours

The distinctive, world-famous, Statue of Liberty stood boldly and proudly on her granite pedestal just off the port bow as the *Queen Mary* made her way into port. The harbor pilot stood on the bridge with Commodore Illingworth, the officer of the deck, and the assigned bridge crewmen.

"The sight of Lady Liberty never ceases to bring a tear to my eyes, especially at times like these," Churchill proclaimed.

"She is a magnificent sculpture and monument."

"Far more than that, I should say. 'Give me your tired, your poor, your huddled masses yearning to breathe free . . .'" Churchill wiped away a tear descending his cheek. "She is hope."

". . . and an inspiring poem," Illingworth added.

The commands from the harbor pilot increased in frequency. Illingworth remained attentive to the ship's state as he tried to show the prime minister appropriate courtesy.

"We will not be docking at our usual pier," Sir Cyril said without looking at Churchill. "The presidential train is waiting for you dockside as soon as the ship and gangway are secure. We are prepared to assist in debarking you, your party, and your baggage as quickly as possible. I understand you are on a tight schedule for your journey to Washington."

"Thank you . . . another wartime conference," Churchill added. The TRIDENT Conference was scheduled to begin the next day and would last two weeks. While many topics would be discussed, the two paramount topics would be the next operation once North Africa was secure and his private discussion with President Roosevelt regarding the rocky start to the Manhattan Project.

As they approached Lower Manhattan, the tugs tied up to the massive ocean liner and expertly maneuvered the ship to a stern-first docking to the south side of Pier 29. The half dozen railcars stood on the tracks at the center of the pier with steam ascending from the locomotive. Churchill thanked the captain and bridge crew for their expertise, then returned to his stateroom.

The baggage had been collected and staged for debarkation. Martin escorted the prime minister to the 'D' Deck port side and the debarkation hatchway.

As a former first lord of the Admiralty, Churchill followed naval tradition. To his surprise, Captain Illingworth stood at the quarterdeck.

"Permission to debark, sir," Churchill said and saluted.

"Permission granted," Illingworth responded and returned the prime minister's salute.

Churchill headed down the gangway and noticed his reception committee for the first time. Harry Hopkins and Bill Stephenson stood at the foot of the gangway, smiling and waving.

Pier 29
Manhattan, New York City
12:30 hours

The prime minister greeted both men enthusiastically.

"Welcome back to the colonies, Mister Churchill," Hopkins added with a chuckle. "The president sent his regards and his train for your conveyance. I'd recommend you board straightaway and settle into the comfort of the salon car. As soon as your party and baggage are loaded, the engineer is up to steam and ready to depart. We have express priority status, so we should be in Washington and the White House in time for supper with the president and first lady."

"Excellent, Harry. Lead away."

They boarded the train. Prime Minister Churchill settled into the president's plush, mounted, swivel chair. When John Martin was satisfied the prime minister was comfortable, he excused himself to ensure the others and baggage made it aboard the train.

"The TRIDENT Conference is ready," Hopkins began with just the prime minister, "and we expect to begin tomorrow afternoon. The president has asked me to discuss with you some unwritten aspects of the agenda." Churchill nodded his head. "He recommends we confine the joint meetings to the field operations and logistics items. He suggested the two of you address the PARAMOUNT issues, or TUBE ALLOYS as you call it, in private this afternoon upon arrival at the White House." PARAMOUNT was the code word classification associated with the Manhattan Project and the atomic bomb development.

"We have two weeks for this conference, so I see no problem whatsoever."

"Excellent. I will radio confirmation as soon as I am able." Churchill nodded. "To the more mundane, the stewards will serve lunch in the dining car as soon as you are ready, and we are underway."

The lurch of the train marked the slow movement of the train off the dock. Hopkins excused himself to check on the arrangements and send the radio message to Washington. Churchill remained content to observe the scenery as the train turned north up the Westside of Manhattan and then across the Hudson River into New Jersey heading south for the District of Columbia.

—

Thursday, 13.May.1943
Oval Office
The White House
Washington, District of Columbia
United States of America
16:30 hours

"Welcome back to Washington, Winston." President Roosevelt had positioned his wheelchair between the two long couches to greet his companion and extended his right hand to the prime minister.

Churchill stepped to his friend, took his proffered hand, and shook it firmly. "Thank you, Franklin. Always a pleasure, I can assure you." Roosevelt gestured to the couch on the right. Churchill sat. "Thank you also for taking the time for a private chat before we begin the TRIDENT Conference."

"I will always make time for you, my dear Winston. So, what is on your mind this fine spring day?"

"First, I brought two relevant messages I received this morning before the *Queen Mary* docked in Manhattan." Prime Minister Churchill retrieved both messages from his jacket inside the left breast pocket and handed them to President Roosevelt.

MOST SECRET - ULTRA

```
MOST SECRET ULTRA
DATE 0910 13 MAY 1943
TO PM
FROM C
RETRANSMISSION
BREAK
MSG RCVD YESTERDAY END
SECRET
DATE 1412 12 MAY 1943
TO OKW OKH
FROM CMDR DAK
COPY SUPREME COMMANDER NORTH AFRICA XX CORPS
ARMORED AFRICA GROUP
BREAK
FIRED LAST CARTRIDGE BREAK HAIL VICTORY BREAK
```

```
HAIL HITLER END
SECRET
DECYPHERED 0826 13 MAY 1943
MOST SECRET ULTRA
```

MOST SECRET - ULTRA

President Roosevelt immediately went to the second message.

SECRET

```
ZZZZ/320247/18AG-PM-AF/5318007/CVSS/159/ZZZZ
SECRET
DATE 12 05 43 1445 HOURS
FROM CINC 18AG
TO PM SC AF
SUBJECT NORTH AFRICA
BREAK
COLONEL GENERAL VON ARNIM SURRENDERED THE
REMAINS OF THE AFRICA CORPS THIS AFTERNOON
BREAK NORTH AFRICA SECURE
END
SECRET
ZZZZ/320247/18AG-PM-AF/5318007/CVSS/159/ZZZZ
```

SECRET

"So, North Africa is finally and fully in Allied hands?"

"Exactly. Unfortunately, two months late to our timeline," Winston noted. "Uncle Joe will not be pleased. He has already spoken out strongly against our Italy next strategy with HUSKY, BAYTOWN, and at least AVALANCHE."

"But we have not amassed sufficient forces for ROUNDUP."

"Exactly the point," Churchill responded. "He thinks in terms of land armies. I have been unable to detect any sensitivity on his part that amphibious operations are not a river crossing. Hitler made exactly the same misjudgment, I must add."

"We cannot and must not dance to Joe's tune. We must make the best choices we can within the constraints we have before us. We did receive word from General Eisenhower that the collection of landing craft, training and preparation of the HUSKY assault forces, and stockpiling of the necessary supplies has set the landing date for HUSKY on the 9th of July."

"I had hoped to do better than that."

"I know, Winston, but we must trust our commanders."

"To be frank and candid, Franklin, I do occasionally wonder if Ike tries too hard for the perfect plan rather than a sufficient plan. As Voltaire observed, 'perfect is the enemy of good.' Nonetheless, did you sanction Eisenhower's HUSKY date?"

"No. You were at sea, and I didn't want to discuss this topic via message traffic . . . best in person."

"Agreed. So, what is your thinking?"

Franklin smiled, held Churchill's eyes, and did not speak. "If we do not trust any one of our generals to meet our objectives, we are obligated to replace them. Have we reached that point?"

This time Winston smiled. "Nicely played, sir. No, I like Ike. He has a keen mind and a certain indescribable *savoir-faire* with people, even with widely disparate, ambitious characters. I have admired that skill since I met him in Washington at the ARCADIA Conference. He was the correct choice, Franklin. He was the correct choice for TORCH. He is also the correct choice for HUSKY."

"And what of ROUNDUP?"

"We are not there, yet, Franklin, are we?"

"No, we are not. We shall see how he does with Italy—Sicily and the mainland. ROUNDUP cannot be executed before the onset of autumnal weather across the Channel. So, it is to be a '44 affair. Have you informed Stalin?"

"No, although I must say, he can easily deduce that fact."

"As I assumed. I would suggest we allow him to ask. I must confess to my mounting frustration, verging upon annoyance, that he refuses to participate in these summit conferences, while he persists in making demands unilaterally as if we are here to serve him."

"Between us, Franklin, I believe Uncle Joe is afraid of airplanes and ships. His transportation means are confined to automobiles or trains."

"That explains a lot. His loss. I know you have tried mightily to inform him of the difficulties of transferring and sustaining an army across the English Channel against a determined adversary. He has proven himself incapable or unwilling to appreciate those complications."

"I would say that assessment is spot on, Franklin. We must take the path and steps that enable us to achieve our strategic objectives in the least time with the least losses."

"I recognize your penchant for the details, and in that light, have you reviewed the HUSKY plan?" the president asked.

Churchill chuckled softly. "You know me well, Franklin. Yes, I have done so just before I boarded the *Queen Mary*. The plan is bold, aggressive, and well structured. Allied Forces is resting the combat troops after closing North Africa. Your USO is due to arrive in North Africa in a few days. The smell of cordite has not yet wafted away. The cinema and entertainment celebrities will be doing their part for a well-deserved respite. They should receive the last of the landing craft by early next month. And, significantly, our deception operations appear to be successful, giving Allied Forces the margins they sought."

"Very good. The TRIDENT agenda will be our final summit review of the plan. You expect it to go well?"

"Yes, I do, Franklin. What is not on the agenda is my concerns within the Manhattan Project."

"I'm listening," the president responded.

"We agreed last year that the project would be a joint development effort."

"Yes, we did."

"While I, we, appreciate the aggressiveness of General Groves, I am sorry to report that the British participants hold a unanimous feeling that they are being largely excluded from the decision-making process. They continue to be surprised by decisions taken beyond their awareness and then informed of the results. That hardly sounds like a collaborative process." Churchill felt the urge to remind his colleague of the unilateral British generosity in transferring British technical secrets, including nuclear weapons development to the United States in 1940, but he resisted the inclination and kept his thought to himself.

"I share your concerns, Winston. When we decided to make this a military development effort, I imagine the military personnel from above and below General Groves fell back to what they know are the control measures associated with highly classified projects. I want to assure you that our agreements of last year remain absolutely and steadfastly in place. I have not authorized any hidden agenda. I also share your frustration with the apparent exclusion of your leaders. If the project team is intentionally or unintentionally excluding your personnel, it is not satisfactory. I will have a private conversation with Secretary Stimson, who is our Cabinet supervisor for the project. If that doesn't achieve the results we need, then I am perfectly willing to gather up the project leaders and instruct them directly."

Churchill nodded his head. "I am grateful for your reassurance, Franklin, and I endorse your initiative."

The two world leaders' conversation turned to more social and personal topics as they continued their private chat before supper was ready to consume. The two men maintained their friendship that enabled frank and direct communications.

—

Saturday, 15.May.1943
USAAF Station F-356
Saffron Walden, Essex, England
United Kingdom
09:20 hours

They had no assigned missions for the day, and the weather would have precluded execution. Thunderstorms, along with periods of heavy rain and high winds, exceeded their mission constraints. Several pilots played games of chess or checkers. A few of their number were reading somewhat tattered paperback books they found in the Mess entertainment room. The squadron remained at Available, but none of the pilots complained. As had become Brian's practice, he leaned back in a wooden chair against the wall to capture whatever sleep or relaxation he could find. The telephone ring brought him back to alertness, although he refused to open his eyes. He heard no sounds of alert. As Brian drifted away back toward his nap, he felt a tap on his knee.

Brian opened his eyes to see Sergeant Ellison bent over toward him. "Excuse me, sir. The Mess sergeant just called to inform you that you have an important telephone call at the Mess."

Oh my God, please don't let anything to have happened to Charlotte or Ian. "Thank you, Sergeant." Brian lowered his chair to the floor, grabbed his hat, and stood. He went to the commander's office and knocked on the open door. Brian waited at the door frame for Major Petersen to look up. "Sergeant Ellison informs me I have an important telephone call at the Mess."

"Sure, sure, looks like we're not going anywhere fast. Take your time, Hunter."

"Thanks, Skipper."

Brian departed the operations building and walked to the Officer's Mess with so many thoughts rushing through his mind. No one occupied the small lobby. Brian went to the message board, found a folded slip of notepaper with his name on the outside thumbtacked to the corkboard, and retrieved it.

A friend
Mayfair 7819
Extension 607

Whew! At least it is not Charlotte. Brian went to one of the open telephone booths and without closing the bifold door. He gave the operator the number and listened to the various switching operators make the necessary connections. "Claridge's. How may I help you?"

"Extension 607," Brian said to the hotel operator. *Who on earth could this be?*

The phone rang twice. "Hello," answered the distinctive voice of Marlene Dietrich. *She is trying so hard for a nice English accent but can't quite mask her native German.* Brian instinctively closed the glass-paneled, bifold door.

"Wow! Marlene, this is Brian Drummond."

"*Guten morgen, mein liebchen,*" she said.

She only reverts to German when she feels safe and among friends. I'm so honored to be counted among her friends. "How long are you in London?"

"We arrived last night, and unfortunately, I must leave in about an hour. I cannot tell you where I'm going, but I can say I will return in one week, and I will have a few days of personal time."

"Excellent."

"If your invitation is still open, Brian, I would sincerely like to meet your wife Charlotte."

"Yes, it is still open. I've talked to Charlotte several times since I returned to England. We would be honored to greet you at Standing Oak Farm. Charlotte is eager to meet you as well." Brian gave her the instructions to reach the farm.

"Does she know of our . . . our connection?"

"Yes, she does, Marlene. She is surprisingly open-minded."

"I know I shall love her." Brian heard a knock at her door. "Just a moment, please," she shouted without covering the phone's mouthpiece. "*Liebchen,* I'm sorry. I must go. I will see you again in one week."

"Excellent. We have a date then."

Marlene blew a kiss to Brian over the telephone and hung up. Brian sat in the booth for a moment, and then he called Charlotte to tell her of the telephone call and Marlene's visit. *This is going to be interesting.*

———

Monday, 17.May.1943
Möhne Reservoir
Westfalen
Deutsches Reich
00:28 hours

The night's mission for No.617 Squadron had been in planning and development for more than a year. The reinforced heavy bomber squadron had 19 Avro Lancaster B.III (Special), four-engine, heavy bombers modified with the Type 464 'Provisioning' system. Each bomber carried a single, special,

9,200-pound, barrel-shaped, UPKEEP depth charge, containing 6,600 pounds of Torpex high explosive material and three hydrostatic detonators set for a 30-foot water depth. The Type 464 system had been developed and proven by Vickers engineer Barnes Neville Wallis, who designed the device for the specific physics of the presented task. The objective of Operation CHASTISE was the destruction of several dams supplying hydroelectric power and water to the Ruhr Valley industrial region of Germany. The UPKEEP devices were designed to skip like a flat stone along the surface of the reservoir to the face of the dam, where it would sink to the designed depth and detonate. The concussive shock, along with the hydrostatic pressure of the contained water, was calculated to breach the dam.

The system spun up the cylindrical barrel bomb to 500 rpm of backspin prior to release and required the aircrews to deliver the UPKEEP devices to a point 800 yards from the dam face, precisely with a 60-foot release height above the water surface and 232 miles per hour (373 km/h) groundspeed. When released, the massive bomb would skip seven times across the water surface of the reservoir, 'touch' the dam face, and then sink to the prescribed depth and detonate.

To achieve the required delivery parameters, the aircraft were modified with two highly directional lights on the underside of the fuselage that would intersect to produce a single spot at exactly 60-foot height above the water surface. They also had a cockpit-sighting device that would be utilized the known distance between the dam's twin towers to establish the release point.

No.617 rehearsed the UPKEEP release procedures numerous times in daylight and then at night in the planned near full moon conditions. The mission plan also called for them to use two different ingress routes to attack two primary dams and three secondary dams supplying electrical power and water to the Ruhr Valley. The squadron had begun launching from their base at RAF Scampton at 21:28 hours on their historical mission.

Squadron commanding officer Wing Commander Guy Penrose Gibson, DSO & Bar, DFC & Bar, flew his AJ-G Lancaster bomber (serial number: ED 932/G) into the valley at the headwaters of the Möhne Reservoir. The near full, waxing moon and cloudless, clear, spring air gave him the best visibility he could hope for in a mission like this one. As they had planned it, Gibson called for the geometry lights. The two dots were roughly ten yards apart—too high. He aligned with the dam on a slight dogleg he would hold until he cleared the finger ridgeline on his left, and then he would bank right into and square up with the dam face. The UPKEEP device was fully spun up and holding at 500 RPM. The system was armed and ready.

Blessedly, Gibson did not encounter any local anti-aircraft fire, as they had anticipated. He cleared the finger, banked right, and aligned on the center of the two towers. The alignment looked good. He was centered between the towers. Both towers were equidistant inside his two ranging bars and growing nicely inside the sight. Gibson gradually descended the aircraft while holding the required airspeed. He listened to the navigator's callouts as he watched the dots on the water slowly approach each other. He placed his left thumb on the special release button on the left side of his control wheel. Gibson rapidly iterated and adjusted his state. The two dots on the surface of the water became one. He held his flight conditions as the towers neared the ranging bars. When each tower centered up under the associated ranging bar, Gibson depressed the red button.

The pronounced upward lurch of the heavy bomber marked the release of the nearly 10,000-pound spinning barrel, special depth charge, and Gibson told the crew what they already knew, "Bomb's away."

The aircraft passed between the towers at mere feet above the top of the dam. Bright balls of anti-aircraft tracer fire began to probe the sky above them. Once clear of the dam, Gibson banked left and began a shallow climb to avoid the surrounding terrain.

Operation CHASTISE became known and popularly referred to as the Dambusters Raid. Five dams were attacked that night. Two dams—Möhne and Eder—were successfully breached and destroyed, releasing 270,000 acre-feet of water, terminating electrical power generation, and causing extensive, fatal flooding downstream. The other three dams were hit but were not breached.

Nineteen aircraft with 133 crewmen of No.617 Squadron took to the air that night—only 11 aircraft and 80 crewmen returned to England.

On Tuesday, 22.June.1943, one month after the Dambusters Raid, the survivors met with King George VI at Buckingham Palace. Wing Commander Gibson received the Victoria Cross—the United Kingdom's highest award for conspicuous gallantry in combat. In addition, 33 other crewmembers received five Distinguished Service Orders, ten Distinguished Flying Crosses, including four with bars (for second and subsequent awards), two Conspicuous Gallantry Medals, and eleven Distinguished Flying Medals, including one with bar.

———

Friday, 21.May.1943
Standing Oak Farm
Winchester, Hampshire, England
United Kingdom
13:30 hours

Charlotte must have been watching for Brian's arrival. Mother and Son stood outside on the fine spring day in Southern England. Brian quickly paid the taxi driver and dropped to his knees as soon as he closed the cab door behind him. He extended his arms to Ian. Charlotte released Ian's hand, and the toddler shuffled awkwardly to his father's waiting arms. Father and Son embraced. Brian kissed his son's cheeks and forehead. He lifted Ian in his arms and then reached for Charlotte. The family embraced as Ian became particularly animated with both his parents holding him.

Edith appeared at the door. "Would you like me to take Ian, Ma'am?"

"Yes, please, Edith. I suspect Brian has something for us to discuss." Brian looked askance at Charlotte, who only giggled. They transferred Ian to Edith, who took the toddler inside.

"You know me so well," Brian said to his smiling wife. He grasped her hand gently and led her to the oak tree. The air was neither warm nor chilly, but it was dry. Neither of them felt the need for a fire for warmth. Charlotte wore a thick, woolen shawl around her shoulders that proved adequate for her. They sat on their bench and enjoyed the scene before them for several seconds. "Marlene expects to arrive here around noon tomorrow. I wanted to ask you one last time if you are comfortable with this visit?"

Charlotte laughed robustly. "My darling husband, you are the one in the middle of this. It is I who should be asking you if you are comfortable with what is about to happen?"

"Uhhhh."

"No need for a response. Yes, I am comfortable, and I'm looking forward to meeting her. Our crew is also eagerly awaiting the opportunity to meet a genuine movie star."

"She is that."

"Brian, please, rest easy, my dear. You know I've met several of your lovers. One of them is becoming an exceptional friend of mine. I do not see Marlene as any different, Brian. I appreciate your honesty and openness with me. I do not want to lose that connection. How long is she going to stay with us? Does she want to do anything while she is here?"

"I've no idea of either answer."

"With Mabel's help, we have obtained sufficient ingredients for a nice supper tomorrow. We have plenty, should she decide to spend the weekend with us. We have the space."

"Yes, we do."

"We have prepared a room for her, should she decide to stay with us."

"Thank you, darling."

"You are most welcome. Now that we have the hard part over, did you manage a bite on your journey, or could you use a spot of lunch?" she asked in an emphasized accent and giggled.

"Thank you, sweetheart, but I did grab a sandwich at Waterloo Station."

—

Saturday, 22.May.1943
Standing Oak Farm
Winchester, Hampshire, England
United Kingdom
11:35 hours

"**I** do believe our guest is on approach, as we say in the flying business," Brian offered at the window.

Charlotte joined her husband at the window. The cab moved along the gravel roadway down the hill. "Here we go," she muttered and moved to retrieve Ian. Charlotte wore a simple light blue dress that complimented her eyes.

Brian wore his uniform without his hat.

The three of them opened the front door and stepped out onto the stone porch to welcome their guest. Charlotte carried Ian on her left hip. The rest of their crew remained inside, dressed in their Sunday best, gathered up in the living room in a line from oldest to youngest. Todd fought with his mother as he wanted to go where Ian was going.

The cab stopped in front of them. Brian stepped forward and opened the passenger door. Marlene paid the fare and stepped out with a small satchel. She wore a simple but elegant, beige, light, pants suit. Her curled blond hair, porcelain skin, light blue, penetrating eyes, and modest pink full lips made her appear very much the movie star she was in life. Brian and Marlene embraced in the European form of greeting. She did not wait for Brian to introduce her to Charlotte and Ian. He managed to take her satchel as she passed him.

Marlene extended her right hand and stepped toward Charlotte. "Charlotte Drummond. I recognize you from the photograph of you that Brian carries."

"I am," Charlotte responded, taking Marlene's hand.

Marlene stepped closer and kissed both of Charlotte's cheeks, and then she kissed Ian's forehead. "And this gorgeous child must be your son Ian."

"It is," answered Charlotte. "Welcome to Standing Oak Farm, Miss Dietrich."

"No, no, that will not do. Please, I prefer Marlene. If we are not friends already, I sincerely hope we shall be so very soon."

"Marlene it is then. If I may, Marlene, the remainder of our crew on the farm are eagerly, if not impatiently, waiting to meet you, if you don't mind."

Marlene smiled broadly. "It would be my pleasure. Lead the way."

Brian led, followed by Marlene, and then Charlotte and Ian. As he stepped inside the open door, Lionel and Mabel were caught just returning to their places in line. He smiled; *they must've been watching at the window.* Brian introduced each of the crew. Marlene spent several minutes talking personally with each person. She asked each of them what they did on the farm and seemed genuinely interested. *She may appear to be the movie star, but she is certainly not acting like a celebrity.*

The table was already set for lunch, and a large dish of Shepherd's Pie sat warming in the oven. Once Marlene had greeted everyone, Charlotte said, "We have prepared lunch if you would like to eat with us."

"I'm famished, darling. Where would you like me to sit, Charlotte?"

"Please sit here," Charlotte answered, patting the chair at the head of the table. Brian and Charlotte had decided to sit across from each other—Brian to Marlene's right and Charlotte to the left. "You are our guest of honor." Brian removed his uniform jacket. When Marlene saw him doing so, she decided to remove her jacket as well, revealing a sheer, see-through blouse with a modest bustier underneath. Brian took her jacket and hung them both up by the front door.

Brian helped get things on the table and served everyone's desired drinks—wine, water, and milk. The crew began to sit at the long table. Brian served each plate to avoid passing the hot dish. The mid-day meal overflowed with laughter, light-hearted banter, and spirited discussion. Marlene took questions and asked her own questions. She made everyone feel like she was part of the group.

When everyone finished, they all helped clear the table, including Marlene. The leftovers were stored, and the dishes and utensils washed. With the lunchtime chores complete, the field crew excused themselves to change clothes and return to their duties.

"Would you care to see a little of our property here?" asked Brian.

"I would love to do so," Marlene replied.

They began to shuffle toward the door when the telephone rang. Charlotte lifted the handset and said, "Winchester 4-3-7-9." Only Charlotte could hear the speaker on the other end of the connection. "Yes, it is." She listened. The caller had something to say that took a score of seconds. "No, I won't." A few more words. "One moment, please." Charlotte covered the mouthpiece and looked directly at their guest. "This is an editor from our local newspaper, the *Hampshire Advertiser.* They heard you were visiting us."

"Probably the cab driver."

Charlotte nodded her head. "They want to send a reporter and photographer to record your visit. That is your choice entirely, Marlene."

"I'm quite used to it," she said and smiled. "I don't mind a few photographs of us, as long as you don't mind. I will be happy to answer a few questions, but I am here to visit you, not carry out some public event."

Again, Charlotte nodded. "Yes, she is visiting us. She has consented to a brief event to take a few photographs and ask a few questions. I will only ask that your reporter recognize that this is private property, and this is her private time. Our guest is not here for any public event. Please respect that fact." Charlotte hung up the telephone handset. Looking directly at Marlene, Charlotte said, "The reporter and photographer will be here in an hour." Marlene nodded and smiled. "Please excuse my forgetfulness. I should have asked early on how much time we will have with you. We have prepared a room for you if you can stay."

"Thank you so much, Charlotte. That is most generous of you. I have an appointment with General Donovan this evening in London, but I would like to spend the night as your guest since I don't know when we shall meet again."

"Excellent."

"We leave Monday morning to return to the States. I should call General Donovan. I will postpone our meeting until tomorrow evening."

Charlotte helped Marlene make the connection with Wild Bill Donovan. She and Brian went outside to give Marlene privacy for her call.

"How do you think it's going?" Charlotte asked Brian in a soft voice.

"Surprisingly well, from my perspective. It is good that we are prepared, but I had not anticipated her staying with us."

Charlotte smiled broadly. "You're welcome." Brian kissed her.

Marlene appeared. "Thank you for the use of your telephone. No problem. All is set."

"Excellent."

"Shall we?" Brian asked and gestured for them to walk on their tour.

To Brian's surprise, Marlene remembered him telling her the story of the lake, the oak tree, and their bench. Charlotte added to the story. They strolled to the top of the hill behind the house. Charlotte pointed to various features of the scene from the summit. Marlene asked quite a few truly engaged questions that Charlotte answered eagerly. By her questions, Marlene demonstrated a rather keen understanding of dairy and farm operations. Charlotte also recounted her side of the aftermath of Brian's landing unconscious in her pond and him eventually hobbling on his crutches to the remains of his Spitfire. Charlotte pointed out the remnants of the broken aircraft spotting the mature field of grass beyond the hill.

"Would you like to go see it?" Charlotte asked.

"No, no thanks. I'm afraid it would bring tears."

"Oh, I know. It does for me even after three years of time. I vividly remember that day . . . that aircraft spiraling just over my head. Fortunately, there wasn't much fuel in the aeroplane. Lionel and Morgan were able to extinguish the fire before it burned too much. And then, I saw the parachute and the limp man suspended beneath the parachute descending into my pond."

They all remained silent, occupied by their individual thoughts.

Marlene broke the silence. "You are a most fortunate and blessed woman, Charlotte."

"I don't know about that, but I am happy . . . well, except for my husband placing himself in danger almost every day of this damnable war."

"We will defeat that little bastard who is destroying the country of my birth."

"None too soon for my liking."

"Nor mine."

"You are lucky beyond description to have Brian in your life. He is a very good man, very caring and compassionate."

"Yes, he is."

"If you will forgive me, Charlotte, I must say he is also a passionate lover."

Charlotte smiled broadly and looked directly into Marlene's eyes. "Yes, he is, and I love him for it."

"You know, I'm standing right here," Brian protested.

Both women laughed heartily like two schoolgirls in some secret girls' club. Their laughter fed on itself, and Brian remained outside. *What the hell is so funny?*

The ringing bell followed shortly after that by the honking of an automobile horn brought their laughter to an end.

"They need us back at the house," Charlotte announced as she suppressed her laughter. "My guess is the newspaper men have arrived."

"You don't have to do this, Marlene," Brian offered.

"I know, but this is the price of fame. If I don't appease them a little, they resort to more intrusive means."

"Then, let's get this done so that you can relax," Charlotte added.

The three of them walked down the hill and to the house. The visitors were indeed the reporter and photographer from the *Hampshire Advertiser*. They seemed to be more star-struck than inquisitive. Marlene answered the questions carefully, simply, and succinctly as the photographer snapped images, mostly of Marlene, from different angles and natural lighting. *She's going longer than I thought she would.* After a couple of last questions, Marlene held up her right hand, palm out, and told them enough. The photographer asked to take a few photographs of Charlotte, Brian, and the three of them in various combinations.

They watched the newspapermen depart over the ridgeline.

"Would you care for some tea and biscuits?" asked Charlotte.

"That would be lovely," said Marlene.

While Charlotte prepared a large pot of tea, she placed a large platter with a variety of homemade cookies on the table. After pouring a 'cuppa' for each of them, Charlotte sat at the kitchen table with Marlene and Brian. Edith had the boys somewhere, so the house was quiet and peaceful.

"It must be getting close to afternoon milking time," Marlene observed.

Both Charlotte and Brian instinctively looked at the large wall clock.

"Yes, it is," replied Charlotte. "How did you become familiar with dairy cows?"

Marlene smiled broadly and mischievously. "A little-known fact behind all the glamor and glitz of Hollywood is my summer holidays spent on my uncle's farm during my school years—my father's brother. I grew up in Berlin with a fairly sheltered childhood, but it was those summers that taught me so much. My sister and I learned all of the farm chores, including milking the dairy cows and goats."

"Would you like to remember your youth? We have plenty of cows." They all laughed. "Yes, I would, if it is not too much trouble."

"No trouble at all, but I doubt you would like to milk the cows in that pant-suit." Charlotte was about three inches taller than Marlene with a similar slender build. "My overalls might be a little longer than you need, but we can roll up the sleeves and legs."

Charlotte retrieved a set of her overalls and a flannel shirt. She led Marlene upstairs to her room. Brian went to their bedroom to change out of his uniform and into his farm clothes. He was ready and sat in the corner chair. Charlotte arrived to change as well.

"What's wrong?" she asked.

"Nothing. I just wanted to watch you take your clothes off."

"You naughty boy." Charlotte did not hesitate or show the slightest modesty.

"I'd jump you right now if we didn't have a guest."

"Later, my stud."

They were both dressed and ready when Marlene descended the stairs in her borrowed farm outfit. They joked about various awkward farm experiences as they walked to the barn. They changed into muck boots as they entered the barn. The men had already begun the afternoon milking and stopped momentarily when Marlene, Charlotte, and Brian entered the expanded milking shed. The cows were now milked with machines, but they still had to take the cows in shifts since they did not have sufficient stalls or machines to do the herd all at once. Charlotte handed Marlene a clean, milk pale, and a stool. She selected three cows and secured them in the old stalls. Marlene took to milking her cow like a seasoned veteran. Brian and Charlotte joined their guest. Marlene drained her cow's utter first. Brian and Charlotte finished shortly thereafter. Marlene wanted to watch them process the milk. Charlotte proudly showed her the process, the various dairy products they made and even gave her a taste of a few of the assortment of cheeses the farm produced.

The first afternoon set the tone for the whole weekend. They talked and talked. Well, Charlotte and Marlene talked, joined intermittently by Edith and Mabel. Brian had never been much of a talker, but he listened and contributed when he felt it appropriate.

Brian drove Marlene to the train station Sunday afternoon to make her appointment with Bill Donovan. They kissed, and she surreptitiously squeezed him, giving him a jolt. They both felt his body react to her touch.

"*Danke schön mein Liebchen*," Marlene whispered in his ear. "It is gratifying to know I still have that effect on you," and she gently squeezed him again. Marlene gave him another peck on the lips and then kissed him more passionately. She giggled mischievously, did not wait for an answer, and winked at him before she boarded her assigned rail car.

Well, that was quite a couple of days.

———

Chapter 7

I never think of the future.
It comes soon enough.
-- Albert Einstein

Monday, 24.May.1943
Federal Reserve Building
2051 Constitution Avenue, Northwest
Washington, District of Columbia
United States of America
15:50 hours

President Roosevelt and Prime Minister Churchill cochaired the next to the last plenary session of the TRIDENT Conference. The combined joint chiefs of staff and their political leaders celebrated the Allied victory in North Africa along with the rapid consolidation of their territorial gains. They also reviewed and approved the operational plans for Operation HUSKY—the invasion of Sicily, scheduled for five weeks hence. They provided notional consent to the general plans for the invasion of Mainland Italy in their strategic effort to eliminate the first of the Axis countries from the victory equation. The group also discussed Pacific operations, both results to date and pending before the next planned summit conference—QUADRANT in Québec this coming August.

The prime minister's duty private secretary for this trip, John Martin, received a gestured signal from one of the security guards. A minute later, Martin returned and whispered in Churchill's right ear. He nodded his head, and then the prime minister raised his hand and said, "Excuse me, gentlemen, it seems an urgent message has arrived."

As Churchill stood, several others stood as well to refill their coffee, tea, water, or juice. Outside the conference room, past the guards, a Royal Navy warrant officer class 1 stood with a case manacled to his left wrist.

"What have you?" asked Churchill.

"A most urgent message from Boniface," the warrant officer stated in a low voice, almost a whisper, "that just arrived from the foreign office, and another 'your eyes only' from the War Cabinet."

Churchill and the courier walked a few steps to the far side of the wide hallway to a narrow display table. The prime minister retrieved his ULTRA key and gestured for the warrant officer to place the case on the table. Churchill unlocked the case and found two single sheet message forms inside.

MOST SECRET - ULTRA

```
MOST SECRET ULTRA
DATE 1610 24 MAY 1942
TO PM UK
FROM FM FO
SUBJECT MOST URGENT ULTRA
SECRET
DATE 0710 24 MAY 1943
TO COMMANDER OF SUBMARINES ALL SUBMARINE
COMMANDS
FROM CINC NAVY
COPY ARMED FORCES HIGH COMMAND NAVY GROUP
COMMAND WEST
BREAK
EFFECTIVE IMMEDIATELY ALL WOLFPACKS ORDERED
TO WITHDRAW BREAK RETURN TO HOMEPORT SAFEST
MEANS POSSIBLE BREAK DO NOT ENGAGE ENEMY BREAK
AVOID ALL CONTACT BREAK SUSPEND REPORTING UNTIL
SAFELY IN PORT BREAK HAIL VICTORY HAIL HITLER
END
SECRET
DECYPHERED 1417 24 MAY 1943
MOST SECRET ULTRA
```

MOST SECRET - ULTRA

The urge to cheer with his loudest voice had to be suppressed. The message offered no explanation. As a milestone in the long-running Battle of the Atlantic and the choking assault of the enemy's submarine offensive, the ULTRA message was a very positive sign, but the prime minister instinctively knew it was not the end. They could not declare victory, as much as he wanted to do so. Churchill placed the first message behind the second in his hand, and then he read the second message.

MOST SECRET – PM EYES ONLY

```
MOST SECRET PM EYES ONLY
```

```
DATE 1537 24 MAY 1943
TO PM UK
FROM WAR CAB
COPY FM FO ADMIRALTY WAR DEPT
BREAK
BONIFACE CONFIRMS GERMANS BELIEVE MAJOR MARTIN
BREAK SIS FIELD SOURCES CONFIRM GERMANS
MOVING ONE ARMOR AND TWO INFANTRY DIVISIONS TO
BALKANS CITING RELIABLE INTELLIGENCE BREAK ALL
OBJECTIVES MET BREAK GOOD LUCK TRIDENT
END
MOST SECRET PM EYES ONLY
```

MOST SECRET - PM EYES ONLY

Churchill smiled to himself, and then he looked directly at the warrant officer and said, "Please standby. I will return these messages to you for proper handling, but I need the joint chiefs to see these."

"Very well, sir."

Churchill folded the messages in half and returned to the conference room. In a loud voice, he said, "Excuse me, again, gentlemen, I need the room cleared except for the president, secretaries and ministers, and the combined joint chiefs." The much more constrained membership all had ULTRA and MAGIC access.

The assorted American and British staff officers and administrative staff left the room as instructed. The prime minister waited for the doors to be closed and secured, and then he handed the messages to President Roosevelt. The president nodded his head and passed the messages to Secretary Knox.

As the others read, Churchill said in a calm voice, "The first one is from Dönitz himself." Hitler relieved and retired Admiral Raeder the prior January and replaced him with Karl Dönitz as the German Navy's commander-in-chief. "Clearly, this is a very positive sign, but I dare say, I doubt we can declare victory."

"There is much more bite in those alligators," declared the first sea lord. "Nonetheless, a positive sign as the prime minister suggests."

"We have much more to learn here," Winston said. "This could be just a temporary regrouping or a refitting of their submarines with some new device or system to counter our tools."

"We all have to watch this one," Churchill said. "I'm with Admiral Pound. We're not done with these damn U-boats."

"What does the second message mean precisely?" President Roosevelt asked.

"For some time now, His Majesty's Government has carried out misinformation and deception operation under the title FORTITUDE," Churchill began. "The campaign has numerous subparts as you well imagine. One of those elements was Operation MINCEMEAT. The principal in the effort was a dead man made out to be Major Martin of the Royal Marines. Major Martin carried fake official papers that pointed at the target for the next pending operation being the Balkans and Greece rather than Sicily. The message from the War Cabinet states that we now have confirmation from ULTRA that the Germans swallowed the misinformation planted in the locked case manacled to Major Martin's left wrist."

"Does General Eisenhower know all of this?"

"Yes, he does. He and a few key members of his staff have been part of Operation FORTITUDE since he became commander of Allied Forces."

"I'm not sure I need to know all that detail. I trust the combined joint chiefs are aware."

"Yes, Mister President," responded General Marshall. "Admiral Stark and I were briefed on the skeleton of FORTITUDE before we entered the war. We have agreed to an even larger umbrella plan called BODYGUARD— Operation BODYGUARD. All of these sub-elements are being absorbed under BODYGUARD. The success of MINCEMEAT directly supports HUSKY and subsequent operations in Europe. The second message means that the Germans are not expecting our assault on Sicily. It doesn't mean the HUSKY force will have an easy go of it, but they should face less opposition than might have otherwise been the case."

"I will also add to General Marshall's cogent remarks," said Churchill, "that we must vigorously and relentlessly protect these deception operations. HUSKY will prove the benefit of MINCEMEAT, and that will establish the value of BODYGUARD for what lays ahead of us. In wartime, truth is so precious that she should always be attended by a bodyguard of lies."

"Well said," Roosevelt commented. "I fully and unequivocally endorse the prime minister's statement. We know the objective before us. We also hold our adversary with the respect due a worthy enemy. A bumpy road lies ahead, yet we shall ultimately prevail with true faith in our noble cause.

"Now, with the wise and flowery platitudes behind us, I feel compelled to state in closing that we have a solid plan. We have endorsed General Eisenhower's operational plan for Sicily and Italy. We have agreed to the general direction and guidance for our assault on the continent. I eagerly await the detailed plan for the final defeat of Nawzees, as the prime minister prefers to pronounce, Germany. We have done, all of you have done, a magnificent job of our collaborative planning and preparation. I will also add here from my perspective that Generals Eisenhower and Alexander have risen fully to the challenges of joint operations. Let us see this to the end."

"Spot on, as we Brits like to say," added Churchill.

"Unless there is any additional business," Roosevelt said, looking around the room. No one indicated they had anything to add. "We are concluded for this session. We shall see you all tomorrow to close this summit conference."

The cacophony of the conference breaking up into small personal groups marked the end of the meeting. Roosevelt and Churchill would have another private supper that night. They were almost done.

—

Wednesday, 26.May.1943
British Overseas Airways Bristol
39° 15' 20" North – 76° 34' 30" West
Baltimore Harbor
Baltimore, Maryland
United States of America
07:55 hours

The Boeing Model 314 flying boat known as the BOAC Bristol sat peacefully at anchor as the motor launches ferried Prime Minister Churchill and his party from the short terminal dock to the aircraft. The prime minister had become quite familiar with the Boeing Model 314 flying boat's configuration and went directly to the first-class forward compartment.

The prime minister and his party were the only passengers on this particular flight. With the prime minister, Generals Marshall, Brooke, and Ismay, Captain Pim, along with Doctor Moran, the prime minister's personal physician, Detective Thompson, the prime minister's bodyguard, his valet Sawyers, and his duty private secretary John Martin and duty lead stenographer Patrick Kinna boarded the aircraft and situated themselves.

The chief steward informed the prime minister the flight called for an eight-and-a-half-hour flight to the Royal Canadian Air Force seaplane base at Botwood, Newfoundland. They expected a two-hour layover to top their fuel and re-provision the aircraft. The night trans-Atlantic flight to Gibraltar was planned for 17 hours and an arrival time in late afternoon the following day.

The generals and prime minister discussed the TRIDENT Conference while en route before lunch. More importantly, they discussed the pending discussions with Eisenhower and Alexander. The latter would retain command of his Middle East and North Africa command, but the British 8th Army would be transferred to Eisenhower's Allied Forces command for Operation HUSKY—the invasion of Sicily—the prelude to the invasion of mainland Italy. They all agreed that Operation MINCEMEAT had gone surprisingly well in deceiving the Germans and Italians. Conditions were ripe for the next step.

This add-on mission grew from Churchill's private discussions with Roosevelt over the course of the TRIDENT Conference. The generals would convey the joint plans and objectives. Churchill volunteered to make the not so slight detour in his return journey back to England to pass along their appreciation for Eisenhower's demonstrated, rather extraordinary negotiation skills and compromise toward mutual satisfaction. The TORCH operation and ensuing North African campaign had gone quite well, even though it had taken longer than expected or planned, but the job was finally done, and they were onto the next step in the ultimate defeat of Italy and Germany. As was his nature, Churchill masked his primary purpose with other activities to include the generals' conference, congratulating the troops for their victory, and a visit to Carthage's ruins that fell to the Romans in 146 BC.

After the meeting with Eisenhower and his staff, the prime minister would head back to England via Gibraltar. By the time he arrived in London, Churchill had been away for exactly a month.

—

Thursday, 27.May.1943
British Overseas Territory Gibraltar
16:17 hours

The BOAC Bristol seaplane alighted on the harbor's calm water and taxied to its assigned anchorage location. Prime Minister Churchill and the other passengers remained seated, as requested by the crew, until the ground crew had secured the aircraft to its anchorage platform. The sounds of the last two Wright R-2600 engines being secured marked the aircraft's readiness for debarkation, but the prime minister waited for the chief steward to inform him for departure. Churchill thanked the crew before stepping through the port side hatch. The aircraft commander stood on the platform to recognize the completion of the mission.

Brooke, Marshall, and Ismay with Prime Minister Churchill departed on the first launch to the dock. The transfer took just over five minutes.

Governor-General of Gibraltar General Noel Mason 'Mac' MacFarlane waited at the dock and greeted the dignitaries as they stepped from the launch to the pier. The prime minister would accompany the governor-general and spend the night as his guest. Appropriate quarters had been arranged for everyone. MacFarlane gestured to the limousine. Another limousine would transport the generals. Staff cars and a truck waited for the remainder of the party and the baggage.

As they drove along the perimeter road around North Front Airfield, the prime minister noticed an unusual aircraft he had not seen before and commanded the driver to go to it.

"That is your transport to Algiers," MacFarlane stated.

When the car stopped, Churchill got out of the limousine. A uniformed squadron leader and flight lieutenant ran from a small building that served as a terminal building. The prime minister did not wait and began to walk around the strange aircraft. The name painted on both sides of the aircraft's nose in script read Ascalon. By the time the prime minister completed one circuit, the two approaching RAF officers had met him. They both saluted Prime Minister Churchill.

"Good afternoon, Prime Minister. I am Squadron Leader Houghton, your pilot, and this is Flight Lieutenant Ritter, who will serve as my co-pilot for tomorrow's flight."

"Nice to meet you, gentlemen," Churchill responded and shook hands with both men. "Pray tell me about your fancy machine."

"We are with 5-1-1 Squadron at RAF Lyneham. We took delivery of this aircraft a month ago. It is the third prototype aircraft and the first model with a triple-rudder configuration to compensate for the wider fuselage. The aircraft is an Avro York, a passenger variant of the Lancaster heavy bomber. We are slated to acquire more of this model, but this one is assigned specifically for your transportation service. Would you like a tour of the interior?"

"First, what of Mister Vanderkloot and Commando?"

"He remains with Transport Command as does the Liberator known as Commando. I was not party to such decisions, sir, but I surmise Command believed this aircraft was better suited to your needs, and I was assigned as your command pilot. I consulted Mister Vanderkloot before we departed Lyneham."

Churchill stared at Squadron Leader Houghton and then smiled. He turned to look at MacFarlane. "Do we have a few minutes to spare, General MacFarlane?"

"Certainly, Prime Minister. May I join you?"

"Of course."

The two RAF pilots opened the aircraft. Houghton pulled the boarding ladder out, secured it, and boarded first to assist the others. Houghton said, "The normal configuration of the York has 13 rows of three seats across. As

I stated earlier, this aircraft has been specifically configured as the prime minister's air transport. There are six rows of wider, more cushioned seats, one on each side of a center aisle way. The loo is through the aft door. A forward bulkhead with a center door marked the extent of the passenger compartment." Houghton opened the door and stepped into a small conference room. A table with four smaller, mounted chairs, two on each side, occupied the compartment's right side. Two plush leather chairs faced each other on the left side. Another bulkhead with a center door marked the forward boundary of the conference room compartment. The next compartment had what appeared to be the galley and provisions storage on the right and an odd, oblong, metal container with several windows installed on the left, opposite the galley. Pointing to the container, Houghton explained, "We call this the egg for obvious reason." He lifted two levers along the long side. The top half opened up like a large clamshell.

"I'll be damned," exclaimed Churchill.

"This device is pressurized to maintain the interior at 8,000 feet equivalent pressure altitude. The egg has a small writing table, reading light, limited snack storage, and it is equipped with adjustable temperature controls, an intercom with this compartment, and a separate channel for the cockpit. It circulates and filters the interior air, so your cigars are acceptable inside. It also has its own water supply."

"That must go. No water. Brandy would be better."

Houghton laughed as though the prime minister had just delivered the punch line of a good joke. The prime minister was not laughing or smiling. "Forward of . . ."

"Excuse me," interrupted the prime minister. "Why do I need this contraption?"

"There are a variety of reasons we may need to climb to high altitude. The aircraft has a service ceiling of 23,000 feet. We must be on oxygen above 10,000 feet. The egg is here for your comfort when the rest of us must don our oxygen masks." Churchill noticeably frowned, furrowed his brow, but nodded his head. "Forward through that door," Houghton said, pointing to another bulkhead and center door, "is the navigator's station on the left and the radio operator's station on the right. A small passageway forward leads to the cockpit, where Flight Lieutenant Ritter and I will be tending to the business of getting you to the church on time."

Churchill smiled broadly at the little quip. "This is quite the machine," he commented.

"Yes, it is. We certainly expect this aircraft will serve your transportation needs in admirable form."

"Any armament?"

"None, sir. We intend to avoid potential intercept zones. We do not have quite the Lancaster's speed, but we are most definitely not as airy and cold as the bomber. We can keep the interior quite comfortable for all the passengers."

"Thank you for the tour of your aircraft, Squadron Leader Houghton and Flight Lieutenant Ritter. We will join you tomorrow morning for the journey to Algiers."

"We will be ready, Prime Minister. Have a good evening, sir." Both men saluted.

Churchill casually returned the salute and departed with General MacFarlane for a nice group dinner and a good night's sleep before the final leg to Algiers.

—

Tuesday, 1.June.1943
USAAF Station 356
Saffron Walden, Essex, England
United Kingdom
16:30 hours

"**R**ather odd time for a mission," observed Sweet.

You didn't fly those dreadful endless missions from dawn 'til dusk during the Battle of Britain, Hunter thought to himself. *If you can see, you can shoot.*

"Yeah, well, we go when they tell us to go," Pete replied. "This afternoon, we are a solo squadron. We are to attack the railroad marshaling yard at Amiens, France. The intelligence folks tell us a large military supply train will be passing through the yard at our target time. No identifiable markings or configuration clues were provided. Regardless of whether the target train is there when we arrive, our orders are to chew up the yard and anything else at that location."

"Anything?" asked Dusty.

"Yes, those are our instructions." Pete briefed their ingress route along with the known anti-aircraft batteries to avoid. The threat of enemy fighter interception remained ever-present; however, the whole squadron would attack the primary target. They would respond to any potential threat. They would hit the target by flights abreast in trail along the rail yard's long axis, roughly 105° heading across the city center and parallel to the River Somme. The late afternoon sun would be over their right shoulder, giving them good target illumination. The spacing between flights would be wider than usual to avoid being hit by ricochets since they would attack from rooftop height. After completing their one pass on the yard, they would peel off into steep, climbing right turns to put as much distance as possible between the rail yard to avoid ricochets and the known anti-aircraft batteries sprinkled on the north side of the city. Petersen briefed the remainder of their mission, including the waypoints, radio frequencies, and pipsqueak code for exit and reentry into the British air defense zone.

The pilots collected the remainder of the flight gear and headed to their aircraft. They launched in short order, and the transit across the Channel was smooth and unchallenged. The squadron crossed the French coast at a sparsely populated stretch of beach between Dieppe and Mers-les-Bains, turned due east, intercepted the River Somme halfway between Abbeville and Amiens, and then they turned southwest along the west bank of the river.

Pete shifted their attack formation of flights in trail with extra spacing and brought each flight to a line abreast of four Thunderbolts each. Amiens was easy to spot even at their treetop height above the ground and high speed.

Brian continuously scanned the sky. *No fighters . . . yet.* And his flight was in perfect position. Hunter saw the tracers erupt from Blue Flight. Billows of steam and black smoke rose from the rail yard. Pete pulled up, rolled right, in a climbing turn. Red Flight held a perfect attack position. More smoke plumes bloomed from the rail yard as Green Flight peeled off into their climbing turn. Brian had his first full-on view of the rail yard. *Several burning rail cars. A locomotive is still spewing steam.* An assembled train stood just in front of him and appeared to be making steam to move out of the attack zone.

"Bandits east high descending."

Brian instinctively looked up over his left shoulder. *They're still a way off.*

"Pectin Able engage. Pectin Baker press the attack."

"Pectin Baker, let's do it."

Hunter placed his pipper short of the locomotive. *It's moving.* Brian let the pipper rise just enough and depressed the trigger. All eight of the 50-caliber machine guns sent streams of mixed ball and incendiary rounds toward the train. Impacts danced across the locomotive. A massive plume of white steam burst out of the top of the locomotive. Brian kept his trigger down and chose to fly through the cloud. His engine coughed and refired as he came out the other side. His pipper remained on the string of railcars. Impact flashes pocked all of the rail cars to the end. Brian pulled up and rolled right. He immediately looked to the east. Able Flight engaged, creating a furball of twisting fighters. Hunter pulled his nose through, heading toward the furball. A brilliant flash from the rail yard caused him to quickly roll left for a glance down. *A massive explosion.* Hunter rolled back out in his climb to the fighter engagement. The shock wave from the explosion violently jolted the QP-G Thunderbolt. *She's still flyin'.*

Brian chose his point of engagement against a squadron of Messerschmitt 109s. *I'm not giving Buddy any slack, but at least I see him behind my left wing. The rest of the division is back there, but I can't wait for 'em.*

A 109 was chasing a Thunderbolt. Whether by design or happenstance, the Thunderbolt rolled sharply to the left directly in front of Hunter, bringing the 109 with him across Brian's nose. Hunter rolled sharply left and pulled hard to get his sight pipper ahead of the German. Satisfied with the lead, Hunter depressed the trigger. The bullet stream arced nicely. Impact flashes danced across the enemy fighter's nose and right wing just before it ripped itself apart. Brian jerked his aircraft left and up to avoid the remains of the German without success as the impacts could be heard and felt on the belly of his fighter. *I'm still flyin'.* Once he was clear, Hunter rolled back to the right, searching for his next target.

"Bandits, southeast high."

Brian had to roll back left. *A squadron of Focke-Wulf 190s closing.*

"Pectin disengage!"

As Brian turned to the north and dove for speed, he saw a few other Thunderbolts doing the same. It would take them a few minutes to reorganize. He kept looking over both shoulders. The 109s were giving chase, and the squadron of Fw190s was behind them. They were all at full throttle, so none of them possessed closure margin. They had no backup or cover squadron, so they were on their own. The 334FS was scattered throughout a couple of square miles as they ran north. Brian continued to scan the sky behind them. The Germans were closing but slowly. They could see the coastline. The squadron gradually tightened up into the beginning of a cohesive formation. *The engine is still going strong. They're still closing. They'll catch us by mid-Channel. At some point, we're going to have to turn and fight. Lord, I hope he doesn't wait too long.* Tracers from ground-based anti-aircraft guns streaked among them. In another minute, they were over the sea. The next time Brian checked his six o'clock, the Germans pulled up and were turning. *They've given up the chase.* Brian waited for another minute to ensure the Germans had indeed given up their pursuit, and then he signaled for Baker Division to join up. Pete did the same and throttled back to offer margin for the join up. They were soon a proper formation of fighters. *We're missing one. It's one of mine. No QP-B — that's Sloppy Butterfield.*

After the intensity over France, landing back at Debden seemed almost mundane. They landed in sequence by section—pairs of Thunderbolts.

Brian reported his probable shrapnel damage to his crew chief. His quick look at the belly of his fighter noted one hole in the right landing gear panel. Brian knew Tomlinson would give the aircraft a thorough examination.

The pilots began to gather outside the operations shack as they completed their intelligence debriefings.

"What happened?" Brian asked Sweet Sweeney.

"Sloppy must've hit an ammo car. The whole damn thing exploded right in front of him. I only saw chunks of his airplane come out the other side of the fireball."

"Damn!"

"Yeah. Most unfortunate. But hey, it was quick."

They remained silent as several others joined them in the lawn chairs outside.

"Why the hell did we run?" Horn Lee asked.

"Yeah, why?'" Buddy added as they looked at Brian.

"We haven't heard from the Skipper yet," Brian answered, "but my guess is, we were low on fuel and ammo, and we just lost one of our guns. He probably guessed we were outnumbered and not in a good position. Looking back, he was right to run. The 109s and 190s had more fuel and more ammo. He brought us all back . . . well, except for Sloppy. Let's be thankful."

Pete Petersen was the last to arrive. He did not waste time in the debate. He dismissed the squadron to reconvene after the evening meal in the Officer's Mess bar to celebrate their fallen comrade's life. They would have much to discuss about the day's mission.

—

Thursday, 3.June.1943
Allied Forces Headquarters
Hôtel Saint George
24 Avenue Souidani Boudjemaâ
Algiers
Algérie Coloniale Française
15:15 hours

The prime minister had arrived in Algiers with General Marshall on Friday the 28th. He had taken some time from military affairs to visit the troops, do some touring of historic sites in the area, and tend to other state matters. Churchill remained directly involved just enough to imprint the concerns of the president and himself.

General Eisenhower stood at the panoramic window staring at the brilliant sparkling specks of sunlight on the surface of the azure blue sea. The mini-conference with the prime minister had gone well, better than anticipated. The planned final session with Prime Minister Churchill would begin in a few minutes.

General Smith knocked and entered. "The prime minister is on his way. We should begin on time."

"Thanks, Beetle." Eisenhower kept his gaze on the exterior.

"Do you need some thinking time?"

"No, no," Ike answered and turned around. "Do you have something?"

"Do you recall a report two days ago on the failure to arrive of BOAC Flight 777 from Lisbon to Bristol?"

"Yes."

"We received confirmation that the flight was indeed intercepted and shot down by eight German Ju-88 maritime fighters." Eisenhower stared intently at Smith and then nodded. "The actor Leslie Howard was on that aircraft, a commercial DC-3, along with 12 other civilian passengers."

"Ashley Wilkes?"

"One and the same . . . of *Gone with the Wind* fame."

"Another casualty of war. Great movie. An accomplished actor."

"Quite so."

"See if you can find an address for his wife and family. I'd like to send them a note of condolence."

"Yes sir. Now, we'd better get you into the meeting room before the prime minister arrives."

Eisenhower and Smith greeted the attendees. General Sir Alan Brooke and General George Marshall represented the combined joint chiefs of staff for this last command review before the execution of Operation HUSKY. Both army chiefs of staff agreed; they had done their part to ensure the success of the pending invasion of Sicily and Italy. The major component commanders organized for Operation HUSKY under General Eisenhower's command were:

-- Allied Deputy Commander-in-Chief Ground Forces General Sir Harold Alexander, also served as Commanding General, 15th Army Group. The 18th Army Group had been disbanded on 15.May.1943, and replaced by the 15th Army Group comprised of the British 8th Army under General Montgomery and the American 7th Army under General Patton,

-- Allied Deputy Commander-in-Chief Naval Forces Admiral of the Fleet Sir Andrew 'ABC' Cunningham, and he remained Commander-in-Chief Mediterranean Fleet, and

-- Allied Deputy Commander-in-Chief Air Forces Air Chief Marshal Sir Arthur William Tedder, GCB, held the collateral position as Commander-in-Chief Mediterranean Air Command.

Also, in attendance by invitation for the final session were Lieutenant General Carl Andrew 'Tooey' Spaatz, USAAF [USMA 1914], Commanding

General 12ᵗʰ Air Force, and Air Vice Marshal Sir John Spencer, Air Officer Commanding-in-Chief No.37 Group.

"It's great to finally meet you, Sir John," Eisenhower said and extended his right hand to Spencer.

"Likewise, General."

"Your group has tallied up quite the record in your short time with us."

"Great pilots, sir."

"With a great commander, Sir John."

Prime Minister Churchill entered the room with General Ismay. He waved modestly to the senior officers and turned immediately to his nephew. "A pleasure to see you again, Sir John. It has been far too long."

"Thank you, Prime Minister. You are a very busy . . . and mobile man." They all chuckled softly.

"And how is my nephew's fighter group doing in your command, General."

"Exceptionally well, if I do say so, Prime Minister. His pilots have performed masterfully in protecting our forces from enemy intrusions."

"Excellent," the prime minister responded. "Now, let's raise the curtain and get this show concluded."

The principals took their seats along the long sides of the rectangular conference table. Prime Minister Churchill sat at the head of the table opposite the large wall map of the Central Mediterranean region. General Eisenhower stepped to the foot of the table at the wall map.

General Eisenhower used a long, red-tipped, wooden pointer and the wall map to summarize the Operation HUSKY plan for landing amphibious, airborne and glider forces on Sicily, Italy. The assault force would be split into the Western and Eastern Task Forces, landing on both sides of Cape Passero in Southeast Sicily. The general also summarized the operating plan for the swift securing of the island with the Eastern Task Force advancing north along the eastern coast, while the Western Task would head northwest to Palermo and then east along the northern coast to Messina.

"Does anyone have any other issues we need to address?" Eisenhower asked.

"I do not want to preempt the generals for their counsel," Churchill jumped in, "but I do believe you and your staff have done a masterful job of planning HUSKY and the subsequent operations. The quicker we subdue Italy, the sooner we can focus our forces on Germany's ultimate defeat. I do believe everyone here knows and understands my concerns about Eastern Europe. Getting to Berlin before the Red Army is, shall we say, imperative. Germany aside, I am pleased to report my most recent communication with the president. On behalf of both the president and myself, General Eisenhower, you are authorized to exploit the tactical situation to execute the subsequent BAYTOWN, SLAPSTICK, and AVALANCHE plans without further review. I will add the keys, as we have discussed earlier, are the ports of Naples and Taranto as well as the aerodrome at Foggia. The president and I agree that we need to leave the landing craft under your command at least through AVALANCHE, and I believe we are all agreed that we must transfer the majority, if not all, of that shipping to England this autumn for training and preparation in support of ROUNDUP. We have a difficult balancing act ahead of us."

"I must add," interjected Sir Alan, "that the balancing act to which the prime minister refers must be weighted to ROUNDUP. Thus, I believe it is vital that Allied Forces recognize that sufficient forces for the Italian peninsular campaign must be on the ground before the end of summer to allow the transfer of landing craft."

"I can assure you, Sir Alan," Eisenhower responded, "the Allied Forces staff is keenly aware and sensitive to the constraints you note. As we did with TORCH, we will do what has to be done to achieve the operational objectives within the specified constraints."

"You have your orders, General," the prime minister stated. "You also have the authority to execute the subsequent operations without further review. I ask this group of generals if there are any further matters to be discussed."

"I think you sank the marker, Prime Minister." General Marshall looked to each set of eyes on him. No one objected or offered further input. "We are unanimous." Looking back at Eisenhower, Marshall added, "You are 'go' for execution of HUSKY and beyond."

"Very well," Eisenhower answered.

"Then, Beetle, let's have that champagne I requested," Churchill said.

Smith smiled and chuckled softly. "Yes sir." He stepped out. He returned a minute later with four stewards carrying buckets of chilled champagne. The corks were popped, the bubbly poured, and toasts made to a successful operation. They had a group dinner planned. Churchill and Brooke planned to fly back to England in the morning. Marshall would fly with the prime minister to England for a quick review with the European Theater of Operations (ETO) and progress of Operation BOLERO before he flew back to the States on Monday. The next gate had been crossed.

—

Wednesday, 9.June.1943
Allied Forces Headquarters
Hôtel Saint George
24 Avenue Souidani Boudjemaâ
Algiers
Algérie Coloniale Française
16:20 hours

The knock on the door of the supreme commander's spacious office broke General Eisenhower's concentration. Chief of Staff General Smith entered. "We just received a confirmation message from London. The prime minister arrived safely."

"Thanks, Beetle. What is the latest on the training status?"

"Well, as a matter of fact, I just checked with the G-3. Both the 7th and 8th Armies are ahead of plan with their parachute, glider, and amphibious landing procedures training. They both had a number of injuries but nothing serious. We are looking good for execution in a month."

"Excellent. We need to keep a close eye on their progress. I want to do a command visit to witness training evolutions for as many units as possible next week for both armies."

"I'll set them up with Monty and George. You've got a few minutes before the press conference you asked me to set up. Are you sure you really want to do this?"

"Thanks to MINCEMEAT, we have the most positive margin we have yet enjoyed. We need the press on our side rather than as adversaries probing us for information. They are going to play their part to an even greater degree as we close on the main event. Now is the time to test them. I want them to trust us when we really need their cooperation."

"You're taking a big risk with the lives of our men."

"I know." Neither man spoke for several seconds. "I want you with me for this affair . . . as my witness . . . in case it goes sideways."

"Sure thing. We'd better go."

Eisenhower and Smith took the stairs to the ground floor and one of the hotel's meeting rooms set up as a pressroom. This time, two, large, serious-looking, armed Military Police guards with Thompson submachine guns at the ready stood in their combat gear at the entrance. The two generals were not quite a minute late to the schedule.

"Close it up," Smith commanded the guards. "No one enters until the doors open."

"Yes sir," the two guards answer in unison.

Eisenhower went directly to the podium. Smith took a position two paces to the left and behind the supreme commander. The seats were half full.

Only vetted and cleared, credentialed, British and American journalists had been authorized to attend. Of that group, only two-thirds of those made it to the pressroom in time—before the doors were secured.

"Why all the security, General?" one of the journalists shouted.

Eisenhower raised his right hand palm out. "The reasons shall become all too apparent. Now, I would like to make a statement to you, off the record." Grumbling among the journalists interrupted Eisenhower's statement. "Please, gentlemen, I acknowledge this is rather unusual. However, if you will allow me to finish my statement, I think the reasons for this, shall we say unprecedented arrangement, should be quite apparent." Eisenhower paused, allowing for any objections. None came. "This is a moment of trust . . . for you . . . and for me. I intend to share information with you that is vital to our next major operation for one reason, so you do not make a mistake and report on anything that might jeopardize the men who will execute that operation. I ask you to respect the lives of those men. If anyone of you is not prepared to accept this responsibility, then I will ask you to do the proper, moral thing here and leave the room now." Eisenhower searched the faces of every man in the room. No one moved or spoke. "Very well. I am trusting each of you to do the morally responsible thing. The men of the Allied Forces—British, French, and American—are trusting you with their lives.

"As you know, the Allied Forces now control all of North Africa from the Atlantic to the Suez Canal. We are resting and refitting our troops. Training for the next operation is well underway. Our next objective is a joint operation involving the glider, parachute, and amphibious landing of the 7th and 8th Armies on the beaches of Southeast Sicily. We will secure Sicily as quickly as possible, and then we intend to quickly use the island as a base of operations to defeat the rest of Italy. Now you know. We are not asking you to be part of any deception. However, I am only asking you to avoid speculating on our next objective or two. You are welcome and invited to report on the men's training and well-being, just avoid our targets and timing. I will take a few questions."

"This is most unusual, General Eisenhower," said a young reporter. "I sense an unseen angle in this request. What is behind this move of yours?"

"There is no hidden purpose. My request is straight and true. It is as it seems."

The young reporter turned to the other reporters, most of whom were older. "Has anyone ever heard of such a thing?"

"No," came a chorus of replies.

"I am sorry if my question seems suspicious."

"But we have nothing else by which to judge your request."

"I understand your inherent suspicion. It is part and parcel of your profession. I can only say I have taken an extraordinary risk for a combat commander. I cannot stop you from reporting exactly what I have just told you. I was advised against this move." Eisenhower glanced over his left shoulder and nodded to Beetle Smith, who did not flinch or twitch. "I want to establish a trust between us. It is important, if not vital, to this operation and future operations, we may be involved in together. I want all of you on our side, not trickling out information by mistake or ignorance that is beneficial to the enemy. You have a right to write what you wish, but I want you to recognize the responsibility and consequence of reporting the wrong things in wartime."

The silence was a strange and extraordinary event among this group. Eisenhower waited patiently for the next question. He saw no need to stimulate them.

"What are we supposed to do with this?"

"Do what you must," Ike responded bluntly.

"What the hell does that mean?" asked another reporter.

"You now know what is coming. You can assume it is coming soon. I will not divulge our planned landing date or time, but rest assured it is coming. I am only asking you to avoid probing the officers or men of the Allied Forces."

"Can we talk about this meeting?" a different British reporter asked.

"I have no means to stop you. I will only state that doing so risks the security and integrity of the Allied Forces. You can be overheard even in friendly social conversation. There should be no doubt that German agents and spies are among us. It only takes one little slip to jeopardize the safety of hundreds of thousands of men. The choice is yours. I am trusting you with vital information because I do not want anyone of you to make a mistake that could risk a single life. Combat is hard and dangerous enough without compounding the threat."

"That is rather stark," observed an unidentified journalist.

"Welcome to my world, gentlemen." Subtle laughter filled the room. "I carry the awesome responsibility for the well-being of the men under my command. Now you do as well. I trust that you are worthy of that responsibility." Eisenhower waited for the next question. He was surprised by the reservation of these hardened journalists. "Very well. Let us go forward together. Thank you for your patience and support, gentlemen." Eisenhower did not wait. He left the room directly, followed by Smith.

—

Monday, 14.June.1943
Headquarters, 8th Air Force
Camp Griffiss
Warren Plantation and Sandy Lane
Bushy Park, Teddington, London, England
United Kingdom
11:10 hours

The large briefing hall was full to standing room only with field grade and general officers. The cacophony of aviators impatiently waiting for the unusual gathering of squadron, group, and wing commanders to begin dissipated quickly when Major General Ira Clarence Eaker, Commanding General 8th Air Force, entered the hall, and the entire hall jumped to attention, some more swiftly than others. Eaker waved his hands for everyone to sit. Major Pete Petersen sat halfway back with his colleagues of the 4th Fighter Group. Eaker nodded for the military police soldiers to close the doors and bar the entrance of any late arrivals.

General Eaker waited for the hall to quiet. "Gentlemen, I will begin this briefing with a news item to illustrate the difficulties of the challenges we face. Yesterday, our bombers flew a mission against the German Navy facilities in Kiel. A total of 76 heavy bombers were dispatched on the raid. They had fighter escort to the range limits of our fighters, roughly the western border of Germany. Twenty-two of their number did not return. It will take a few days or weeks to ascertain how many of the crews survived. A moment of silence for our fallen, please."

The room remained stone cold silent. Many of the pilots bowed their heads, presumably in prayer.

"I say this to preface the difficult days that lay ahead. From this point on, this briefing is classified SECRET. You will treat the information accordingly.

"In January, the combined joint chiefs and our political leaders approved Operation POINTBLANK, our concentrated integrated bombing campaign against all targets in Axis territory involved with fighter production and operations. The British shall strike by night. We shall strike by day. We will keep up an unrelenting pressure on the enemy's fighter defenses. The target lists have been compiled from the best of our collective intelligence agencies. The purpose of POINTBLANK is the diminishment or elimination of the enemy's fighter intercept capacity.

"Until now, our fighter escort capability has been successful to the border of Germany. I wish to personally assure you that the Army's command in Europe, including the 8th Air Force, have stressed our urgent need for a capable fighter to stay with the bombers beyond the border. That aircraft is nearing the completion of its development. We expect initial deliveries through the rest of this year and next. The new aircraft will give us unprecedented escort capability. Unfortunately, POINTBLANK cannot wait for the new aircraft, which means we must do the best we can with the equipment we have."

Eaker paused, paced a few times, and seemed to search the faces and eyes looking at him. He returned to the podium.

"Orders will be issued as we go. You are to brief your pilots on the overall objectives of POINTBLANK and ensure they understand the importance of these missions. These next few months are going to tax our leadership skills, and I want each of you to be prepared."

"Maybe we should bomb at night," some unidentified officer shouted.

"Yeah, the British don't have the fighter problem we do," offered another.

Eaker held up both hands for quiet. "We are not going to debate the benefits of daylight bombing. We all know this is tough, guys, but POINTBLANK serves several strategic objectives. By reducing the enemy's capacity to build and operate its fighter aircraft, we gain air superiority for the inevitable invasion of Europe and ending the war sooner, and we diminish their capability to intercept our bombers. This campaign is vital to the overall war effort, and every crewmember must appreciate their part of the process. We already see fewer German fighter aircraft over France and the Low Countries. The same will be true over Germany as we prosecute POINTBLANK.

"You all are the leaders of the 8th Air Force. The nation and freedom itself depend upon each of you to lead your flight crews through these difficult months ahead. Rest assured, we will do everything we can to minimize the risks but as General Sherman . . ." Numerous hissing and boos interrupted the general, but he chose not to react. "As General Sherman observed so succinctly, war is hell. We must blast through hell to get to the other side of the River Styx.

"I wanted you all to hear this message directly from me, not in the words of some teletype. You know what has to be done. Let's get this done. You are dismissed." General Eaker did not hesitate and strode smartly out of the hall.

The myriad conversations erupted into a dissonance of unintelligible words as the officers began to stand and make their way to the now open doors. Pete kept his thoughts to himself as they boarded one of several buses that would take them to Teddington Station and the return to their various airbases.

—

Wednesday, 16.June.1943
Combined Services Detailed Interrogation Centre
Trent Park House
Cockfosters Road
Enfield, London, England
United Kingdom
09:00 hours

The two allied intelligence chiefs, Generals Donovan and Menzies, were driven from Broadway House to the Trent Park interrogation center for a dual purpose; first, briefing Big Bill Donovan on the facility and its operations, and second, to discuss the latest information yield from work done there.

The spacious manor house sat on 800 acres of land with a history dating back to the 14th Century and King Henry IV. The last owner, Sir Philip Sassoon, passed away in June 1939. The government requisitioned the estate as the war in Europe began.

Donovan noticed the street sign that immediately induced a revelation. "Ah, that," he said, pointing to the passing street sign, "is why they call the center Cockfosters Cage."

Menzies chuckled audibly. "Precisely. It is also referred to as Camp Number 11."

"Which implies there are at least ten other such places," Donovan observed.

"Part of the continuing subterfuge, I'm afraid. We have nine units at various locations, of which this is but one. We've considered building more, but fortunately, with your cooperation, we have been able to ship the less productive subjects to internment in America to make sufficient space for incoming captives."

The three-story brick manor was larger than Bill had imagined. The evidence of purpose was well camouflaged, making it difficult for the casual observer to know what happened inside the facility. As they drove into the large gravel parking area at what appeared to be the front entrance, Bill noticed a single British Army colonel standing at attention three-paces in front of the closed main door. The colonel remained at attention as the two intelligence chiefs exited the limousine.

"Good morning, C," the colonel said and saluted as the two generals stepped toward him.

Both generals returned the salute. "General Donovan," Menzies said, "may I introduce Colonel Tom Kendrick. Colonel, this is Brigadier Donovan, director of the OSS."

Colonel Thomas Joseph 'Tom' Kendrick was a career intelligence officer within MI6. He had been serving in the Secret Intelligence Service since the Great War.

"A pleasure to finally meet you, General," Kendrick said.

"An honor, Colonel."

"Colonel Kendrick," C continued, "was the founder of MI19 and led the establishment of the organization we will shortly discuss."

With the war in Europe less than a year old, British intelligence recognized the need for a specialized unit to interrogate enemy prisoners of war. MI19 created a layered, systematic process to filter and focus intelligence assets to glean as much intelligence as possible from prisoners of war.

"I eagerly anticipate hearing more," Donovan responded.

"Shall we hop to it, then," Kendrick said, gesturing to the door that miraculously opened as they approached. "As requested, we have allotted two hours for General Donovan's briefing. The other chiefs are due here at 11 for my latest findings report."

The foyer was unmanned, although it was not open to the interior. Donovan surmised the security measures behind this facility were beyond the walls. Kendrick gestured to a door on the left side of the foyer. The colonel opened the door to allow Menzies and Donovan to enter first. It was a small, closed room with no other openings and was configured as a conference or briefing room within ten chairs around the center rectangular table. Donovan followed Menzies to two middle chairs facing the door that was now closed and sat. Kendrick took the center chair opposite Donovan.

"We don't receive many visitors beyond the personnel employed here and, of course, the prisoners of war themselves. Everything you see or hear this morning is jointly classified MOST SECRET – ANGEL and must be treated as sensitive compartmented material.

"Cockfosters began with mostly a few captured *Kriegsmarine* officers, but *Luftwaffe* pilots soon dominated those interned here. We learned early on that aggressive interrogation means were not a high yield endeavor . . . sometimes necessary and appropriate. We carefully crafted a process that has been utilized successfully for the last three years. The process entails using conventional, nonphysical interrogation techniques in the first induction session once a prisoner of war arrives in England. Those initial techniques may be extended depending upon specific results, but eventually, the captives are divided up and sent to one of the nine CSDIC facilities depending upon their back. We want to put the individual with his kind, to develop connections with other prisoners with similar experience—army with army, navy with navy, and so forth. As we began to accumulate general officers, Cockfosters evolved into a facility for them. We have found that decision to be a very productive move. We will discuss some of the current yield at the meeting later this morning. Any questions so far?"

"I'm eager to learn how you do this. One immediate query, I understand you have several Americans on your staff, correct?"

"Yes sir. Only Americans. We have a half dozen at this facility and at least one at the other facilities except for two. We," Kendrick said, nodding to Menzies, "have only allowed American intelligence officers inside—no others. To the rest of the world, these facilities and the unit I am responsible for do not exist."

"Understood. Why do you call these places cages?"

Kendrick appeared to chuckle softly without making a sound. "It's a frame of reference that evolved. I suppose it's much like the circus or the zoo. The officers who remain in the Cages are under constant observation whether they recognize it or not. They are on display."

"Are you going to offer an example or show me the process?" Donovan asked.

"If there are no other questions to this stage, we'll move to the specific techniques." Kendrick paused. Neither general spoke. "I'll start at the broad, and we can bore in as you wish. The summary version is we collect these men in groups that they have an affinity to, and what we lead them to believe is just a simple detention facility. We apply stimulus of various kinds—newspapers, magazines, or simply comments by presumed staff workers, and then we simply listen to the discussions that ensue. We have every room, every gathering place, inside or outside on the grounds, wired with state-of-the-art listening devices. At this point, if you have no questions, I suggest we head to the basement. We can't enter the confinement area, so the best I can do is show you some samples of the device we employ. Hopefully, that will suffice. I also want you to see the listening stations and how they work. Because of the nature of the work our listeners do, I must ask that we have no conversations that might distract them from their work." Donovan nodded his agreement.

Kendrick stood. Menzies and Donovan followed the colonel across the foyer, through another door, and down a closed corridor with three closed doors. He opened the door on the right. "Please close the door behind you," Kendrick commanded.

The small room contained only the top of a steel circular staircase. Kendrick descended the stairs. Donovan followed. Menzies closed and latched the door, and then he followed. Donovan heard an electronic deadbolt engage. He wondered how that works? At the bottom, Kendrick held up his right index finger to his lips. It was another rectangular room with six closed doors. He chose the far left door that opened to a small conference room padded with sound insulation. Kendrick waited for the door to close and motioned to the chairs. He whispered, "We use this room for team meetings to discuss various operational matters." Kendrick pulled a small box from a small cabinet. He removed a small circular device with two unattached wires. He continued to whisper. "This is a conventional listening device installed in multiple positions in every room accessible by the prisoners." Donovan recognized the device. It was similar, if not exact, to devices used by the FBI and OSS. Donovan returned it to Kendrick, who placed it back in the box. The MI19 chief withdrew two more devices. One looked like a piece of bark. Another looked like a rock. A third device appeared to be a flower blossom. "These are samples of camouflaged devices we deploy at numerous spots around the grounds accessible to the prisoners. They talk. We listen.

"Next, we will go into a listening room. It is one of three such stations on this site. The other sites have virtually identical installations and procedures. The supervisor has a routing station that indicates voice-activated devices. The supervisor promptly routes to a specific listener. To be frank, many of our listeners are German Jews who fled their homeland to avoid the K-Zs. They transcribe the conversations. Most conversations are superfluous and are of no use. But then, we capture some gems. The operators and experts immediately analyze those relevant conversations on-site before they are passed to the Broadway House desk analysts. What happens to the intelligence beyond that point is past my knowledge. Now, to remain on track, let us get the mechanics out of the way." The generals nodded their heads. "We are going to enter one of our listening rooms. We will not be able to talk . . . even at a whisper. I want you to see the equipment, including the supervisor's console, and observe the activities. These are active operations. We should spend a few minutes in the room, and then I suggest we return to this room for a few more key points. Is this reasonable?"

"Yes, certainly," Donovan answered.

Without another word, they stood and followed Kendrick to a key-locked door that the colonel opened. Inside with the door shut, Donovan quickly surveyed the large, windowless room. Three rows of a dozen workstations nearly filled the room. Each workstation appeared to be identical, with a small array of lights and a half dozen dials with switches and nobs. All of the stations were active with an operator, and females in various uniforms manned about a third of the positions. He saw no one in civilian attire. They walked slowly and quietly down the left row. The operators had relatively large, insulated headphones with a large pad of paper and a jar of pencils. No one could be observed looking around; they were all listening intently.

Six large consoles that had to be the supervisor positions spanned the room's length along the wall opposite from the individual workstations. Each large console was different, with a diagram of what had to be their assigned area. Two stations were floor plans with several lights in each room. The other four stations had different sections of the grounds with lights that presumably marked exterior microphone locations. Bill Donovan was amazed at how quiet the room was. Only the soft click of switches could be heard.

Kendrick gestured for them to leave. The generals followed the colonel back to the basement conference room. When the door latched behind them, they sat, and Kendrick continued, "I would like to add a couple of comments that may prove helpful for the pending chiefs meeting. Cockfosters evolved to specialize in general and senior staff officer prisoners. We currently hold 39 generals and colonels. All of them are *Wehrmacht* career officers. Just a note here, one of the London Cage units focuses on SS officers to include *Waffen-SS, SD, Gestapo*, and other captured black shirts. As a new officer arrives, he takes a few days to take stock of his situation, but within a few days, he finds affinity with one of two groups—pro-Nazi and anti-Nazi. The former group's tacit leader is *General der Panzertruppe* Ludwig Crüwell, who was captured a year ago in North Africa. The latter group focus is *General der Panzertruppe* Ritter von Thoma, who was captured last November, also in North Africa. In our transcripts, we use a three-letter designator for the speaker. For example, CRU is Crüwell's designator, and THO is Thoma's reference.

"That is the extent of my preparatory briefing. Any questions to this point?"

"How do you know who is speaking?" Donovan asked.

"The operators gain the ability to recognize the voice, tone, accent, speech affectations, and word choices. It is quite like recognizing the operator of a telegraph key. We worked very hard to corroborate the identification early on, but we are convinced of the reliability. We do cross-check with physical observation when we can do so without being detected."

"I presume these German generals are being well treated."

"Yes, they are. Some believe they are treated too well. Thus, our ability to get them to relax and talk amongst themselves. They know they are confined, but our treatment plays to the notion that they are no longer important to the war effort and can let down their guard."

"Makes sense, actually."

Kendrick glanced at his wristwatch. "It's a quarter to 11. I'd suggest we make our way to the main conference. The others will be arriving soon." He did not wait for a response.

Bill Donovan took a relief break and then rejoined the group before the others arrived.

11:00 hours

The first to arrive other than those present was Lieutenant Colonel Norman Richard Crockatt, DSO, MC, Director of MI9, responsible Clandestine Operations, Escape and Evasion, followed by Lord Selborne, representing SOE. Shortly thereafter, MI5 Director-General Sir David Petrie, CIE, CVO, CBE, KPM, the head of the Security Service, entered and completed the intelligence review committee. The attendees all knew each other from multiple meetings, and those who had not yet met General Donovan were properly introduced.

"Thank you for coming, gentlemen. We have a couple of significant findings to discuss this morning. But first, this one we have discussed before, but I offer it for General Donovan's information, as the typical yield from our operations.

MOST SECRET - ANGEL

```
Excerpt of conversation: THO, SPO & LIE; 2nd
June 1943; 14:37
    SPO When are those damn vengeance weapons
          coming?
    THO The last I heard, they had not solved
          the stabilisation issue.  Who knows?
    LIE We are not that far from the centre of
          London.
    THO True.
    SPO They could easily hit us when they come.
    LIE Is there anything we can do to stop
          them?
    THO Stop the war.
    LIE And how do we do that?
    THO I wish I had an easy answer, but we are
          prisoners of war and have no control
          or authority anymore.  The Peenemunde
          Research Center's development work
          has been most impressive, and only
          the leader knows when they will be
          deployed.
    SPO We have heard stories.
    THO Most of them are probably true.  On my
          last visit, I witnessed a test flight
          of a massive four-story-high rocket.
```

```
            That test did not go well that day,
            but they are still working on the
            stabilisation, as I said.
        SPO They also have a pilotless flying bomb,
            a rocket plane fighter-interceptor, a
            guided glidebomb, and a rocket-powered
            guided bomb.
        THO Yes.  I have not seen the other weapons,
            but I have heard of them also.
                End of relevant conversation.
```

MOST SECRET - ANGEL

"I will add here, General Donovan," interjected General Menzies, "the conversation recorded in that particular transcript has convinced the prime minister to take action against the enemy program."

"If field officers know of these things, I would say our earlier technical information is accurate," Bill observed.

"That is our assessment as well."

"Who has access to ANGEL, if I may ask?"

"The men in this room, the prime minister, War Cabinet, service ministers, and the service chiefs. Access is tightly controlled."

"Rightly so."

Sir Stewart waited for any other comments from Big Bill. He nodded to Kendrick.

"The next two transcripts are more recent take for the committee's review. The first one between Thoma and Cramer was recorded two days ago at a remote bench under a mature elm tree at the far end of the grounds." Kendrick passed the next paper to Sir Stewart, who in turn passed it to Donovan and so on.

MOST SECRET - ANGEL

```
        Excerpt of conversation: THO & CRA; 14th June
        1943; 15:23
            THO Well, here we are, Hans.  Welcome to
                England.
            CRA They held me in London for several
                weeks.  I guess they are done with me.
            THO Yes, like the rest of us.  The war
                is done for us.  I understand you
```

were collected with the others during
the surrender of the Africa Corps in
Tunisia.

CRA Exactly. A tragic end to a glorious
combat corps. The mad corporal gave
Rommel and von Arnim his usual stand or
die order. The bastard! He fought in
the last war, but he has the audacity
of a mad man. Can you imagine, some of
our best armour generals.

THO One of the attempts has to succeed.

CRA You would think. You were captured in
November of '42.

THO Correct. My luck ran out in Egypt right
after the second El Alamein.

CRA Then, Ritter, you may not have heard
that a serious attempt by von Tresckow
failed. They managed to get a bomb
on the corporal's plane, but the
pressure transducer detonator failed to
activate. They retrieved the bomb and
were not discovered.

THO We have heard nothing about that here.

CRA There are others. Other news you may
not have heard. The 6th Army under
Paulus surrendered at Stalingrad last
January.

THO Poor fellows.

CRA Most will not survive. The mad corporal
promoted him to field marshal to keep
him from surrendering, but they had no
ammunition, no food, no supplies, just
as it happened to us in Tunisia. We
are being choked, starved, frozen, and
beaten. The end is inevitable, I'm
afraid.

THO I had that feeling last year. We were
beaten at El Alamein not by the enemy
but by our lack of supplies, mainly
fuel and ammunition.

```
CRA It was worse for us after they chased
    us across the desert of Cyrenaica and
    Tripolitania to Tunisia, and then we
    were literally abandoned.
THO There is nothing we can do from here,
    but I certainly hope one of the groups
    is successful, and we can end this
    damnable war before that mad man
    destroys the fatherland.
CRA You are not alone in that thought.  I
    think most of the professional Army
    wants to sue for peace before our
    fatherland vanishes.  He is going to
    burn the house down.
THO I wish it was most of the Army.  I must
    be blunt and frank here, Hans.  Cruwell
    is here.
CRA Ludwig?
THO Yes.  He still believes along with
    others among us.  National Socialism
    has corrupted the minds of more than
    just party members.
         End of relevant conversation.
```

MOST SECRET - ANGEL

"I must add here," Kendrick said, "Thoma and Cramer thought they were secluded and secure. Knowing each other throughout their service careers, they instinctively recognize that the SD or Gestapo is not listening. It is our assessment that they both know more than we have been able to detect. We shall work carefully to extract that information. We have seen and heard Thoma enough to know that he has deep love and commitment to Germany and an intense hatred of National Socialism."

"We may be able to glean enough to be helpful," Sir Stewart added. "We are looking at other avenues."

"As are we," contributed Big Bill.

"I doubt our bevy of double agents will have knowledge in this arena," Sir David said, "but I would like to discreetly query them on what they might know. I also think we might be of assistance with the interrogation of the internees."

"Agreed," Menzies responded. "Please coordinate with Colonel Kendrick." Petrie nodded his agreement. "Both the OSS and MI6 have sources and agents in Germany. The Thoma-Cramer exchange suggests the anti-Hitler, anti-Nazi movement is more pervasive than we know or imagined." Menzies looked to Donovan for a response.

"We agree completely. We know there are assassination and coup d'état initiatives within Germany in both military and political circles, but I think it safe to say we do not know about all of them. SOE experience with the White Rose is a good example."

"I was just going to mention that mission," contributed Lord Selborne. "We took the risk to connect with the Munich student group, and it ended abruptly for reasons we do not yet know. Our operator came very close to compromise and capture. He is safe now. We will, of course, strive to ascertain whether his presence or identity were compromised, but he will be precluded from entering Germany until we know more. The point here is we must be cautious in approaching dissident groups within Germany. Yes, they want to be rid of Hitler and National Socialism, but the risk of challenging the conflict between their anti-Nazi sentiments and their loyalty to the fatherland is an excessive risk, it seems to me."

"Agreed," Donovan affirmed.

"And we as well," added C. "We shall have to treat each potential group or contact with great care . . . and jointly, so we minimize the potential for a misstep."

"Yeah, lives are at stake," said Big Bill. "If I may, I think the prime minister and president need to be made aware of this content."

"Unless there is an objection, MI6 agrees." Menzies checked each set of eyes to receive consent. "Very well. Would you prefer a transmitted or hand-carry copy, General?" C asked Big Bill.

"I am due to return to Washington tomorrow. I'd prefer a hand-carry copy if it's no trouble."

"We will make it so," Sir Stewart said and looked to Kendrick to receive a confirmatory head nod. "You will have your copy before we leave." C again nodded to Kendrick to continue.

"The last message we have this morning was recorded yesterday," Kendrick said and passed the piece of paper, "is a conversation recorded yesterday."

MOST SECRET - ANGEL

Excerpt of conversation: NEU & BAS; 15th June
1943; 10:08

```
BAS Can we discuss our recent intelligence
    now?
NEU As long as we are careful.  We are
    outside, so we can ensure no one is
    listening.  What concerns you?
BAS We discussed the threatened invasion by
    the Western Allies.  The last report I
    saw was they were focused on Greece or
    the Balkans.
NEU Yes.  Correct.  Just before the Africa
    Corps' surrender, Military Intelligence
    retrieved the body of an unfortunate
    fellow who was apparently blown
    overboard and drowned.  Documents he was
    carrying confirm the enemy's intention
    to invade Greece or the Balkans.
BAS Why?
NEU Good question, Gerhard.  According to
    the intelligence analysis, the British
    want to protect their influence over
    Greece and the Mediterranean.
BAS But I heard the leader is convinced they
    will attack at Calais.
NEU So they say.
         End of relevant conversation.
```

MOST SECRET - ANGEL

"This is MINCEMEAT," declared Menzies. "I must confess to the gratification that the operation conceived many months ago has been swallowed whole. It is amazing that a full circle concept returns home in the candid thoughts of two Luftwaffe generals.

"Well done," Lord Selborne added.

Sir David said, "Quite so."

"The prime minister will be pleased," Menzies thought aloud.

"And to General Eisenhower," Donovan contributed, "with the HUSKY operation within weeks of execution."

"We will need to scrub the source information before disseminating this information beyond the ANGEL access list," commanded Sir Stewart.

"Broadway House will take it from here. We will see to the distribution. Please convey our gratitude to your teams, Colonel Kendrick."

"Hear, hear," said Lord Selborne.

"My apologies, before we adjourn," commented Donovan, "you gave a couple of the designators. Do you have a list of the others used in these excerpts?"

"Yes sir." Kendrick retrieved a folder from a leather case and removed a single piece of yellow message paper. "This is our current focus group that should cover the subjects of the transcripts discussed this morning." The colonel passed the paper to General Donovan.

MOST SECRET - ANGEL

```
Current focus list; 14th June 1943; 08:15
   BAS Generalmajor Gerhard Bassenge
         - Luftwaffe (9 May 1943)
   BRO Generalmajor Friedrich Freiherr von
         Broich
         - Heer (12 May 1943)
   CRA General der Panzertruppe Hans Cramer
         - Heer (12 May 1943)
   CRU General der Panzertruppe Ludwig Crüwell
         - Heer (29 May 1942)
   LIE Generalmajor Kurt Freiherr von
         Liebenstein
         - Heer (13 May 1943)
   NEU Generalleutnant Georg Neuffer
         - Luftwaffe (9 May 1943)
   SPO Generalmajor Hans Graf von Sponeck
         - Heer (12 May 1943)
   THO General der Panzertruppe Wilhelm Josef
         Ritter von Thoma
         - Heer (4 November 1942)
```

MOST SECRET - ANGEL

"Thank you, Colonel." Donovan paused. "I must say, this is a very impressive operation and technique. I suspect we will learn much more as we accumulate more generals. Thank you for spending the extra time with me."

The committee broke up. Donovan made sure to personally thank each man for the contributions of their respective units. Menzies and Donovan did not discuss the ANGEL information on the drive back to Broadway House in the Westminster District of London. Instead, they talked about various newspaper reports like two businessmen en route to their next meeting.

—

Thursday, 17.June.1943
USAAF Station 356
Saffron Walden, Essex, England
United Kingdom
09:15 hours

"**W**e need to form up in a few minutes for today's inspection tour, but first, I am to inform each of you that the initial warning and mission orders for Operation POINTBLANK have been issued."

"Man, I don't envy those bomber fellas at all," mumbled Horn Lee.

Petersen ignored the interruption. "Our turn is coming up. We've got to give the bombardment chaps clean transit as far as we can cover them. Yeah, they've got a tough job, and our task is to make it just a little bit easier while we are able. I've done what I was asked to do. Now, since you misfits are all dressed up in your Sunday finest, let's get outside and in formation. Our visitors today are Lieutenant General Devers, commander of the ETO, and U.S. Ambassador Winant. This shouldn't take long. We have no planned missions this afternoon, and I anticipate that we will be given the afternoon off once we're done with the inspection formation." Cheers and applause punctuated Pete's statement.

Lieutenant General Jacob Loucks 'Jake' Devers, USA [USMA 1909] assumed command of the European Theater of Operations, U.S. Army (ETO), the previous month after his predecessor was killed in a B-24 crash on a mountain in Iceland.

"Come on, you ingrates," Pete admonished, "get outside."

"What the hell does that mean?" asked Second Lieutenant John Henry 'Jack' Jarvis from Austin, Texas, one of the new guys and now Dusty Langford's wingman.

"It means the skipper thinks we are ungrateful," Dusty replied as they shuffled outside.

The pilots lined up in two files – 'A' Division in front and 'B' Division behind them. The skipper stood in front of the formation facing them. "Attention!" he commanded. "Dress right, dress!" he ordered to get the two files lined up and spaced properly. Satisfied, he said, "Parade Rest," to allow a slightly more relaxed stance. Petersen continued to glance to his right to monitor the progress of their visitors. They started with the group staff, and then the maintenance and administration squadrons. The three fighter squadrons of the 4th Fighter Group were at the tail end, with 336FS first and 334FS last. Petersen looked straight ahead and came to a position of attention. "Ah-ten-hut!" he commanded. He quickly scanned the squadron and then executed a smart about-face.

The general was in his pinks & greens service uniform with his silver stars visible on his epaulets. Ambassador Winant, who was the taller of the two, wore a light grey business suit with an almost luminescent solid blue necktie and a snappy fedora that matched his suit.

Pete reported the squadron ready for inspection. Winant led Devers and Petersen along the first file, and then they came to Brian as the leader of 'B' Division. "Great to see you again . . . Captain is it now," Winant said.

"Yes sir. Captain now."

"How is your wife Charlotte?"

"Just great, sir. Unfortunately, we don't have camp followers anymore."

Winant laughed robustly. "Quite so, Brian. Keep up the great work."

"Yes sir."

Winant stepped to Buddy Courtland next to Brian.

General Devers faced Brian. "The highest scoring ace of the ETO," Devers said.

"Only one since our transfer, sir," Brian responded.

Devers smiled. "Humility is an admirable attribute, Captain."

"Thank you, sir."

"We have high expectations for you. Fly the hell out of those machines," the general said, pointing over Brian's shoulder at the P-47s parked behind the formation.

"Will do, sir."

Pete followed the general and just winked at Brian as he passed. Brian could not look, but he assumed that Pete was receiving the general's impressions. After several minutes, Pete returned to the center-front of the formation. He looked to his right, presumably waiting for Winant and Devers to separate sufficiently on their way back to the airbase operations building. He faced the squadron. "At ease," he commanded, allowing the pilots to take a more relaxed position without moving their right feet. "The general indicated he was satisfied with his inspection. We passed. Our guests were enamored with our hero." Buddy gave Brian an elbow in the ribs that the 'B' Division leader chose not to react to in the slightest way. "I'll need to give Group a few minutes to allow the dignitaries to depart, and then I'll check on our status." No one responded. Pete took one more glance to his right and looked back. "Dismissed."

The formation broke, and the pilots filed into the operations building. No one chose to jab Brian about the special attention he attracted, and he was just fine with that.

They waited nearly 20 minutes for the stand down from Group. Pete released the squadron for the remainder of the day. To Brian's surprise, the whole squadron, minus Pete Petersen, decided to head into London for a good ol' American cheeseburger, French fries, and a Coca-Cola at the Eagle Club, with time for a couple of beers at Shepherd's Pub. They had to be back on the airbase by midnight and ready to fly in the morning.

—

Chapter 8

The man who is tenacious of purpose in a rightful cause
is not shaken from his firm resolve
by the frenzy of his fellow citizens
clamoring for what is wrong, or
by the tyrant's threatening countenance.

-- Quintus Horatius Flaccus

Friday, 18.June.1943
Cabinet War Rooms
New Public Offices
Whitehall, London, England
United Kingdom
22:00 hours

The War Cabinet and Defense Committee assembled for the late Friday evening meeting. Prime Minister Churchill had forgone his usual departure for the weekend at Chequers to hear the report of Doctor Reginald Victor 'RV' Jones, PhD (Physics). Also in attendance were Duncan Sandys and the prime minister's science advisor Lord Cherwell, The Prof, otherwise known as Frederick Alexander Lindemann.

The prime minister did not wait for the cabinet secretary to open the meeting. Churchill commanded perhaps a little more sharply than he intended, "Your report, Doctor Jones, if you please."

Jones stood and moved to the center of the open end of the 'U'-shaped table. "We have just completed our analysis of the most recent aerial photographic reconnaissance from the Baltic coast special site in Northeastern Germany." Jones uncovered a very large photographic print. He retrieved the red-tipped, long pointer. "This is the primary of several concrete revetments at the German research and development site at Peenemünde in Mecklenburg. I draw particular attention to these soot or burn marks on the concrete floor. Please notice the radial marks appears as high-energy outflow from the stand at the center. We've seen these markers before, but it was not this particular photographic plate that we believe we captured the source of the marks. This shadow is a large, bullet-shaped, cylindrical object. Based on the dimensional analysis of this object shadow, we have sketched it." Jones pulled a smaller card with a drawn image and general dimensions.

"A rocket," observed Lord President of the Council Sir John Anderson, GCB, GCSI, GCIE, PC, Member of Parliament for the Combined Scottish Universities.

"Yes. That is what it appears . . . a very big and powerful rocket. We have not yet established the designation, yet, but we believe this is one of what Hitler has referred to as his vengeance weapons. This object is distinctly different from the pilotless airplane bomb we identified earlier."

"What is its purpose?" asked Deputy Prime Minister and Dominions Secretary Clement Richard Attlee, PC, and Member of Parliament for Limehouse.

"We are still developing our rocket technology and knowledge. That said, our analysis suggests it is a ballistic rocket that is capable of delivering a one-ton explosive warhead to a range of roughly 190 miles, 300 kilometers."

"They can't reach us from Northeast Germany," Anderson added.

"No, but they certainly can from Holland, Belgium, and Northern France."

"Indeed," Attlee said.

"We don't need to find out. We must strike this snake before it strikes us," Churchill declared. "Minister Sandys, I presume you have this information. How is your planning progressing?"

Duncan Sandys responded, "Yes, we have the information. We are adjusting our planning. The team will have an initial plan by the end of the month. All of the services are involved. We continue to confer with both MI6 and the OSS to ensure we have the most comprehensive plan. As it is evolving, we have taken a much broader approach than military attack to include our assessment of countermeasures."

"Military attack would suffice for now," Churchill barked. "We don't need a demonstration of this weapon if that is what it is." The prime minister looked directly at Lord Cherwell. "Pray tell, Professor, what is your assessment?"

Cherwell cleared his throat. "We are aware that not everyone agrees with Doctor Jones's analysis, but the physics is accurate to the best of our knowledge. We looked for other explanations. The doubters point to a variety of possibilities; after all, we have no direct evidence of flight."

"The intelligence lads are searching," interjected Secretary of State for Foreign Affairs Robert Anthony Eden, MC, PC, and Member of Parliament for Warwick and Leamington. As the Foreign Minister, Eden had direct ministerial responsibility for the Secret Intelligence Service (MI6) and through MI6 for coordination with the OSS.

"I'm sure they are," added Cherwell. "Until we have seen one of these things in action, the doubts will persist. Nonetheless, as for me, I believe Doctor Jones has illuminated the most likely explanation. I would also like to add that the Oslo Report validates RV's analysis. This is not new work by the Germans. They have devoted considerable resources to this development task, as indicated by the sophistication of that facility. This is very important to the Germans. I think, Prime Minister, that you hit the nail squarely; we do not need a demonstration."

"Is there sufficient evidence to act now?" Churchill asked.

"If I may, sirs," interjected General Brooke. He paused for any objection. None came. "Doctor Jones, has the Air Intelligence Branch seen, detected, suspected, or even heard rumors of any other test or development sites for the German rocket program, if that is what it is?"

"No sir."

Sir Alan nodded his head. "Then, I would suggest to the War Cabinet and the Defense Committee that this may well be a devil-we-know moment. While the evidence is not conclusive beyond any doubt, I tend to agree with the Air Ministry's analysis. The sketch appears to be the shadow in the Peenemünde photograph, and in my novice opinion, the sketch appears to be a very large rocket. We know where they are. When we attack, as I believe we most assuredly will, they will move and disperse this research facility to an untold number of hidden places. I respectfully suggest we keep a reasonably close, but not too close, eye on this place until we have conclusive evidence that they are approaching operational status; then we strike and strike hard."

Several smaller, nondescript, muffled conversations broke out. Churchill simply stared at General Brooke. The prime minister smacked his open hand like a gavel on the table. "Gentlemen, please, we all need to benefit from the collective minds. Sir Alan has offered a worthy suggestion. What say you?"

"I, for one," Eden spoke, "think Sir Alan has made an appropriate observation. As soon as we attack, they have proof of our knowledge. Trying to intercede or obstruct their taking such a large rocket operational will become significantly more difficult. From what we've seen, this thing," he said, pointing at the photograph, "could be quite mobile, which would complicate countermeasures."

"The thought of a one-ton warhead coming at us from 200 miles away is not a pleasant image to have in one's thoughts," Churchill added. The prime minister quickly looked at all of the attendees. "Unless there is an objection, I do believe we can at least wait until we hear Minister Sandys report at the end of the month. Hopefully, we have some more intelligence information on this topic. Are we in agreement?" Churchill carefully looked at each voting member of the War Cabinet and Defense Committee. He received a head nod, a raised hand, a thumb's up, or an affirmative word from every member. "Very well. Thank you, Doctor Jones, Lord Cherwell, and Minister Sandys, for your contributions. We will reconvene when new information arises or when your report," he said, looking directly at his son-in-law, "is ready for presentation.

We cannot allow this matter to hang over our heads like Damocles' sword. I shall wait on pins and needles for the plan. We are adjourned."

Duncan waited until the other ministers and generals departed. He followed his father-in-law to the below ground prime minister's office.

Churchill noticed his son-in-law. "Yes, Duncan."

"There are many sides to this rocket matter."

"I'm certain there is, Duncan, but the people don't care. The thought of one-ton, fast bombs dropping from the heavens cannot be explained away. Our task is to keep them safe. After enduring The Blitz, another more sinister version might well prove to be too much."

"Sinister?" Duncan asked.

"If I understand Doctor Jones properly, these things will launch into a ballistic arc, which they will come down from space at supersonic speed. The people could see bombers. They will not see or hear these things until they explode."

Sandys nodded his head. "Yes, I see your point. Sinister it is. The team is addressing all known aspects."

"I anxiously await your findings."

"We will not disappoint."

"I'm sure you won't, but the Sword of Damocles is not comfortable, Duncan."

"We shall do our best to relieve the discomfort."

"Thank you, Duncan. Please give Diana our best wishes. You really must join us at Chequers for a weekend. We miss her. We miss you both."

"I will tell Diana tonight."

———

Thursday, 24.June.1943
Oval Office
The White House
Washington, District of Columbia
United States of America
12:30 hours

The president sat at the Hoover Desk reading the latest situation report from Admiral Nimitz on the Pacific Ocean Area campaign's progress. The distinctive knock on the contoured door announced only one person. Private Secretary to the President Grace Tully opened the door. "Doctor Bush has arrived, Mister President."

"Please show him in, Grace." President Roosevelt laid down the report and wheeled himself in front of the desk, as Director Office of Scientific Research and Development (OSRD) Vannevar 'Van' Bush entered the famous office. The door closed behind him.

"Good day, Mister President," Van Bush greeted the president in a cheery, ebullient manner.

"And to you, Van. Thank you for joining me for lunch." They shook hands. "We will take a working lunch in the Study." The president wheeled himself toward the side interior door. Director Bush followed Roosevelt. A small, two-place, mobile table had been set. A steward stood by the table and waited for the president's signal to uncover the two dishes—chicken cordon bleu with mashed potatoes and green beans.

Roosevelt waited for both men to savor a bite of the chicken and the steward to retire, leaving the two men alone. "I wanted a calm, more social conversation with you regarding our progress on the Manhattan Project."

Bush finished chewing another bite and took a sip of his iced tea. "Yes sir. As a summary, I would say, thanks to Doctor Fermi, we have confirmed the physics to an essential unanimous consensus among the nuclear physicists. His on-going experiments have also resolved a few of the remaining enrichment questions. In short, we now know what has to be done to achieve the result; however, we are still working on the how. Oppenheimer has led the scientist to the collective agreement that we will pursue both uranium and plutonium cores, at least for now. The engineers continue to work hard on the enrichment process to yield sufficient Uranium-235, the isotope we need, for experimentation and production. Producing Plutonium-239 has proven to be easier with a substantially higher yield factor. We feel we have a fairly clear path to producing a working device; however, the problem remains generating sufficient material for critical mass. We have not yet resolved the engineering involved in the plutonium device. Numerous developmental experiments are planned to find the means to retain safety while achieving critical mass at the moment required."

"Critical mass?" asked Roosevelt.

"Yes sir. It is the physicist term for the point at which a mass of fissile material generates sufficient neutrons to divide other atoms producing more neutrons, inducing the 'critical,' self-sustaining, chain reaction. A collateral product is heat—the heat of fission. The physicists describe that fact as the 'k' factor, or effective neutron multiplication factor. The theoretical physics suggests a rapid, or near instantaneous, creation of a supercritical mass, or a k factor greater than one, will create a very rapid release of massive heat—an explosion. The physics is good. We're still working on the engineering to achieve the physics in a controlled, stable, and safe manner."

"That's a lot to digest."

"Yes sir, it is. We're talking about physical processes that occur at the atomic level and take place in a few milliseconds. It is a lot to comprehend. Doctor Fermi's experiments have been the essential element of 'seeing' the physics. Oppenheimer and his team are feverishly trying to solve the engineering challenges, while the Army builds the massive production facilities necessary for refining these materials to sufficient purity and quantity for sustainable assembly. Plutonium appears to be a far more attractive fissile material, but problems of safely producing, on command, a supercritical mass are proving more difficult than initially thought. In short, plutonium is a better material for our purposes, but it's also a more finicky material—volatile and unstable."

Roosevelt lapsed into contemplation, taking a few more bites of his lunch and allowing Doctor Bush to eat his meal. After several minutes, Roosevelt placed his knife and fork on the edges of his plate and took a good gulp of his iced tea. "So, if I understand your description, the uranium device is easier to achieve but less attractive from a supply stream perspective."

"Exactly."

"And the team has decided to produce both types?"

"Yes, an all-the-eggs-not-in-one-basket thing." Both men chuckled softly at the image. "The team sees the plutonium device as more attractive but more difficult to achieve."

"How soon? When will they have a workable device?"

"The answer to your question has far less certainty. General Groves feels one to two years. Oppenheimer maintains his opinion that we are perhaps two to four years from a functional, deliverable device."

"That is too long. An awful lot more men are going to die."

"I can assure you, Mister President, the team feels the urgency. The Manhattan Project Military Policy Committee, which I chair for Secretary Stimson, decided last month to alter our design focus from Germany to Japan."

"Yes, Henry Stimson briefed me after the meeting. I concurred. Japan imposes additional constraints that don't preclude use with Germany. Handling Japan includes Germany, although the inverse is not true."

"Exactly. I might add that my personal chats with Oppenheimer suggest our shift of design focus does cause some personnel consternation, especially among the European refugee scientists on the team."

"Henry mentioned that as well. I trust Groves is handling any disgruntled-ness among the team."

"Yes, I do believe he is."

"In round numbers, we are talking about two years before we can use this thing to end the war."

"Yes sir, but even that is no guarantee. There are more than a few serious obstacles that could trip us up, but that is as I understand our progress."

They ate a few more bites. "How are Phoebe and the boys handling all this pressure on you?"

"The burdens we carry pale in comparison to all those young men on the frontlines."

Roosevelt smiled broadly. The two men finished their lunch, discussed other mutual matters of personal or professional interest until the president's schedule demanded his attention.

—

Tuesday, 29.June.1943
No.10 Downing Street
Whitehall, London, England
United Kingdom
16:30 hours

Minister Duncan Sandys made his presentation to the combined War Cabinet and Defense Committee.

"Thank you for your comprehensive report, Mister Sandys," announced Cabinet Secretary and Secretary to the War Cabinet Sir Edward Ettingdene Bridges, KCB, MC. "Questions, gentlemen?"

"I will add to Sir Edward's gratitude," Prime Minister Churchill said firmly and calmly. "Well done, Duncan. We clearly have our task laid out before us. Did I understand correctly from your comments before the meeting that you have new information? I did not note that information in your report."

"Excuse me, Prime Minister. Yes, we did. MI6 received information and sketches from direct sources that give us much detail about the Peenemünde facilities that we cannot see in our aerial photography. We have incorporated that information in our targeting data to the Air Ministry. The source information also confirmed the shadow object . . . ," Sandys paused to find a single page in his papers. "Excuse me. I wanted to get the same words." He searched the page for the phrase he sought. "Here it is. The source reported seeing perhaps a half dozen times in the last nine months, quote, a large bullet with fins and a long tail of flame going out the bottom rising into the sky beyond sight, unquote. An additional sketch in the package confirms the shape of our shadow sketch presented two weeks ago and offers new details we could not ascertain in the aerial photograph. This additional data combined with what we already have conclusively establishes the purpose of the object. We continue to refine our performance analysis."

"How reliable is the source or sources?" Attlee asked.

"MI6 believes the source is very reliable with the observations offered," Sandys answered. "Further, the facility sketches where they have commonality with what we see in the photograph are identical; they match. We are now convinced we have direct evidence of a major German rocket program like none other. The American OSS and Army G-2 agree that the evidence is pretty solid. They also agree with our performance analysis. I should add here that the OSS was instrumental in connecting us with Doctor Robert Goddard, who gave us good mathematical analysis for rocket motor scaling. We are missing critical elements for the analytical equations. We will keep looking, but this is the best we have so far."

Churchill looked at General Brooke. "You voiced the wait-and-see perspective, Sir Alan," the prime minister said. "Does Minister Sandys' report and information alter your opinion?"

"The discovered cockroach nest effect remains valid. Allow me to ask Minister Sandys, when or how do we determine how close they are to operational deployment?"

"Hard to say," Duncan responded. "Could be weeks, months, or even years. All of our available data suggest the Germans have achieved a stable platform. The open question is their guidance performance. Will the thing go where they want it to go—the aiming equation?"

"Well," Sir Alan said and paused, "I have to agree with our statement of two weeks ago. We do not need a demonstration of the effects of this weapon. We should be ahead of the Germans."

"To be clear, General Brooke," said Churchill, "you have seen enough?"

"Yes, Prime Minister, I have. It is worth the risk. We will deal with the cockroaches."

Churchill then looked at the chief of the air staff. "I assume the Air Force has picked up the lance."

Air Chief Marshal Sir Charles Portal leaned forward, resting his elbows on the table. "Yes, we have, Prime Minister. We have opened Operation HYDRA. We should be prepared to launch a 600-ship raid on the Peenemünde site in two weeks' time. However, we have a complication. The 8th Air Force is focused on POINTBLANK. To their side, they are far more sensitive to German fighter capabilities than we are."

"Can you reach some compromise with General Eaker?"

"We have been working on it. The issue is not whether but when. They agree that Peenemunde is a worthy and necessary target. It is just one of the priorities. They see the rocket threat as a potential or eventual threat, not immediate. They see the German fighter capacity every single day, and the deeper they penetrate into Germany, the more severe the threat realization.

It is my understanding that American industry is working on a long-range fighter design to escort their bombers during daylight raids, but the new fighter aeroplane is roughly six months away. They seek to diminish their losses during unprotected fighter engagements."

"Their choice to fly daylight raids," interjected Anderson in an almost muttered voice.

Sir Charles smiled more in annoyance than humor. "Minister, we have discussed day versus night bombing multitudinous times. I do believe the War Cabinet appreciates the risk-benefit assessment. I do not fault the Americans for seeking the benefits of daylight bombing with their sophisticated bombsight, and my heart aches at the losses they suffer on virtually a daily basis."

"We suffer horrendous losses even at night," interjected Minister of Labor and National Service Ernest Bevin, Member of Parliament for Wandsworth Central.

"Enough," Churchill commanded. "This is not some board game we are playing. We will not get into any tit-for-tat with our allies. I will say as much sternness as my words will allow, God bless the Americans for standing to the mark and taking on the burdens of daylight bombing. Because of their sacrifices, we can bomb Germany or any other target we choose, around the clock." Churchill looked at Sir Charles and Secretary of State for Air Sir Archibald Henry Macdonald 'Archie' Sinclair, Bart, Kt, CMG, PC, Member of Parliament for Caithness and Sutherland. "Do what you can to find a solution with the Americans. I believe the War Cabinet is in unanimous agreement that we cannot afford to wait for the Nawzees to use this damnable weapon because it will most assuredly be aimed at us . . . and the Home Islands. If you do not find a reasonable compromise within two weeks, I must hear a report of your efforts. If need be, I will take this matter up with President Roosevelt. We simply cannot wait until it is convenient. We need to disrupt the Nawzee program to bring this bloody rocket to an operational state before they use it on us. Am I clear?"

"Yes sir," responded Portal. Sinclair nodded his head in agreement.

Churchill scanned the War Cabinet members. "Would anyone else like to review the Operation HYDRA plan before execution?"

Attlee chuckled softly. "We trust your judgment, Winston. We know you will represent us well."

Churchill scanned the group again and received no objection. "Very well, then. Thank you for your report, Minister Sandys. I eagerly anticipate your plan when it is ready to execute," he said to the chief of the air staff.

The special meeting adjourned.

—

Thursday, 8. July. 1943
Il-Palazz tal-Granmastru
Valletta, Crown Colony of Malta
17:10 hours

General Eisenhower flew to Malta, the largest of three inhabited islands in the colony's archipelago. A U.S. Army staff car drove him to the Grandmaster's Palace. He met and had a private meeting with Governor Field Marshal Lord Gort, VC, GCB, CBE, DSO, MVO, MC, 6th Viscount Gort of Galway, who was born John Standish Surtees Prendergast Vereker and led the British Expeditionary Force during those harrowing days of the Battle of France and the evacuation at Dunkirk.

Lord Gort's aide announced the arrival of General Alexander and Admiral Cunningham. Both men stood to welcome the commanders of the ground and naval forces for Operation HUSKY. Chief of the Air Forces Air Chief Marshal Tedder remained in Algiers to lead the air campaign, since all of the air units were stationed in North Africa.

"Congratulations for your field marshal's baton, Sir," Alexander said as he shook Gort's proffered right hand.

"Well done," Cunningham added, as he shook hands with Lord Gort.

"Thank you, Harold and Andrew. Welcome to Malta."

"Thank you, Sir." Alexander looked at Eisenhower. "I just arrived, so I'm a bit behind, Ike. What is our status."

"Both the Eastern and Western Landing Forces will commence their amphibious landing day after tomorrow. Both Forces are in position to arrive in the early morning hours before sunrise. The airborne and glider units will commence their landing operations tomorrow night, although we are tickling the weather abort threshold. They will make the attempt with the decision based on immediate conditions. Unless the sea states preclude landing craft beaching, we will proceed. It is going to be rather tricky, I must say. George is aboard *Monrovia* [USS *Monrovia* (APA-31)], and Monty is aboard HMS *Antwerp*. They're maneuvering to position."

"The last report I received this morning indicated the winds and sea state are expected to remain below our no-go threshold," added Cunningham.

"Good, so we remain a go for landings," Eisenhower noted.

"Yes, for now," Sir Andrew added. "As you indicated, Ike, this is going to be close to the edge. We've agreed not to employ preparatory naval shore fire to preserve as much surprise as possible, but I remain exceptionally uneasy."

"These operations are never without risk," Alexander added. "The field commanders understand the risk. The intelligence remains consistent with our planning." Sir Harold smiled. "Your impressive naval guns won't alter the weather."

All four flag officers nervously chuckled.

"And the weather seems to be our biggest threat at the moment," Harold observed.

"The airborne units are slated to jump just after midnight tomorrow night. The transports will begin offloading their troops three hours before dawn on the 10th, and your big guns will be available immediately should the troops run into unexpected resistance. We've argued this openly. It is a bold plan, not without substantial risk, but we have done our best to mitigate those risks. In just over 24-hours, the success of HUSKY will be up to the sergeants. We have done our part. We have a good plan."

"We have prepared," said Lord Gort, "your operations room per your instructions and your advance staff work. The Lascaris War Rooms are well underground beneath the Lascaris Battery at Fort Lascaris, overlooking Grand Harbor. Our air and coastal defense control centers occupy some of the space, but there is plenty of room should you need to expand your operations center. We have been outfitting your spaces with all of the communications, maps, and operational equipment you requested."

"Excellent. We should probably have a good inspection before supper if you don't mind, Lord Gort. But, before we go I received news confirming the Germans initiated a major armor counterattack at Kursk. The Red Army is giving ground as they redeploy their forces. This battle is shaping up to be a significant test of the Red Army's resilience."

"Or the death throe convulsions of the Germans," Lord Gort interjected.

"I would not be so quick to write off the Germans," responded Sir Harold. "They're not done yet."

"So far, the Russians appear to be doing everything correctly. We'll know in a couple of weeks. But we must not forget this is 190 miles of a 1,500-mile front between the Germans and Soviets. We'll need to keep an eye on this engagement, but we've a much more pressing task ahead of us. Now, let's get our inspection of the operations center done."

Two well-appointed staff cars waited for them outside the palace. Gort and Eisenhower took the first vehicle. Alexander and Cunningham took the second car. They did not have far to drive. On the backside of the imposing fort from the harbor, a rather non-descript square entrance did not display the purpose of what lay inside, except for the two heavily armed, serious-looking guards. Even though the various guards recognized the governor of Malta, they still carefully checked the four senior officers' identification. Once past the security checkpoint, Field Marshal Lord Gort led his guests into the underground tunnels and conducted a running narration of the Lascaris War Rooms' various elements. They eventually came to the Allied Forces' working spaces. The senior officers talked with multiple officers and men that were the initial staff. They spent an hour underground before heading back to the palace for an exquisitely prepared evening meal and more social conversation.

—

Friday, 9.July.1943
USAAF Station F-356
Saffron Walden, Essex, England
United Kingdom
09:30 hours

The squadron had no assigned or scheduled mission for the day, but they remained on duty in standby status. The request from Group seemed a bit odd, but the affected pilots complied. Nine of their number had served in the Royal Air Force, only two of them during the Battle of Britain, and they were asked to be in the operations shack. Peterson, Hickerson, Stonestreet, Langford, Forcier, Courtland, Morton, Sweeney, and Drummond sat patiently waiting for whatever this meeting was supposed to address. Even Major Peterson did not know, or at least, he was not admitting to knowing the purpose.

A staff sergeant entered the building and stopped in front of the group. "Good morning, gentlemen. I'm Staff Sergeant Zabrowski. I'm the admin chief on the 4th Group staff. Please give me a moment." Zabrowski appeared to be ticking off the attendees on his clipboard. He then scanned the entire list. "By our records, each of you served in the Royal Air Force before your transfer to the Army Air Forces." He paused, perhaps for an acknowledgment, but he received silence. "Also, I do believe Captains Langford and Drummond were serving in RAF Fighter Command during the period of July 10th to October 31st of 1940. I am to inform you, and your Army records will so reflect, that qualified personnel have been awarded a campaign medal the British government calls the 1939–1943 Star. Captains Langford and Drummond are further entitled to add the Battle of Britain clasp to the ribbon. Do each of you agree with this assessment?" Zabrowski received affirmative words and head nods from all nine. "Very well. I will order the appropriate medals for each of you. As a foreign award, the medal should be worn above your right breast pocket under your RAF pilot wings. I also should remind you that all members of the squadron are entitled to wear the American Campaign Medal and the Europe-Africa-Middle East Campaign Medal under your pilot's wings. Do you have any questions?"

"I think your information has been straight forward, Sergeant," Pete responded. "Thank you very much for taking the time to inform us properly."

"Yes sir. My honor, sir. Thank you for your service and commitment, sirs. Good day, gentlemen," the sergeant said and departed.

"How about that," Langford noted. "We get a medal for being there."

"It's more than that, Dusty. Great Britain has chosen to recognize our service. Let us just be grateful."

"Hear, hear," Brian added. A few of the interior bunch rose and went outside. Brian leaned back in his chair against the wall. Hick and Jimmy took up a game of checkers. Brian closed his eyes, tried to ignore the muffled conversations, and drifted off to a combat nap.

After an indeterminate amount of time, Brian returned to awareness by a touch on his knee. He opened his eyes to see an apprehensive expression on Sergeant Tomlinson hovering over him.

"Excuse me, Sir. We completed the change out of the turbosupercharger and the intercooler heat exchanger. We need you to fly a check flight to certify proper operation."

Brian lowered his chair, stood, and hugged Tomlinson. He whispered, "Thank you, Larson. I need a free flight."

Tomlinson appeared confused and a bit surprised. "You're welcome, Sir." The sergeant spun to return to the aircraft.

Hunter grabbed his flight gear and stopped at Peterson's office. "Maintenance flight, Skipper."

"Wink, wink," he responded and exaggerated the action. He gestured as if he was shooing an annoying fly.

Brian took off, banked left, and climbed toward their training area. As he passed 7,000 feet altitude, Brian advanced the boost lever and checked the turbocharger RPM was less than 18,000. He retarded and advanced the boost level several times. Hunter tried different throttle settings and ensured the turbo-supercharger RPM did not exceed 18,250 RPM, and the boost lever did not exceed the throttle position. Brian advanced the throttle and boost levers together and separately. Satisfied the engine and supercharger were performing properly, he radioed the sector controller that he was complete and transiting southwest toward Southampton. The controller cleared Pectin Red for transit.

The nearly cloudless sky over Southern England gave Brian an easy line of sight to recognize the unique shape of Southampton Harbor and the Isle of Wight. He initiated a high-speed descent toward his objective northeast of the estuary. Brian maintained redline airspeed. He eventually saw his objective and adjusted his flight path to be at treetop height at full speed. As he passed directly over the top of the main house of Standing Oak Farm, Brian rolled 90° left and pulled smoothly back on the stick to maximum 'g.' He kept the engine at full throttle for another pass. His second time around, he saw everyone outside in the courtyard. They were all waving. They knew who was buzzing their home. Brian extended to the south, pulled up, into the first half of a loop—what the aviators called a Half Cuban Eight. As he passed through the inverted position, he continued the loop to a 45° nose down, rolled out of the inverted position to an upright attitude with his nose pointed short of the pond. As his speed rapidly increased, Brian adjusted his path, so he leveled out as low as possible, clear of the treetops. Everyone remained outside. Charlotte held Ian on her left hip as she waved. He leveled out with his throttle at full power. Brian rocked his wings to wave at his family and crew. As he passed over the house, Brian pulled up to 45°, zeroed his angle of attack, rolled two full times, and turned to the northeast.

"Carmen, Pectin Red, five miles southwest for landing."

"Pectin Red, Carmen, the pattern is open. Winds 2-2-0 at 7. Cleared to land 2-8."

"Roger, Carmen. Cleared to land 2-8."

Brian banked left, configured his aircraft for landing, and set a nice 500 feet per minute descent line for the approach end of runway 28. Brian pulled the canopy open. One quick check. Gas – Main selected, just under half a tank, plenty. Undercarriage – gear down and locked. Mixture – full-forward, rich. Prop – full forward. Speed – 115, on speed. As he passed over the numbers, Brian pulled his throttle back to the idle stop, flared, and made a nice three-point landing.

After Brian taxied to his spot and braked to a stop, Tomlinson signaled that the chocks were in place. Brian shut down and secured the aircraft. Larson waited for him on the left side, at the canopy edge. "How did she do, Captain?"

"Perfect, Larson. I ran her through her paces." Brian had a small sheet of paper from his kneeboard. "I took a couple of power checkpoints for the record."

"Thank you, Sir. We'll get her checked out and fuel topped off, just in case you get launched."

Brian stood in the cockpit. Tomlinson jumped off the wing. Hunter extracted himself. As he stepped into the operations building, Sergeant Ellison said, "Skipper wants to see you." Brian nodded his acknowledgment.

Peterson's door was open. Brian knocked on the door jam. "Excuse me, Sir. Sergeant Ellison said you wanted to see me."

Pete gestured for Brian to come in and close the door. He then gestured for Hunter to take a seat. "How did the maintenance check flight go?"

"New turbosupercharger worked perfectly."

"Good. I received a call from Group. They informed me that one of our aircraft conducted an impromptu airshow to the east of Winchester. I said we only had one aircraft airborne, and I knew that aircraft could not have been the errant machine. This is where you are going to fess up to whatever it was you did."

Brian swallowed hard. "It was me, Skipper."

"And you did what?"

"A couple of low passes over Charlotte and the farm crew."

"Sounds of freedom?"

"Yes sir. Exactly."

"Thank you for not trying to blow smoke up my ass. Now, this is where you are going to tell me you are not going to use the government's aircraft and fuel for your personal pleasure."

"Yes sir."

"No. I want you to say it."

"Yes sir. I will not use the government's aircraft and fuel for my personal pleasure."

Peterson stared at Drummond. He nodded his head. "We are not going to discuss this again, and you are not going to mention your little escapade to anyone."

"Yes sir."

"Now, get out of here and leave the door open."

Brian did as instructed. Several pilots queried him on what the private chat with the Skipper had concerned. Brian did as he was ordered and simply shook his head.

—

Saturday, 10.July.1943
USS Samuel Chase *(APA-26)*
37° 2' 7" North – 14° 14' 4" East
off Gela, Sicily
Regno d'Italia
05:30 hours

The half-moon would have helped illumination, but moonset occurred at 00:44. H-Hour initiated the main force landings at 02:45. The initial landings of the 1st Infantry Division had been successfully completed by 03:35 at the DIME landing beach straggling the Gela pier. A bomb from a Ju-87 *Stuka* hit the U.S. Navy destroyer, USS *Maddox*, under flare light, and the warship sank in short order with most of her crew. Wild Bill Donovan had been forced to alter his original plan with all the excitement and confusion of the pre-dawn landing and the less-than-ideal illumination from his transfer from the Western Task Force flagship USS *Monrovia* to the *Samuel Chase*. Morning twilight that began at 04:39 gave them sufficient illumination for the Navy to have confidence they could move the general safely. Donovan arrived shortly before sunrise that came at 05:46.

Dressed in his field uniform and wearing a brigadier general's single stars, Donovan climbed the anchorage, ladder, and gangway to the quarterdeck.

In true naval tradition, Bill saluted the flag and faced the officer of the deck. "Permission to come aboard, sir."

The U.S. Coast Guard lieutenant junior grade responded, "Permission granted. Welcome aboard, General Donovan. Lieutenant Commander Donovan is expecting you on the bridge. Do you need an escort?"

"No, thank you, Lieutenant. I know the way."

The main deck of the *Samuel Chase* remained a beehive of activity. Donovan surveyed all that was going on as he made his way up to the bridge.

Twenty-nine-year-old Lieutenant Commander David Rumsey Donovan, USN, was the oldest child of Bill and Ruth Donovan and older brother to Patricia. He was the senior U.S. Navy amphibious task force planning staff officer aboard *Samuel Chase* to coordinate any last-minute adjustments as the landing operations progressed. David had also been part of the naval task force that executed the TORCH landings at Oran.

Bill found his son on the starboard bridge leaning over the railing, observing the continuing troop and supply offloading into landing craft headed for the DIME beachhead. The younger Donovan was so intent upon the operations below him that he did not notice his father's arrival. Wild Bill waited for several minutes and noted the first rays of sunrise on the eastern horizon. Bill placed his hand on David's right shoulder.

"Not now!" protested David and waved off the interloper.

Wild Bill did not object and waited patiently. The sunrise was progressing nicely, and the massive armada came into view for the first time. After several additional minutes, he then stepped to the railing to his son's left to see what David was so attentive to below him. Landing craft were rising and falling alongside, making the transfer dangerous and a matter of timing. A half dozen minutes later, David must have sensed someone next to him. He took a quick glance and did a double take.

"Dad!" David exclaimed and turned to embrace his father. "Why didn't you say something?"

"You're working, David. I'm just an observer. I didn't want to interrupt your attention."

"Yeah," David said, gesturing with his thumb over his right shoulder. "This sea state is making the offloading process quite difficult. We got the first wave off without incident, but these continuing operations are proving far more problematic than we had hoped. Thank God these Coast Guardsmen are as skilled as they are. So far, so good, but we are falling behind our timeline."

Wild Bill gestured over the railing and then turned to look at the activity. David joined him. Pallets of ammunition hung above the landing craft on the crane cable. They could see the Utility Landing Craft (LCU) crew working feverishly to maintain the landing craft's position alongside the ship. The crane crew supervisor used a complex hand sign language to direct the operator at the crane's controls to inch the load closer and closer to the deck on the LCU. He had to judge the motion and timing of the LCU's movement along with the rate variations of the crane's winch. They had to raise the load several times to avoid slamming it into the sides of the LCU. Several times, David twitched as if he felt 'drop it now.' His son's gyrations reminded him of a football coach reacting to his player's actions on the field.

David eventually stood straight up and turned to his father. "I can't do anything to help them. Do you want to go to the wardroom for a mug of coffee?"

"Your choice, Son. You're the working man here."

David gestured for his father to follow him. In the wardroom, David served up two mugs of coffee. They sat at the long rectangular table. They were the only ones remaining. Others came to get coffee, a pastry, or both and left.

"I didn't know you'd be in on this," David said.

"Well, to be candid, I didn't know I would be able to make it either. Fortunately, General Patton is a fan of the OSS. He made the decision. I had hoped to make it across from *Monrovia* before H-Hour, but this morning's enemy action altered my plans."

"Why are you here?"

Wild Bill smiled. "I wanted to see my son."

"I'm so glad you did, Dad. It has been too long."

"Yes, far too long. As I am sure you can imagine, we have business in this affair and especially the next few steps."

"Next few?"

"I'm fairly certain you can imagine what will happen after Sicily. Your services are going to be hard-pressed until we get firmly established on the Continent and headed to Berlin."

"That is not close."

"Probably not, but it is inevitable. Our job is to collect the information necessary to make it sooner rather than later."

"I wish I could talk to you about the OSS and what you do. Maybe after the war."

"Perhaps. None of us can predict how all of this is going to play out. Certain steps are predetermined. It is only a matter of when and where. The Red Army is on the offensive now. I suspect . . ." Bill chose the less specific word to avoid the inevitable questions. ". . . the Germans know the end is approaching."

"How soon?"

"It is not my place to say, but we are talking years, not months."

David thought about his father's response. He nodded his head several times. "We will do our duty."

"We all will, David. We all will. I wanted to tell you how so very proud I am of you and your service, Son."

"Thanks, Dad. How long do I have you?"

"A few hours. A launch should be back to pick me up after the noon meal. A destroyer will take a few of us back to Malta. I'm supposed to meet with General Eisenhower tomorrow."

Father and son spent the few hours they had together conversing about family matters. David had not seen his mother or sister in a longer time than his father. Letters were good, appreciated, and important but could never replace a warm hug. They used their available time wisely. Bill shadowed David as the young officer went about performing his duties. Bill Donovan enjoyed the noon meal with the officers still aboard *Samuel Chase*, and then he departed by launch to perform his own duties.

As the turmoil and uncertainty of the invasion's early stages passed, the fleet settled into a routine of progression. The Western Task Force and American 7th Army, in parallel with the Eastern Task Force and the British 8th Army, consolidated their beachhead footholds quickly. The campaign to subdue Sicily would take five weeks to complete. Powerful elements within the Italian military would not wait for the conquest of Sicily to be concluded before they made secret overtures to the Allies to end their participation in the Axis of Steel. The end was moving another notch closer.

—

Thursday, 15.July.1943
Selfridges & Co
400 Oxford Street
Marylebone, London
United Kingdom
16:15 hours

The prime minister followed the physical security procedures without complaint or comment. Armed Army guards protected a non-descript door in the basement of the world-famous department store founded by American transplant Harry Gordon Selfridge, Sr., and opened for business on 15.March.1909. The prime minister's duty private secretary John Peck stopped at the basement anteroom, where he would wait for Churchill's return.

The senior guard recognized the prime minister, and he was expected at the secure site. The guard opened the door and closed it behind Churchill.

Inside the small room, the prime minister descended in a sole, dedicated freight elevator by himself 200 feet down below the famous department store.

A U.S. Army captain and technical sergeant greeted Churchill when the elevator stopped, and the security gate rose. They both wore the shoulder patch of the 805th Signal Service Company, U.S. Army Signal Corps. "Welcome to SWOD, Prime Minister."

"Thank you, Captain. If I have been informed properly, this telephone system became active this morning."

"Correct, Sir."

"So I can keep up, what does SWOD stand for in this instance."

The captain smiled. "Nothing fancy. It is just an acronym for the location—the four streets bounding Selfridge's department store—our cover."

Knowledgeable individuals had already begun to refer to the underground facility as SWOD, named after the four roads that enclosed the Selfridge store: Somerset, Wigmore, Orchard, and Duke.

"Ah . . . very well. I shall remember that. Now, I am told this device of yours is called SIGSALY. What on earth does that mean?"

Again, the captain smiled. "That name is not an acronym as we so often use in the military. It is simply a code word assigned by the Army Signal Corps. The system was developed by Bell Laboratories and has quite a few nicknames—X System, Project X, Ciphony I, RC-220-T1, and occasionally we refer to this monster as the Green Hornet."

"Green Hornet?"

"A super-hero character on an American radio program and recently a comic book hero, but we all think the name comes from the distinctive buzz the machine makes in operation. Would you like to see it and hear it?"

"Yes, indeed. I understood I would also have the opportunity to use the system."

"Yes sir. President Roosevelt and Secretary Stimson were unavailable, but General Marshall is scheduled for a SIGSALY call at 16:45." The captain turned to what looked like a watertight hatch on a ship with a long handle and six mechanically connected hatch dogs. He lifted the long arm unlocking the door. The prime minister, the captain, and lastly, the sergeant stepped through the hatch into a larger than expected concrete room. Floor to ceiling, green, electronic cabinets formed a large 'U.' Each cabinet unit had different dials, switches, instruments, and lights. The buzz on the equipment emitted a humming buzz that was indeed quite distinctive.

"All of this for a single telephone?" Churchill asked.

"Not exactly, Sir. This is the base station for England. Over the next few weeks, we will install remote station trunk lines to the U.S. Embassy,

No.10, the Cabinet War Rooms, London Station, and five spare lines for later assignment. The U.S. base station is located in the basement of the Pentagon building with remote stations at the White House, the State Department, and the E Street Complex?"

"OSS?"

"Yes sir. This is a speech decipherment system that's based on a One-Time Pad or OTP process to avoid repeat sequences and a sophisticated synchronization algorithm to enable a specific link. The system has a control feature to enable isolated one-to-one links as well as multi-station conference calls. The system has been tested in the lab with all stations active on a single call, but the duty controller must enable any configuration beyond a singular link. Specific commands must be activated for multi-station calls. Now, I notice the time, and I need to show you the telephone unit itself," he said and pointed to a metallic booth in the corner of the room with a single door and one thick window. The captain opened the door. "This is actually a sound-proof booth, well, at least as insulated as we can reasonably make it." A small desk, more like a built-in counter, filled the side with the window. A green desk telephone unit was the only object on the desk. A well-cushioned leather swivel chair was obviously the operational seat—two wooden, straight back chairs sat at the back of the booth, one in each corner opposite the desk. "The three big lights at the top identify the status of the telephone. Red means the system is inoperative. Yellow means the process of connecting with the specified station is underway. Green means the system is operative, and it confirms the system to be synchronized with the intended station or stations. When you lift the receiver, you'll hear a be-bonk sound that audibly confirms synchronization." The captain lifted the handset and pointed to a bar button on the inside of the handset handle. "This button is your talk button. You depress it to activate the send mode. It overrides everything else, but the last button activated has command."

"So I don't do anything?" asked Churchill.

"No sir. You simply tell the duty operator whom you wish to connect with, and he takes it from there. You simply wait for the green light. This button," the captain said, pointing to a small button in the lower-left corner labeled SPEAKER, "activates a speaker function that overrides the handset, enabling others to hear what is being said and for anyone in the booth to speak on the call."

"Not the usual use of a telephone, but I think I understand," Churchill said.

"No sir. It's different, but the difference is necessary to accommodate the electronics that encrypts your voice."

"A small price to pay for security," the prime minister commented.

"Yes sir. It's nearly time for your call with General Marshall at the Pentagon building. Do you have any questions before we begin?"

"It seems fairly straight forward to me."

The captain closed the door, leaving Churchill in silence. The prime minister saw the red light illuminate. Perhaps ten seconds later, the yellow light lit up. Prime Minister Churchill waited patiently. When the green light illuminated, he heard an odd repetitive clanging that he interpreted as the ring tone. Winston lifted the handset and listened to the be-bonk.

"This is General Marshall at the Pentagon," the voice came through surprisingly loud and clear.

"George, this is Winston in London."

"Great to hear you, Prime Minister. It appears this SIGSALY system is working."

"Indeed!"

"President Roosevelt and Secretary Stimson apologize for not being able to participate in this inaugural exercise."

"Quite all right, I must say, General. Please convey my sincere congratulations to the president and the secretary for a job well done. I'm certain this system will be of extraordinary value to us in the coming months."

"I think we have accomplished the objective of this call, Prime Minister. Do you have anything else you wish to discuss?"

"No. I'll make a comment, though. The Red Army appears to be gaining the upper hand at Kursk. They may well bloody Gerry's nose in this one."

"It does appear so, Prime Minister. We're watching as close as we can."

"Thank you, General. Best regards to all."

"You're most welcome. Until the next time, then."

The be-bonk came again, and the light on the desk unit turned red. Prime Minister Churchill hung up the handset and left the booth, closing the door behind him.

The captain stood between the electronics console and the hatch. "Was your call satisfactory?"

"It most certainly was, Captain. My compliments to your unit for bringing this system into operation. When will the remote units become operational?"

"I don't have the schedule, Sir. I'll check to see if the installation schedule has been established. However, I'm certain it'll be in the next month or two."

"The sooner, the better, Captain. This is a godsend. In my line of work, it helps immensely to hear the voices and tones."

"We'll do our best, Sir."

With that, Prime Minister Churchill thanked the captain for his instruction and took the elevator up to meet John Peck and get on with the rest of his day.

—

Sunday, 18.July.1943
Shangri-La
Naval Support Facility Thurmont
Catoctin Mountains
Thurmont, Frederick, Maryland
United States of America
15:30 hours

"Good afternoon, Mister President," General Bill Donovan said as he entered the rustic country estate.

"Welcome back to Shangri-La, Bill. How was your trip?"

"Informative and successful, I would summarize. I was able to observe the HUSKY landings, very impressive. The update I received this morning indicated the 7th Army broke through German and Italian defenses. They are headed to Palermo. Monty's 8th Army is facing stiffer resistance with the difficult terrain on the eastern axis of advance more favorable to the defense. The competitiveness between Patton and Montgomery is a force of nature. Ike has been able to channel that energy toward the objective. The 15th Army Group is on track.

"I was able to witness the landings, well, as much as I could see in the pre-dawn darkness. The Axis forces were quite active in their efforts to stop the invasion but were unsuccessful. During morning twilight on D-Day, I was able to convince the Navy to transfer me to the USS *Samuel Chase*, a fast transport, carrying elements of the Big Red One, the 1st Infantry Division, and their combat supplies. My son David served as an Allied Forces staff officer aboard. I was able to spend a few hours watching him work during the early part of the landings."

"Excellent, Bill. I'm so glad you were able to connect with David."

"None of the family had seen him in nearly a year, so it was good to see him finally. I left in the afternoon of D-Day to meet with General Eisenhower the following day. Ike was most pleased to receive my report that we have detected rumblings within the Italian military to end Mussolini's domination of the country. We know the King is favorably inclined, perhaps even sympathetic to such a move. They now know Sicily was not a feint, and mainland Italy is next. I recommended to Eisenhower that he prepare to hear secret diplomatic overtures from the Italian military."

"Unconditional surrender is our objective."

"Yes sir. He is keenly aware, as are we. We don't yet know what the Italians have in mind or how deep their support is within the military. I urged General Eisenhower to keep an open mind until we hear what they propose."

"That doesn't sound like unconditional surrender to me, Bill. We're not going to amend our policy. The Italians freely and openly embraced Nazi Germany in their intent to dominate the world. The Italians invaded several countries on their own, specifically France and Greece . . . among others."

"Yes sir. We don't know what they are thinking, but what if they offered to join us against the Germans?"

President Roosevelt looked intently at General Donovan. "I see your point. Having the Italians switch sides might give us significant intelligence against the Germans."

"Precisely. I'm only suggesting we keep an open mind until we know exactly what they're thinking."

"Churchill might be a problem. He has been quite adamant on the unconditional surrender for the Axis countries. An armistice did not work 25 years ago. We cannot accept a repeat of those mistakes."

"Understood, Sir. Would you support me making a private approach to Prime Minister Churchill?"

"Carefully . . . very carefully, yes, it's worth the gesture to see if there is any common ground."

"Very well. With the Constellation airliners, I can get there and back in a couple of days. General Eisenhower is not going to do anything without specific guidance. I would suggest we leave it at that level for now."

"Fine. I'm good with that."

"Then so it shall be done. I will, of course, inform you of the outcome, if I can return before Mister Churchill messages you." They both laughed at the image in their minds. Winston was, after all, a communicator *extraordinaire*. "As we discussed, I asked for a few minutes of your time to demonstrate a few of our gadgets. Do you recall my telling you about Major Fairbairn, 'Bill' Fairbairn?"

"The Englishman from China . . . Shanghai Police, as I recall."

"Yes, exactly. He has been instrumental in our development and training of clandestine agents to operate behind enemy lines. Major Fairbairn is the operator. He knows how to use these gadgets. I took the liberty of bringing our director of Research and Development, Doctor Lovell, who is the genius behind the gadgets you will see this afternoon."

As the director of the OSS Research and Development Department, Doctor Stanley Platt Lovell, PhD (Chemistry), served as the leader and mastermind behind the special operations tools used in the field. The OSS R&D Department was the rough equivalent of the Q Branch of MI6.

"Yes, after you mentioned it, I've been looking forward to this display. How do you want to do this?"

"Lovell and Fairbairn have chosen a range of items for you in the conference room."

"No demonstrations?" Roosevelt's mischievous smile did not cause Donovan to miss a beat.

"We cannot or should not do the explosives, but if the Secret Service has no objection, we've set up a protected target if you would like a demonstration of the firearms."

"I've only heard distant stories about such things.

"Well then, let's replace those stories with the real items."

Donovan pushed the president's wheelchair to the conference room. He introduced the president to Doctor Lovell and Major Fairbairn. The OSS men quickly and expertly described a wide variety of special operations equipment, including a button that was a compass, miniature cameras, radios, and detonators of various types that were triggered by timers, pressure, or even sound levels. They had a camera that was a matchbox. The display had a microdot film sample, both the actual dot and an enlarged print of what the microdot recorded. They had a hand grenade the size and shape of a baseball; explosives that appeared like lumps of coal, dog and mule feces, and disguised as bags of Chinese flour. They had a selection of semi-automatic pistols with and without silencers that were removable with threaded fittings, including a Colt M1911, a German Lugar, a Webley Self-Loading Pistol, and a Walther PPK 32. The last items were a conventional, standard M3 submachine gun, commonly referred to as a 'grease gun,' and the other version had an integral silencer.

As the president requested, they went outside on the covered porch. Major Fairbairn took two pistols, the M1911, and the PPK, as well as both versions of the M3. Both on-duty Secret Service agents stayed very close, and they were not shy about their agitation with firearms so close to their charge. Fairbairn fired several shots from each weapon with and without the silencers.

"That is most impressive, Major. I had no idea that these silencers worked so well. The metallic sound of the slide is louder than the muzzle report."

"We can thank Doctor Lovell for that particular refinement. Silencers have been around since 1902. None of the earlier versions were that good, but Doctor Lovell's versions are incredibly effective."

"You give me too much credit, Major." Lovell looked first at Donovan and then at Roosevelt. "I have a magnificent group of highly skilled and innovative engineers in the R&D Department, thanks in full measure to General Donovan."

Wild Bill chuckled. "Now, you give me too much credit, Stan." Donovan held President Roosevelt's eyes. "These items make our field agents all the more effective at doing what we need them to do. I wanted you to have a feel for the equipment side of our special operations capability. Our cooperation with British MI6 and SOE has produced a potent force that offers valuable support to the line combat units. This," Will Bill said, pointing at the weapons, "is the manifestation of the vision we set in place two years ago. There is more to come."

President Roosevelt congratulated the OSS men for their work. He also thanked his Secret Service detail for their tolerance and concern. General Donovan thanked the president for his time, interest, and support.

—

Sunday, 25.July.1943
Allied Forces Headquarters
Hôtel Saint George
24 Avenue Souidani Boudjemaâ
Algiers
Algérie Coloniale Française
18:45 hours

The unscheduled meeting request had been marked 'urgent,' and the sender amplified the word. Supreme Commander General Eisenhower and Allied Forces G-2 General Strong waited not so patiently.

"They are running quite late," Ike noted.

"Yes sir, but they said it was important."

"Indeed, they did. I assume from your words that you don't know the topic."

"Correct. I've no idea what this is about."

Ike stood from the plush leather chair and stepped to the picture window. The sun was low on the western horizon. The air remained clear and warm. He noticed movement below and to his right at the entry portico. "They're here," he muttered. Ike watched the two visitors disappear into the building. Eisenhower was already standing, so he remained. Strong stood as well. Both men moved toward the suite door to greet their visitors.

"Welcome back to Allied Forces Headquarters, gentlemen," Eisenhower said as both men entered the supreme commander's office.

Robert Daniel 'Bob' Murphy had been serving as President Roosevelt's personal representative in North Africa and the Mediterranean region with an equivalent rank of minister to French North Africa since the autumn of 1942. He used his language and diplomatic skills to tamp down divisions within the Free French forces that now operated as part of Allied Forces.

Lieutenant Colonel William Alfred 'Bill' Eddy, USMC, wore his service uniform along with the Navy Cross, the Distinguished Service Cross, two Silver Stars, and two Purple Hearts he had been awarded while serving as the intelligence officer for the 6th Marines and in combat at Belleau Wood. His fluency in Arabic gained him the attention of General Donovan and the OSS as well as a cover assignment as naval attaché in Tangier, Morocco, in December 1941. Together, Murphy and Eddy provided invaluable intelligence prior to the TORCH landings.

They shook hands. Eddy had not met General Strong, so the proper introductions were made. Eisenhower gestured to the circle of leather chairs. All four men sat.

Eddy began, "My apologies, General. My plane from Cairo was late. The pilot claimed unforecast headwinds."

"These things happen, Bill. We have all been victims at one time or another. So, what was so urgent to bring you all the way to Algiers?" Eisenhower asked, jumping to the matter at hand.

"I will open," responded Eddy, "since it was my contact that initiated our actions. Just days after D-Day for HUSKY, I was contacted by an Italian intelligence agent in Cairo. At first, I was very suspicious. I asked for a day or two to think about things. He agreed. I used that time to discuss the overture with Bob," Bill said, nodding to Murphy.

"I made protected contact," Bob picked up the lance, "with three different, disassociated Italians I knew here in Algiers and Tunis. Each of them, in their own words and ways, indicated the military had lost faith with Mussolini in what they saw as the tragedy of ineptitude of Mussolini's dealing with North Africa. Based on that, I communicated with Bill that the overture was likely *bona fide*."

"With that, I re-initiated contact. He trusted me, and as a consequence, the dissidents chose him and me to open a clandestine dialogue." Eddy paused to offer an opening for any questions or comments at this stage. "While we discussed a number of aspects of Italy's situation, the conversation boiled down to one question," he said, looking directly at General Eisenhower, "are you willing to discuss surrender terms? Before I could get the information to you, the situation inside Italy has changed."

"I have confirmed with my Italian contacts that two hours ago, the King dismissed Mussolini, and a squad of *Carabinieri* loyal to the King arrested Mussolini as he departed the palace."

"Is he secure?"

"We don't know about that," Murphy answered. "We may know more about the arrest in a few days. I think the arrest of Mussolini is indicative of their gesture."

"OK. Please carefully communicate with your sources, both of you, that we are open to hearing their proposal. You may also add that we are encouraged by Mussolini's arrest and trust the Italian authorities will do everything possible to ensure he stands trial for his crimes."

"Forgive me, General. Should you not seek guidance from the president, or the government?" asked Murphy.

Eisenhower smiled. "I already have. I didn't expect it, but the president anticipated the potential."

"Very well. It shall be done." Murphy looked at Eddy and received a confirmatory head nod.

"While you're still here, perhaps you should hear this." Eisenhower stood, went to the intercom box on his desk, and pushed the selected lever. "Please find General Smith and ask him to come to my office as soon as possible. If he is not available within a few minutes, please let me know how long it will take him to arrive."

"Yes sir," came the scratchy, tinny reply.

Eisenhower had barely sat back down when General Smith entered.

"Yes sir," Smith said.

"Beetle, I think you know Bob Murphy and Bill Eddy."

Smith affirmed Eisenhower's statement and shook hands with both visitors before he sat in an empty chair.

"I want you to prepare to meet with a representative of the Italian government as my personal representative in the next few days."

"Has something happened?"

"Mussolini has been deposed and arrested. Bob and Bill have received the first feelers. I've instructed them to inform their Italian contacts that we're amenable to hearing their proposal."

"Good news. I'll be prepared to go wherever necessary at a moment's notice."

"Excellent." Eisenhower looked at Murphy and Eddy. "Thank you for your extraordinary efforts. Let's move quickly. We can save lives."

The men agreed, said their good-byes, and departed to pursue their instructions.

—

Thursday, 29. July. 1943
Allied Forces Headquarters
Hôtel Saint George
24 Avenue Souidani Boudjemaâ
Algiers
Algérie Coloniale Française
07:15 hours

"**W**elcome back, Beetle," Eisenhower said as General Smith entered the office.

"Thanks, Ike. Interesting trip. I arrived before dawn this morning." Eisenhower gestured to the leather chairs. "I met with Brigadier Castellano in Lisbon at the Swiss Embassy several times over two days. Castellano was the personal representative of Field Marshal Badoglio, appointed by the King to be prime minister. As the intelligence folks indicated, they are seeking terms. It took a few hours of conversation to build some confidence that my discussions with him were genuine. He also felt the need to confer with Rome and presumably with Badoglio several times. I remained patient with his sense of necessity. To be blunt, Ike, they want to avoid unconditional surrender, partly to save face, but I think, more importantly, to preclude provoking the Germans any more than required. They are walking a very fine line."

"OK. So what do they propose?"

"They suggest a secret armistice to end Italian belligerence. In exchange, they offer material intelligence on German military dispositions, operating procedures, and associated logistics provisions."

"Allied policy is unconditional surrender."

"They know that in vivid detail. If you will permit me, Ike, I see benefit to a deal with the Italians. Looming large in my thinking is the demands of ROUNDUP and the inevitable drawdown of combat units in Italy to support ROUNDUP. We got the French to join us in TORCH, and I think we are agreed that despite the difficulties of getting the French to be unified, their participation helped us beat the Germans. I think the Italians can help us liberate Italy and tighten the vice on Germany."

"With that assessment, you recommend I favorably endorse the Italian initiative with Washington and London."

Smith stared intently at Eisenhower's unblinking eyes and expressionless face. "Yes. It's worth the risk, as it was for TORCH," Smith stated with solemnity. Eisenhower nodded but did not answer his chief of staff. "Since I've been out of the loop for a few days, how are things on Sicily?"

"Pretty good, actually. The 7th Army is quite channelized, moving down the coast road on the north side of the island—not easy going. The island's terrain is not conducive to the armor operations favored by both Monty and George. The 8ᵗʰ Army is facing stiffer resistance, but they are progressing north toward Messina." Eisenhower stood and went to the window as he often did when he was thinking. Smith did not intrude on his thinking time. Eisenhower turned away from the window but did not move to the chairs. "What's the next step?"

"We both agreed we needed to confer with our respective governments. Thanks to Colonel Eddy, the OSS field agents in Rome will serve as our secure communications conduit until a more substantive link can be established. I expect to hear something from Castellano over the weekend, and if this proceeds, we'll probably meet again next week."

"OK. That gives us a few days to coordinate with Washington and London. Put together a summary message of your talks with Castellano along with your recommendations, and then, let's talk before we send it. I'm inclined to agree with you—the benefits appear to outweigh the risks. We may have a more receptive attitude than we think. I was working on something last night, noticed the time and had the duty comm guys dial up the radio. The president gave another Fireside Chat last night. Well, it was early this morning here."

"Yeah, I guess, two o'clock in the morning, as I recall."

"It was dark outside."

"Indeed."

"If my notes are correct, the president told the world, 'The first crack in the Axis has come. The criminal, corrupt fascist regime in Italy is going to pieces.' For some odd reason, I thought we all agreed to keep any contact secret."

"So much for secrecy."

"Guess it doesn't apply to presidents." They both laughed. "Regardless, I do believe the president is a bit premature."

"Yeah, I'd say. We don't even have the framework of an agreement."

"True, but I interpret the president's words as he is predisposed at least, unless they have information we don't. Anyway, let's get the message prepared so that we can take the first formal step."

"You've got it, Chief. I'll get right on it."

The beginning of the end, at least in part, had finally arrived. Now, they simply had to ascertain how to exploit this change in condition.

—

Chapter 9

He had decided to live forever or
die in the attempt,
and his one mission each time he went up
was to come down alive.
-- Joseph Heller, *Catch-22*

Sunday, 1.August.1943
Ploesti Oil Refinery Complex
Ploesti, Prahova
German Occupied Romania

Operation TIDAL WAVE grew from earlier general plans once the planning transitioned to the detailed phase in preparation for execution. Their target for the mission was the nine oil refineries in a complex around Ploesti, Romania, which were estimated to produce one-third of all oil-based products for the German war machine. The planners used the experience of a pioneering bombing raid conducted by the Halverson Project (HalPro) on 12.June.1942. They modified their aircraft to incorporate a bomb bay auxiliary fuel tank, raising the aircraft fuel capacity to 3,100 gallons of aviation-grade gasoline (AvGas). The aircrews conducted sand table studies and several dress rehearsals in the month before the mission, a 2,400-mile round trip against a heavily defended target.

The plan called for the 2nd Bombardment Wing (2BW) to takeoff from Benghazi, fly north to the Greek island of Corfu in the Adriatic Sea near Greece and Albania's border. The wing would turn northeast to their target until they reached their initial point. They would have to climb over the 9,000-foot Pindus Mountains. Clear of the mountains, the massive bombers would descend to treetop height to approach the targets to avoid enemy anti-aircraft radar and minimize their exposure to an array of anti-aircraft guns. They planned to execute a right hook at the initial point east of Ploesti to attack from the north. The mission plan also called for strict radio silence to preclude detection by the Germans.

Early in the morning, the 2nd Bombardment Wing's five bombardment groups, involving 177 of the planned 178 modified B-24D Liberator heavy bombers, launched from airfields around Benghazi. One aircraft crashed on takeoff. The difficulties of executing the plan affected the 2BW from the get-go. Many fully loaded heavy bombers took off in short order kicking up voluminous dust clouds that sandblasted following aircraft. The aircraft carrying the lead navigator dropped out of formation and crashed into the sea for unknown reasons. The directed radio silence made the adjustments confusing and challenging to achieve. Clouds over the mountains disrupted the formations and altered the timing of the various Groups, but they pressed on with the attack. The German and Romanian air defenses worked them over without mercy.

Historians argue the mission was a failure, not worth the cost, since despite suffering severe damage to cracking towers, collecting and storage tanks, and the interconnecting pipelines, the Germans and Romanians had the refineries back up to full production within weeks of the attack. The disruption of fuel supplies affected German combat operations, but the disturbance was temporary. The cost versus benefit was undoubtedly debatable. Of the 177 aircraft that successfully launched on the Ploesti raid, 162 made it to the target and delivered their bombs. Only 88 bombers returned to Benghazi; 53 aircraft were shot down; of the airplanes that did return, 55 were seriously damaged, some beyond repair. A total of 1,751 men took to the air that morning; 310 were killed, and 190 were captured or interned. What cannot be debated or denied is the extraordinary heroism, courage, ingenuity, perseverance, and commitment by the aircrews to their mission.

Five pilots were awarded the Medal of Honor for their conspicuous gallantry and intrepidity during the mission—more than any other single mission in history. They were: Colonel Leon William Johnson USAAF [USMA 1926]; Colonel John Riley Kane, USAAF; Lieutenant Colonel Addison Earl Baker, USAAF; Major John Louis Jerstad, USAAF; and Second Lieutenant Lloyd Herbert Hughes, USAAF. The last three pilots were awarded the Medal of Honor posthumously. In addition, members of the 2BW on the Ploesti Raid were awarded 16 Distinguished Service Crosses, 10 Silver Stars, 841 Distinguished Flying Crosses, and one Soldiers Medal, along with the Distinguished Unit Citation (DUC) for the entire mission.

—

Tuesday, 3.August.1943
15th Evacuation Hospital
Gela, Caltanissetta, Sicily
Occupied Italy
10:25 hours

Lieutenant General Patton decided to show the stars in person for the wounded soldiers at various medical support units. He dressed in the field uniform he had become known for and recognized by for several years now—riding boots and britches, dual pistols holstered on his hips, long-sleeve khaki shirt with field scarf, and a strapless helmet with three bright silver stars. His field scarf was cinched up properly and tucked into his shirt. He wore three stars on his collar points and only one row of ribbons of his many awarded medals above the left breast pocket—Distinguished Service Cross, Distinguished Service Medal, and Silver Star with Oak Leaf Cluster. The general carried leather gloves in his left hand, even though it was summertime and not needed for warmth.

The troops at this hospital had been seriously wounded, made it through two or more medical evacuation stages, and reach the final in-theater evacuation point. They were awaiting their boarding orders for a medical evacuation ship back to the United States.

General Patton talked to each conscious soldier and prayed on one knee beside the cots with unconscious soldiers. He pinned a Purple Heart on each wounded man—conscious or not. The general knelt and silently said a prayer for the comatose warriors struggling to survive their severe wounds.

Then, Patton came to Private Charles Herman Kuhl, 18 years old, assigned to 'L' Company, 26th Infantry Regiment, 1st Infantry Division, sitting on a stool at the far end of the field tent infirmary.

General Patton was not satisfied with the diagnosis of "battlefield fatigue" and slapped Kuhl several times with his gloves. In a loud, growling voice, he ordered Kuhl out of the tent and out of the presence of wounded soldiers, and then he ordered the doctors to send the man back to the front immediately. The incident shocked those who witnessed the event.

—

Friday, 6.August.1943
Euston Station
Camden, London, England
United Kingdom
00:20 hours

The train's departure just after midnight would place Churchill and his entourage in Glasgow at midday and Greenock at mid-afternoon for an evening set sail time for the Atlantic transit. The object of this trip was the QUADRANT Conference in Québec City, Canada. The train would take them north to Greenock, Scotland, where they would board the RMS *Queen Mary* for the crossing of the North Atlantic to Halifax, Nova Scotia. The last leg of the journey by train from Halifax to Québec City would take 18 hours. Churchill had decided on an unusually large, 250-person entourage since the agenda called for a wide variety of topics ranging from agriculture and banking to logistics, manufacturing, and of course, military affairs. For this conference, Prime Minister Churchill decided to take Clementine and their youngest daughter, 20-year-old Mary. They boarded the prime minister's railcar.

Churchill looked at his private secretary for this journey, John Martin. "Please let me know as soon as everyone is on board, and we are ready to depart."

"I'm tired, Papa," Mary said. "I'm going to bed." She gave her father and mother a hug and kiss on the cheek. She had a separate compartment.

"I think I'l do the same, Winnie." As was their traditional practice, wife and husband utilized separate bedrooms, or in this case, separate compartments.

Winston kissed Clementine and watched her depart the lounge compartment. He turned to the liquor cabinet and poured himself a nice, healthy quantity of Hine Cognac and sat in one of the plush leather chairs to consider his thoughts about what lay ahead in Québec.

The train gently jolted into movement before Martin returned. "The train is loaded," Martin said.

"So I gathered since we're moving. Would you care for a brandy?"

"If you'll permit me, Prime Minister, I'd prefer to retire for what is left of the night."

"Sure, sure, certainly. I'll see you in the morning, John. Good night."

Churchill was left to himself and his thoughts. The night rail journey to Glasgow would take the planned 12 hours to complete before they took a local train to Greenock, and then they would board a launch to the ship at anchor.

———

Friday, 6.August.1943
RMS Queen Mary
55° 58' 22" North – 4° 44' 49" West
River Clyde Anchorage
Greenock, Renfrewshire, Scotland
United Kingdom
17:30 hours

Winston stood with Clementine and Mary on the Sun Deck as they enjoyed the magnificent Scottish terrain passing to the ship's stern.

"So I don't forget, please allow me to remind both of you that we must remain in the first-class area of the ship. The ship is carrying several thousand prisoners of war being transferred from Britain to Canada and America. We do not need to tempt any of them."

"How do we know where they are?" Clemmie asked.

"There are signs and a guard posted at each boundary hatchway. Do not go beyond that point for any reason without an escort."

Mary nodded her head, but her attention was beyond the ship. "It is such beautiful countryside."

"It certainly is, darling," Clementine added.

The prime minister remained present, but barely so. He had seen the terrain more than a few times, and his pending initial review of the newly renamed Operation OVERLORD plan occupied his thoughts. This was Mary's first transit out of the Clyde Estuary, and the sights captivated her.

"I think it's time to make our way to the dining room," announced Clementine.

"I'm not too keen on this early evening meal schedule," Winston added, "but rules are rules."

The family enjoyed and did not rush a delightful meal. The Churchill's returned to their cabin. Winston poured a modest Drambuie liqueur each for Clementine and Mary, and cognac for himself.

"We will most assuredly eat well on this voyage," Mary noted with a touch of humor.

"I suspect you are correct."

"Thank you, Papa, for allowing me to come with you on this trip."

"It is our pleasure to have you with us, dear one," her father said.

Mary went to the cabin's right porthole. Out of curiosity, Clementine and then Winston joined their daughter at the left porthole. "What do you see that is so interesting, Mary?" Winston asked.

"The water, the trees, the mountains. I see this scenery, and I can forget the war. This is peace and tranquility. I am so grateful this part of our country has not been touched by war. Beautiful, simply beautiful."

"It is that," Winston responded.

"Did you say you had an appointment this evening," Clementine whispered to her husband as they both continued to enjoy the scenery with Mary.

"Yes, Clemmie. I'm afraid it is so. But I want to enjoy our *digestif* before I must go."

Neither of the women acknowledged the subtle maneuvering of the great ship now that they were nearing the open sea. Winston saw no reason to inform them of the anti-submarine procedures. Without taking her gaze off the passing scenery of the Isle of Arran outside the stateroom porthole, Mary asked, "What should I expect with this conference, Papa?"

"Very good question, my dear. The agenda calls for several general sessions that you should be able to listen to if you wish. Of course, others will be rightfully closed. We're expected at Springwood, President Roosevelt's country estate in Hyde Park, New York, for a few days before the conference begins. You will get to meet the president and possibly his wife, Eleanor. There are plenty of things to see and do in Québec City. I am certain Prime Minister King will have escorts and tour guides for you to learn about and see the historic and important part of Canada. After the conference, we have planned a little holiday adventure for a few days in the mountains. My friend, Colonel Frank Clarke, will escort us to his mountain retreat known as *La Cabane de Montmorency* on the Montmorency River in the Laurentian Mountains. It is roughly four thousand feet above sea level, they tell me, so that it will be cooler than at sea level."

"It sounds exciting, doesn't it, Mummy."

"Yes, dear, it does," Clementine responded. "It will be a welcome relief for your father and quite distant from the war," she paused for several seconds and then mumbled, "at least for a few days."

Winston went to the bar and refilled his glass. He sat in a nice, overstuffed chair, watched the ladies who continued their absorption of the passing scenery and enjoyed this cognac. A knock at the door commanded his attention.

"Excuse me, Prime Minister," said John Martin. "Mister Eden asked me to convey a message, and it is nearly time for your meeting with General Morgan."

"Would you care to come in for a cognac?"

"No, thank you, Sir. I'd prefer you step out into the passageway."

Clementine was looking at him, but Mary was not. Winston held up one finger. He closed the door behind him.

"Mister Eden asked me to inform you that our embassy in Tangiers was contacted by the Italian assistant commercial attaché requesting peace terms."

"Well, well, they are casting the net wider." Churchill had participated in numerous meetings, secure telephone calls, and classified message exchanges since the initial contact with Colonel Eddy. Two of those SIGSALY telephone calls were with President Roosevelt privately. An initial draft of an armistice agreement was generated by General Eisenhower and circulated in London and Washington. While the agreement was not finalized, it had come together nicely. Only a few members of the War Cabinet, selected members of the American Cabinet, and the combined joint chiefs of staff knew the details of the discussions with the Italians. "Please ask Eden to inform the War Cabinet and Secretary Hull of this additional contact. The diplomats need to carefully sort out how this contact fits. Eden will know what that means. If he would like further discussion, I can meet with him after I meet with Morgan."

"Very well, Sir." Martin left to carry out his instructions.

Winston returned to the stateroom and bade the ladies goodnight. They would probably be fast asleep by the time he retired for the evening. Clementine came to him and kissed her husband goodnight. Mary remained focused on the retreating and darkening scenery.

—

Saturday, 7.August.1943
Standing Oak Farm
Winchester, Hampshire, England
United Kingdom
13:30 hours

Brian was the last to arrive. For unknown reasons, he had not been released for his scheduled and approved leave until mid-morning, causing him to miss the first of a series of trains across London to Winchester.

Charlotte stood with Ian, who was doing surprisingly well standing for a 26-month-old toddler. Linda and Jonathan stood outside as well as beside Charlotte, almost like a receiving line.

"I'm so sorry I'm late," Brian said as he exited the taxi. "I'd planned to be here to welcome you to the farm."

"Charlotte did quite an admirable job of that," Jonathan proclaimed.

Brian knelt to accept a hug and kiss from their son. He then hugged and kissed his wife before he did the same with Linda, although in a less familiar or intimate manner, and then he embraced his brother-in-arms. "Welcome to Standing Oak Farm," Brian announced in a bold and commanding voice.

"This is such a beautiful place," Linda observed.

"My thoughts precisely," Brian added with a smile, "ever since our hero pulled my sorry arse," he said, using the British word and pronunciation, "out of the pond," gesturing over his shoulder, "I've been infatuated with this enchanted place situated perfectly in the countryside of Hampshire." They all laughed at Brian's attempt at a British dialect, including Brian. "Will y'all be able to spend the weekend with us?" he asked, returning to his American accent.

"That is the plan, mate," Jonathan answered.

"I'm sorry, darling," Charlotte said, "but we went ahead with lunch without you. Are you hungry?"

"No, not necessary, I'm not starving. I was the one who was late, so I can wait for the evening meal. Charlotte and I had talked about a horseback tour of our property. The horses are not exactly riding ponies, but they are most agreeable horses."

Knowing the plan given to them, the crew had all four horses saddled. Edith took Ian. The two couples mounted up and headed out at a comfortable and sustainable saunter. Charlotte insisted upon showing Linda the remnants of Brian's Spitfire fighter in the north field from that incredible day at the end of July 1940. The RAF had stripped the shredded remnants of the aircraft of any surviving usable parts years ago and offered to remove the remaining wreckage, but Charlotte declined, choosing to leave the twisted and burnt aluminum as a makeshift monument. They also traversed the Harris and Brownfield additions. By the time they made it back to the house, it was afternoon milking time. Jacob tended the horses. Horace and Lionel tended to the milking machines, while Charlotte and Brian taught Linda and Jonathan the process of hand milking the cows. Neither of the Kensington's had milked a cow, so the teaching was filled with humor and joy.

With the evening milking complete, Lionel, Horace, and Jacob processed the afternoon's milk yield. Charlotte and Linda joined Edith and Mabel in completing the evening meal. Jonathan and Brian stood on the front porch.

"I knew you were divinely protected," Jonathan said. Brian shrugged and looked confused. "There is no possible way you should have survived the break-up of your Spit in the first place and especially landing in the pond unconscious, set aside the opening of your parachute in the process."

"Well, there is that."

"And then, to be rescued by a gorgeous woman."

"Yes, I have been blessed for some reason. I do not question it. I just accept it, and I show my gratitude at every opportunity."

"You have always been lucky."

"Better lucky than good." Both pilots laughed. "There is so much of that day, that moment, that I still don't understand, but I have learned to accept the facts as they have been recounted for me. But Charlotte means so much more to me."

"Neither of us needs any distractions in our line of work."

"Do you feel Linda is a distraction?"

Jonathan did not answer, as he was considering the question and whether or how to respond. "Sometimes. Yes."

"How so?"

"It's not so much anything she does or doesn't do. It is more what I do to myself. I find myself thinking of her, especially during long-range escort missions."

"Not good, my friend, but I must confess, you are not alone. It sounds like Allied Forces are making good progress on Sicily," Brian said, changing the subject.

"So the press reports tell us."

Charlotte opened the front door. "Dinner is ready, boys. Call the men."

"Yes, dear."

Brian and Jonathan helped the men finish. They would deliver the load after dinner. The crew cleaned up the barn, cleaned themselves, and headed to the house. They had a simple but delicious meal, and everyone made their guests feel they were part of the crew. The laughter was good for all of them.

The evening meal took a little longer than usual, but it had to come to an end. Horace, Lionel, and Jacob excused themselves to make the evening's deliveries and headed home. Edith and Mabel tended the dishes while the Kensingtons and Drummonds entertained the toddlers. As the boys began to wear themselves out at a little past bedtime, everyone said their goodnights.

"It's a nice summer evening," observed Linda. "Would anyone be interested in a modest fire, more for light than warmth, at the oak tree I've heard so much about?"

"Works for me," Charlotte responded.

The four of them strolled down the gravel pathway. Brian made quick work on a small fire in the pit. The bench proved large enough for all four of them, although they were shoulder to shoulder, not tight but touching. Brian and Jonathan sat at each end of the bench.

"We have an announcement," Linda said. "Your invitation for this weekend visit came at a fortuitous time." No one spoke, not wanting to interrupt Linda's train of thought. "Jonathan and I," she said, grasping her husband's hand, "are pregnant." The congratulatory words and hugs gushed out among the four of them. "I missed my cycle three weeks ago, and the rabbit died three days ago. With invitation in hand, we decided that you would be the first to know."

"Thank you for the honor, Linda," offered Charlotte. "With the absence of our men, the day of conception should be easily marked."

Linda and Charlotte laughed. Jonathan and Brian did not. "You are quite correct—easily," Linda responded. "That day is the 28th of April. Jonathan had one day off, which was the first I'd seen him in nearly three months. The baby is due around the 26th of January."

"That is so exciting." Brian put another couple of small logs on the fire. "Can I change the subject?" asked Charlotte.

"Sure. Of course," Linda said.

"Brian tells me you knew Anne Booth and Virginia North."

Jeremy Morrison had engaged Anne and Virginia while Brian was in training before the war began. Anne and Brian maintained a relationship until the two women were arrested and executed for espionage.

"Yes, I did," Linda responded. "Anne and I had been friends since our early school days."

"Can you tell me a little about them? I've met all of his lovers," Charlotte said, leaning forward and looking at Jonathan, "including your sister. But I never had the opportunity to meet Miss Booth."

"Whoa! You have met his lovers," Linda said, as she leaned forward to connect with Brian's eyes.

"Surely, my sex life is not a worthy topic," protested Brian.

"Sounds exciting to me," Jonathan added.

The ladies laughed. "She was a good woman, Charlotte. I don't know how she got mixed up with the Germans, but that is what led to her demise."

"She was hanged?"

"Yes, both Anne and Virginia were executed for espionage and treason. I never got to talk to her about whatever it was that got her in trouble. It is so hard for me to imagine. I never saw a hint of dissatisfaction or disloyalty in her—not ever."

"She was a prostitute?"

"Yes, as was Virginia. They were both proud and unashamed of their profession. She liked to refer to herself as a courtesan, but a prostitute nonetheless, high end or not."

Charlotte looked at Brian. "And it was Jeremy Morrison who introduced you?"

"Yes, although introduced is a rather loose term. He had arranged a blind date meeting. It was not until later that I learned she was a professional woman."

"She loved the business," Linda added. "She always told me the good far outweighed the bad."

"Did you ever consider joining them?" Jonathan perked up at Charlotte's question.

"Sure. They both seemed very happy, and they made very good wages, and even better when you consider they were getting paid handsomely for enjoying pleasure. But I could never bring myself to do it. Just my friendship with them brought me the intensity of police questioning just because of my friendship and association with Anne and Virginia."

"That couldn't have been pleasant."

"No, it wasn't. I resented those interrogation episodes, but Jonathan helped me understand and to place them in perspective. Why do you ask about Anne?"

"Just curious. Every single one of Brian's female friends has impressed me. Incredible women. Anne was the only one I did not know about in life."

"I think you would've liked her, Charlotte. Everybody liked her, which is probably one of the reasons she was so successful as a courtesan."

"I'm sure I would have as well. It also makes me more curious about how she got in so much trouble that it claimed her life."

"We probably won't know what that was until well after the war when those documents are declassified," Jonathan interjected.

"It was Lord Morrison, who introduced Jonathan and me."

"Small world."

"Indeed."

They turned to discussions of the farm and even the Drummond's airline, which fascinated Jonathan more than Linda. They talked for another hour until the fire was rendered to glowing coals. When they decided to call it a night, Brian poured a small pail of water on the coals to extinguish them.

Both couples retired to their respective bedrooms for the night.

—

Saturday, 7.August.1943
RMS Queen Mary
55° 23' North -- 16° 15' West
At sea
21:45 hours

Winston went to Captain Pim's Map Room for a 22:00 scheduled private meeting with General Morgan. For this discussion, only the two men were present.

"Good evening, Prime Minister."

"And a very good evening to you, General Morgan." As the prime minister sat at the head of the small rectangular table, he said, "Let's see what you've got so far."

Morgan stood at the opposite end of the table in front of a large English Channel map. "First, I'm not sure if you are aware, but the combined joint chiefs of staff have opened a new classified compartment for the current planning. Henceforth, our planning will be classified TOP SECRET – BIGOT, Sensitive Compartmented Information. As you and President Roosevelt agreed last week, the new title for our work is Operation OVERLORD. We have made all of the appropriate adjustments. General Eisenhower controls the access list."

"Presumably, both the president and I are on the access list."

Morgan chuckled nervously. "Yes, of course, Sir. That is how I am here."

"I didn't know about the new compartment, but I do now. Proceed."

"This is a BIGOT briefing in its entirety." Churchill nodded. "First," Morgan continued, "we have set aside planning for this year. The earliest weather window is in early May next year, so we start there. Second, we have examined the astronomical tables for the sun, moon, tide, and average weather conditions. Third, we surveyed the potential landing beaches for six initial simultaneous divisions in the first phase, with a total of 20 divisions, five armored and 15 infantry, by D+30. Fourth, we need a beach gradient sufficient to deploy the Mulberry harbors within a mile of the mean high tide line. Fifth, and perhaps the hardest constraint, we have to run a series of tabletop simulations of German deployments to yield a three-to-one Allied advantage at D+1, D+10, and D+30.

In essence, we must be able to land and deploy combat units faster than the enemy can redeploy their units."

"Most of that sounds familiar."

Morgan nodded his head. "None of the potential Atlantic beaches gave us the surf requirements until into July, and as you can imagine, the local surf experienced depends upon storms in the North Atlantic, which we cannot predict except statistically and thus does not give us sufficient confidence. We considered four remaining sites for the landings: Brittany, Cotentin, Normandy, and the Pas de Calais. We disqualified beaches within 30 miles either side of Calais since that is the object of our deception campaign and plays to the Germans' predisposition. The preponderance of enemy forces are garrisoned in Northeast France. Brittany and Cotentin are both peninsulas, and as such, they are susceptible to channelization and minority force blockage. The Germans would be able to use an inferior force to bottle up our invasion force, so those sites were rejected."

"What about Dieppe?" the prime minister asked.

"It passes on several of the requirements but fails on the beach gradient factor, which we would have difficulty with sustainment of the invasion. The beaches in and around Dieppe were disqualified for that reason." Morgan paused in case the prime minister had any follow-up questions. None came. "We have created the skeletal plan for the air campaign, special operations work, the naval blockade of the Channel, and of course the all-important logistics plan. We have created scalable algorithms to help us 'see,'" he said with air quotes, "the logistics demand should we need more assault divisions as well as slower or faster deployment of follow-on forces based on combat type, in other words, infantry, armor, engineer, air defense, and whatnot."

"Excellent. That brings me back to that first impression." Morgan displayed a puzzled expression. "As I recall, you mentioned six combat divisions in the initial assault."

"Correct, sir."

Churchill lapsed into thought for several seconds, and Morgan did not twitch or interrupt. "I cannot see how that number could possibly be enough. That force would be far too small to deal with the so-called Atlantic Wall's coastal defenses and the inevitable counterattack by experienced, combat-hardened German front line troops. There are at least two fully configured and manned *Waffen-SS Panzer* divisions in Northern France. They have proven themselves to be quite fanatical in Russia. They will be the same here. We need perhaps double the number of the initial assault divisions not just to break the counterattacks but also to advance into offensive operations to liberate France and head to Berlin."

Morgan cleared his throat. "The difficulty we face is available shipping to move a force that size. At least at the moment, the constraint is not the actual transport ships but the landing craft to put our forces across the surf and beach lines. We simply do not have and are not projected to have the number of landing craft necessary for a larger assault force."

"Then we must build more." Morgan smiled nervously as if he was not quite sure how to confront the prime minister with reality. Churchill did not ignore the general's unease. "You are telling me our power projection capacity is controlled by amphibious landing craft."

"Yes sir. That is precisely the point. And further, we are going to be hard-pressed to keep them all operating for such a sustained time for meeting the follow-on deployment objectives."

"Have you discussed all this with the chiefs? Oh wait! Of course, you have. We have a few days at sea before we arrive in Québec. I want to explore this some more with the chiefs."

"Yes sir. We are at your service."

Churchill waved his left hand dismissively as if swatting a fly. "Have you considered the transfer of landing craft from the Mediterranean and perhaps from the Pacific Theater?"

"Yes sir. A majority but not all from the Mediterranean." Churchill shook his head vigorously and clearly in disagreement. "To my knowledge, no demands have been made for the redeployment of American resources in the Pacific region. Further, we are also using the best production yields from the Americans, and they could fail to meet that rate."

"That was my next question. Well, this will simply not do. We, none of us, can afford to get bogged down on the beaches by having insufficient forces to break through the defenses and inevitable counterattacks. We must have a stronger force. If we need more landing craft, then so be it. We must find more." Churchill stared past Morgan at the map. Morgan waited for a reaction. "How soon can we have the Mulberry Harbors in place to preclude the need for landing craft?"

"So much depends upon sufficient beachhead to protect the installation and operation."

"Yes, yes," the prime minister said impatiently, "but when?"

"Our current operating estimate is D+20."

"Not acceptable. We must do better. We will examine the details of the harbor plan as well. If we can get the Mulberry Harbors operating sooner, we can relieve the pressure on the landing craft capacity."

"We are prepared to discuss it all, Prime Minister."

"Yes, yes, you certainly are. My apologies if you felt under my barrage, General Morgan. I recognize you are developing a plan with the resources and constraints you are given. However, that is also the point of planning, to identify our choke points so that we can mitigate those risks." Morgan nodded his head. "I think we are done for this evening. I have much to consider and contemplate. I want to discuss the OVERLORD plan with the chiefs tomorrow before lunch. Please see to it."

"Yes sir. I will coordinate with Mister Martin for the time."

"Thank you for your time and expertise, General. I know this is not easy, but it is a vital process."

They secured the room and returned to their staterooms for what was left of the night.

—

Tuesday, 10.August.1943
93rd Evacuation Hospital
Santo Stefano di Camastra, Messina, Sicily
Occupied Italy
10:25 hours

General Patton's slapping incident of August 3rd at the 15th Evacuation Hospital repeated a week later. There were fewer differences than there were similarities between the two incidents. The second event's object was a different soldier, Private Paul Grady Bennett, 21, of C Battery, 17th Field Artillery Regiment, 1st Infantry Division, who was diagnosed with "shell shock." Again, General Patton slapped the soldier with his gloves, growled that he was a coward, and reached for the Peacemaker revolver holstered on his right hip, threatening to execute the soldier himself for cowardice in the face of the enemy. His aide-de-camp restrained him, and Patton yelled his orders for the soldier to be immediately removed from the tent and sent back to the front, as his aide guided the general out of the tent.

A week apart, the two incidents occurred decades before the military and medical professions understood Post Traumatic Stress Disorder (PTSD). Also reflecting upon the state of knowledge at the time, the Veterans Administration issued a memorandum dated 26.July.1943, requesting approval to perform a prefrontal lobotomy treatment for veteran PTSD patients. Permission was eventually granted. VA doctors performed extraordinarily invasive frontal lobotomies from 1.April.1947 to 30.September.1950, on more than 1,464 veterans at 50 hospitals in their contemporary attempt to treat what eventually became known as Post Traumatic Stress Disorder.

Many people who served underarms, especially in times of war, see the Patton slapping incidents in a far different light. War is killing. Killing is never easy for the vast majority of human beings. War is hell on earth, as General Sherman so succinctly and directly proclaimed. More than a few believed General Patton was correct and his actions appropriately complemented the sacrifices of so many soldiers.

—

Tuesday, 17.August.1943
USAAF Station 356
Saffron Walden, Essex, England
United Kingdom

The squadron had partially briefed the complex mission yesterday evening, since the plan called for an early pre-dawn final detailed mission briefing. They had only been informed the mission was a long-range bomber escort task and would require an early morning briefing. The raid had originally been planned for the 7th of August but had to be postponed several times due to inadequate weather. After the evening briefing, the pilots were confined to base and urged to get a good night's sleep. Tomorrow was going to be a long hard day.

When the pilots departed their quarters before dawn, dense fog blanketed the base—not a good sign. All three squadrons of the 4th Fighter Group had breakfast and completed the detailed mission briefing together.

Commanding Officer, 4th Fighter Group (4FG), Colonel Edward Wharton 'Trunk' Anderson, USAAF, briefed the Group as a whole and would lead the Group as a unit for this mission. The Group pilots learned together that the mission was the first major daylight bombing raid under Operation POINTBLANK and the 84th mission of the Army Air Forces 8th Air Force. The 1st Bombardment Wing with 12 groups totaling 230 B-17 heavy bombers would attack several precious ball-bearing plants in Schweinfurt, Germany, and return to their bases in England. The 4th Bombardment Wing, with seven groups totaling 146 B-17 aircraft, was assigned to bomb the Messerschmitt fighter production complex at Regensburg, Germany, and recover at Allied bases in North Africa.

The 4th Bomb Wing had the farthest distance to go and thus the tightest time window to make their landing bases before dusk. The 4th Wing would launch first. The 1st Wing would launch two and a half hours later in a planned effort to catch German fighter aircraft on the ground refueling and rearming after engaging the 4th Wing. The scheduled launch time for the 1st Wing was 08:00.

The entire 4th Fighter Group, including Brian's 334th Fighter Squadron, was one of four fighter groups—two RAF groups and two AAF groups—

assigned to cover the mission's penetration segment. The 4th Group segment assignment was to escort the 1st Bombardment Wing from the coastline across Belgium to Eupen, near the border with Germany—the farthest extent of fighter coverage. When the Group reached their bingo fuel quantity, they would return to base, refuel and rearm, and get back up to pick up the bomb wing on the way home. Since they were the farthest out, they would cover the closest, last leg from the Belgian coast to England. The bomber formation would have another 45 minutes of unescorted transit to reach their assigned target and then 45 more long minutes to reach their fighter escort cover at the German border.

The fighter pilots had remained unusually quiet and somber when they recognized what the bombers were going to be dealing with beyond the range of the protective coverage of their fighters. Each of them felt a responsibility, although it was beyond their capacity to help.

Colonel Curtis Emerson LeMay, USAAF, leading the 4th Wing, was mindful of his Wing's tight mission timing. Despite the fog, LeMay decided to take the risk and launch, an hour late to plan but still within the time window for the mission.

Brigadier General Robert Boyd 'Bob' Williams, USAAF, led the 1st Bombardment Wing and proved more cautious given the low visibility. He was concerned about being able to recover abort aircraft in the low visibility conditions. The fog began to lift in late morning and became a low overcast sufficient for an airplane that had to turn back shortly after takeoff to land safely. Satisfied they had adequate conditions, he ordered the launch. The first bombers of the 1st Wing rolled down the runways at 11:18, three-plus hours late to plan. The mission plan had already become disconnected by the weather and the 4th Wing's tardy take-off—the consequences would be felt all too soon.

11:25 hours

Pete gathered up the pilots. "OK, gentlemen. It's show time. The First Wing has begun launching the bombers. We'll throttle up in 20 minutes. Let's mount up."

The pilots collected the last bits of their flight equipment and headed to the aircraft. They had plenty of time.

Larson Tomlinson stood at the aft root of the left wing as Brian rounded the tail. "So, they're going to launch you guys in this soup," he observed.

"Yep. These machines fly just fine in clouds. Can't do much, but they fly."

"Bird's ready, Captain. I checked her really well . . . a couple of times. I've got every drop of fuel I can get in the tanks."

"Thanks, Larson."

"So much so, the bird's been pissing fuel as it warms and expands."

"We're going to launch in a few minutes, so it should be fine."

Brian climbed up and jumped into the cockpit. Tomlinson followed up on the left wing to assist with connections and strapping into his parachute and seat. When he was ready, he gave Tomlinson a thumb's up. Larson jumped down off the wing and ran around the left wing to grab the fire extinguisher and be prepared for start.

Brian waited patiently for several minutes for the squadron start signal. When it came, Brian stepped through his start and pre-takeoff checks. They taxied out, completed their run-up checks, and took to the runway.

11:45 hours

The 334th Fighter Squadron P-47 Thunderbolts took off in sections. They initiated a wide climbing turn that they would maintain for the cloud penetration until they broke out on top of the overcast. As soon as the Group joined up, they turned to take a beeline to their rendezvous point.

On a clear day, they would have expected to see the condensation trails from the engine exhausts of the bomber and fighter formation. The mission briefing called for the bombers to be stacked from 23,000 to 26,500 feet. The 48 Thunderbolts of the 4th Group were passing 15,000 feet. Another cloud layer appeared as a solid overcast at something like 20,000 feet. *This is not going to be good*, Brian thought. The mission plan continued to be disrupted. Nothing seemed to be going according to plan. They leveled off at 18,000 feet below the cloud deck. While they were still in pursuit, Anderson sent his second section up to check the layer's depth and see if the bombers might be above the layer. The cloud layer began to break up below them while they were over the North Sea. The scout section returned a few minutes later, and apparently, hand signaled Anderson that there was nothing above the cloud layer. They stayed below the clouds. As they approached the Belgian coastline, dark lines ahead of them resolved into the rear bombers of the 1st Wing. Nearly 100 Spitfires of 11 and 83 Groups passed them in the opposite direction, having been relieved of the bomber escort duty by the 78th Fighter Group. They had several miles to close and take up their escort position.

The radio chatter told them the escort fighters were already engaged in opposing enemy fighters. Anderson broadcast the approach of the 4th Group. "Horn, Upper, we're closing at six."

"Roger, Upper . . ." Everyone heard the distinct staccato of his guns firing. "Sorry Upper, *Le Boche* are being a bit feisty today. We've got them occupied. Take the high cover."

"Wilco, Horn."

The clouds above them were thinning and breaking up. The massive formation of 230 B-17 bombers remained at 17,000 feet. As they had briefed, Anderson and his division along with the 336th Squadron, callsign Shirtblue, would take the center position above the lead section of bombers. They began broad 'S' turns to maintain their speed differential and position over the bombers. The 335th Squadron, callsign Greenbelt, took the right flank, and the 334th took the left flank. German flak shells sporadically burst among the bombers but did not appear to affect their progress. Brian's head and eyes remained in constant motion scanning the scene around them along with glances at his instrument panel. The engine's robust roar and vibration told him what he needed to know about his steed.

The 78FG remained engaged, dealing with what looked like four Bf109 squadrons. The various furballs gradually drifted behind the advancing bombers, which made Brian even more alert and apprehensive. *Something is going to pop. I can feel it.* Brian noticed elements of 78FG rose up and reconstituted their units at the rear of the formation. Then, their call came.

"Bandits, two o'clock, two fingers below the horizon."

"Greenbelt, Upper, take 'em. Shirtblue, shift right."

The 16 Jugs of 335FS rolled to engage what looked like a squadron of Fw190 fighters closing fast. The 336FS drifted to the right to cover the right flank just in case other Germans appeared. It also meant they would move forward a little. Brian wanted to watch the right flank engagement, but he was experienced enough to know he could not do so. *They're out there somewhere. I can feel it.* They did not have to wait long. Another squadron of Fw190s appeared from a patch of cumulous clouds below and off to the left from them.

"Bandits, eight o'clock low, just under those clouds," Brian radioed.

"You're closest, Hunter," broadcast Pete. "Take 'em. We'll follow you to engage."

Brian quickly hand signaled he was rolling left. The other seven Thunderbolts of his division followed with Pete's 'A' Division following Brian's flight for a head-on engagement with the climbing 190s. They kept coming, clearly intent upon the engagement. They're probably going to attempt a blow by to get at the bombers. "Make you shots count," commanded Brian. He placed his sight pipper on the closing lead 190. Brian depressed his firing button with all eight Browning M2, 50-caliber, heavy machine guns erupting from both wings. Just a second later, Brian saw the muzzle flashes from the German's guns, but a bevy of bright flashes burst on the German's nose and left wing. He kept adjusting his pipper as they closed. The flashes continued until he saw the left wing move, waver, and an instant later folded up over the canopy causing the German to enter a violent tight spiral. Brian pulled up sharply to avoid the shrapnel he knew was coming directly at him. As soon as he felt he was clear, Brian rolled inverted to witness the melee below him. His wingman and the section were trying to stay with him. The German formation had scattered as their leader's aircraft disintegrated.

As he arced over the scene, aircraft seemed to be everywhere. One Thunderbolt and two 190s were smoking, but they were all still in the fight. Pete's 'A' Division joined the fight. The Germans were at a disadvantage from the outset, but they fought valiantly. Several 190s tried to break for the bombers, but they were immediately engaged. One of the break-a-ways exploded in a huge ball of fire. A large black smoke trail followed the other one with bright flame coming from the engine; he dove sharply to escape.

Picking out a worthy target, Brian pulled his nose down, rolling upright, and adjusted his flight path for a good pursuit intercept. He took a quick scan. *Buddy's in a good position.* He checked his target. He glanced on the other side and saw an Fw190 rolled toward them. Brian quickly evaluated whether he could make a pass on the target he was closing on before the approaching German. *Nope. Not good enough.* Brian rolled sharply and pulled his nose up to oppose the single diving German. Before they closed for even a long-range shot, the German pulled up sharply and rolled right away. Brian tracked him briefly but then looked over both shoulders. The Germans were disengaging.

"Pectin, disengage," commanded Pete.

"Rejoin in position," Trunk radioed.

Brian quickly located the bomber formation above and behind his right wing. He rolled smoothly to a good rendezvous line. He throttled back a little to give his division some power margin for the rejoin. Courtland maintained a good spread position. *Good man.* Red 2 Section was closing from the west. Yellow Flight was farther away to the east, but they had already joined up and held a good pursuit line.

Before 'B' Division completed their rendezvous, they heard, "Bandits, 10 o'clock high."

"Shirtblue, Upper, they're all yours. Pectin, take the high cover."

The 336FS climbed and turned to engage the inbound enemy fighters—a squadron of Bf109s with black noses. Oddly, as soon as the Germans saw a cover squadron closing, the Germans turned to stand off and parallel the bomber formation like a pack of wolves stalking a large flock of sheep. Shirtblue turned to parallel as well, placing them between the Germans and the bomber formation. They climbed to gain a superior position. The Germans did not respond in kind.

They're bait. Brian feverishly scanned above and below the formation, and all around. *They're setting us up for others to get closer with our attention on these guys.* Brian's instincts were electrified and taut. *These guys are biding their time. They've throttled back to match the bombers' speed. They're waiting. These bastards know we can't go much farther.* Brian kept his eyes scanning.

"Shirtblue, Upper, pull it back, take the left flank." A few miles farther on, another Bf109 squadron, this one with green noses, took a position off the right flank of the formation, matching the bombers' speed.

Colonel Anderson must have sensed the same things Brian did. "Upper, these guys are waiting. Greenbelt, engage the bandits to your right. Shirtblue, engage the bandits to your left." The two flank squadrons turned to intercept their assigned targets. No sooner had the intercept line been established, both German squadrons rolled away.

The clouds had broken up to scattered coverage. Ten miles on, Brian saw the city that matched their aerial photographs—Eupen, Belgium. Germany stood on the eastern edge, although there was no line on the ground. Brian watched Trunk's Thunderbolt descend and joining the lead B-17 just forward of the bomber's left wing. *He's probably giving the general a salute.* The extent of their range had been reached.

Anderson pulled up smoothly, gently, and rolled left. "Upper, we are bingo. RTB." All three squadron commanders led their squadrons. They joined up on Trunk's Thunderbolt, heading east-northeast toward England. The entire Group had not yet completed their disengagement, and they saw first one, then two, three, and four German squadrons climbing to a suitable perch position ahead of the bomber formation. The wolves were preparing to feast on the flock. The bombers droned on their penetration route. The sinking, nauseating sensation in Brian's gut was undeniable. He had never felt so helpless. He was sure they all felt the same way. The 1st Bombardment Wing had another 45 minutes under the looming onslaught ahead of them before reaching their targets. The return of the 4th Fighter Group was unopposed and uneventful. Even the overcast that had blanketed Southeast England had broken up. There were still clouds, but geographic navigation was easy.

15:40 hours

The Group landed as they had taken off, landing by sections. They had not lost a single fighter, but they had left their flock to the wolves.

The ground crews swarmed over the fighters to refuel and rearm the aircraft. The pilots debriefed the sortie with the intelligence folks. They all voiced, to a man, the terrible feeling they had as they left the bombers to the German fighters. The P-47s could go farther than the Spitfires, but they could not go far enough. A dozen 4th Fighter Group pilots were given provisional credit for an aerial victory, along with two shared and five probable wins, including Brian's 23rd victory. Considerable bravado accompanied the recognition of Brian's event. A couple of the squadron pilots received shrapnel damage from the German fighter's break-up, but they all sung Brian's praises. As he had done with his other victories, Brian did not participate in the revelry.

The squadron's fighters were all reported ready before they were needed. Several telephone calls to Group eventually established their second sortie launch time.

17:05 hours

The 4FG launched as they had done at noon. They met what was left of the 1st Bombardment Wing near the Belgian coastline. They relieved the RAF No.83 Group Spitfires as the escort. No German fighters appeared. The sight of the Wing was devastating. In addition to being far fewer than they had left at Eupen, a dozen bombers had smoke trails, although thankfully no obvious fires. An uncounted number of bombers had one or more engines shut down, and the propellers feathered as well as chunks and pieces missing—elevators, rudders, ailerons, flaps, and at least one bomber with a red painted tail gunner's station. Many had large holes in their wings, stabilizers, and fuselages. They had taken an incredible pounding that made their sense of guilt all the more intense.

The 4th Fighter Group held their escort positions with solemnity and respect. None of them wanted to repeat Mission 84 ever again.

Unfortunately, history would record their wishes were not fulfilled. The mission plan into Germany's heartland was going to be complicated even before the first engine started. The weather disruption that morning made a difficult plan fearsome. Despite all the deviations from the plan, the 8th Air Force had successfully flown Mission 84. The bomb damage assessment took several days to accomplish. History recorded that the 4th Bombardment Wing hit their target and destroyed the Messerschmitt works, putting a serious dent in German fighter production. The 1st Bombardment Wing had been less successful against a more dispersed set of precision targets and the terrible carnage of their ingress.

Of the total of 376 heavy bombers on the Mission 84 Schweinfurt-Regensburg Raid, 60 B-17s (16%) did not return; 55 lost in combat and 552 airmen were killed, captured, or missing. Most of the surviving 1st Wing aircraft were damaged to various degrees and returned to England with seven more aircrewmen killed and another 21 wounded. The losses were appalling no matter who observed them or from whatever perspective. While the precision of the high-altitude daylight bombing, especially on Regensburg, was impressive, the loss rate was staggering and hardly justifiable as a reasonable cost. The terrible losses that day caused everyone to reconsider whether unescorted daylight bombing without long-range fighter escort was even sustainable. The flak encountered was one thing. The decimation of unopposed enemy fighters was orders of magnitude more punishing. The losses during the Schweinfurt-Regensburg raid led Allied leaders to re-think the feasibility of unescorted, long-range, daylight raids into Germany.

A second raid on Schweinfurt took place on 14.October.1943 with similar results. This type of bombing mission would be temporarily suspended after the second raid on Schweinfurt sustained 20% casualties. All of the national leaders realize such losses were not sustainable, not even for the United States. The national priority for a long-range fighter increased substantially.

—

Tuesday, 17.August.1943
La Citadelle de Québec
1 Côte de la Citadelle
Ville de Québec, Québec
Dominion of Canada
15:20 hours

Prime Minister William Lyon Mackenzie King, CMG, PC, had been prime minister of Canada almost as long as Roosevelt had been president of the United States. He preferred being called Mackenzie for informal conversations. King stood behind two sturdy, oak armchairs, dressed in a medium gray business suit with a light blue necktie. Churchill walked beside Roosevelt in his usual traveling wheelchair as Harry Hopkins pushed the president. "Welcome to Canada and the QUADRANT Conference, Mister President, Prime Minister," he announced with a strong voice and an extended right hand. King looked at Hopkins and gestured to the gap between the two chairs after shaking hands and giving the usual cordialities. Harry rolled the president's chair between the two armchairs and locked the wheel to keep the chair from rolling on the old citadel's slightly sloped stone rampart deck. King gestured for Churchill to take the chair to Roosevelt's right. He took the left chair. The three leaders were left alone.

"I thought we could enjoy this delightful, warm, summer day and the view before we begin our more serious discussions. This location in the grand citadel is known as the King's Bastion offering commanding views of the St. Lawrence River and the approaches from seaward."

In 1932, Canada and the United States signed the St. Lawrence Seaway Treaty to build a series of locks, canals, bridges, and associated structures and facilities to enable sea-going shipping access to the Great Lakes and the heartlands of Canada and the United States. Unfortunately, the treaty failed to gain the constitutionally required two-thirds vote threshold for ratification by the U.S. Senate. The resistance could not be overcome until subsequent administrations, but the Seaway would eventually be built and put into operation.

"Magnificent, Mackenzie. This fort has quite the history."

"It is my first time at this beautiful place," Roosevelt added.

"The gateway to the St. Lawrence Seaway . . . if we ever get that far," observed King.

"I am sorry, Mackenzie. We need the system for the war effort alone, but the realities of democracy stand in the way."

"The Senate."

"Exactly. We had a majority in '34, just not the required two-thirds to ratify the treaty."

"I truly appreciate your continuing efforts to overcome the resistance, Franklin. The surveys and engineering are pretty much complete. Now, we just need the political will, a treaty, and funding to get the system built.

"We needed the Seaway system years ago," Roosevelt said.

"It just makes sense."

Roosevelt laughed softly. "We know it's the right thing to do, but politics are selfish for both of us. Moving our war supplies directly from the plants in the Great Lakes region alone would save weeks or months."

"We can use every day we can find," Churchill contributed. "BOLERO is progressing well, but it is never fast enough."

All three men nodded their heads in agreement. They watched the ships moving in both directions on the St. Lawrence River below the dominant fort.

"Where are we on TUBE ALLOYS?" asked King.

Churchill picked up the answer. "Franklin and I had a very productive series of chats at Hyde Park before making our way up here. Correct me if I misrepresent our discussions, Franklin." Roosevelt nodded his consent. "I do believe we have a draft agreement for the three of us to sign during the conference. We've agreed on the monopoly of Canadian uranium production so that we will focus our entire collective efforts on the Manhattan Project. We will subordinate TUBE ALLOYS to the Manhattan Project."

"We've agreed that is a joint development effort," interjected Roosevelt. "While I believe it is essential to have a unitary command for such a time-critical and ambitious scientific endeavor, we will share the data and products of development. In our efforts to dispatch Germany first, I should also note that the 8th Air Force stepped up the execution of POINTBLANK today with a major daylight bombing raid into the heart of Germany, attacking the ball bearing plant at Schweinfurt and Messerschmitt fighter production facility at Regensburg. Initial reports suggest they hit their targets, but the losses were heavier than expected."

"Bomber Command was planned to do a follow-up night raid on the same targets, but we had to divert our resources to a night raid on an extraordinary German weapons development complex on a Baltic island in Northeast Germany." Both King and Roosevelt looked at Churchill as if to say, well, what's the rest of the story? "The facility on the island of Peenemünde. We have hard photographic and physical evidence the research center has been the source for major rocket programs. The evidence is less solid that Heisenberg has conducted some nuclear development research in the area and probably supported by the center."

"What kind of rockets?" asked King.

"One is definitely a flying bomb with wings. The other is a large, streamlined, bullet-shaped, ballistic missile that will likely propel a one-ton explosive warhead 200 miles or so. We've been planning this raid for weeks now, and the required conditions en route and over the target came together for tonight."

"I presume you've shared this information with our intelligence folks," Roosevelt said.

"Yes, absolutely . . . with both national services."

"Then we await the results," King commented.

"Yes, precisely." Churchill shifted in his chair to look directly at both leaders. "We have considerable serious work ahead of us. I'm reticent to say this, but of the three of us, England will be the first of us to face these dreadful weapons. We endured the Blitz and survived, but these new weapons bring a whole new dimension to warfare."

"Terrible times," King said.

"Quite so," added Roosevelt.

"Indeed," Churchill said. He noticed Private Secretary John Peck approaching with a single sheet of paper in his left hand. Winston raised his left hand to signal the other two leaders to halt their discussion.

Peck whispered to the prime minister's right ear. "This just arrived, sir," he said softly.

RESTRICTED

```
RESTRICTED
DATE 1405 17 AUGUST 1943
TO PM UK
FROM GOC 15AG
COPY WARCAB WARMIN CIGS SCAFHQ
BREAK
SICILY COMPLETELY UNDER OUR CONTROL BREAK LAST
ENEMY SOLDIER FLUNG OUT AT 1000 BDST BREAK ALL
HUSKY OBJECTIVES MET BREAK GOOD LUCK QUADRANT
END
RESTRICTED
```

RESTRICTED

Churchill handed the message to Roosevelt, who in turn passed it to King.

"Congratulations to the Allied Forces," announced King.

Churchill leaned forward and turned again. He held Roosevelt's eyes. "Do you think the Italian overtures are genuine and sincere?"

"Hard to say, Winston. Generals Marshall and Eisenhower believe the discussions are worth exploring."

"Yes, as does Alexander and Montgomery. It costs us nothing at this stage."

"We agreed in Casablanca," Roosevelt interjected, "to no negotiated surrender . . . nothing but unconditional surrender for the Axis powers."

"Yes, we did, Franklin, but as I said, hearing what the Italians have in mind costs us nothing. Further, I would like to suggest that turning the Italians to help us with the Germans would relieve more than a few divisions for OVERLORD."

Roosevelt contemplated Churchill's words. "You've a point there, Winston. Yet, what will Uncle Joe think? We told him no negotiated surrender."

"That is a complication, Franklin. However, based on my previous discussions with Uncle Joe, I believe I can convince him of the wisdom associated with turning the Italians to our side."

"An awful lot depends upon the success of that conversation."

"Indeed!"

"The last thing we need at this stage of the war is the Soviets negotiating a separate peace agreement with the Germans," Roosevelt observed, "because they suspect we are doing the same without them. They know the Germans are far more obsessed with them than they are with us."

"There is that dimension that affects us all." Churchill paused to gather his thoughts. "We've got to reassure him that the primary, if not ultimate, objective is Germany. The bloody bastard of a corporal has made his intentions quite clear. He seeks to eradicate communism. You will recall Rudolf Hess crashed in Scotland in May of '41. He claimed he was speaking for Hitler and the Nawzee Party. He actually asked for us to join the Germans against the Reds."

"But you didn't think it was real," Roosevelt said.

"Correct. We assessed it as a bit deranged, although it was a most tempting option."

"So," said King, "what makes you think the Italians are any different from Hess's offer?"

"First, the agents that Allied Forces are in contact with are general staff officers and senior diplomats, not just a deputy political leader, acting on his own. Second, the overtures are far broader, consistent, and singularly focused on the Germans, not the Soviets."

"Do you think you can gain the concurrence of Stalin?" King asked.

"That is the salient question, isn't it?" Churchill looked off to some distant point. "Just past performance, he will rant and rave, and stomp around like a mountain guerilla on an alpha male display, and then he will seek some concessions that serves his political objectives."

"If anyone can negotiate that minefield," Roosevelt said, "it will be you, Winston."

"Thanks, Franklin. I'll take that task on after this conference. Until then, I suggest we green light General Eisenhower's initiative to see what the Italians have in mind."

"Agreed," Roosevelt said.

"Likewise," added King.

Their aides approached to notify the leaders the scheduled first introductory plenary session was ready to begin. All three of them took one last look at the scenery across the river to the south bank and beyond. They moved slowly to the large conference room set up for their meeting. The room used to be one of the fort's ammunition magazines. The QUADRANT Conference began.

—

Tuesday, 17.August.1943
Heeresversuchsanstalt Peenemünde
Peenemünde, Usedom, Pomerania
Deutsches Reich
19:50 hours

The German Army Research Center at Peenemünde had begun comprehensive development and experimentation of rocket propulsion, guidance, and associated technologies in 1937 when German rocket research had been collected up at the new center. The British prime minister and the War Cabinet had decided at their 29.June meeting and set in motion Operation HYDRA—the bombing and special operations campaign to slow down or derail the German rocket program. The 18/19.August night's bombing raid was the first raid on the Peenemünde facilities. The raid had been planned for some weeks in an effort to coordinate with the 8th Air Force. Bomber Command was supposed to fly a mission that night back to Schweinfurt and Regensburg to complement the day's effort by the Americans, but Peenemünde took priority. The plan called for three waves through the night, involving 324 Lancasters, 218 Halifaxes, and 54 Stirlings along with Mosquito pathfinder aircraft, using the night bombing techniques proven at Essen and the Krupp Works raid on 5.March.1943. The very northern tip of Usedom Island offered near-perfect geography for the H2S ground-mapping radar. They would have weather en route, but conditions over the target were perfect for the full scope of heavy bombing procedures, which would be ably applied.

The raid was exceptionally successful and proved the vulnerability of the German rocket program. The British success that night instigated a crash effort by the Germans to move the manufacturing and assembly operations into an underground tunnel complex built into the Hartz Mountains, and the nearby Sachsenhausen concentration camp provided the forced slave labor for the manufacturing process.

The raid also demonstrated that Berlin was well within the range of Allied bombers and portended what was to come for the German capital.

—

Wednesday, 18.August.1943
Allied Forces Headquarters (AFHQ)
Hôtel Saint George
24 Avenue Souidani Boudjemaâ
Algiers
Algérie Coloniale Française
15:00 hours

Lieutenant General Patton entered General Eisenhower's spacious office. Eisenhower sat at the middle of a long side of a rectangular conference table. Lieutenant General Omar Nelson Bradley, USA [USMA 1915], II Corps Commanding General sat to Eisenhower's right, and Major General Beetle Smith, sat to Ike's left. Patton saluted Eisenhower, and Ike returned the salute and said, "Have a seat, George."

"This can't be good."

The three-seated generals sat stone-faced and did not respond as Patton took the center seat opposite Eisenhower.

"At a time like this, I would rather be congratulating you on a successful combat operation, but that is not why we're here." Patton did not react in any form. "I received reports of two incidents earlier in the month where you slapped and threatened to execute two separate soldiers in the tents of two different field hospitals."

"They were cowards, Ike, cowards on the battlefield in the face of the enemy. And those damn doctors were coddling the bastards."

"George," Ike said more forcefully than he intended, took a deep breath, and calmed his tone, "you are confirming the incidents."

"Yes, of course, I am, Ike. I shoulda shot the bastards for cowardice on the battlefield, and . . . ," he stopped when Eisenhower held up his right hand palm out with fire in his eyes.

Eisenhower tapped the wooden tabletop with both index fingers several times as he looked at the folder in front of him. "I have been struggling to keep the wolves at bay, George. The War Department ordered a general court-martial, but I convinced the chief to let me handle the situation." Patton nodded his head as if it was a good thing. "Your detractors, at least those who are aware of what happened at those hospitals in Sicily, want your head on a pike. So, upfront, I have prepared a reprimand letter that I will hold until some unspecified, undetermined time. You are hereby relieved of command of the 7th Army. I will state in front of these witnesses," Ike said, looking at Bradley and Smith, "what you did in Sicily to those two soldiers was wrong and brought discredit to the Army."

"Ike, they were fucking cowards," Patton shouted, "yellow belly cowards, I tell you . . . on the battlefield, in the face of the enemy. There were good, brave men who fought valiantly and were seriously wounded in those tents. Neither one of those cowards had a single wound—no injury. They deserved to be shot for cowardice."

"Shut the hell up, George. Your damn mouth is your own worst enemy. Now, that is the worst of it. I have a proposition for you." Patton's angry glare dissipated. "In spite of your poor judgment and transgressions, George, you can be useful, but you are going to have to play the role of an aggrieved and humbled general." Patton's puzzled expression brought a smile to Eisenhower. "As you know, we have begun serious, detailed planning for OVERLORD, including the overall deception support plan called Operation BODYGUARD for ETO activities. Part of that planning is an active tactical operations deception program to deflect as much of the German line divisions in France from our intended landing beaches. Operation FORTITUDE is the working deception plan focused on the Pas de Calais. Our planning to date has rejected Calais as an option for OVERLORD, mainly because we believe Hitler is convinced that is where we will land. We have strong indications, probably reflecting the German planning for their SEALION amphibious invasion plan for England in 1940, that they are predisposed to the notion that Calais is the most likely for our invasion beach. We want to reinforce their inclinations subtly." Patton gestured 'so' that amplified his puzzled expression. "You will publicly apologize in person to the two soldiers, to every person present in those two hospital tents, to both medical units, and to the 7th Army headquarters staff. You will be sent back to England as soon as those tasks are complete. You will be asked to give several public relations speeches to local community groups that will be well publicized."

"Is all this necessary, Ike?"

"Yes, George, it is, unless you wish to retire or be given a training command back in the states."

"I'm at your mercy. I'll do whatever you ask of me to get back in the fight. I must be a part of our ultimate victory."

"You are going to walk a very fine line. It will be leaked to several prominent American journalists in a couple of months that you were relieved of command and reprimanded for conduct unbecoming a general officer in slapping those two soldiers. There will be public outrage and calls for your dismissal. The publicity will be far more for German consumption than anyone else. With this effort, we want to convince the Germans you are leading an entire army group building up in Southeast England for a cross-Channel amphibious invasion at Calais. This will be in parallel to an essentially identical effort in Scotland intended to point at Norway. Your portion of the BODYGUARD and FORTITUDE efforts is called Operation QUICKSILVER. You will be given command of an imaginary army group, designated the First U.S. Army Group (FUSAG). Decoy tanks, trucks, artillery pieces, aircraft, bivouacs and such will be deployed at numerous sites in Southeast England. You will be given scripts for your active parts in the QUICKSILVER plan. So, given that information, what is your choice?"

"The choices you are offering me beyond humiliation are: retire, a stateside training command, or this fake army group."

"George, I am not going to argue the point, and this is not a negotiation. There is a proper way to deal with cowardice on the battlefield, and that does not include 18th Century actions. We all know you see yourself as an old guard, but you are a general in the modern Army of the 20th Century. You may view my orders as humiliating, and that is your choice, but I am trying to make lemonade from the lemons you presented me. I am trying to save you from a general court-martial and a dishonorable discharge, if not time in Leavenworth."

"Ike . . . !"

"No, George, stop, damn it! This is not a debate or a negotiation. What is your choice?"

"The first two take me out of action for the rest of the war. The third one gives me at least some faint hope of returning to a combat command."

"Correct. I can make no offers or promises beyond these, George. It will be up to the OVERLORD expeditionary force commander to decide what happens as the forces on the continent expand for the attack on Germany itself. If you do your part in QUICKSILVER correctly, it will be your best shot at returning to a combat command."

"Then, the decision is made."

"Before we finish here, I strongly and emphatically encourage you to stay strictly to your part. Keep your mouth shut except as the QUICKSILVER plan directs you. Your best hope is to make the Germans believe you are in command of the lead army group invasion force."

"I will do my part, Ike, and hope for the best. I want . . . I need a combat command for the drive into Germany."

"I know, George. Just keep your mouth shut and do your part. Now, you have some sincere apologies to prepare, and I suggest you get on with it as soon as possible. I want the apologies complete in two to three weeks."

"It will be done."

"Very well. Good luck, George. You are dismissed, General."

Patton stood, pushed his chair under the table, and he came to attention and saluted. Eisenhower returned Patton's salute. General Patton performed a proper, military, about-face, and left the office.

"What did you think?" Eisenhower asked Bradley and Smith.

"George is George," Bradley responded promptly, then added. "I think you drove the nail squarely, Ike. I'll chat with George in a few days to get a feel for his mood and mind. He'll be OK. Above all else, he wants to command an armored infantry army into Germany. The *pièce de résistance* for him would be to accept the sword of Rommel or Guderian in surrender."

"Keep me posted."

"I will."

Lieutenant General George Patton swallowed his pride and faithfully performed his assigned duties from Eisenhower's admonition. He apologized to each soldier at issue in the privacy of his office. Patton went to each division in the 7th Army and issued a heartfelt apology. The men of several of those divisions shouted and chanted their support for the general. Patton would go on to perform his part in Operation QUICKSILVER, and arguably, he was a significant contributor to the success of Operation OVERLORD, ten months later.

—

Chapter 10

What is art? Prostitution.

-- Charles Baudelaire

Friday, 3.September.1943
Allied Forces Encampment Fairfield
Cassibile, Siracusa, Sicily
Occupied Italy
15:20 hours

After ten days of talks with various representatives of the new Italian government in a variety of locations, the Articles of Armistice between the Kingdom of Italy and the Allied Forces had been negotiated and resolved. *Brigadiere Generale* Giuseppe Castellano, assigned to the Italian general staff, arrived dressed in an ill-fitting dark business suit at the appointed time to represent King Victor Emmanuel III and *Maresciallo d'Italia* Pietro Badoglio, newly appointed prime minister after Mussolini's ouster and arrest on the 25th of July. The Armistice document was presented for signing by Brigadier Castellano and General Smith on behalf of General Eisenhower.

```
FAIRFIELD CAMP
SICILY
September 3, 1943
The following conditions of an Armistice are
presented by
General Dwight D. Eisenhower,
Commander-in-Chief of the Allied Forces, acting
by authority of the Governments of the United
States and Great Britain and in the interest of
the United Nations, and are accepted by
Marshal Pietro Badoglio
Head of the Italian Government
1.   Immediate cessation of all hostile activity
        by the Italian armed forces.
2.   Italy will use its best endeavors to deny,
        to the Germans, facilities that might be
        used against the United Nations.
3.   All prisoners or internees of the United
        Nations to be immediately turned over to
        the Allied Commander in Chief, and none of
```

these may now or at any time be evacuated
to Germany.

4. Immediate transfer of the Italian Fleet
    and Italian aircraft to such points as may
    be designated by the Allied Commander in
    Chief, with details of disarmament to be
    prescribed by him.

5. Italian merchant shipping may be
    requisitioned by the Allied Commander in
    Chief to meet the needs of his military-
    naval program.

6. Immediate surrender of Corsica and of
    all Italian territory, both islands and
    mainland, to the Allies, for such use as
    operational bases and other purposes as
    the Allies may see fit.

7. Immediate guarantee of the free use by the
    Allies of all airfields and naval ports in
    Italian territory, regardless of the rate
    of evacuation of the Italian territory by
    the German forces. These ports and fields
    to be protected by Italian armed forces
    until this function is taken over by the
    Allies.

8. Immediate withdrawal to Italy of Italian
    armed forces from all participation in the
    current war from whatever areas in which
    they may be now engaged.

9. Guarantee by the Italian Government that if
    necessary it will employ all its available
    armed forces to insure prompt and exact
    compliance with all the provisions of this
    armistice.

10. The Commander in Chief of the Allied
    Forces reserves to himself the right to
    take any measure which in his opinion may
    be necessary for the protection of the
    interests of the Allied Forces for the
    prosecution of the war, and the Italian
    Government binds itself to take such

administrative or other action as the
Commander in Chief may require, and in
particular the Commander in Chief will
establish Allied Military Government over
such parts of Italian territory as he may
deem necessary in the military interests
of the Allied Nations.

11. The Commander in Chief of the Allied Forces
    will have a full right to impose measures
    of disarmament, demobilization, and
    demilitarization.

12. Other conditions of a political, economic
    and financial nature with which Italy will
    be bound to comply will be transmitted at
    a later date.

   The conditions of the present Armistice
will not be made public without prior approval
of the Allied Commander-in-Chief. The English
will be considered the official text.

MARSHAL PIETRO BADOGLIO
Head of Italian Government
By:

GUISEPPE CASTELLANO
Brigadier General, attached to The Italian High
Command

—

DWIGHT D. EISENHOWER
General, U.S. Army
Commander in Chief, Allied Forces
By:

WALTER B. SMITH
Major General, U.S. Army
Chief of Staff

Also present at the armistice signing ceremony were:
-- Maurice Harold Macmillan, MP – British Resident Minister, AFHQ,

-- Robert Daniel Murphy – Personal Representative of the President of the United States,

-- Major General Lowell Ward Rooks, USA, Assistant Chief of Staff, G-3, AFHQ

-- Commodore Royer Mylius Dick, Royal Navy, Chief of Staff to the CinC Mediterranean,

-- Brigadier Kenneth Strong – Assistant Chief of Staff, G-2, AFHQ

-- Franco Montanari – Official Italian Interpreter.

The small group witnessed the capitulation of Italy—the first of the Axis nations to fall. The Italians recognized reality when their North Africa forces surrendered along with the German *Afrikakorps*. They also had incontrovertible proof they were next when the Allies invaded and captured Sicily. The Allies sought Italian assistance as they did with the Vichy French in Operation TORCH ten months previous. Intelligence indicated the Germans were going to continue to fight in Italy.

After the official armistice document was signed, General Eisenhower joined the group to celebrate with champagne and simple *hors d'œuvre* prepared by the officer's mess cooks. Beyond the congratulatory conversations, Eisenhower managed to take Castellano aside with Montanari.

Through the interpreter, Eisenhower said, "I trust Marshal Badoglio is committed to the armistice."

"Yes sir, he is," Castellano said in Italian.

"The 8th Army is landing in Calabria as we speak."

"That was expected, General. We will do our part to help. Marshal Badoglio has sent emissaries with private messages to the regional commanders in anticipation of your offensive. We expect their cooperation but anticipate there will be a few resisters."

General Eisenhower wanted to share Allied plans for the Italian peninsula campaign, but he did not have the confidence in the security of such information, although Castellano had comported himself well during the negotiations. Ike became an advocate for backing-off the original Allied position of unconditional surrender largely because of Badoglio's willingness to join the Allied side against the Germans and Castellano's faithful conduct during the discussions. President Roosevelt and Prime Minister Churchill ultimately accepted Eisenhower's arguments on behalf of an armistice rather than unconditional surrender.

"What of Mussolini?" Ike asked.

Castellano did not need Montanari's translation. He turned his head to the left away from Eisenhower and spit on the grass. "That mad man has been successfully moved last week from prison to the Hotel Albergo Freugio in the Gran Sasso Mountains east of Rome. The hotel can only be reached by cable car, so it is much easier to secure. We are concerned Hitler, or the Nazis may attempt to rescue him. The King is prepared to transfer custody of that mad man to you when that action becomes more feasible."

"Very well. We want him to face trial for his crimes. We also trust you will do your utmost to keep him securely incarcerated."

"We will, Sir. We have Army detachments permanently positioned at both stations of the cable car system and at the hotel. We want him to feel justice for what he has done to our great country."

"Good. Now, I'm afraid I must go. Enjoy the celebration and safe journey, General. Thank you for your contributions to this armistice. You have saved lives and spared your ancient country from destruction."

Eisenhower shook hands with Castellano and Montanari, and then he waved to Beetle Smith to signal his departure. Time would tell the tale whether this was a wise move.

—

Wednesday, 8.September.1943
Oval Office
The White House
Washington, District of Columbia
United States of America
16:30 hours

"**W**e just received confirmation that the Germans reacted to Marshal Badoglio's public statement of surrender. They sent combat troops into Rome, Naples, and probably other cities," the president stated as the two leaders conversed alone at the couches.

"To be expected, I'm afraid," the prime minister replied. "We expected the Germans to react. They clearly do not intend to abandon the Italian peninsula even though the Italians have left them. At least the new government has Mussolini in custody. They have commandeered the Hotel Albergo high in the Gran Sasso as his makeshift confinement. They only access is by cable car, so he should be secure."

"He needs to stand trial."

"Absolutely. Agreed. As soon as we can arrange a tribunal. I might add that we also received confirmation that King Victor Emmanuel III and Marshal Badoglio have led the fledgling government out of Rome. General Eisenhower has extended protection to the new Italian government. They have evacuated Rome and are making their way across the peninsula to the Adriatic port of Pescara. As we understand their plan, the king and government will move south behind our lines. Montgomery's 8th Army should liberate Brindisi in a few days.

It appears they will settle in Brindisi under Allied Forces protection. We should gain confirmation from General Eisenhower as soon as they are reestablished."

"As we agreed, General Eisenhower made the public radio address to announce the Italian surrender. I understand the formal surrender document will be signed later this month."

"That is my understanding, as well."

"What do you hear of BAYTOWN?" the president asked, regarding Operation BAYTOWN, the extension of the HUSKY forces onto mainland Italy.

"General Montgomery and the 8th Army moved swiftly with the crossing of the Messina Strait and taking Reggio, the city opposite Messina. They have also secured the military aerodrome at Reggio, our first on the mainland. I am informed that Allied Forces will execute AVALANCHE and SLAPSTICK tomorrow morning—good plans, good intelligence. We shall soon see if our new Italian friends have given us valuable information. The prevailing opinion so far is the Italians have been forthright and effusive."

Operation AVALANCHE was the amphibious landing of the 5th Army, commanded by Lieutenant General Mark Wayne Clark, USA [USMA 1917], at Salerno, south of Naples. Operation SLAPSTICK was the landing of British airborne and naval forces on the east coast to secure the vast Taranto naval base.

"Excellent. I must say we must make quick work of the Germans in Italy in order to shift our attention to OVERLORD. I think we both agree AVALANCHE will not get us Germany; only OVERLORD can do that part of our strategic objective."

"Yes, my dear Franklin, we are in full agreement. Italy ties down important German infantry and armor divisions that are not readily moved to Northern France."

"True, but as we discussed in Québec City, we need those landing craft and 5th and 8th Armies for OVERLORD."

"Respectfully, Franklin, we are not there yet. I am encouraged by your direction to redouble the industrial capacity of the United States to produce and deliver the additional landing craft, as well as raise the additional divisions we need for the push to Berlin. To be candid, we are walking a very thin line. For all our successes in the last two years, we have a long hard road ahead, and we simply must beat the Russians to Berlin, or we shall have an entirely different problem on our hands. I am still not comfortable with our initial assault, Franklin . . . no, I will confess that I am dreadfully afraid that our assault will have an insufficient force to avoid a stalemate. I have a mortal fear, a primal terror, of being consumed in another Passchendaele. The slaughter, the senseless slaughter, it is nauseating even to this day, 26 years hence. A quarter of a million young men, a quarter of a million, lost in just three months of to and fro, with no gain, only the consumption of young men." Tears descended unabashedly down Churchill's cheeks. He did not attempt to wipe them away. "We simply cannot allow it to happen again."

The Battle of Passchendaele, also known as the Third Battle of Ypres, took place between 31.July and 10.November.1917 (3 months, 1 week and 3 days) in the Ypres Salient centered on the little Belgian village of Passchendaele. Fifty British divisions faced off against 80 German divisions. The seesaw battle achieved nothing beyond the infliction of 400,000 casualties on each side. The memories of those three months have haunted British military and political leaders for decades—the senselessness of the mind-boggling slaughter. The British could not and would not forget.

Roosevelt nodded his head several times and held Winston's watery eyes. "I have always admired your passion, Winston. Let it suffice to say I share your apprehension. We have committed to finding the forces and equipment we need to do OVERLORD properly."

"Thank you, Franklin."

"You are much more engaged in these military plans than I am, Winston. I truly trust your judgment in such matters. We shall both rely on superior reasoning in these affairs."

"Thank you again."

"You are most welcome. Now, would you care to freshen up before cocktail hour and supper?"

"I suppose I should. After all, I must be on my best form . . . the combined joint chiefs and their associated ministers, well except Admiral Pound. Quite the gathering."

"How is Sir Dudley?"

"Not well, I'm afraid. He is under doctors' care at the Embassy. Lord Moran informs me these are likely his end of days."

"Very sad. He lost his wife Betty in July . . . devastated him. Sir Dudley has been such a stalwart advocate for sea power and an accomplished first sea lord."

"Yes, yes, so true. I have known and trusted him for most of my professional life. A noble leader of men . . . without question." Tears returned to Winston's cheeks. "Now, I'm afraid I've made a fool of myself with this blathering."

"Quite the contrary, my friend. Once again, I admire your passion. You are a most remarkable man."

Churchill stood, shook Franklin's proffered right hand, bowed, and departed the Oval Office for the residence to prepare for the evening's social event with the defense staff.

———

Tuesday, 14.September.1943
OSS London Station
Nos. 70-72 Grosvenor Street
Mayfair, London, England
United Kingdom
15:35 hours

Captain Brian Drummond patiently stepped through the unusually elaborate security procedures to validate his identity and gain access to the interior. An army sergeant appeared to be in charge and performed all of the checks. Four, serious-looking, attentive, well-armed soldiers occupied the corners of the security anteroom. Brian wore a fresh, pinks and greens, service uniform with only his silver Army wings over his left breast pocket and his gold RAF wings over his right breast pocket. Once his identification was complete and he was approved, Brian waited. The audible electronic deadbolt locks signified a change.

An Army second lieutenant in service uniform with Intelligence Branch lapel insignia appeared. "Captain Drummond, would you follow me please." They passed through another interior room that seemed to be a secure waiting room and another heavy electronic locked door. Brian followed the lieutenant up two flights of stairs, down the left corridor, to the end of the hall and a door with an engraved brass sign.

**Chief
of
Station**

Brian recognized one of the two men in the large, well-appointed office—Brigadier General Bill Donovan. The other man was attired in an Army pinks and greens service uniform with a bird colonel's rank insignia.

"Welcome to London Station, Brian," Donovan greeted their guest with an extended right hand. Brian saluted first and then shook the general's hand.

"Thank you, sir."

"I'd like to introduce David Bruce, our chief of station here." The two men shook hands.

David Kirkpatrick Este Bruce was a lawyer who had served in the Maryland House of Delegates in the 30s and chief of the American Red Cross War Mission in London during The Blitz. His dispatches home helped shape American public opinion, much like the broadcasts of Ed Murrow. Donovan selected Bruce to be chief of mission earlier in the year.

Donovan gestured to the comfortable chairs around a low, round coffee table. "Was Charlotte able to join you?" asked Bill.

"Yes sir. We checked into the Dorchester. I will pick her up before dinner."

"Excellent," Bill said. "I look forward to finally meeting your famous wife."

"She's quite confused as to why she was invited," Brian added.

Donovan smiled. "I think your wife is more famous than you, hotshot." Brian smiled and nodded his head. "Plus, Marlene speaks very highly of Charlotte Drummond."

"You know about that?"

"Yes, I do. I wasn't so sure it was a good idea, but as you now know well, Marlene can be a very determined woman."

Brian chuckled softly. "Yes, I do know that."

"In addition to meeting your wife, I wanted to chat about a few topics with David present, so he is up to speed." Brian nodded his agreement. "I wanted to tell you that your airline is doing a great job supporting our operations. In fact, one of your BAS Connies flew me . . . well, and nearly a full planeload of American, British, and Canadian personnel across the Atlantic. I must say it is an elegant mode of transportation. I do believe we have a great, mutually beneficial enterprise. I hope and trust you are as happy with our relationship."

Brian wanted to acknowledge the BAS weak point. "We have tried to improve our unscheduled fulfillment rate."

"And that effort has been duly noted. I wanted to hear a little of your experience with the bomber escort missions."

Why does that matter to the OSS or the intelligence apparatus? "Well, there are two primary aspects. Within the range of our P-47Ds, we're doing pretty good at protecting the bombers. However, for bombing missions deep into Germany, beyond the range of the P-47D, it is gut-wrenching. We were one of a bunch of fighter squadrons escorting the 1st Bombardment Wing as part of the Army Air Forces Schweinfurt-Regensburg mission back in mid-August. We were doing fine until we reached our bingo fuel level and had to leave the bombers. Several German squadrons stood off, stalking the bomber formation. They knew we would have to leave them at the German border. We had to watch as the Germans pounced. Some of the guys in my squadron talked to a few of the bomber pilots on that mission. They had to deal with the enemy fighters all the way to the target and all the way out until we refueled and rearmed, and returned back up there to meet them. The damage and losses were staggering."

"Our agents, the British and us, have managed to collect up a few of the downed airmen and repatriate them, but we can't be everywhere. What can be done to help?"

"They tell us a longer-range fighter is in production. We are supposed to transition early next year. I've no idea how you could possibly position agents on the ground since bailout is such a happenstance kind of thing."

"We'll continue to do our part to help. I will add a note to my trip report about the pressing need for a long-range fighter. Another related topic, as you may know, Allied Forces landed major forces at several spots in Southern Italy. The Italians have surrendered and joined us against the Germans. As a consequence, the Germans have occupied Rome and deployed several special weapons."

"We've seen the *Stars & Stripes* announcement of the Salerno landings, but we've not heard anything about special weapons."

"One of these new weapons is an armor-piercing glide bomb called a Fritz-X. It is radio-controlled by an operator in the release aircraft using a flare in the tail. The other one is a Henschel Hs293, a rocket-propelled, radio-controlled, flying bomb. Because it is not a freefall bomb like the Fritz-X, it has a longer range, but it is still guided by an operator tracking the tail flare to the target. Five days ago, they dropped a Fritz-X on the Italian battleship *Roma* in Taranto Harbor, did some serious damage, but they didn't sink the ship. Two days later, another Fritz-X hit the number three main turret of the light cruiser *Savannah*, but the warhead did not detonate until it passed through the ship and out the bottom, undoubtedly saving the ship."

"Wow! Those are some impressive weapons." Brian considered the challenge of intercepting such weapons. "At face value, the weak spots appear to be the carrier aircraft and the controller on board. The radio control link is also a vulnerability."

"The British signals intelligence branch is working feverishly to identify the radio properties and develop a jammer. Do you think you could intercept either of those weapons in flight?"

"We can't dive as fast as a bomb, so no, I don't think we could intercept a Fritz-X as you call it. Our ability to intercept one of those Hs293 missiles would depend upon the speed it can achieve. Rocket-propelled suggests a higher speed than we can attain. Since they are both clear weather, line-of-sight weapons, I dare say any opportunity to intercept would have to be quite fortuitous."

"OK. That is good information. I leave tomorrow for Southern Italy to see how the OSS is doing in support of the offensive. I'm not particularly keen on witnessing the capabilities of those weapons, but that seems to be where they are employing them at present."

"Good luck, General."

"Thanks, Brian. Now, one last question before we break to get ready for dinner. Have you reconsidered coming to work for us?"

Brian laughed heartily. "No one can say you are not persistent, General."

David Bruce joined the laughter. "That is a serious understatement, Brian. He's strong-armed me into joining his magic circus."

"Now, wait a minute, I think you two are ganging up on me. I've never forced either of you to do anything you didn't want to do."

"True," Bruce added. "You may not realize, Bill, but you are a hard person to say no to in any discussion."

Donovan looked at Brian and gestured with his eyes and head, as if to say, well? "Before you answer, I would like to add in my defense that working as the air arm of the OSS would enable us to expand the operations of BAS beyond transportation. You know it would be exciting work."

"I'm certain it would, General, but I like what I'm doing. What is the old saying, a bird in hand . . . as my Mom used to tell me. I'm good at what I do. I don't think I would be much of a transport driver. I like being a shooter far better than being a target."

"The offer remains open until this affair is over."

"Thank you, Sir. I truly appreciate the confidence you show in me."

"Very well, for now," Donovan pronounced. "Let's get you back to the Dorchester to retrieve your bride. We'll meet you at the chief of station's residence."

17:25 hours

Bruce picked up his cue. "I've arranged for one of the station's limousines to return you to the Dorchester, Brian," Bruce said. "The driver will wait for you and Mrs. Drummond, and then he will transport you to the chief's residence," he added, as if the place was not where he lived.

"Please put Charlotte's mind at ease, Brian. She is not walking into some ambush. I wanted to talk with you during my stop en route to Italy, and I thought it would be a perfect opportunity to meet Charlotte, which I might add, I've wanted to do since she pulled your sorry ass out of her pond."

Brian laughed robustly. "Sorry ass, indeed! I will reassure her. Perhaps, someday, if you can spare a day or a weekend, you can visit our farm and see that very pond of which you speak," Brian said with laughter in his voice.

"I would love to be your guest. I will look for the soonest opportunity. Now, off with you. We'll see you in an hour or so. By the way, so there are no worries, the driver is at your disposal tonight." Donovan glanced at Bruce and received a confirmatory head nod. "Very well, then, we are adjourned. See you in an hour or so."

"Yes sir." Brian stood and saluted the general. All three men shook hands. Bruce escorted Brian to the waiting limousine parked with the engine running in the small courtyard behind the building.

—

Monday, 20.September.1943
Euston Station
Camden, London, England
United Kingdom
18:10 hours

The QUADRANT Conference had gone exceptionally well. The president did not show the same degree of interest in the military plans for OVERLORD, but in his way, he endorsed Churchill's comments on the operations plan as reviewed in Québec City. Roosevelt and Churchill also reached a secret agreement on nuclear collaboration known as the Hyde Park *aide-mémoire*. The memorandum was so secret that essential personnel in both countries were not aware of the contents until years later.

Sir Dudley Pound had been in deteriorating health since July and suffered two strokes while in Québec City. He resigned his post as first sea lord of the Admiralty on the 10th. The doctors tended to the admiral on the voyage back to Great Britain and the railway journey to London.

Admiral Cunningham would take his new post as Admiral Pound's replacement. General Eisenhower put up a token resistance, but ultimately, he fully supported Sir Andrew's promotion. Admiral Cunningham's deputy and commander of the HUSKY Eastern Task Force Admiral Sir Bertram Home Ramsay KCB, KBE, MVO, DL, ably replaced Cunningham as the Allied Forces, Naval Forces Commander. Admiral Ramsay had planned and executed Operation DYNAMO—the successful evacuation of the BEF from Dunkirk in 1940.

The train arrived at a closed platform established for just this purpose. A platoon of doctors and nurses stood calmly in readiness forward of the prime minister's railcar. The train had barely come to a stop. The medical team moved swiftly to extract the first sea lord from the railcar.

The prime minister moved with urgent purpose to be on the platform at the boarding stairs as they moved Admiral Pound off the train for transport to the hospital. He stayed with the admiral until the ambulance departed. His limousine was waiting. The prime minister went directly to Number 10 for the waiting War Cabinet for his report on the QUADRANT Conference results along with collateral discussions.

———

Wednesday, 29.September.1943
HMS Nelson
35° 53' 19" North - 14° 30' 41" East
Grand Harbor
Valletta, Crown Colony of Malta
15:30 hours

By prior coordination and agreement with the battleship's captain, the standard naval custom of announcing the boarding of a flag officer or dignitary was suspended. Prime Minister Badoglio boarded the British battleship without honors, and only a colonel aide and a major interpreter. General Eisenhower stood on the quarterdeck with the Royal Navy lieutenant officer of the deck.

"Welcome aboard *Nelson*, Marshal Badoglio," Ike said and extended his right hand to the Italian prime minister, dressed in his service uniform with full regalia.

"Thank you, General Eisenhower," Badoglio responded in heavily accented English. The two men shook hands.

Eisenhower led the prime minister to the officer's wardroom for the signing ceremony. "Let us dispense with the business of this occasion first, and then I would like to have a private chat if you agree."

The marshal's interpreter translated Eisenhower's words into Italian. Badoglio nodded his head and answered in halting English, "Certainly."

General Eisenhower nodded to General Smith, who opened the leather folio in front of Marshal Badoglio. An Italian translation was provided *pro forma* for the master English document. The marshal appeared to be satisfied with his preview reading. He signed the amended armistice document. Beetle lifted the open folio and placed it before the supreme commander. Ike signed the document. Beetle blotted the signatures and closed the folio. The two leaders were left with only their respective interpreters.

Once the room was clear and the doors closed, Eisenhower began, "First, thank you for finding your way to our side. We look forward to working with you and your government to ending the scourge of dictatorial fascism." He paused to allow the translation into Italian. "Second, what do you know about Mussolini's status?"

The marshal answered in Italian. Eisenhower's interpreter said softly but clearly. "As you know and our negotiations neared conclusion, we moved Mussolini on the 27th to the Hotel Albergo in the Emperor's Field, a ski resort in the Gran Sasso of the Apennine Mountains. It is accessible only by cable car. On the 12th, a German special operations unit executed a masterful glider assault to rescue Mussolini."

At 14:00 [A] CET {08:00 [R] EST}, Sunday, 12.September.1943, *Waffen-SS Hauptsturmführer* Otto Skorzeny led *SS-Sonderverband z.b.V. Friedenthal* in a bold rescue of Mussolini on Hitler's orders. The team utilized DFS-230C gliders and the prevailing wind to minimize their ground speed for landing on the short, rough, mountain top field in front of the hotel. The Italian guards were caught by surprise and did not offer any resistance. Mussolini was flown off the mountain in a Fieseler Fi156 *Storch*, short takeoff and landing aircraft.

"We believe he is in Northern Italy under German protection."

"We would prefer to have him back in custody to stand trial for his crimes. We will be looking for him as well. If we find him, our special operations personnel may be able to help recover him." Badoglio nodded his head with the translation. "How are your government and the King doing after your move?"

By prior agreement with Allied Forces, Prime Minister Badoglio publicly announced Italy's surrender on Wednesday, 8.September.1943. The Germans immediately sent combat troops into Rome and Naples. The Italians recognized the situation was untenable and decided to move the government.

Badoglio smiled. "Brindisi is not Rome, but the accommodations are adequate. The government is functional. We are most grateful for Allied assistance and protection. On behalf of the King and the Italian government, thank you very much for your support."

"You are most welcome. We look forward to your government's contributions to the speedy defeat of German forces that occupy your country. We are making good progress in retaking Naples and should have control by the end of the week. More facilities would be available in Naples."

"Not necessary," Badoglio responded. "We are functional in Brindisi for now. We would prefer to return to Rome as soon as possible."

"Very well, then. Now that we have the formal armistice documents we just signed, we will work to get a State Department diplomat in place as soon as possible. Until then and for the foreseeable future, I have established a desk officer in my headquarters dedicated to the coordination task with your government."

"Yes," the prime minister said in English, and then he switched back to Italian. "The communications means have been sufficient and satisfactory."

"Excellent. Great to have you with us, Marshal."

They concluded their discussions. Marshal Badoglio departed the battleship without fanfare.

—

Wednesday, 29.September.1943
USAAF Station F-356
Saffron Walden, Essex, England
United Kingdom
19:45 hours

The 4th Fighter Group pilots had gathered in the Officer's Mess Bar after supper to enjoy their usual raucous camaraderie. The 334th and 335th had flown separate ground attack missions into Northern France. The 336th had remained on alert all day without a launch. That fact alone made them the common objective of light-hearted jabs from the others who had flown. Brian never found such revelry attractive, rewarding, or satisfying, but he always enjoyed the talk of flying and learning from the experiences of others. The missions flown this day were successful from their perspective, and they had lost no one, some aircraft damage, but no losses.

One of the Mess privates entered, looked for Brian, and when he found him, he weaved his way through the sea of pilots to Brian sitting at a corner table with several members of his division. "Excuse me, Sir. A woman named Charlotte is on the phone in booth two for you."

"Thank you, Private." He stood. "Excuse me, gentlemen." Brian made his way to the lobby. Three of the six telephone booths were occupied. Two doors were open. The booth with the brass numeral '2' over the closed door remained unoccupied. Brian opened the door, stepped in, sat down on the small integral bench seat, and lifted the handset to his ear. "Charlotte?"

"Yes, darling, it's me."

"Is everyone OK?"

"Yes, everyone is quite all right and in good health."

"OK. I'm listening."

"I received the weekly reports from both Bobby and Jonas. In summary, all is right with the Drummond world. Bobby has improved the unscheduled fulfillment rate to 76% while improving the scheduled fulfillment rate by a couple of points. Our oil revenues are up by nearly 250% as the government's demand for oil is unbounded. Jonas says the government will pay top dollar for all the oil we are willing to sell."

"Good news, I'd say."

"Yes, I knew you would like to know. I'll respond accordingly. But, the reason for my call this Wednesday evening is an invitation we received."

"Invitation?"

"Yes. We have been invited to lunch with Lord and Lady Selborne this coming Saturday."

"Why? Do you know who they are?"

"I don't know. They didn't say. No, I don't, although we are apparently neighbors of sorts, and I surmise they know who you are. As I understand the information from the *Hampshire Advertiser*, Lord Selborne is the 3rd Earl of Selborne and the Minister of Economic Warfare." Brian thought about but rejected telling his wife about the secret offensive branch of the ministry Selborne ran known by its internal name—Special Operations Executive (SOE).

"The OSS works with them."

"What do you want me to tell them?" Charlotte asked with somber clarity. "Do you think General Donovan put Lord Selborne up to this?"

"If he is behind this invitation, he did not confide in me."

"And?"

"Well, if you are comfortable with such an engagement, I'd say let's do it."

"Can you get leave for the day . . . or perhaps the weekend?"

"We will never know unless I ask."

"Then should I wait until you ask Major Peterson?"

"Would you go if I could not get leave to join you?"

The silence suggested Charlotte was thinking about Brian's query. "I would prefer not, but I suppose I would, if for no other reason than to learn their purpose."

"There you have it. I'd suggest we respond in the affirmative with the proviso that I might not get leave for any one of multiple reasons."

"Are you sure?"

"Yes. I'll do my best to get there. I'm curious, too."

The couple exchanged their lovelies and wished each other goodnight. Brian hung up the handset and sat in the booth for a few minutes. *I wonder what that invitation is all about?* Brian took a deep breath and exhaled audibly. He turned to the bar and refreshed his beer. The pilots were not done for the night.

—

Thursday, 30.September.1943
Hotel Luna Convento
Via Pantaleone Comite
Amalfi, Salerno, Campania
Regno d'Italia
10:45 hours

General Donovan made it safely to the location he had been given. The rather modest hotel showed no signs of damage. A small, cardboard, hand-printed sign indicated the location was correct. Two stern-looking, well-armed, Military Police soldiers stood guard blocking his entry.

"ID card, Sir."

Before Wild Bill could produce his identification card, Major Alfredo Stephano Morelli appeared. "He's cleared, Corporal. For your benefit, this is none other than General Bill Donovan, Director of the OSS." Both soldiers saluted. Donovan returned the salute. "Welcome to Amalfi Station."

"Thanks, Al." The two men shook hands. Donovan followed Morelli up three flights of stairs to wooden numerals '4-1-7' on the door and a small cardboard sign that simply indicated 'C-O-S.'

"Sorry about all that, General. We're still getting things organized, and we are dependent upon the Military Police battalion for security until we get our own security in place." Morelli opened the door and gestured for Donovan to enter. The major followed, closed, and locked the door. He then gestured to the wooden chairs around a round table.

"Thanks again, Al. I've been traveling for a couple of days now, so please give me a quick summary of events over the last few days."

"Sure thing. All three operations—BAYTOWN, AVALANCHE, and SLAPSTICK—are progressing well. Most of the heavy combat action is in front of the 5th Army, so we have been less effective. The 8th Army is advancing up the east coast more quickly and had to be pulled up to keep from getting too far ahead of the 5th and exposing their flank. We generally keep the commanders informed of where our agents are located to avoid any friendly fire. Corsica has gone exceptionally well. The front team should have the island secure within the week. General Clark expects to take Naples tomorrow or the next day, but not soon enough to stop the Germans from destroying a good portion of the port facilities."

"How bad?"

"Worse than we hoped, I'm afraid. Our guys tried to create some diversions to distract the German sabotage teams. We had some limited success, but nowhere near enough to save the port. The 5th Army was just not fast enough in their advance."

"How long will it take to get the port repaired and operational?"

"According to the engineer battalion . . . perhaps two to four weeks."

"Too long."

"They understand that. I'm sure they will strive to improve that estimate. I believe they will try to get the easy ones up first to at least achieve partial operations. But the water must be cleared of mines before anything can be utilized."

"OK. Keep headquarters informed. As I'm sure you are aware, the port facilities are crucial for Allied Forces and swiftly negating the Germans, and thus quite sensitive to both Washington and London."

"Gotcha."

"What about Capri?"

"The team landed at dawn. They encountered no German resistance. They had a few close calls with the local constabulary, but no shots were fired. The police are now cooperating. I expect a radio call at any minute that the island is secure."

"I'd like to head over there now," Donovan announced.

"We commandeered several speed boats. Some of the boats are at Capri with the team. It will take about an hour to get there. I'd like to send a driver and two of our armed agents with you, just in case."

Donovan stood and gestured for them to go. Morelli signaled his aide. The guards joined them as they walked across the coast road. The coxswain for the speed boat was already in the boat with the engine warming up. Morelli remained. They cast off, made their way out of the dock area, and then increased speed to nearly, if not full speed, heading west-southwest along the coast.

———

Thursday, 30.September.1943
Villa Il Fortino
Via Sopramonte
Isla di Capri, Campania
Regno d'Italia
15:20 hours

The boat trip took 55 minutes, pretty good even though they encountered larger swells when their course exposed them to the north wind and made for a briefly rougher ride. The coxswain knew precisely where he was going—*Porto Turistico di Capri* on the island's north side. An OSS man had been waiting for the boat to tie up at the dock. The coxswain and guards would stay with the boat for his return to Amalfi. They used a commandeered Fiat sedan. The streets were not laid out with automobiles in mind, and some parts were barely wide enough for the small Fiat.

Agent Captain Jedediah Abraham 'Jed' North, the OSS front team leader sent to Amalfi, stood at the pedestrian gateway to an elegant, undamaged, and well-maintained villa with subtle yellow and white accents. The villa was embedded in the lush landscaping of conifer trees, shrubs, and multitudinous plants blooming in colors of the rainbow. The various types of healthy shrubs offered many textures, shades of green, and some even added blossoms.

"Is the villa secure?"

The property was owned by a friend, a good friend—Edmona 'Mona' Williams née Strader. In 1926, she married her third husband, Harrison Charles Williams, an American entrepreneur, investor, and multi-millionaire. When the newspapers reported the Allied landings on mainland Italy, Mona had called Donovan directly and asked him to do what he could to protect *Il Fortino* on Capri as best he could. Donovan had agreed. The villa had been situated on a prominence east of the rocky escarpment that essentially bisected the island. The OSS would use the villa as a rest and relaxation facility for the remainder of the war, fulfilling his commitment to Mona.

"Yes sir. We did have a surprise when we arrived, however." Donovan gestured impatiently for North to continue. "We managed to snag a German dignitary trying to make his getaway out the backdoor, so to speak."

"Are you going to tell me who?" asked Donovan with more impatience.

"Count von Bismarck." Donovan did not react in any form. "Actually, Albrecht Karl."

Bill Donovan knew him as *Graf* von Bismarck-Schönhausen; born Albrecht Edzard Heinrich 'Eddie' Karl, and one of Mona Williams' many lovers with 'Eddie' being the current version. Whether Mona's husband knew of his wife's current lover, Donovan knew not; and it did not matter other than as potential leverage, if needed.

"I presume you are insinuating some relation?"

"I had to do a little homework with one of our trusted Italian friends, since Albrecht has not been particularly forthcoming with information. He is the youngest son of Herbert von Bismarck, and the grandson of Chancellor Marshal von Bismarck, Otto von Bismarck."

"And why is he here?"

"He claims he was house-sitting for the owner."

"Does that sound reasonable?"

"No, it doesn't fit. I don't know who the owner is, and I'm not sure it matters, but a German count house-sitting in Italy does not make sense."

"Do you have him in custody?"

"Yes sir. He's under guard in one of the bedrooms."

"Excellent. I'd like to talk to him alone."

"Yes sir. Whenever you're ready."

Donovan gestured to the interior. North led the way. An armed guard stood at one of the doors. North nodded subtly to the guard, who in turn opened the door, allowing Donovan into the room and closing the door behind him. Bill retrieved and placed a straight back wooden chair across and six feet away from their captive.

"Normally, I would extend my hand to you as our guest, but these are not normal times, and this is not a normal situation. Allow me to introduce myself. My name is Donovan, Bill Donovan. Your name is?" The man simply stared out the window without acknowledging Donovan's statement. "Eddie, may I call you Eddie?" The man did not twitch. "We can do this the easy way or the hard way, Eddie. It's your choice entirely. The hard way is I will declare you a prisoner of war, or perhaps even an enemy spy, and the best you can get is confinement in a camp somewhere in mosquito-infested Mississippi. Or you can cooperate, answer my questions, and I could release you, allowing you to return to your country. So, what is your choice?"

The man finally looked at Donovan and held his eyes. "I am not a combatant," he said in heavily German-accented English.

"I know that, but the military police authorities do not, and they will accept my declaration."

"What do you want to know?"

"Let's start with your name."

"My familial name is Karl. My given name is Albrecht."

"OK. I'll accept that for now. Why were you here?"

"I told the other interrogator. I was watching the villa for a friend."

"Who might that friend be?"

"The owner."

"Name please."

"Williams. Mrs. Williams."

"Fine. We're making progress. Now, how do you know this Mrs. Williams, you say?"

"She is and has been a friend of mine." Both stared at each other as if searching the other's eyes for answers. "You know who I am, don't you?" added Eddie.

"Yes."

"And you know who Mrs. Williams is also?"

"Yes. She is a friend of mine as you say, which is why I'm here. Your presence was fortuitous for us, and I do believe you'll eventually agree that it's lucky for you as well. Thank you for telling the truth. Now, here's what's going to happen. You'll remain under the protection of the OSS for another day or so. I'll turn you over to a professional interrogator. I'm not one of those. He's going to ask you several particular questions."

"What about?" Eddie interrupted.

"Mostly about how you were able to move from Germany to Capri and back. He will ask you about the security procedures to allow your travel."

"You are asking me to betray my country."

"Absolutely not, Eddie. We will ask you to defend your country. I can't imagine you support the brutal dictator or his political party who currently dominate your country in every way. I imagine you would like to do your part to return your country to democracy, peace, and prosperity. Your grandfather was a nationalist in the truest form, but he was never a dictator, nor did he advocate for the taking of innocent lives." Count von Bismarck nodded his head in agreement. "When we're done, you'll be given another set of choices. We can release you to return to Germany, or we can accept your defection and situate you in New York City, closer to Mona and her affections." Eddie's demeanor picked up, and he actually smiled noticeably. "Do you have any questions for me before we move to the next phase?"

"No questions, but I would like to say, I may have met you in New York before this war. I do not recall exactly. Your face seems familiar. If my misty memory serves, you were a founding partner of a law firm that bears your name in New York City, Wall Street, to be more precise."

This time Donovan smiled. "Your memory is not so misty as you claim." Bill stood, looking down at Eddie, who remained seated. "Thank you again, Eddie. I look forward to helping you move on from here." Donovan did not wait for an answer and departed the confinement room.

North was waiting for him outside the room. So that both North and the guard could hear him, Donovan said, "He is to remain in our custody. Count von Bismarck is now cooperating, so please take good care of him and ensure his safety." Donovan gestured with a head nod for North to follow him. The two men did not speak until they reached the entry foyer. Bill turned to face Jed and look him in the eyes. "I think you will find him far more compliant. Do you have a professional interrogator with your team?'"

"No sir."

"I will try to get one out here as soon as possible. Do you feel comfortable taking on that task until we get a proper interrogator out here?"

"I suppose so."

"That is not an inspiring or encouraging response, Jed."

"I've not been trained in the interrogation of prisoners, Sir. I'm a field officer."

"Eddie is in the mood. I don't want empty time until we can get an interrogator engaged. Talk to him about his family, his friends, his education, his relationships. Avoid discussing his travels, his knowledge of security procedures, his politics or feelings about the German regime, or anything even remotely related to his patriotism or affinity for his country. If you have any questions, doubts, concerns, worries, or apprehension, please contact me, or Ned Buxton, directly and immediately. I do not want this screwed up."

"Yes sir."

"Now, I've got to skedaddle. I'll be in Amalfi and then at 5th Army headquarters for the next couple of days. Thank you for your great work, Jed."

Donovan departed the villa and reversed his transport. Morelli was waiting for the director's return. In the privacy of Morelli's makeshift office, Bill recounted what had happened at *Il Fortino*. Team Amalfi did have two trained interrogators who were working on other tasks. Donovan directed

Morelli to deploy one of the interrogators to Capri as soon as possible. He also gave very explicit instructions for the questioning of Count von Bismarck as a friendly source and potential defector rather than as a prisoner of war or adversary. Donovan also ordered a report of results as well as his required consent for disposition of their 'guest.' Bill waited patiently as Al issued the necessary orders. Once complete, they turned to the other support tasks that Amalfi Station had on-going as part of the Allied Forces operations in Italy.

—

Thursday, 30.September.1943
No.10 Downing Street
Whitehall, London, England
United Kingdom
23:45 hours

Winston worked in the office on the endless paperwork and reports. What struck him the most was the Admiralty's weekly shipping report. He smiled to himself. Just then, duty Private Secretary Anthony Bevir knocked and entered the prime minister's office.

"I just read the most extraordinary report from the Admiralty," the prime minister announced. "We did not lose a single ship in the last three months. From those dreadful and mortally threatening early days of the war, this is a remarkable accomplishment and another positive sign."

"Congratulations, Sir."

"Not to me, Tony, to the Navy, to the entire Allied cause." Bevir nodded his agreement. "Now, you came in here with a purposeful expression. What have you?"

"The Admiralty duty officer called to inform you that their midget submarine attack on the *Tirpitz* in the early morning hours of the 22nd was more successful than originally thought. They did not sink the battleship; however, the damage has instigated a much greater repair effort than the original battle damage assessment suggested."

"Not perfect news, but definitely on the positive side of the ledger."

"We also received this message," Bevir said and handed the classified message folder to Churchill.

MOST SECRET

```
MOST SECRET
DATE 2028 30 SEP 1943
```

```
TO FOR MIN
FROM EMBASSY STOCKHOLM
COPY PM UK
BREAK
PROF DR NIELS BOHR AND BROTHER HARALD ARRIVED
SAFELY BREAK GUESTS COMFORTABLE BREAK AWAITING
INSTRUCTIONS
END
MOST SECRET
```

MOST SECRET

"More good news," the prime minister announced. "Please notify the War Cabinet; we need a special meeting in the morning. I do not want to wait for our regular afternoon meeting. We have some decisions to take on a number of matters."

"It will be done, Sir. Would 10 o'clock be reasonable?"

"Yes, yes, I just need to make sure Sawyers knows."

"Would you like me to inform Sawyers?"

"Yes, please. Thank you, Tony. I'm going to get through some more of this paper."

"Very well, Sir. I will be right outside if you need me."

Bevir departed and closed the door. Churchill turned his attention back to his reading.

—

Chapter 11

Men,
not having been able to cure death, misery, and ignorance,
have imagined to make themselves happy
by not thinking of these things.
-- Blaise Pascal

Saturday, 2.October.1943
Temple Manor
Sotherington Lane
Selborne, Hampshire, England
United Kingdom
12:15 hours

Charlotte had suggested the horses as a last-century transportation mode, and Brian thought it had rustic elegance. He remained in his pinks and greens service uniform with just his wings and no ribbons. Horseback enabled a more direct route without roadblock checkpoints, less than in the hairy days of 1940 but still impediments to timely travel. Plus, they had plenty of grass for the horses and avoided the constant balancing act of fuel rationing. To Brian's surprise, Charlotte had a rather sophisticated riding outfit from boots and britches to an elegant burgundy blazer. They left the farm with plenty of time for a slow ride to Temple Manor. Their meandering route enabled them to check on several elements of their collective farm holdings on the way to Temple Manor. Charlotte took a few minutes to describe how she wanted to modify the Brownfield property residence as a self-sustaining dormitory of sorts until building materials became more readily available to build bungalows for farmworkers in her effort to improve support for their growing workforce.

A low rock wall marked the boundary of what they understood to be the Selborne property. They passed through a narrow but dense forest belt and into open farm fields. They could not see the manor house but knew the general direction. They both correctly deduced the cart paths ultimately led to the manor house, or at least the support buildings. Their deduction proved correct.

The manor house was modest by earldom standards, at least that Charlotte and Brian were aware of in their knowledge. The main building was larger and older than Standing Oak Farm. The main house was not particularly ornate or extravagant, but it was impressive, nonetheless. A footman appeared in uniform from the main entrance door under the large, pillared portico. Another similarly attired footman appeared before the Drummonds' horses came to a halt. Each footman took the reins at the bit before Charlotte and Brian dismounted.

As they came around the horses, a slender, distinguished-looking man in a medium blue business suit, white shirt, and no necktie approached with an elegant woman wearing a light pink half-sleeved dress walked toward the Drummonds. "Captain and Mrs. Drummond, welcome to Temple Manor." The two couples completed their introductions. They entered the house and proceeded to an expansive library. A modest fire in the impressive huge stone fireplace kept the room at a very comfortable temperature. Tea was offered and accepted by everyone.

Lady Selborne, Grace Palmer née Ridley, was the fifth and youngest child of Matthew White Ridley, 1ˢᵗ Viscount Ridley, and Mary Georgiana Marjoribank. Grace became the Countess of Selborne when her husband was elevated to the earldom.

"I must say, Captain, I add my accolades for your accomplishments in the air. As one of The Few as the press likes to refer to your comrades who served during those harrowing months, you are a bit of a rarity, and you have increased your tally since your transfer to the 8ᵗʰ Air Force last year."

"Thank you, Sir."

"I know your name in various news reports, but I only recently learned that we share a common friend," Lord Selborne said and looked at Charlotte, "and we share a common boundary."

I think he's referring to Wild Bill Donovan, Brian thought. *I'm not sure if Charlotte knows the connection, and I'd rather not illuminate the relationship, or show my ignorance, if I'm wrong.*

"Yes, we do, Lord Selborne," Charlotte responded, "once we acquired the Brownfield property."

"I see from the property line that you are transforming pasture to farming."

"Yes sir. The demand for vegetables to meet wartime requirements is growing. We will be farming suitable fields on both the Brownfield and Harris properties we now own. We have also expanded our dairy holdings as well as our dairy products."

"We know," said Lady Selborne. "We enjoy your cheeses, milk, and cottage cheese. We truly appreciate the quality of your products."

"Thank you very much, Lady Selborne. We do strive to deliver the best products we can."

Cecil changed the subject. "I must add my gratitude to you," he said to Brian, "for your airline. General Donovan has been exceptionally generous to make space available on your aircraft."

Brian wanted to say, *they are not my aircraft. The government, the OSS, and General Donovan have paid for them and also paid for us to operate them.* "They are the best aircraft available for flying across the Atlantic."

"Have you flown them?"

"Not yet, but I am certain I will. I have my hands full flying my fighter aircraft. Mister Sales manages the airline business for me, and Charlotte supervises since I'm often unavailable."

Selborne looked at Charlotte. "You are a woman of many talents, I must say, Mrs. Drummond. And you are a holder of the George Cross, as well, awarded by King George himself."

"For saving my sorry ass from her pond," Brian added.

"Language, Brian," Charlotte chastised him. "And it is our pond now."

They all laughed in good humor.

"Sorry. My apologies. My language gets a bit coarse these days."

"Quite understandable, my dear fellow. These are troubled times."

They discussed farming, although the Selbornes were understandably more distant from the actual work. Lord Selborne offered to connect their farm superintendent with Charlotte, the default superintendent of Standing Oak Farm.

The butler appeared. "Lord and Lady Selborne, lunch is ready to be served."

The large dining room table was set for four at one end. The lunch menu included pork chops with brown gravy, roasted Brussels sprouts, and scalloped potatoes. For dessert, they were served healthy slices of homemade cheesecake.

As they enjoyed sherry and before they left the table, Lady Selborne stated, "I'm so happy you enjoyed the meal. I must say our chef extended herself. The entire meal, including the dessert, was produced entirely from ingredients grown by our farm and yours. She had to substitute our honey for the sugar in the cheesecake, but the entire meal was homegrown between us."

"We are expanding products," Charlotte added, "but we do not have meat."

"We have limited meat, mostly for our consumption," said Lord Selborne. "Perhaps we can set up a mutually beneficial barter system since you have products we do not and vice versa."

Charlotte smiled broadly. "I am certain we can find appropriate accommodation, Sir. We would be most grateful." She looked at Brian and nodded her head.

It's time. "Thank you so much for your gracious invitation and hospitality, Lord Selborne. I'm afraid we must go. The afternoon chores are pending. Perhaps, someday soon, you will allow us to reciprocate your courtesy."

"We would be honored to visit Standing Oak Farm. Thank you for coming. We look forward to knowing our neighbors better with each visit."

The horses were waiting for them exactly where they had left them, at the entry portico. They said their good-byes and mounted up. Charlotte and

Brian did not talk, lost in their private thoughts, until they were halfway across the Brownfield property.

"What did you think?" asked Brian.

"I thought it was a very nice afternoon and an excellent meal." They both chuckled as they walked their horses. "I didn't detect any ulterior motive for the luncheon. Did you?"

"No. I was listening for even a hint. I detected none."

"Do you think Lord Selborne was serious when he suggested bartering our food?"

"Yes, I do. I think it will be a great opportunity to access more protein for our family and our crew."

"Yes, well then, I'd better study up on market pricing in these difficult days."

"I have faith you can handle it, my sweet," Brian said softly.

Charlotte looked over at him as they rode side-by-side. "Oh my, you must want some of my affections."

Brian returned her smile. "Now, there's an idea I can get into once we get everyone settled tonight."

"You naughty boy." Charlotte took off at a gallop. Brian tried to catch up.

—

Thursday, 7.October.1943
No.10 Annexe
New Public Offices
Whitehall, London, England
United Kingdom
08:15 hours

Winston remained in his robe, in bed, finishing the last of his breakfast of poached eggs on toast with roasted potato cubes and blood sausage. Peck announced the arrival of Lord Cherwell.

"My apologies for interrupting your morning routine, Winston. I have a full schedule today, and this news just could not wait. I wanted you to hear it from me directly. Doctor Bohr arrived in Scotland early this morning, but he nearly did not survive the trip. He was in a thermal protective bag suspended in the bomb bay of a Special Activities Mosquito for the flight from Sweden across Norway and the North Sea. Somehow, the communications system failed, or Niels did not understand the pilot, but he failed to don his oxygen mask for the high-altitude portion of the flight. When they landed, he was unconscious—hypoxic and hypothermic. Fortunately, the RAF had an expert medical team waiting that worked quickly to revive Doctor Bohr. He is safe now. The extraction flight could have turned out far worse, and it was a close call."

"Thank goodness we did not kill him."

"Indeed!"

"Where is he now?"

"He is being treated and checked at a military hospital in Edinburgh. The doctors want a couple of days of observation before they clear him for travel. The Home Office has already issued his refugee identification credentials. I am happy to report that he should be fully recovered and able to meet with you on Tuesday at Number 10. MI6, with the assistance of MI5, will interview him several times over the weekend to complete their first phase questioning."

"Thank you, Prof. I look forward to finally meeting Doctor Bohr. I trust you will be here for the meeting."

"Absolutely. I wouldn't miss the opportunity. It's been more than a week since I've seen you, and I understand congratulations are in order. Naples has fallen to the Allied advance, and you have concluded the surrender of Italy."

"Allied Forces."

"Yes, of course, the troops in the field. Now, if you will excuse me, I have a crucial meeting at the Royal Society in a few minutes, and I'm already going to be late for the introductions."

"Yes, yes, of course, Prof, be off with you. Thank you for stopping by and for the news."

Lord Cherwell departed promptly. Churchill placed his breakfast tray aside and rang for Sawyers. His valet arrived in short order. As Sawyers removed the tray, Winston said, "I think it's time to get on with the day," meaning he would take his morning hot bath and then dress for the day.

"Excuse me, Sir, you might want to wait a bit longer. Miss Sarah and Miss Pamela just arrived, asking for a quick word."

"Is anything the matter?" Churchill straightened the covers and his robe as if he needed to be more presentable.

"They did not say, Sir. Yes, of course, let me see them, and then I'll have my bath."

"Very well, Sir."

As soon as Sawyers cleared the door with the breakfast tray, Daughter Sarah and Daughter-in-Law Pamela entered. "Good morning, Papa," Sarah said boldly and with unusual cheeriness.

"Good morning to both of you. How are you two this fine morning?"

"Fine, Papa, fine," Sarah blurted impatiently.

"And how are your husbands?"

"Frankly, I don't know. I've not heard from Vic in several months."

Winston wanted to jump into their dysfunctional marriage, and he wanted to explore the apparent growing relationship with Gil Winant. But he resisted the urge. "Oh dear."

"Not to worry, Papa. We're happy."

Papa Churchill looked at Pamela. "It's has been many months since we've heard from Randolph. Do you have any more recent information regarding your husband?"

"Yes, Papa," Pamela said, using the familiar moniker the other Churchill children used. "I got a rather strange letter a few weeks ago that led me to believe he is no longer in Egypt. One sentence said something about the Balkans being gorgeous this time of year."

Winston knew where his son was but could not speak of it. Randolph was in the early stages of transferring from the general staff to a special mission with Tito's partisans in Yugoslavia. They had not left yet, but they were preparing for the mission. "I'm fairly certain he is safe wherever he is, or we would have heard something from the War Office."

"I hope so. It did seem rather odd."

"And what do I owe this gracious visit. Surely you didn't delay my bath to query me about Randolph's location."

Sarah jumped into the response. "Pamela just heard that Averell departed for the Soviet Union. Is he going to be gone long?"

"I didn't expect him to leave so soon. I surmise he has returned to Washington for instructions. Averell will be installed as Ambassador Harriman at the end of the month."

Pamela's expression turned instantly dark.

Winston had seen the newspaper reports and heard the gossip of what so many believed to be a not very well-hidden affair between Pamela and Averell Harriman. He felt the unique remorse of a father for his son, but he also recognized that Randolph was not an easy man to be around, set aside live within marriage, but still, this was his only son on the outside and deployed to a war zone.

"So it's true?" Pamela asked.

"I'm afraid so, my dear. Why do you ask?" Winston said, giving his daughter-in-law an opening if she wanted to talk or confide in him.

"I . . . we were just curious is all," responded Pamela.

"I can confirm his assignment as ambassador, but I cannot disclose his posting date other than at the end of October."

"Thank you, Papa. We'll leave you, so you can get on with your bath."

Both women leaned over and kissed Winston on the cheek. They went to the door.

"Please call Sawyers."

"We will, Papa," Sarah said. "Have a great and successful day."

—

Friday, 8.October.1943
26th Air Depot Group
USAAF Station LG-209
Deversoir, Fayed, Ismailia Governorate
Egypt

The airbase sat on the Suez Canal west bank at the north end of the Great Bitter Lake, 12 miles south-southeast of Ismailia and 72 miles northeast of Cairo. It had served as a Royal Air Force base since the 1930s. The U.S. Army Air Forces stationed various units there in mid-1942.

On 22.July.1943, a Romanian air force pilot defected alone in a nearly new, freshly delivered, Junkers Ju88D-1 long-range photoreconnaissance aircraft, a variant based on the Ju88A-4. The aircraft, serial number 430650, had all of 50 flight hours on it when it landed on Cyprus. The British flew the plane to learn as much as possible. Through diplomatic negotiations, the British turned over the aircraft to the AAF for formal engineering evaluation.

Major Warner Eugene 'Tutor' Newby, USAAF, had arrived at Deversoir, Egypt, on 1.July.1942. He was a qualified aircraft commander of B-25 Mitchell medium bombers and a combat bomber pilot assigned to the 81st Bombardment Squadron, 12th Bombardment Group, 9th Air Force. Newby flew his first combat mission on 16.August.1942. The squadron transferred to Station LG-088, southwest of Alexandria, on 18.October.1942. Newby completed his 25-combat mission tour requirement in February 1943, and as a degreed engineer, he was reassigned as the Depot Engineering Officer for the 26th Air Depot Group at Deversoir, Egypt. Major Newby was given the task of performing sufficient evaluation flights to know the aircraft's capabilities and to prepare to fly the Ju88D-1 aircraft back to the United States for full exploitation.

The process yielded several changes including the incorporation of P-38 drop tanks for extra fuel they would need for the longest legs of their ferry mission. They removed the guns to reduce weight and drag, and removed all unnecessary equipment to reduce weight further. The removed items would be sent to the United States by other means. They also pasted English labels for the various necessary flight instruments above the associated indicators as well as painting U.S. markings over the Romania insignia. They discovered and disabled hidden explosive charges just aft of the wing junction installed to destroy the aircraft in the event of a forced landing, to prevent the plane from falling into enemy hands. Major Newby had noted for the record that the aircraft had 'more damned gadgets than any plane I had ever seen.' He also declared that the Ju88D-1 was the 'heaviest and most vicious airplane I had ever flown.' The aircraft was given the name *Baksheesh*, Persian for 'something for nothing'—quite appropriate.

The Ju88D-1 was configured for a crew of four—pilot, observer, or bombardier in the bomber variant, radio operator/rear gunner, and a rear/lower gunner. The aircraft did not have a second set of controls; however, Newby wanted a copilot for the ferry mission to assist with navigation, the radios and flying when the need arose.

07:05 hours

"Tower, Baksheesh, ready for takeoff," Newby radioed.

"Baksheesh, winds three zero five at 12. You are cleared for takeoff. God be with you."

"Baksheesh cleared for takeoff. Thank you, fellas." Newby looked over his right shoulder to the observer's seat to the right and behind him. First Lieutenant G.W. Cook, USAAF, gave the major a thumb's up. Newby taxied onto the duty runway and pushed the throttles forward smoothly to about halfway. When the tail rose off the runway, and he had rudder effectiveness, Newby advanced the throttles to takeoff power. The aircraft lifted off the runway nicely. Once the aircraft's configuration was cleaned up and their cruise climb established, Newby banked the airplane and headed south.

The planned route of flight would take them to South Sudan before they turned west. They would skirt the southern edge of the Sahara Desert, across the continent to Senegal. The longest leg, and the shortest distance across the South Atlantic Ocean, was from Dakar, Senegal, to Natal, Brazil. Once safely in South America, they worked their way north across the Caribbean Sea and into the United States to Dayton, Ohio.

Major Newby and Lieutenant Cook accomplished the trans-Africa, trans-Atlantic flight in 5 ½ days. The ferry mission covered 12,000 miles at an average speed of 240 miles per hour and broken into legs ranging from 900 to nearly 1500 miles. The journey was not without incident as they were intercepted numerous times by fighters sent up to check out the German aircraft with American markings. They delivered the aircraft safely to Wright Field, Dayton, Ohio, for exploitation.

Warner Newby was the older brother of the author's mother. He went on to successfully manage the wing improvement program of the B-52

Stratofortress, achieving the rank of major general and finishing his career as the commanding general of Vandenberg Air Force Base.

—

Monday, 11.October.1943
USAAF Station F-356
Saffron Walden, Essex, England
United Kingdom
09:15 hours

The Germans routed their vital supply trains across rail lines progressively farther from the coast because of marauding Allied fighters and diminished air defenses for Northern France and Belgium. Today's mission would be toward their range limit and deeper into France to hit a railway switching yard in Northeast Reims. Their primary target was expected to be a full train with three armored, anti-aircraft railcars—front, rear, and middle. Anything moving in the switching yard would be their secondary targets. Petersen specifically stated that they were to avoid engaging enemy fighters, if at all possible since it would divert them from their primary mission. No matter how they cut it, this RHUBARB 306 mission was going to be dicey. Also, as a consequence of the range, they would take a low-level beeline track to the target without their usual doglegs to confuse the enemy. The range alone made them more defensive in mindset than any of them felt comfortable with, but they instinctively knew their target had to be pretty important. On the positive side, they would have a cover fighter squadron over the Channel in case they were being chased.

Pete moved Rolo Stanfield to be the 2nd Section leader of Yellow Flight. This sortie would be the first ground-attack mission for the two new replacement pilots. Second Lieutenant Lewis Adrian 'Antler' Henricks of Ithaca, New York, took the position as Sweet Sweeny's wingman, and Second Lieutenant Billy Bob 'Boy' Williams of Birmingham, Alabama, joined the squadron last month as Rolo's wingman.

The squadron launched and crossed the Channel without difficulty. They crossed the coastline between Wissant and Escalles, southwest of Calais. Minor, ineffective, anti-aircraft ground fire from a distance did not pose much of a threat but could not be ignored. They made their initial point of Bazancourt, northeast of Reims, for a wide right hook into their target, attacking from the southeast and giving them their best chance to run for it. In their turn, they shifted to staggered divisions in trail, with each division in a line abreast once they rolled out of the turn. Hunter's Red Flight took the east side behind Pete's Blue Flight with the Green and Yellow Flights on the west side equidistant between the east side flights.

"Bandits, three o'clock high," Salt broadcast. Brian glanced up, and to his right, as certainly all the others did as well. A squadron of 109s dove to intercept them.

"Press on," radioed Pete. "One pass and we run for it. Don't engage unless necessary."

Streams of tracers began to extend out from a train on the north side of the railyard. *That must be our primary target.* A switching engine with smoke and steam rising from it and pulling three railcars lay between the attackers and their primary target. Hunter placed his sight pipper short of the last car and squeezed his trigger. All eight guns sent lethal streams of projectiles downrange. Impact flashes and puffs of smoke or splintered wood appeared all along the small train. Brian bunted his pipper slightly at the locomotive to give it extra rounds. The flashes covered the length of the engine. A huge billow of steam and smoke burst from the engine firebox and boiler. Hunter quickly adjusted his pipper to the rear gun car. Only one of the quad-20mm mounts on the rear car was firing and not at him. Brian fired. The flashes on the armor and metal of the gun mount marked Brian's success. That mount stopped firing as well. To his left, a railcar burst like a large, white, chrysanthemum blossom. Someone hit an incendiary ammunition car.

Hunter pulled up and hard to avoid the white-hot fragments. As soon as he cleared the explosion, he rolled nearly inverted and pulled back to get back down to the tops of buildings and trees. Once he was stable, he looked up to the right. The Germans were closer on a good pursuit line but still not close enough to engage. Hunter looked back to the left. The other three aircraft of his Red Flight were still with him. Over the countryside, they shifted on command signal to their aerial combat formation. Yellow Flight remained out of position since Hunter could not give them a power margin to close. Hunter gradually moved 'B' Division closer to 'A' Division, but they had the same problem—insufficient closure margin. They were still ahead of the Germans. *It's going to be a toss-up whether we make the Channel before the Germans catch us.* Pete kept them running for the coast.

As they approached the Channel, Pete radioed, "Tiptoe, Pectin, we've got an angry tail."

"Roger Pectin, we've got 'em. We'll clean 'em off you."

Whew! That is a welcome radio call.

The P-47 cover squadron passed over the top of them in the opposite direction. The Germans had no choice but to abandon their pursuit of 334FS to defend themselves. The fighters of 334FS were over the water and clear of the threat. At about mid-Channel, Pete throttled back to provide the rest of the squadron the power margin to close up for a more orderly formation. They passed east of London.

"Carmen, Pectin, five miles south for landing by sections."

"Roger Pectin. Winds 2-9-0 at 8. Cleared to land 3-5."

"Roger, Carmen. Cleared to land 3-5."

Pete signaled for sections in trail for a straight in due to their low fuel state. They spaced themselves accordingly. Buddy was behind and below Hunter's right wing—perfect. All 16 members of the squadron survived the mission and landed safely without incident.

Tomlinson waited for Brian at the trailing edge, left wing root. "My quick check showed no damage, and all eight guns fired."

"Sounds right to me, Larson."

"Very well, sir. We'll give her a good inspection, refuel, and rearm her."

"Thanks, Larson."

Brian deposited his flight gear on his peg, and then he walked to the intelligence shack for his debriefing. It was not a perfect mission, but it was a successful one. They all came home with no wounds, and they hit their target deep in France. They continued to be grateful for and toast the Red Army for drawing off so much of the *Luftwaffe* they once faced.

—

Tuesday, 12.October.1943
No.10 Downing Street
Whitehall, London, England
United Kingdom
16:00 hours

Lord Cherwell arrived with their guest from Copenhagen, Denmark, via Sweden and Scotland. Winston waited in the entrance hall.

"Prime Minister Churchill," the Prof began, "I am pleased to introduce Professor Doctor Niels Henrik David Bohr, one of the preeminent theoretical physicists in the world."

"It is a genuine honor to finally meet you, Mister Churchill," Bohr said, as the two men shook hands.

The prime minister led the two men to the Blue Room. A steward served fresh champagne flutes with Winston's favorite—Pol Roger 1928. "A toast to your safe arrival."

"Hear, hear." They responded. The three men sat in the gorgeous blue upholstered couches.

"As the leader of His Majesty's Government," Bohr said, looking directly at the prime minister, "I would like to convey my deepest and sincerest gratitude for rescuing my family and me from those damned Nazi bastards. From your agents in Copenhagen through Professor Lindemann, you have been most generous, and I will be forever grateful."

"We are also grateful that we were able to help. The Nawzees are losing the war. The end for them is inevitable. Unfortunately, that reality makes them more desperate and vindictive. To be candid, Professor, I would have preferred extracting you and your family before the Gestapo turned its attention on you."

"I just never believed the Germans would abuse Denmark as they have done."

"It is far worse in Eastern Europe."

"I know not of any of that."

Churchill nodded his head. "The Nawzees did not want you to know. They were too bloody close. As you wish to know, we will make our evidence available to you, especially to those of your faith."

This time Bohr nodded his head in agreement.

"You are safe to practice your religion as you choose without fear. There is no obligation incumbent upon our assistance to you and your family. As one of the preeminent physicists in the world, we are thankful that your intellect could be preserved. Professor Lindemann informs me that you are current and knowledgeable regarding the German and Allied efforts to exploit the energy stored in the atom."

"Yes, I am."

"You know and are known by most of the physicists involved in the research, including Werner Heisenberg."

"Perhaps so. I've not gone through any list. I've had many discussions with Doctor Heisenberg over the years, and your intelligence people have asked me rather expansive questions that I have answered as thoroughly and forthrightly as I possibly can. I stand ready to assist you in any manner I am able. I must confess that I held considerable skepticism regarding the feasibility of an explosive release of energy. I eagerly anticipate learning more as you are able or willing to share with me."

"We need to thoroughly debrief you, as your knowledge is of utmost concern to the Allied effort. I know our American cousins will want to join us for your interviews. Let it suffice to say, for now, that we initiated a research and development program we call TUBE ALLOYS for the exploration of atomic energy, both in the potential for a military explosive as well as a sustainable energy source. Once we have completed the preponderance of our interviews, President Roosevelt, Prime Minister King of Canada, and I would appreciate your perspective on the program. Professor Lindemann has informed me regarding your doubts about the attainment of a military explosive. We are now convinced it is possible, and we are working on the engineering to achieve such a device. I can also assure you we are far more concerned, and I will say apprehensive, about Germany's progress on such a weapon. I think you will find if you have not already deduced that our disquiet about Germany is paramount in our thinking."

"I am only now becoming aware of why you are so concerned. I can promise you I will do what I am able to assist you in that endeavor."

The three men continued their conversations through the rest of the afternoon, into cocktail hour, across dinner, and then for a majority of the evening as they discussed family, friends, mutual acquaintances, and other matters of the world. Bohr closed the evening by again expressing his gratitude for the rescue of his family.

—

Wednesday, 13.October.1943
Office of the Director, Office of Strategic Services
National Institutes of Health Building
2430 E Street Northwest
Washington, District of Columbia
United States of America
14:50 hours

The knock on the door was followed by Ned Buxton's entry into Donovan's ground floor corner office. Ned closed the door behind him. Wild Bill looked up from the latest field report he was reading.

"We just received MAGIC confirmation that the Japanese executed 98 captured Americans a week ago on Wake Island. The report alleges the captives were attempting to make radio contact with U.S. forces."

"Those men were just trying to survive."

"Quite so."

"Make sure the war crimes desk notes confirmation classified sources—plural. We can't make the MAGIC intercept part of the record, but we should record confirmation for the war crimes tribunal."

"I'll see to it," Ned responded. "One more news item, we received confirmation from London Station that Doctor Bohr arrived safely in London, but not without a scare." Ned paused. Bill waited for the rest of the story. "During transit across the North Sea in the belly of a Mosquito, the good doctor didn't get his oxygen mask on for the high altitude portion of the journey. He arrived in Scotland unconscious, but they revived him apparently without permanent injury."

"Thank goodness to Lady Luck."

Buxton nodded his head. "I wanted to catch you before your meeting with General Groves." Donovan nodded his head and checked his desk clock.

The Groves meeting was scheduled for 15:30. "Have you been able to read the two Hitler profile reports?"

The OSS had commissioned two separate psychological profiles. The first titled "Analysis of the Personality of Adolph Hitler: With Predictions of His Future Behavior and Suggestions for Dealing with Him Now and After Germany's Surrender" had been created by Doctor Henry Alexander Murray, MD, MA (biology), PhD (biochemistry). Doctor Murray used a wide variety of sources, including defectors with first-hand knowledge of the subject. The Murray study was the pioneering work for what would eventually become known as criminal profiling in use to this very day. A companion but separate psychological study titled "A Psychological Analysis of Adolph Hitler: His Life and Legend" by Doctor Walter Charles Langer, PhD (Psychology). Langer studied under Anna Freud and met her famous father several times before the family had to flee Nazi-dominated Austria. Langer was also the younger brother of Deputy Chief OSS Research and Analysis Branch William Leonard Langer, PhD (history).

"I'll have to move them up on my reading list," Wild Bill declared.

"I think you will find them very interesting. I don't think the reports alter our view of Hitler, but they add heft to our assessment. Both reports are pretty clear that there should be little hope that Hitler will surrender. He will likely attempt to burn the house down around him. We have seen his several stand-or-die orders to his field generals, not least of which Field Marshal Paulus at Stalingrad and Field Marshal Rommel in North Africa."

"I need to read them sooner rather than later. You might ask Bill Langer to prepare a presidential summary of the reports. We'll need to brief the leadership, including the president. We also need to share these reports with the British."

"I'll take care of it. Now, you've got about ten minutes until your Groves meeting. I'll leave you to it, in case you have any last-minute prep to do."

"Thanks, Ned."

Buxton departed and closed the door behind him. Bill took one last look at his notes for the meeting. He was ready.

15:30 hours

General Groves arrived spot on time and was announced.

"Thank you for considering our intelligence needs, Bill."

"No problem, Dick. That's what we're here for today. How can we help?"

"We discussed the Alsos Mission a few months ago. The first team is on the ground in Italy. They've scoured the University of Naples without finding much other than a few abstract clues. Doctor Fermi informs us that the bulk of the atomic physics research was accomplished at the Universities of Rome and Pisa, so we are eager to get there before the material can be destroyed."

"Understood. The urgency is appreciated. We can't improve the combat advance. We do have special teams operating behind the lines. If we knew exactly what we are seeking and where the material is, we could carry out a special operations mission, but we must know what and where we are supposed to look. Without the focus, I'm afraid it is far too risky for the action team."

"From what we can see and what we hear," Groves said, "the Germans are not going after an explosive variant with the same aggressiveness as we are. However, what haunts our thoughts and nightmares is what we cannot see. Based on Doctor Fermi's counsel, we are guardedly optimistic we will find substantive information on the Italian, and indirectly we hope, on the German development programs. We recognize that we probably won't know for sure until we see the Heisenberg group's actual research papers and facilities. I think a priority should be the capture or assassination of Heisenberg—the head of the snake."

"We are getting closer to Heisenberg but nowhere near close enough. I would like to imbed a few of our operational agents with your Alsos Mission to stay with you as we learn more."

"We anticipated that potential, Bill. But I must confide in you, such a candidate must have better than a lay understanding of the physics and must have a good working handle on the languages—Italian, German, and probably French."

"I'm working on what I think are or will be good candidates. If you are agreeable, Dick, perhaps we can discuss the candidates at next month's meeting, and if you concur, we'll promptly get them in place. I want to make sure whoever the agents are that they are fully trained in the clandestine arts just in case the situation presents. Those agents we have in Italy, France, and Germany who are aware of our atomic research interest know of the capture-or-kill orders for Heisenberg and the other German scientific leaders."

"They also know such information cannot fall into German hands?" Groves asked.

"Yes, they do . . . in very explicit detail."

"Excellent. I'm in the process of gaining War Department approval for Colonel Boris Pash to lead the unit."

Colonel Boris Theodore Pash, USAR, CIC, had been assigned to the Western Defense Command, the IX Corps Area that included California. He had been born Boris Fedorovich Pashkovsky in San Francisco to émigré parents and anglicized his name early in life. Pash had been selected by

Groves to investigate the Manhattan Project's chief scientist, Doctor Robert Oppenheimer, for his interest in and ties to communist front organizations. Groves had confidence in Pash's skills, judgment, and leadership.

"I know of him. I have an eye on him as well, given his knowledge of Russia from his parents."

"Good man. Colonel Pash knows we are working together to learn more about the German program, so I don't anticipate any problems there. I must say that as we learn more, our worries abate just a little, but Germany remains our primary concern."

"And ours, I can assure you. Now, if I may, how is your project moving along?"

"I believe we all agree that we have a handle on the science, but the engineering is proving more of a challenge. The production facilities at Oak Ridge and Hanford are moving along nicely. We shall soon have high-grade materials for experimentation and testing."

"Are you going to test the thing once you have a feasible design?" Donovan asked.

"That is an on-going debate. The purity requirements are so high that the proper materials are quite scarce. Some want to trust the designs to avoid wasting any precious material. At any rate, it is not a decision we must take now. The project's focus is on the production capacity and resolving engineering matters."

"And beating the Germans to the trigger pull."

"Yes, exactly. That motive drives us all."

The two men continued their discussions about uranium supplies, physical security including Doctor Bohr's safety, and the collection of rare materials the scientists requested for their experimentation. Dick Groves knew he had a tiger by the tail, and so did Bill Donovan from an entirely different perspective. Fortunately, the two leaders maintained a good and productive working relationship as they each pursued the objectives assigned to them.

—

Friday, 15.October.1943
Headquarters, 8ᵗʰ Air Force
USAAF Station AAF-586 (Camp Griffiss, code name: Widewing)
Warren Plantation and Sandy Lane
Bushy Park, Teddington, Middlesex, England
United Kingdom
09:10 hours

Newly promoted Lieutenant General Eaker gathered his staff and commanders, including Commanding Generals Major General William

Ellsworth 'Bill' Kepner, USAAF, of the 8th Fighter Command, and Major General Frederick Lewis 'Fred' Anderson Jr., USAAF [USMA 1928] of the 8th Bomber Command.

"Well, gentlemen," Eaker began, "yesterday's bombing mission proved just as costly as the August version. We lost 60 of 291 bombers on the raid—21 percent. We are losing pilots, crews, and aircraft faster than the Army can replace them. While our aircraft have encountered fewer enemy fighters over France, the Germans appear to have withdrawn squadrons to defend the fatherland. Our bomber crews see the result. We maintain a 25-mission threshold for transfer from combat assignments, and yet the current average life expectancy of our bombers crews is barely 15 missions. I think we all recognize that we face a morale crisis that can't be ignored. Further, we have been assigned strategic objectives by our leadership in conjunction with our British comrades and given the resources to do the job."

"What do you expect from us, General?" interjected General Anderson.

"What I expect, General, is for each of you to do what has to be done to improve morale. I think we're seeing evidence of the crews losing their focus on the mission."

"Easily said," Anderson continued. "I doubt any of us would disagree that falling morale is affecting performance. We see increasing numbers at sick call. We've even seen more than a few instances of self-inflicted wounds to avoid the flight schedule."

"And it must stop. We don't enjoy the luxury of excess crew resources. We need all the men to perform their duty. The majority of our pilots and crews are doing just that."

"It's hard to describe the nauseating feeling of dread these fellas experience with watching the German fighters standing off at a distance just waiting for our fighter escort to leave us. It's inhuman."

"What do you propose?"

"I'd suggest we confine ourselves to targets within the range limits of our fighters. There are plenty of targets within fighter range. We've already rejected abandoning daylight bombing for the night, like the Brits, so that option is out. We've also discussed drop . . ."

"Stop, Fred!" commanded Eaker. "We're not some development squadron. Our country gave us a mission and the tools to do that mission. When they see fit to give us better tools, we'll utilize those tools. Until then, we'll do what we've been ordered to do with the tools we have." Eaker stared at Anderson for several seconds and then took a deep breath that he slowly exhaled. "These are not easy times. Our mission is not an easy one. POINTBLANK is a full-on joint effort by the British and us to blunt German offensive fighter capabilities. The enemy's fighter production, supplies, armaments, fuel, and oil are in Germany. The 15th Air Force took a terrible pounding but hit the Ploesti oil refinery complex hard. While we don't have conclusive evidence just yet, I do believe we're bleeding them."

"General Eaker, they're bleeding us too," Anderson said. "The question is who is going to pass out first from blood loss."

Eaker held up his right hand, palm out. "We all acknowledge that your guys are hurting. The sooner we cut down Gerry's ability to put fighters in the air, the sooner the sky will belong to us. We've adjusted the fighter escort launch times to optimize their fuel. We're doing the best that can be done. I'm asking each of you to take the weekend to think about how to improve morale. We'll meet again Monday morning to discuss your ideas. Dismissed." Eaker nearly jumped to his feet and left the room before the others could stand.

Neither Anderson nor Kepner rose. Sitting next to each other, they spoke in muffled tones. "Do you see anything else that we can do to extend escort coverage?" Anderson asked Kepner.

"He," Bill said, nodding to the door, "won't let us modify our fighters for drop tanks," observed Kepner. "The best I can see is the new Mustangs they tell me will have auxiliary fuel capability built-in. They also tell me to expect deliveries to begin next month. If the information I have been given is correct, the drop tanks should give us sufficient range to cover you across all of Germany and into Poland."

"None too soon for my boys. These uncovered daylight raids are literally killing us."

"I know, Fred. It's taking a toll on my guys too. They know in gory detail what our lack of range is doing to your crews. They're desperate and angry that they can't do more. They see those damn Germans waiting like vultures, and it tears their hearts out when they have to say good-bye. My guys pressure me for drop tanks too. You heard the chief as I did. He's not budging on the tools-we're-given thing."

"This is just the aerial version of trench warfare from the last war. Who will be the last man standing?"

The two men sat by themselves in silence for several minutes. Anderson was the first to stand.

"Let me know if there is anything else we can do to help," Kepner said to Anderson's back as he stood.

———

Saturday, 16. October. 1943
Oval Office
The White House
Washington, District of Columbia
United States of America
16:30 hours

Admiral Leahy and Harry Hopkins sat in straight back chairs on the other side of the Hoover Desk from President Roosevelt.

"The prime minister and I agreed that we would establish a war crimes tribunal at the conclusion of hostilities with both Germany and Japan. We are both insistent upon accountability for the perpetrators of the atrocities we continue to document. The tribunals will be a part of their unconditional surrender. We are determined not to repeat the mistakes of the Versailles Treaty and the last war. General Donovan and the OSS have created a specific desk officer who has established a listing of perpetrators as we know them or learn of them, and a catalog filing system to preserve the intelligence and evidence as we collect it."

"Seems quite appropriate, Mister President," Leahy said.

"I want you both to be fully aware of these agreements, just in case something should happen to me. The unconditional surrender of the Axis remains our objective. However, we must punish the perpetrators, not the population."

"But the population enabled the perpetrators," Hopkins protested.

"Yes, they did, but we have no ability to sort out the enablers. There are others within Germany, and I dare say Japan as well, who did not support the regime, like the tragic story of the Scholl siblings MI6 and the SOE reported last winter. We do not want to punish the whole population. That was our mistake after the last war. I confess my growing apprehension with Henry's pastoral advocacy." Roosevelt lapsed into contemplation.

Secretary of the Treasury Henry Morgenthau, Jr., had been in his position since Roosevelt's initial inauguration. He had consistently argued for rendering Germany to an agrarian society and against allowing any industrialization or maintaining any standing army even for their own defense. He also had, on occasion, suggested that Germany should be broken up into smaller independent states. Roosevelt appreciated Morgenthau's service at Treasury, but he could not agree with Henry's encouragement of Germany's incapacitation. Both Winston and Franklin thought the best approach to post-war Germany was a healthy, vibrant, peaceful, and democratic nation welcomed into the family of respectful countries rather than a resentful society bent upon retribution.

"We've done that once," the president said. "We don't want to make another try of it. We will respect the German people, while we will charge, try, convict, and punish, before the people of the world, those who led them to the abyss."

"Secretary Morgenthau is not alone in those thoughts," Harry mumbled.

Roosevelt chuckled softly. "Therein lies the challenges for all leaders in these dangerous years. Henry Wallace has voiced his support for Morgenthau's pastoral proposal, and a significant faction within the party supports Wallace. We cannot ignore the Morgenthau plan."

"We have faith you are up to the challenge, Mister President," Bill Leahy commented.

"It'll take more than just me. In that aspect, my vision of the post-war world is comparatively solidified from the United Nations to the de-colonization of indigenous peoples. The wild card in all this is the Soviet Union. Prime Minister Churchill is becoming progressively more convinced that Premier Stalin has no intentions of liberating Eastern Europe, but rather to occupy those countries as some kind of buffer between them and Germany. He has voiced an opinion to me that Stalin may have a strategic objective of spreading his brand of communism throughout the world; in other words, world domination using the new found strength of the Red Army."

"Is he really serious?" Bill asked.

"He'd be choosing different words to express his opinion, if he was just thinking aloud, he'd not have used the words he has used. So, yes, I think he is quite serious. The Red Army hasn't yet reached the pre-war borders, so we do not yet have physical proof of their intentions, but I can't ignore the strength of his opinion. Too many want to believe Stalin. I trust Winston. His instincts are surprisingly accurate as they've been for well more than ten years that I know of in this affair."

"Has the prime minister proposed a response?" asked Leahy.

"Yes, get to Berlin first and meet the Russians as far east as we can, to avoid or diminish the question."

"Easier said than done," observed Bill.

"Quite so. That's exactly Winston's point."

"We can't get there until we get a substantial force on the ground in Northern Europe—OVERLORD."

"Precisely, but that's not so easily accomplished either. The difficulty I face with Winston is that I have no reason not to trust Premier Stalin until I have a reason not to do so. I'm caught between Stalin's denials and my inclination to believe him, and my trust in Winston's judgment. It's going to be an arduous few years of trying to balance these opposing forces. The risk that we face in Winston's prophesy is, once we see Stalin's intentions or strategic objective, it'll be too late to do anything about it short of war."

"War with the Soviet Union?" Leahy said with incredulity.

"That's the implication. Not an attractive thought. But Winston is seriously concerned about the autonomy of Poland and other Eastern European states. He believes Ukraine wants its independence from Russia, which in part explains the broad-scale support the Germans enjoyed and squandered in Ukraine."

"What do you want to do?" asked Leahy.

"About the only option we have is to execute OVERLORD as soon as humanly possible and strive to achieve what Churchill suggests. I'll have to walk a very fine line between Churchill and Stalin. I'll have to employ my many charms to dampen whatever hegemonic desires Uncle Joe may possess."

"Is the OSS trying to determine Soviet intentions?" Hopkins asked.

"Yes. I've had several conversations with General Donovan. They're working hard on the question. As I told the general, this situation is precisely what I envisioned strategic intelligence to accomplish."

"Not an easy question to answer," Leahy observed.

"No, it's not, but that is the task."

The three men turned their attention to other military matters as the afternoon waned.

—

Friday, 22.October.1943
Llanion Barracks
Pembroke Dock, South Wales
United Kingdom
15:20 hours

The American 28th Infantry Division (28ID) had been mobilized from the Pennsylvania Army National Guard to federal service on 17.February.1941. The division had served in France during the Great War and already possessed a storied history. General Pershing had dubbed the division the Iron Division and was also known as the Keystone Division for its solid red keystone shaped shoulder insignia.

The 28ID arrived at Pembroke Dock on the Milford Haven Estuary in Southwest Wales. The personnel of the division debarked from their ships using a carefully planned and orchestrated schedule. They formed up on the pier into their squads, platoons, and companies, and marched in formation for the one mile distance to Llanion Barracks. The post had been vacated and turned over to the 28ID as part of Operation BOLERO. The division would continue its training for an eventual combat deployment to the European Continent for the liberation of France and Germany's defeat.

One member of the 28ID was Staff Sergeant Herbert Davis 'Herb' Parlier from Reedley, California—the author's paternal uncle, the oldest of the two younger brothers of the author's father. The division would land in France across the Normandy beachhead and entered combat operations on the 22nd of July—six weeks after the OVERLORD landings and nine months after arriving in Great Britain. The Germans who faced the division would refer to the unit as *die Blutiger Eimer Abteilung* —the Bloody Bucket Division—in recognition of the shoulder patch they wore. The moniker stuck with the division for reasons other than the Germans intended.

—

Chapter 12

Whoe'er excels in what we prize,
appears a hero in our eyes.
-- Jonathan Swift

Wednesday, 3.November.1943
USAAF Station 512
St. Mawgan, Cornwall, England
United Kingdom
15:20 hours

Brian landed his P-47 Thunderbolt smoothly on the massive runway, the largest runway he had yet seen. He followed the ground controller's guidance signals to the designated parking spot for his fighter. A ground crewman gave him hand gestures, guiding him to the precise spot they wanted. Brian braked to a stop, set the parking brake, and waited for the crewman to chock his main wheels and signal engine shutdown. He secured his avionics, switched off all of his electrical equipment, and then pulled the mixture level back to CUTOFF. The big radial engine clanked to a stop. Brian switched off the magnetos, his oxygen supply, and then he unstrapped and removed his helmet, goggles, and oxygen mask, leaving everything in the cockpit since he would only stay for a few hours.

The ground crewman, an Army corporal in mechanic's overalls, stood at the trailing edge, left wing root. Brian jumped down. "We don't see many of these," the corporal said, gesturing to the hulky P-47, "out here. How can we help you, Captain?"

"I came out here to meet an inbound transport aircraft from the states."

"Do you need service?"

"Just fuel. Please top 'er off. Thanks. She's loaded with ammunition, so be careful."

The corporal signaled for the base fuel truck. He faced Brian and said, "If you will come with me, we'll get you into base ops." A private driving a Jeep picked them up and dropped them off at the large, 'V'-shaped, white building with the control tower above the apex.

Before Brian could step out of the Jeep, Charlotte burst through the double doors, ran to Brian, and leaped into his waiting arms. They embraced tightly as Edith emerged from the building holding Ian's little right hand as the 29-month-old toddler waddled along beside his nanny. He immediately set Charlotte down, released her, and spun her around. "When did he start walking so well?" he said, with discernible pride.

"You've seen him walking."

"Yeah, but not like that," Brian professed, pointing to Edith and Ian.

"You've not been home for a month, my darling husband. If you made it home more often, you could watch our son grow up."

"There is a war on, Charlotte." Brian knelt, holding his arms out to his son. Edith released Ian's hand. The boy did his best to run, although quite awkwardly and choppily, to his father. Brian wrapped his arms around Ian, as the boy wrapped his arms around his father's neck. Brian lifted him and faced Charlotte. "He's growing up so fast."

"I'm no expert, but I think that is what children do."

Brian looked at Edith. "Thank you for coming, and thank you ever so much for taking such great care of Ian for us both."

"It is my honor, Mister Drummond."

"I saw this aeroplane when you flew over the farm last summer, but up close it looks so much bigger and fatter," Charlotte asked, pointing at the Thunderbolt. They all laughed.

Brian turned to make sure which aircraft she was pointing to and answered, "Yep. That's it—the P-47 Thunderbolt."

"It's so big and fat," Charlotte repeated.

Brian laughed hard for several seconds, so much so Ian looked at him strangely, got scared, and began to cry. Edith reached for and took Ian into her arms, stepping back a couple of paces to calm Ian. "I'm sorry," Brian said to Ian, although the boy could not understand. He calmed himself and put his arm around Charlotte. "Yes, it is. She's a beast. Some of the guys call 'em Jugs."

Charlotte giggled softly and uneasily. "Why on earth would they call an aeroplane jugs?"

"Some say it is short for juggernaut. But I think it is because the engine has 18 air-cooled cylinders the mechanics call jugs. The designer found a big, powerful engine, and then they built an aircraft around the engine."

"I'm not quite sure what an air-cooled cylinder is, but I guess that makes sense."

"Have you seen a motorcycle engine?" Brian asked Charlotte.

"Yes."

"Well, imagine one of those cylinders with fins on it, about five times that size, and then 18 of them."

"Wow!"

"Yeah, the engine in the Thunderbolt produces 2,200 horsepower at full power, more than ten times the power of our lorry."

"Captain." Brian heard a male voice behind him shout. He turned to see a sergeant standing at the door, holding the door open. "The aircraft you're waiting on is on final approach."

Brian gave the man a thumb's up. The sergeant disappeared back into the operations building. Brian checked the windsock. The tail of the windsock was pointing in the likely direction of approach. He saw a speck in the distance.

"You said this is one of your aircraft," Charlotte observed.

"It's one of our aircraft . . . yes . . . one of our new aircraft making its inaugural trans-Atlantic flight. Bobby Joe Sales is likely flying it if I guess correctly."

"It'll be nice to meet him finally."

They watched the speck grow larger and larger. Brian easily made out the four wing-mounted engines and the triple vertical tail. The aircraft flared. The puffs of smoke marked the main wheel touchdown and then the nose wheel touchdown before the sound of contact, and the idling engines arrived. They watched the aircraft rollout past them with Bainbridge Air Services (BAS) painted in big blue letters along the sleek, streamlined fuselage above the row of passenger windows.

"My gosh, that is much bigger than I imagined, so much bigger than your Thunderbolt."

"Yes, it is. The aircraft is called a Constellation or Connie, a most impressive transport aircraft, from what I'm told."

The aircraft taxied to a position perpendicular to and just to the right of Brian's Thunderbolt. The transport had four engines that were bigger and more powerful than the engine in his fighter. A single air-stair was towed to the rear, left side door, and pushed to the aircraft's side. Once the air-stairs were in place, the door opened. A female, uniformed attendant stood in the doorway and handed several papers to the operations sergeant. The woman stepped back inside the fuselage. The sergeant stood just outside the door and appeared to tick off what had to be a manifest with each person's name as he exited the aircraft. Generals, admirals, colonels, and captains deplaned and walked to the operations building. Brian counted what he thought was two-dozen senior officers—a lot of stars from one to four. Junior officers, probably aides, followed the flag officers.

Bobby was the first person he recognized departing the aircraft. He jogged over to Brian. Ground crews began unloading the baggage and what cargo there was on board. Brian introduced Charlotte, Edith, and Ian to Bobby Joe Sales, President of Bainbridge Air Services. Before they finished, Brian watched Gertrude Bainbridge descend the air-stairs. He waved to her, and she waved back.

Brian immediately looked at Bobby. "You brought Gertie?"

"Yep. She's classified as flight crew to get her past the priority system." Bobby smiled broadly as Gertrude walked toward them. "You won't believe who else was part of the crew." Just then, the tall, lanky figure of Howard Hughes appeared in the open hatch.

"I'll be damned."

"Yeah . . . none other. He insisted upon coming along on this inaugural flight. Since he was the only one of us who has actually made the Atlantic transit, it seemed like a good idea. He's a helluva pilot, Brian."

Charlotte must have sensed the stir. "Who is that?" she asked.

"Howard Hughes," answered Brian.

"The movie producer?"

"Among other things, yes. He was instrumental in helping us acquire this aircraft," Brian said, gesturing to the aircraft, "and others like her."

Bobby added, "He did a lot more than that. Howard helped us get the airline running efficiently."

Gertrude went directly to Charlotte and grasped her shoulders. "I know you are Brian's Charlotte."

"Yes," Charlotte answered with a shocked expression. The two women embraced. "And you must be the famous Mrs. Bainbridge . . . for whom the air service company is named."

Gertie chuckled softly. "Oh no, my dear. That honor belongs to my deceased husband. "This," Gertie gestured toward the Constellation, "was Brian's idea." Gertrude released Charlotte and embraced Brian. "So this is England."

Brian laughed. "Indeed, it is, Gertie. Welcome to England."

"That flight is far too long. I don't think I can do it again."

"Why did you do it in the first place?" Brian asked innocently.

"I figured if I was going to meet Charlotte and Ian, this was the time. Bobby was so gracious to designate me as a member of the crew for this inaugural flight. I'm not getting any younger, Brian, and I saw this as probably my only opportunity to see where you've been hiding out for nearly five years. Worse, I had no idea when you would bring Charlotte and Ian to see me, so I just had to come see them."

Howard stepped toward them, held Charlotte's eyes, extended his right hand to her, gently grasped Charlotte's right hand, bent over, and kissed the back of her hand several times. "You are Charlotte Drummond, and I am Howard Hughes."

"A pleasure to meet you, Mister Hughes," Charlotte responded. Howard finally released her hand.

"Please . . . Howard, we're friends, no?" Hughes looked at Brian. "My God, man, you married up, my friend."

"Thanks, Howard. I agree without question. She resisted my charms for the longest time."

"But I eventually succumbed," Charlotte offered with a giggle, "to his infinite *charisma* and magnetism."

While Howard introduced himself to Edith and Ian, Brian met BAS Chief Pilot Lawrence Earl 'Larry' Hollis, Copilots Cord Zekiel Dallion and Francis June 'Franny' Billings, and Constellation Flight Engineers Barbara Lee Simington and Michael 'Mike' Reinhold. He was also introduced to BAS Chief Stewardess Jane Sara Simmons, and two Stewardesses Nicole Ann George and Tori Lofton. After a little chitchat, the crew excused themselves, so they could find something to eat and get some much-needed rest.

As the crew excused themselves and went to the small bus, Brian looked at Bobby. "Quite a few women."

"Indeed. A little more than 60 percent of our cockpit crews are women. It has been nearly impossible to find male pilots. The ones we have generally have some medical disqualification for military service that does not preclude them from maintaining their flightworthy status. With the WASPs gobbling up the qualified female pilots, it's getting harder to find women who are already trained."

"Wasps?" Brian asked.

"Women's Auxiliary Service Pilots," Bobby explained. "Jackie Cochran returned from England and was apparently charged by Hap Arnold to create a group of female pilots to ferry aircraft. The intention was to relieve male pilots of more routine flying tasks so they could be deployed to combat squadrons."

"I met Jackie a few times," added Brian.

"Helluva pilot."

"So I hear," Brian responded. With his mind on other issues, he gestured toward the operations building.

By prior arrangement with the base commander, Brian had requested the use of the main conference room. The remaining group made their way into the operations building and the assigned conference room. As those so inclined grabbed a mug of coffee and settled into their seats around the rectangular table, Ian began to fidget.

Edith announced, "I'd better get our young Master Ian outside so he does not disturb your meeting."

Brian waited for the door to close behind Edith and Ian before he spoke. "I don't have much time. I need to return to Debden before dusk this evening, which to do so I need to take off in about 30 to 40 minutes. Thank you for this inaugural flight. I trust you had no difficulty with the mission."

"None, Brian," Bobby responded. "The flight legs we flew were like clockwork, thanks to Howard's assistance and Hollis' planning. Thank you, Howard," he said, looking directly at Hughes.

"My pleasure," Howard offered. "I appreciate being included in the new flight crew and glad to help."

"Thank you, Howard," Brian added. "With so many important burdens in your life, we're most grateful you could take the time to help."

"I could not pass up the opportunity to meet Charlotte," Hughes said. Everyone giggled and laughed.

"I'd like to believe I was the objective of your motivation, but . . . ," Charlotte paused in her thought, and then continued, "I recognize your importance to the success of Bainbridge Air Services. So, I will add my gratitude to my husband's words. Thank you."

"Too bad you cannot take a familiarization flight with us," added Bobby. "At least you can take a tour of the aircraft. Most impressive, I must say."

"It'll have to wait for another time. I wanted to hear about the expansion of our airline."

"So far, so good is the short answer. Howard and his connections with TWA have helped enormously with scheduling and training. Zero nine three, outside, is our first L-49, but we've taken delivery of two others. Our hangars at Wichita Municipal are nearly complete. They should be done by the end of this year. The Connies are a whole higher dimension of our operations. We've received all of the Beech Model 18s, eight of the planned 12 Lockheed Model 18 Lodestars, and the first three of the Connies."

"How are operations?" asked Brian.

"Net positive and looking good would be my answer. Our principal customer is consuming virtually all of our capacity so far. Our overall load factor has remained in the 93% range plus or minus a couple of points. The hard part for us has been predicting and ticketing available seating."

"I would agree," Howard added. "BAS has a significant complicating factor that TWA, American, and other commercial airlines don't have. Your primary customer hasn't been particularly successful in scheduling their transportation needs. I mentioned it to Bill the other day, and he said he'd have his guys work on the predictability of their transportation needs."

"How are the routes maturing?" Brian asked.

"To be frank," Bobby began, "establishing the routes has been the most difficult. The routes for our primary customer have been the easiest. They've regular transfers that we service. They rarely fill an aircraft. It's easy enough when they do. The trick for us is filling the available seats when they don't. We run into some difficulties from time to time, but we get them sorted out quickly. We do have a few regular routes we can schedule and ticket. We're gettin' the hang of things. And, most important, we're making a good profit."

They discussed the details of airline operations from scheduling to maintenance, logistics, and even the administrative details like hiring, payroll, training, and certification. Brian was satisfied that the airline operations were maturing nicely, and Bobby was in firm control of the process.

Brian glanced at Howard, who very subtly nodded his head. Brian smiled. Looking at Howard, Brian asked, "How is TWA doing?"

Hughes laughed. "Doing good, since you asked. There is plenty of business for all of us. Wild Bill wanted a less well known, less public, airline for his purposes."

"Who is Wild Bill?" Charlotte asked.

"It's one of the nicknames they call Bill Donovan. You met him in London last September."

"They call him a lot of things," Howard added. "Bill is a good man with an impossible job and the world stacked against him. Just after he became COI in 1941, he told me what he wanted, and we discussed it. He told me about this fighter pilot he met during his first official unofficial tour of England. When we learned that you, a hotshot pilot, inherited a few aircraft and a fledgling air service company, he knew what had to be done, and he asked me to help. And here we are."

"We're most grateful for your assistance," Brian said. He glanced at his wristwatch.

Charlotte waved her left hand over her head like an enthusiastic schoolgirl. Everyone looked at Charlotte. "Before my dear husband blows this pop stand, as he likes to say . . ." Everyone laughed heartily. "I simply must know, Mister Hughes, are you going to make any more movies?" Again, everyone laughed.

"It's time for me to leave," Brian added quickly, "but I simply must hear the answer to my wife's query."

Hughes smiled, nodded his head several times, and replied, "Aviation seems to be my interest of late, but the simple and direct answer is yes. I haven't lost my interest in movie making."

"The first movie I saw of yours was *The Front Page*. I was fascinated. But it was *Hell's Angels* that I didn't see until seven years after it was first released in England—the epic scale of it all." Charlotte smiled broadly and shook her head.

"That one is still my favorite." Howard smiled at Charlotte and winked.

"Anything in the works, if I may ask?" asked Charlotte.

"Yes. Several movies are in various stages of production. One very special movie we've been working on for several years now premiered in San Francisco last February, but we've been having a bit of a tussle with the censors who seek to impose their Puritanical beliefs on everyone."

"Is that *The Outlaw*?" asked Charlotte.

"Yes."

"I've seen the movie posters, although the movie has not yet been released in Britain that I know of today."

"Yeah," Howard continued. "We began general release in February, but we pulled it rather than have the censors stifle sales."

"Their objections might enhance sales," offered Charlotte.

"We considered that potential, but for most movies, the United States is the primary and largest markets. I considered going it alone, but ultimately, I balked. We've been negotiating with Will Hayes and his MPAA since we pulled the movie from general distribution. Jane Russell is truly a phenomenal actress. She doesn't deserve this. We don't deserve this, but the MPAA has gained enormous power in our deeply religious, socially conservative society, and they object to cleavage." They all laughed, some more nervously than others.

"We all look forward to your next movie," added Brian, feeling the need to change the subject. "Now, I really must be going. Y'all can carry on without me. There's a war on after all."

They all stood as Brian did. He said goodbye to everyone. Brian held Charlotte's hand as they walked outside to the car. Ian was still asleep, but Edith got out of the vehicle. Brian leaned into the car, stroked Ian's cheek several times and kissed his forehead. "Goodbye, my son," he whispered. Brian stood back and softly latched the door. He looked at Edith and said, "Thank you for all you do, Edith, for Ian, for Charlotte, and for the household. We genuinely treasure all that you do."

"Thank you very much, Mister Drummond."

Brian nodded his recognition and turned to Charlotte. He extended his arms and embraced her, holding her tightly, he whispered in her ear, "I love you very much, my sweet. I'm sorry I can't stay to help, but please take good care of our guests."

"I will, my darling. Please be safe."

They kissed passionately. Brian touched Charlotte's cheek with a gentle caress.

The group stood outside the operations building door as Brian waved and then walked to his fighter. The ground crew saw him approach the aircraft and the crew chief ran out to support the start. Brian did a quick check of the aircraft, including the main fuel tank. Satisfied, Brian jumped up on the left wing root, looked back one more time, and waved. Edith had Ian in her arms and straddling her left hip. They all waved back, including Edith. She even took Ian's hand and waved for him.

Brian strapped in, completed his pre-start checks, signaled the crew chief, and received an acknowledgment that he was ready for the start. Brian checked the Mixture RICH, Prop full forward, and cracked the throttle. He primed the engine and depressed the starter button. The starter motor whined. The big radial turned over and fired off. Once Brian completed his pre-takeoff checks, he called for taxi, waved one last time, and released the brakes.

When he was ready, Brian requested clearance for takeoff and several low passes, traffic permitting. The tower indicated they had no inbounds, the pattern was his, and he was cleared for takeoff.

Brian kept the fighter just off the runway as he accelerated rapidly, sucked up the landing gear, and at the end of the runway, he pulled up smoothly into a gentle wingover. The aircraft accelerated nicely on the backside of the wingover. He leveled off just off the ground with the throttle full open, and then he lined up to pass between the tower and the Connie. Everyone remained outside and waved as the Jug roared past. Clear on the other side, Brian popped up just enough to roll left into a hard, steep turn, pulling back just enough to turn through three-quarters of a turn without losing too much airspeed. He lined up to pass directly over the Connie and directly at the group. He extended out just enough to allow him a modest turn. He lined up on the runway. As soon as he was clear of obstacles, he dropped to just off the runway and kept the throttle full forward. Brian stayed low until the upwind numbers, and then pulled up into a 45-degree climb and completed a victory roll before he turned to the heading for home base. *Another good day.*

—

Saturday, 13.November.1943
HMS Renown
50° 21' 44" North – 4° 10' 14" West
Royal Navy Anchorage Plymouth
Plymouth, Devonshire, England
United Kingdom
12:00 hours

"**U**nderway! Shift the colors," came the broadcast command, as they weighed anchor and began to move out of the harbor.

Prime Minister Churchill, attired in his preferred uniform as an RAF air commodore, stood on the battleship's port wing of the flag bridge along with First Sea Lord ABC Cunningham and daughter Sarah dressed in the uniform of a Women's Auxiliary Air Force section officer, the equivalent of a male RAF flying officer. Sarah had been given an extended leave of absence from her duties in the Photographic Interpretation Unit at RAF Medmenham and would serve as the prime minister's *aide-de-camp* for both the SEXTANT (Cairo) and EUREKA (Tehran) Conferences. The Cairo meeting would involve Churchill, Roosevelt, and Chinese Nationalist

Generalissimo Chiang Kai-shek since Stalin had refused to participate because the Chinese were not part of the European campaign and the Soviets were not part of the Pacific operations. Both Roosevelt and Churchill were grateful that Stalin had finally agreed to attend a summit meeting outside the Soviet Union, even if it forced them to stage a separate summit conference in Tehran.

"It's great to be back at sea," Admiral Cunningham said more to himself than anyone else.

"Indeed!" added Churchill. "This is a very historic place," he added without focusing on any particular feature of the sprawling His Majesty's Naval Base, Devonport."

Two destroyers led the battleship out of Plymouth harbor. Other destroyers churned the water of the Channel undoubtedly sweeping the sea for possible German U-boats that might be lurking—not likely but possible. Once they cleared the anti-submarine defenses, the water at the stern of the capital ship began to boil, and the ship increased speed.

"I'm getting chilly, Papa," Sarah said. "I'm going below to warm up with some tea." Sarah kissed her father on the cheek and departed.

A squadron of Spitfire fighters passed low at high speed from north to south, and then they split with one division climbing to the east and the other division climbing to the west. They would escort the small flotilla until the ships were up to full speed and into the open ocean.

"There is something very encouraging about the sound and sight of those aircraft," the prime minister observed.

"So true. They are always impressive to watch." The two leaders observed the evolving naval formation develop. "The Red Army is making good progress," the first sea lord added.

"Yes, they are. They crossed the Dnieper and liberated Kiev. That's a damn sight better than where they were two years ago. The Germans are still putting up a helluva fight. I think the outcome now is inevitable. It is only a question of how long and at what cost."

"The Oshima report left me with the impression that OVERLORD is not going to be a piece of cake."

Lieutenant General Baron Hiroshi Oshima, former military attaché to Berlin and now Japanese ambassador to Germany, took copious notes on a recent, German-hosted, four-day tour of the Atlantic Wall fortifications and German troop deployments. He wrote a 20-page classified report that he sent to Tokyo. Unbeknownst to the Germans or the Japanese, American decryption services intercepted and decoded the message. The deciphered and translated report was distributed within the MAGIC compartment.

"MI6 has validated portions of the report. The OSS has duplicated some and added their validation of other sections. The collected opinion in the report is that it is genuine and accurate, giving us exceptional intelligence regarding German dispositions and defense preparations. The hard part for the intelligence chaps is parsing and sanitizing the information into a useful form for the planners."

"They will sort it out," the admiral suggested. "It seems the most immediate difficulty is the air war."

"The U-boats are not the menace they were in 1940, but they remain a threat. The Germans have decided to defend Italy without the Italians. My guess is they don't want us on the other side of the Alps from the fatherland. Bomber Command will begin the aerial battle of Berlin on the 18th. POINTBLANK remains the primary focus of our American cousins."

"And rightly so. The German fighters are cutting them to ribbons."

"Yes, which is also why they will not be joining us for Berlin, at least not initially," Churchill said. "They are determined to deplete the fighters through POINTBLANK. We are helping as we can. We have convinced the American leadership that we must deviate like our continuing efforts on Peenemünde and our pending focus on Berlin. But the inevitable root question remains how quickly we can get a sufficient force on the Continent and race to Berlin? If we could meet the Soviets at the Polish eastern border, I would breathe a sigh of relief. We owe it to the Poles after we failed to jump to their defense when this whole dreadful affair began."

"They are far closer to that point than we are," observed Cunningham.

"Yes, they are. We must focus on next spring and ensuring OVERLORD is successful. We have much work ahead of us to achieve that objective." Without skipping a beat, the prime minister continued, "Now, I'm afraid the wind across the deck and the late autumnal chill are more than my old, tired body can tolerate. I'll leave you to it. I'm going to find Section Officer Churchill for a brandy."

"I'm with you, Prime Minister. My overcoat is no longer sufficient."

Both men stepped through the hatch to the flag bridge, and the admiral dogged it behind them.

———

Saturday, 13.November.1943
USS Iowa (BB-61)
Pier 12
Norfolk Naval Station
Norfolk, Virginia
United States of America
08:00 hours

"**U**nited States arriving," the ship's 1MC broadcast as the Boatswain of the Deck piped the president aboard, and the sideboys saluted. The four assigned seamen made their way with some difficulty carrying the president in his wheelchair from the quarterdeck to the flag bridge. Two wooden platforms had been constructed and installed, one on each wing of the flag bridge, to allow the president to see over the solid railings. They positioned him on the starboard box, secured his wheelchair, and retired to the bridge to stand in readiness to move the president into the flag stateroom when he was ready. On the bridge wing with the president, in addition to the ever-present Secret Service detail, were the services secretaries and joint chiefs, all of whom would participate in the upcoming summit conferences.

"Underway. Shift the colors," came the 1MC message to signal the last of the mooring lines securing the ship to the pier had been cast off.

The impressive new battleship had been tasked to transport the president to the SEXTANT Conference in Cairo with Churchill and Chiang Kei-Shek, and the EUREKA Conference with Churchill and Josef Stalin. The Soviet premier refused to attend the Cairo Conference, forcing the Western Allies to add the subsequent meeting.

President Roosevelt watched with keen interest as the battleship moved away from the pier and slowly moved into the channel through Hampton Roads. Gray ships were everywhere, tied up at the many piers and anchored in the anchorage portion of the waters. The sight of the rapidly growing Atlantic Fleet inspired considerable awe. The president remained on his observation box and very attentive until the ship passed through the anti-submarine defenses at the mouth of the Chesapeake Bay and into the open ocean. The destroyer screen had already deployed and swept the area. He counted six nimble destroyers arrayed ahead of them.

Once they were into the open ocean and their speed was increasing, the president signaled that he wished to withdraw to the warmth of his stateroom. The four seamen made quick work of the transport task, and the president settled into a daily routine.

—

Sunday, 14.November.1943
USS Iowa
34° 20' North – 40° 58' West
Western Atlantic
13:55 hours

The ship's klaxon gonged repeatedly. "This is not a drill. This is not a drill. General Quarters! General Quarters! All hands man your battle stations. Torpedo wake, starboard side." The ship heeled heavily to port as it executed a hard turn to starboard.

The president's secret service agents burst into the flag stateroom. The lead agent shouted, "Our station is the interior conference room, Mister President." They did not wait for the president's acknowledgment and lifted him in his wheelchair. They carried him through the hatch to the adjoining interior conference room. A rumble could be felt as the massive warship increase speed and leveled out. "They spotted a torpedo wake, sir."

"It's not hit us yet."

"No, Mister President."

"I'm not too keen on going for a swim in the middle of the Atlantic."

"None of us are, sir."

The rumbling stopped, and the ship heeled less to starboard. Minutes passed as the two Secret Service agents and president stared at the walls—no portals, no view of the outside world. Roosevelt began to fidget in his wheelchair, frustrated by his forced inactivity. The security agent tried to ignore the president's mounting irritation.

"I'm reluctant to bother the captain during a situation, Mister President," the lead agent finally volunteered. "They've not changed the material condition status, which means they are still working the situation."

Roosevelt stared at the agent with an admixture of disbelief and resentment. "I can't just sit here doing nothing," the president protested.

"I'll go check with the captain," the lead agent stated.

Ten minutes later, the president's chief bodyguard returned with the captain of the Iowa, Captain John Livingstone McCrea, USN [USNA 1915]. McCrea and Franklin Roosevelt had a history together, with the former having served as the staff secretary for the ARCADIA Conference in Washington a couple of weeks after the Pearl Harbor attack. He had also served as *aide-de-camp* to CNO Stark and naval aide to President Roosevelt. During the latter assignment, McCrea established the president's map room in the White House. He accompanied the president and his entourage to the SYMBOL Conference in Casablanca, before becoming the first captain of *Iowa* when she became operational in February. And now, McCrea was the captain of the magnificent battleship.

"Pardon the imposition, Mister President," McCrea began. "Our lookouts spotted a torpedo wake, and we had to take evasive action. The torpedo appeared to have come from one of our escort destroyers that caused us to respond with our main battery guns as if it had been an intentional event."

"Intentional?" Roosevelt asked.

"Yes sir. We had no choice but to assume it was an attempted assassination."

"Assassination?"

"Yes sir. It took us a few minutes to exchange signal lamp messages to determine that the torpedo launch was an unfortunate accident."

"Accident?"

"Yes sir. The crew of the William D. Porter had been conducting a combat drill, and they accidentally launched a live torpedo that just happened to be aimed in our direction. It took us several minutes and numerous signal lamp messages to ascertain that the firing had been a terrible training accident."

"Is everything OK, then?" asked the president.

"We believe so, Mister President, but we have a couple of clean-up items to clear before we can secure from general quarters."

"May I return to my paperwork?"

"Yes sir," responded McCrea. "It is safe to do so, Mister President. The all-clear should come over the 1MC shortly. We have already returned to our proper course and speed. Our ETA at Gibraltar and Malta remains unchanged. We'll make up this little distraction."

"Thank you, John. I know we are in good hands."

"Thank you, Mister President. Is there anything else I can do for you?"

"No, John. Please tend to the ship's business."

McCrea saluted and departed. Roosevelt nodded his head to the flag stateroom. The duty Secret Service agents moved the president back to his desk. Fifteen minutes passed before the boatswain of the watch broadcast over the 1MC to the entire ship, "All clear. Secure from general quarters. Set Condition Yankee, all stations."

"Well, that was enough excitement for one day," Roosevelt said aloud to himself, as he stared out the adjacent portal at the passing clouds. Unfortunately, the stateroom's portals were built for an ambulatory person, so Franklin was relegated to seeing just clouds. He took a deep, cleansing breath and returned to his paperwork. He still had three briefing binders to review for his preparations. The first summit conference in Cairo would focus on Pacific and Asian strategy. Stalin had rejected the joint proposal from the two Western leaders for a full joint conference, stating that China was not his concern and Japan would not get his attention until Germany was defeated. They had reluctantly conceded to Stalin's intransigence, which meant they would both be on the road longer than they wanted. By prior agreement with the prime minister, the Manhattan Project would not be discussed or even mentioned at either summit conference.

Following the *Iowa* incident, the Navy ordered the USS *William D Porter* and her crew to U.S. Naval Station Bermuda for an inquiry into the event. The destroyer's commanding officer, Lieutenant Commander Wilfred Aves Walter, USN, was not relieved of command following the investigation and remained in command of the *Porter* until 30.May.1944. Chief Torpedoman Lawton Dawson, USN, failed to follow established procedures and remove the torpedo's primer that enabled it to fire in the direction of *Iowa*. The Navy later court-martialed Dawson, convicted and sentenced him to hard labor. President Roosevelt intervened in Dawson's case, declaring the incident had been an accident. Walter later went on to command other ships and eventually became a rear admiral.

—

Thursday, 18.November.1943
Il-Palazz Sant'Anton
Attard, Crown Colony of Malta
14:30 hours

In the first of two preparatory meetings before the SEXTANT and EUREKA Conferences, Allied Forces Supreme Commander General Eisenhower sat down at the conference table with Prime Minister Churchill and the British Joint Chiefs—First Sea Lord Admiral of the Fleet Sir Andrew Cunningham, Chief of the Imperial General Staff General Sir Alan Brooke, and Chief of the Air Staff Air Chief Marshal Sir Charles Portal. They also invited Governor Field Marshal Lord Gort to attend as well, and he was present.

"Gentlemen," Churchill stated, "we have the SEXTANT Conference in Cairo in a week. There have been some concerns about security, but I think we have finally settled those worries. We will meet with the Chinese leader to discuss the Pacific region campaign primarily. The generalissimo will not have his staff with him, so the talks will be with the leaders only. However, in Tehran, Premier Stalin will have his full staff with him. Each of you can expect to interact extensively with your American and Soviet counterparts. We have several plenary sessions planned for all of us. That said, as the first order of business, General Eisenhower, would you be so kind to give us your latest assessment of the Mediterranean zone of operations?"

"Certainly, Prime Minister," Eisenhower began. "The engineers are working overtime to restore Naples harbor for our logistics use. The progress so far suggests another month or two before we have sufficient capacity to support combat operations without the beachhead at Salerno. We have secured

Naples and the territory south of Naples. The 15th Army Group has moved north of Naples. Lead elements of the 5th Army have entered the Liri Valley. Intelligence suggests the Germans may attempt to hold a trans-peninsular line in the vicinity of Cassino. We have not yet engaged those defensive preparations. So far, so good."

"Thank you, General," Churchill said. "Any questions?" None came from the British chiefs. "I am certain you will keep us posted as Allied Forces move north."

"Yes sir."

"I'm encouraged by the swift progress Allied Forces have made with our advance on Rome. Marshal Badoglio has proven himself a man of his word. Yet, several thoughts, or perhaps concerns or worries, have haunted my thoughts of sorts. It's not my intention to deflect us from the immediate challenges we have directly ahead of us. However, the prospects of OVERLORD loom large in my thinking, but the potential costs cause more disquiet. We haven't solved the question of sufficient forces, which leaves me cold on the current operation plan. We must take care that the tides do not run red with the blood of American and British youth, or the beaches are choked with their bodies."

No one spoke for a handful of seconds. The image offered by the prime minister made all of them uncomfortable. The whole point of their detailed planning was to achieve the objectives with the minimum costs possible.

Churchill continued, "Our ultimate objective remains and will remain the unconditional surrender of Germany and Japan. The objective is in sight. My thoughts have turned progressively toward the post-war status. The president and I agree that we must keep a wary eye on Premier Stalin and the Soviets. My impressions of the Soviet leader's intention are solidifying, and I suspect that they will present an amenable face to us, while they secretly hold no intentions of liberating the countries of Eastern Europe. To put my premonition in rather stark terms, I see one hegemonic dictatorship replacing the one we're striving to defeat. If that my intuition proves correct, we're caught between a very large rock and the abyss in that we need the Red Army to command the preponderance of German attention. I'm fretting enough about 20 divisions in France. Our situation would change dramatically if the Germans added 100 divisions from the East to the defense of the West. In short, we need the Red Army to stay in the fight."

Churchill continued but changed the focus of his comments. "If we're to save as much of Eastern Europe as possible and, specifically, our pre-war ally Poland, we must meet the Red Army as far east as possible. I see our advance more through the Balkans to the Black Sea. We clearly won't be quick enough to help Ukrainians or the Baltic countries achieve independence, but perhaps we can save Poland, Czechoslovakia, and Hungary. There are fewer German divisions in the Balkans than in the Soviet Union, France, or Italy."

"There is also far more mountainous terrain between the Adriatic and Baltic Seas," observed Brooke.

"That fact is understood, Sir Alan, but we must find an answer. We can't fail our Polish allies, again."

"We understand the political motives, Prime Minister," responded Brooke, "but soldiers must face the realities of the battlefield."

"Then, is it your counsel that we should abandon the potential of a Balkans offensive in favor of OVERLORD?"

"No sir. My counsel is unity. Whatever the differences between you and the president must be resolved and agreed long before our troops are engaged in combat to achieve the objective."

"I raise this question here and now because I expect we shall have time in Cairo, outside the SEXTANT Conference, to discuss the way forward before we arrive in Tehran. We won't be able to discuss this matter at the EUREKA Conference, but I'd like to know where each of you stands on a Balkans campaign in lieu of the cross-Channel operation. Admiral Cunningham, as the senior service, what say you?"

"Either approach is workable from the Navy's perspective. A Balkans campaign represents a more difficult supply line protection challenge. The landing craft or amphibious aspects are simply a point of focus matter for the Navy. The Navy can support either."

"General Brooke?"

"As I stated earlier," the chief of the Imperial General Staff began, "the war objective is a political matter. We'll do what our coalition leaders decide. There are ramifications and benefits to each approach. BOLERO is gathering our forces in England rather than North Africa or Italy. BOLERO is preparation for OVERLORD. Should we shift our focus to a Balkans campaign, we'll have a major logistics challenge of moving the BOLERO forces to the Mediterranean—not a trivial challenge. Planning for OVERLORD is progressing steadily. Moving the BOLERO forces to the Med will likely extend our execution date. As it is, we're already nearly a year behind our original joint execution date. Further, if we get bogged down in the mountains and fail to reach the northern plain before the Russians, the Red Army might well penetrate Poland before we could block them. We might well be facing the left flank of the Red Army rather than the right flank of the Germans. That would leave us with no substantive force between the Red Army and the Atlantic Ocean. If you're asking for my counsel, I see the cross-Channel operation as more supportable with wider offensive potential than the channelized ground operation through the mountainous terrain of the Balkans. The Army favors the cross-Channel operation."

"Air Chief Marshal Portal?"

"We don't have the aerodrome facilities in Italy and North Africa to enable air operations in support of a major ground offensive through the Balkans. The air forces would also need to shift major forces from England to North Africa. I can't place a timeline upon the necessary shift of forces, but I think General Brooke accurately stated the consequences. I think we can all see your concerns," Sir Charles said, "however, if our objective is Berlin, I see the shortest path to that objective as across the Channel."

"Lord Gort, with your combat experience, what is your opinion?"

"Thank you for the courtesy of your query. It is outside my charter. However, your military counsel seems wise and grounded in reality. The mountainous terrain between the Adriatic and Baltic presents a significant risk and complication to offensive operations. Mountains favor the defense."

"Thank you, Lord Gort. General Eisenhower, your turn."

"I have no reason to question your intuition, Prime Minister, and if your supposition is correct, to be frank, we're altering our objective from the unconditional surrender of Germany to the thwarting of Soviet hegemonic designs. Is that what we have all agreed to do?"

"I see your point, General. I would answer by saying that the thwarting of the Soviets, as you say, is an interim objective on the road to defeating Germany. I also see it as separating Germany from the majority of her armed forces."

"I see considerable risk in an attempt to make a thrust through the Balkans, not least of which is not making it to the Baltic before the Red Army makes it into Poland. That potential would leave us in a very precarious position." Eisenhower paused to allow for comment or debate. None came. "The Red Army could and might well block us. Shifting our axis of advance from Poland to Hungary and Austria would add significant additional complication. A Balkans campaign, while noble in objective and intent, offers far more risk than benefit. I must also add that once we initiated BOLERO in the UK, I think we committed to the cross-Channel invasion. From a higher perspective, OVERLORD gives us near-optimal armor terrain, enabling rapid advance. OVERLORD gives us the best shot at getting to Berlin before the Soviets but does virtually nothing for Eastern Europe. Lastly, I know the president remains quite concerned about the second front and helping the Soviets. He knows we will face criticism with Stalin and wants that second front as soon as possible. To close my remarks, I stand with General Brooke; we'll execute what you and the president decide."

"Well, that makes it unanimous. I do not argue with your assessments. I also note that none of you have argued against my apprehension regarding

Soviet hegemonic intentions. I must note here that President Roosevelt is not as convinced as I am of Soviet intentions. I'm searching for a path forward to defeat Germany and protect the Central European countries—Poland, Hungary, Czechoslovakia, Yugoslavia, and Greece—from Soviet domination and occupation. We missed the summer window. So now, we must look to the spring window. The Tehran Conference will be crucial on a host of levels, not least of which will be achieving a common approach. We don' have much leverage with Stalin and the Soviet Union, but we shall do our best to find a peaceful, post-war solution for everyone."

Prime Minister Churchill and Governor Lord Gort had other commitments. They departed. The flag officers remained for another hour or so, conferring in a less rigorous or formal manner until it was time for them to adjourn. The group would reconvene at the governor's palace for cocktails, supper, and social intercourse.

———

Saturday, 20.November.1943
Betio Island, Tarawa Atoll, Gilbert Islands

The U.S. Fifth Fleet under the command of Vice Admiral Ray Spruance arrived in the darkness of the pre-dawn hours to execute Operation GALVANIC. In morning twilight, an artillery duel began between four, 8-inch, shore battery guns of the Imperial Japanese 6th Yokosuka Special Naval Landing Force and the 16-inch, main battery guns of the battleships USS *Maryland* and USS *Colorado*. The American battleships made quick work of the shore battery guns, but the defenders were well prepared and dug in.

09:00 hours

The lead elements of the 2nd Marine Division began their amphibious landings across Red and Black Beaches on Betio—a 0.6 square mile island in the southwest corner of the triangular shaped Tarawa Atoll. The Battle of Tarawa was underway.

The bloody battle lasted four horrific days, but by the 24th, the island defenses had been defeated, and the heavily damaged runway was in American hands. The Navy Construction Battalion—the Seabees—had begun their work repairing the runway as the Marines secured parts of the airfield. The Army Air Forces units arrived shortly after the island was secured, and within weeks, began combat operations against many other Japanese targets in the Central Pacific. The Battle of Tarawa set the tone of what lay ahead in the campaign to defeat Imperial Japan.

Four Marines were awarded the Medal of Honor for conspicuous gallantry on Betio Island—Colonel David Monroe Shoup, USMC; First Lieutenant Alexander Bonnyman, Jr., USMC; First Lieutenant William Dean Hawkins, USMC; and Staff Sergeant William James Bordelon, USMC; the last three of them were awarded posthumously. Colonel Shoup went on to be promoted eventually to 4-star general and became the 22nd Commandant of the Marine Corps.

—

Saturday, 20.November.1943
Guest Villa No. 1 (the White House)
Carthage, Tunis
Tunisia
14:15 hours

General Eisenhower met President Roosevelt and the American joint chiefs as they were transferred ashore once the USS *Iowa* anchored in Algiers harbor. The destroyer screen would rotate with two of the six destroyers patrolling the waters outside Algiers harbor, while the others would enter port to give the crews shore liberty.

Eisenhower flew with the president and his military chief of staff to Tunis in the supreme commander's dedicated C-54 VIP transport aircraft. A separate C-54 carried the American joint chiefs—Army Chief of Staff General Marshall; Chief of Naval Operations Admiral King, and Chief of the Army Air Forces General Arnold.

They discussed the upcoming conferences with the Chinese and Soviets. General Eisenhower provided the status briefing he had delivered with the prime minister and the British joint chiefs. Ike did not discuss Prime Minister Churchill's Balkan proposal; he recognized that he had been allowed access to the British, but it was the prime minister's political domain that he felt obligated to protect. After the summit discussions, the president and chiefs took a vehicle tour of the Carthaginian ruins and recalled the Punic Wars between Carthage and Rome.

The group enjoyed an exquisite dinner before the president retired to his suite and invited Ike to join him for a private chat.

"You've done an exemplary job leading Allied Forces, Ike."

"Thank you, Mister President."

"This seemed like an appropriate time for you and I to have this talk. I want you to know that I recognize the difficult, thin, wavy line you must walk between the British and us. Combined staffs are never easy. But you've shown us all how it should be done. We are grateful for your skills, Ike."

"Thank you, sir."

"Besides singing your praises . . ." Both men chuckled. ". . . I wanted to discuss two matters with you privately. First, I need your candid assessment of the way forward. We agreed to strike Italy with the expectation they would quickly collapse. Our assumptions have proven correct so far. Italy is at least notionally on our side now."

"I'd suggest our relationship with Italy is better than that. Marshal Badoglio has delivered what he's promised and has been frank with us when he cannot deliver. The Italians are in a very difficult position between their old ally and their new ally. Fortunately, the government made a successful, functional move behind our lines."

"I appreciate your perspective. The bottom line is that Italy is out of the war as an Axis adversary." Eisenhower nodded. "I think we also agreed that Berlin doesn't lie through Italy." Again, Ike nodded. "With that as a premise, Prime Minister Churchill is pressing me regarding our primary thrust to defeat Germany should be through the Balkans to the Baltic Sea in an effort to cut off the Soviet advance into Central and Western Europe. He believes Stalin holds intentions to expand the Soviet Union beyond the pre-war borders. Despite Stalin's assurances to liberate rather than occupy the countries they take from the Germans, Churchill thinks the Soviets will use sham elections to dominate those countries. It seems to me that if we were successful in such an offensive, we would have the bulk of the German armed forces between the Red Army and us on one side with the remainder of the German military on the other side. I understand his point. To be candid and to share with you privately, I have the impression he's more concerned about blunting the Soviet's advance rather than defeating the Germans. I would not say that to him, but that is my impression. In some ways, you're closer to him than me. If you can or will, I would appreciate your insight."

Eisenhower hesitated and cleared his throat more to buy time for thought. "If you'll allow me some circumspection," Eisenhower paused to receive a confirmatory head nod, "I think he's seeking a means to kill two birds with one stone, as we say in the country. I've no basis to doubt his impressions of Marshal Stalin's post-war intentions. From a military offensive perspective, the terrain of the Balkans favors the defense. The Germans could bottle us up with a fairly small but determined force. Further, if the prime minister is correct, Marshal Stalin might not take kindly to us interfering with his plans."

"Thank you for your thoughts, Ike." Roosevelt smiled in a rather mischievous manner. "I'll postpone this discussion until after I get a feel for Marshal Stalin. We'll deal with it then. At this juncture, I'll say that the OVERLORD planning appears to be progressing well, which brings me to my second topic.

"Prime Minister Churchill and I have been discussing the leadership of OVERLORD. There are several candidates on both sides of the Atlantic. You're one of those candidates. Have you been following the COSSAC planning?"

"Yes sir . . . not as close as I need to but close enough."

"And what are your impressions at the current state of planning?"

"I'm not satisfied that we've sufficient combat forces in the initial landing phase. The follow-on logistics plan appears to be adequate for the build-up of forces, and I like the Mulberry harbor approach to supply the combat divisions. However, we'll not be able to rely on the beachhead as our only point of substantive supply. I confess that I've not devoted the proper oversight of the planning process to address the initial landing concerns. I do believe Prime Minister Churchill and others in the defense establishment have voiced their apprehension about getting bogged down at the beachhead with insufficient combat power to break any potential stalemate and to restrict our capacity to reinforce our units."

"Have you been able to examine the alternatives to a cross-Channel operation?"

"We've discussed the possibility of the Balkan axis of advance and the exclusion of Italy and a trans-Alps approach peripherally. We've also looked at Atlantic and South France beachheads." Eisenhower paused to think. "As succinctly as possible, the balance of numerous opposing factors is difficult and the best guess. We've used the same techniques in assessing our plans beginning with TORCH a year ago. From my perspective, the key, if not dominant, factor is the rapidity that an operational plan can amplify the combat forces." Eisenhower paused for Roosevelt to respond. The president remained attentive and silent. "From my perspective, the shortest path to Berlin is via Calais. The intelligence we have tells us the Germans have deployed the preponderance of their combat forces to defend against a Calais invasion. We must reinforce their predisposition with FORTITUDE."

"So, you favor OVERLORD?"

"Yes sir. It's the best we're going to do in maximizing our strengths and minimizing our weaknesses against the German defenders . . . and balancing the Red Army for that matter."

"Now to the salient question, are you prepared to assume command of OVERLORD?"

General Eisenhower stared at President Roosevelt without expression. "I know General Marshall wants the posting."

"Yes, he does, but I need him to continue doing what he has done since the beginning of the war in Europe. The British have offered Brooke, Alexander, and Montgomery. All of them can do the job, Ike, but you're the one who has stood to the mark. Prime Minister Churchill and I have had numerous generalized conversations. The decision is looming, and I expect we'll make that decision in early December, shortly after we get home from the Tehran Summit Conference. So, to my question, General?"

"I'm a soldier, Mister President. I serve at your will."

Roosevelt chuckled softly and nodded his head. "I'll take that as a yes." The president extended his right hand. The two men shook hands. "I must add that Prime Minister Churchill speaks very highly of your skills, Ike. I don't need to convince him. But I know he feels a duty to speak on behalf of his generals, and I must honor that need. You enjoy his full confidence as well as mine, and the assignment will not be a hard sell."

"Thank you for your confidence, Mister President. We'll get the job done."

The two men continued to chat for another hour about family and the social elements of their times.

—

Sunday, 21.November.1943
Office of the Director, Office of Strategic Services
National Institutes of Health Building
2430 E Street Northwest]
Washington, District of Columbia
United States of America
15:20 hours

"Thank you for coming into the office on your Sunday, Ned," Donovan acknowledged.

"At your service, General."

"A couple of items fell in place this afternoon, and as you know, I leave early tomorrow morning for India, and I wanted to discuss both items with you eye-to-eye before I left. By the way, I'm going to use one of the Bainbridge Constellations for the trip, and I'm taking three field teams with me. I figured these fellas are heading off to clandestine war, and at least we can treat them to a comfortable ride."

"Sounds right to me."

"Do you know the Boston Red Sox catcher Moe Berg?"

Morris 'Moe' Berg had a checkered career as a Major League Baseball catcher. He began his professional baseball career with the Brooklyn Robins. Berg traveled extensively during the offseasons. He spoke several languages, including German and Italian. After Pearl Harbor, Berg worked for Nelson Rockefeller and the Office of the Coordinator of Inter-American Affairs (OIAA). He accepted an invitation to join the Special Operations Branch (SO) of the

OSS the previous August. General Donovan tapped him for a unique special mission.

"Sure, not great, but passable enough to play for 15 seasons."

"That's him. Moe speaks several languages and recently completed his special operations training course at Camp X." The secret joint training facility in Ontario, Canada, had been established by the Canadian, British and American clandestine services in December 1941. "He agreed this morning to his assignment to the Alsos Mission. He will be our direct liaison. I just finished discussing Moe's assignment with Dick Groves, who agreed with the posting, and tomorrow he will assign a selected physicist from his project team to teach Moe the elements of nuclear physics he needs to know for this task. He's a pretty sharp cookie. He also has the skills to execute the capture or kill directive against Heisenberg."

"You're sure?"

"Yes. He did exceptionally well at Camp X."

"Do I need to do any follow-up while you're in Asia?"

"No. I was just waiting for Groves's consent. Personnel already has his orders ready for both the additional training and deployment. They'll issue the orders tomorrow. The second matter was the Drew Pearson disclosure condemning Patton for the slapping incidents last August. The radio broadcast went perfectly well, just the right amount of disapproval without irreparably tainting the general. The script for the general as part of FORTITUDE was issued last week. The Pearson broadcast completed our portion of the program. I'd like you to task an analyst to watch public opinion now that the incidents are public. We need to keep track to make sure public opinion does not go too far in one direction or the other. We don't need the general excoriated, just humiliated a little. Patton's status is an important part of selling FORTITUDE to the Germans."

"Gotcha. We'll get the correct analyst watching the media and giving us a weekly summary," Buxton responded. "Good luck on your trip, Bill."

"Thanks, Ned."

———

Monday, 22.November.1943
Villa Alexander Kirk near Hotel Mena
No. 3 Tolombat Street
Cairo
Egypt
20:40 hours

United States Ambassador to Egypt Alexander Comstock Kirk had been the chief American diplomat in Egypt since March 1941. As the American

Charge d'Affaires in Berlin, he wrote an unusual letter directly to the president dated 29.July.1940, as the ferocious intensity of the Battle of Britain mounted toward its pinnacle, that warned of the consequences should England fall to the Nazis either by peace overtures and negotiations, or by armed conflict and invasion.

Shortly after he arrived at his posting in Cairo, Kirk leased the palace of Tewhida Yegen née Isma'il, a granddaughter of Khedive of Egypt Isma'il Pasha, to be used as the ambassador's residence. The spacious, well-appointed villa in an exclusive neighborhood made an excellent diplomatic, social venue.

The ambassador and his wife hosted a wonderful supper for the combined diplomatic and defense conference participants, followed by a social hour. By prior agreement, the prime minister and the president quietly retired to the ambassador's library for a private conversation between them.

"The initial meeting with Generalissimo Chang went quite well, I think," Churchill offered.

"I agree. My take as well, although it seems there is never enough. We're supporting operations in China as best we can. Just as we agreed that Berlin doesn't lie through Italy, Tokyo doesn't lie through China. We must do our best to support the Chinese but remain focused on the objective in the Pacific."

"From my perspective, Franklin, you are doing more than enough. Yes, the Chinese will always want more. However, your forces in the Pacific are executing a dual-axis of advance campaign that in itself is verging upon unprecedented."

"Yes, well, perhaps I should be embarrassed to have bowed to General MacArthur's insistent demand to stroke his ego through his return to the Philippines, but we saw sufficient potential benefit to see a path to Tokyo through the Philippines and Formosa to justify the approval."

"You'll not hear a word of criticism from me, Franklin."

"Thank you, Winston, but the thought does haunt me, although I must say, so does the island-hopping plan of Admiral Nimitz. The message I received this morning reports brutal fighting at Tarawa that began two days ago, and the island is not secure yet. The Japanese aren't going to go quietly."

"Neither will the Germans," Churchill stated. Both men thought for a few moments. "You'll meet Uncle Joe in a week or so. He's very charming when he wants to be. As his first meeting with you, he'll work his charms on you to gain your support. He's also likely to say all the right things about supporting free, democratic elections and ending their occupation as quickly as possible once the war is done."

"But you don't believe him," challenged Roosevelt.

"As you well know, Franklin, at the diplomatic level, so much depends upon trust and perception. Uncle Joe is purported to have proclaimed, and I paraphrased here, that those who vote decide nothing. Those who count the votes decide everything. His minions will be counting the votes."

"What about observers?"

"I raised the potential in the last meeting I had with him, and he summarily dismissed it as unnecessary. I don't know if we'll get to the elections in the occupied countries, but if it does, we should be prepared to confront the matter."

"We've very little leverage with Stalin or the Soviets in general. We surely cannot risk war with our erstwhile ally."

"Not former just yet, but he's moving in that direction. Our intelligence from Ukraine, behind the front lines, conclusively documents the brutal retribution being exacted by the NKGB and NKVD on Ukrainians for their early support of the Nawzees. I am concerned that by the time we have conclusive evidence of Soviet intentions in Poland and other Central and Eastern European countries, it will be too late for us to intervene short of war."

"We declared our intentions in the Atlantic Charter of August 1941. This war has inflicted an incalculable toll on all peoples of the world. War with the Soviet Union is not an option."

"That's what Chamberlain said about Germany in 1938, and here we are. I've proposed to the military chiefs an alternative to OVERLORD, namely a primary thrust through the Balkans north to the Baltic Sea to limit the Red Army's advance, protect Poland and Central Europe, and defeat Germany from the east rather than the expected west."

"It's something to discuss, Winston, but first, we must convince Stalin that OVERLORD will be the second front he sought for several years. You know he's going to press us for our plans. We're not prepared to present a Balkans alternative, and I can't support raising such a potential at the summit level without thinking things through."

"Very well. The option is not on the table for EUREKA. This meeting with Stalin will be the first time both of us will be face-to-face with Uncle Joe. I'm eager to gain your assessment of the Soviet dictator. I'll also say I'm not warm on OVERLORD either. I see too many opportunities to stumble, and every obstacle we're not able to broach rapidly moves the Red Army farther and farther west. You may not share my apprehension regarding Soviet intentions, but I'll close my private remarks by urging you not to get seduced by his friendly façade. He's a dangerous man."

"I hold no illusions, Winston. We'll have plenty of opportunities to confer after the Tehran Conference, but we've the remainder of the SEXTANT

Conference still ahead of us and the next session tomorrow. I'm not as resilient as you, Winston, and perhaps as I once was. Unless you've other issues of urgency, I'm afraid I need my rest before tomorrow's session."

"Yes, of course, Franklin."

The two leaders adjourned for the evening and retired to their respective villas. Churchill had reluctantly become a prophet in the 1930s, and he once again sounded the clarion of warning.

—

Chapter 13

The rose is fairest when 'tis budding new, and
hope is brightest when it dawns from fears.
-- Walter Scott

Monday, 29.November.1943
British Embassy
198 Ferdowsi Avenue
Tehran, Iran
12:30 hours

The private lunch between Roosevelt and Churchill was arranged on short notice after the first plenary session of the EUREKA Summit Conference on Sunday and the American Embassy dinner. Churchill had not been pleased and was frankly disturbed by his excoriation by the Stalin-Roosevelt tag team. The ambassador's private dining room had been allocated for the luncheon.

After their lunch meal had been served, the doors were closed, and the two leaders were left alone. They ate their meal sporadically amid their discussions.

"Thank you for agreeing to this private luncheon, Franklin."

"My honor, Winston. Your request sounded rather urgent."

"Yes, well, I suppose the matter is rather urgent from my perspective. Perhaps mistakenly, I've been under the impression that you and I held a special relationship, one of genuine friendship, camaraderie, and connection. In that light, what happened yesterday was extraordinarily disturbing. My impression, whatever friendship may have existed between us was illusory—vanished in an instant."

"Winston . . . my friend . . . if that was your impression, I must offer my most heartfelt apology. That was never my intention. Yes, I feel exactly the same about our friendship. I may have gotten carried away with my desire to forge a personal relationship with Joe."

"A noble objective, I must say, Franklin. However, I don't quite appreciate the need to further your relationship with Joe at my expense."

"That was never my purpose. I'll confess to my serious concern about Stalin's intentions when this sordid affair is done. You've candidly shared your assessment. I fear what the world might look like if your assessment of Stalin and the Soviets is accurate."

"I share your concern, Franklin. I've no interest in painting the course one way or another. I'm only interested in being prepared for what lies ahead of us, to the best of our ability. My early discussions with Stalin and Molotov were quite positive and encouraging when their fate remained very much in question, as even they confessed, they were on the razor's edge. I detected a shift in their attitude when they stopped the German advance on Moscow. However, the demonstrable change occurred with the German 6th Army's surrender at Stalingrad."

"What do you think his objective is?"

Churchill smiled broadly and shook his head. His expression turned stone cold before he answered. "At the risk of sounding facetious, I'll answer with sincere candor . . . world domination."

Roosevelt chuckled nervously. "Seriously?"

"Franklin, we've known each other for a few years now. I'd love to say, of course, I was joking. But alas, I can't offer such a claim. I've discussed post-war restoration with Joe several times now. We'll discuss that topic again this afternoon. Allow me to predict what you'll experience. He'll be charming and yet mystifyingly indirect. He'll say all the right things, but he'll not agree to restore the countries the Red Army liberates. I've seen it already in just the discussion of the eastern border of Poland. We started at the pre-war border. He started at the border between German and Russian occupied Poland. As the war progresses and the Red Army advances farther to the west, the Soviet border demands will move farther to the west as well."

"Is that a suspicion or your true belief?" the president asked.

"I don't want it to be true. I pray night after night that I'm wrong. The signs that I see that I detect, that I feel, all point in the wrong direction. I must confess to my inability to dream of a new, peaceful, post-war world until after the Blitz ended and German attention on Russia became clear. My image of the post-war world darkened with each successive exchange. Yet, I'm the eternal optimist. I continue to hope that we can apply sufficient pressure for him to give up his hegemonic inclinations."

"There's a fine balance, Winston. We both agree we must keep the Soviets in this fight. Even though we've all mutually agreed that there will be no negotiated surrender—only unconditional surrender to all of the allied nations, you, yourself, reported the potential for the Soviets to seek an independent cessation of violence."

"Yes, I did," Churchill responded. "Yet, while that potential will always exist until the Nawzees are vanquished, I believe Uncle Joe has an unbridled ambition to replace Hitler as the dominant force in Europe."

"You can't be serious."

"I most assuredly am, I'm afraid. While he has said all the right things in our post-war discussions, there's a detectable undercurrent running beneath the surface that tells me he has no intentions to liberate Eastern Europe. He intends to dominate and subjugate all of the countries he can take from the Nawzees. He talks about free and fair elections, but I suspect the only candidates that will make it to the ballot will be vetted and approved by the Soviets. I do believe you can see where that would go. Free and fair are not words in his lexicon."

"This is my first opportunity to get the measure of the man," Roosevelt stated.

"You should have that open and unfettered opportunity, my friend. If you need me to be your whipping boy to enable that opportunity, then so be it. I just want to ensure we hadn't gotten crosswise."

"No, we haven't. My apologies, Winston, if my actions caused you that degree of apprehension. While we're alone, I wanted to ask directly and frankly about your assessment of General Eisenhower."

Churchill smiled. "In short, Franklin, he has performed well above my expectations. I find him an exceptional listener, a curious student, and an exemplary negotiator and collaborationist. He has done an extraordinary job of bringing dissimilar, even disparate, personalities together into a cohesive headquarters staff. I like how he thinks and handles people."

"Thank you for sharing that with me, Winston."

"The question implies you're considering Ike as the supreme commander?"

"You proposed Brooke and Alexander."

"Yes. I could offer others, and I understand Marshall has expressed interest as well, Franklin."

"Yes, he has, but I told him that was not an option. I like George exactly where he is, as a most effective chief of staff."

"That is exactly how I feel with Sir Alan and Sir Harold. Sir Alan seriously wants the assignment. Any one of the four of them would be perfect for the job, but frankly, I believe Ike deserves the mission given his magnificent performance as the supreme commander of Allied Forces on TORCH, HUSKY, and AVALANCHE. He has proven himself as a worthy joint forces commander."

"I'm inclined to agree with you. We need to put a peg in the ground."

"Agreed."

"I've got a few remaining political boxes to check off as soon as I get back to Washington. I'm also going to stop in Algiers to talk to Eisenhower one last time. I expect we should make the announcement before Christmas."

"I'm in complete agreement, Franklin. The COSSAC staff is finalizing the plans nicely, and we need a commander, sooner the better. The May target date for the first window is closer than we think."

"Quite so."

"Uncle Joe is going to press hard for the sooner option. He has been consistent in that demand. As I've noted before, Franklin, Joe can be very charming and deceptive when he wants something, and he definitely wants us to draw off 20 or 50 German divisions to help him in his push west."

"Where will he stop?" the president asked.

"When he meets our forces . . ."

"Wherever that might be."

"Yes. If he could reach the Atlantic before we execute OVERLORD, he'd eagerly do so."

"All of Europe?"

"Yes. He is very ambitious, and his ambition is far greater than his political ideology. Please ask General Donovan for an update on the current focus and intentions of Uncle Joe's Comintern operations. They're openly planning on world domination. He uses his communist ideology as an excuse to shield his hegemony, and it's not confined to Europe. We've told him he needed to help in Asia. He's consistently repeated back to me, Germany first. He feels no threat from the Japanese, not like we do. There is zero doubt to my thinking that he'll turn his armies on Asia, when the time comes."

"What are you suggesting, Winston?"

"I feel like we are being torn apart by two massive teams of four monstrous horses. We are damned if we do or damned if we don't. On the one hand, I strongly urge us to meet the Russians as far east as we possibly can, but on the other hand, I'll confess my mortal fear of being bogged down on the landing beaches. I'm scared to death of another Passchendaele. We must deflect as many German divisions as possible with our deception operations to get our troops on the ground in Normandy in overwhelming numbers before the enemy figures out our plan and moves those divisions around Calais to react. The challenge for us over the next few months will be finding the correct balance to execute the plan."

"There's no such thing as perfect."

"True. But we must search for that point as far along toward perfect as we possibly can—too many precious lives are at stake."

"So, what's our position for this afternoon's meeting and Uncle Joe?"

"As I understand the constraints so far, our earliest window is May, and BOLERO will barely get us to our threshold for the execution of OVERLORD by that time. Uncle Joe will likely put on a demonstration that May is far too late and wants it in the next few months."

"That's not likely given winter weather."

"Exactly, but he doesn't care. He wants an easier go of it for the Red Army. The Germans are far more focused on the communists than on us."

"The easier for the Soviets, the faster they move west."

"Precisely."

"Then, we'll do what is best for our troops, our joint forces, and the success of the operation." Roosevelt checked his wristwatch. "I note the time,"

Roosevelt said. "Our second plenary session of our conference is scheduled to begin in a few hours, and I'm conscious of your naptime."

"Naptime is quite precious, Franklin, very rejuvenating."

"So, you've told me many times."

Churchill chuckled softly. "Yes, I have, haven't I? In that vein, if you'll excuse me, Franklin, I shall retire to my upstairs suite. I shall meet you again at the Soviet Embassy on Nofel Loshato Street, and Uncle Joe is our host for the second session and dinner tonight." Roosevelt nodded his head in agreement. "To close our luncheon, I'd like to ask you to soften your jabs at my expense to garner favor with Joe Stalin. You're perfectly capable of charming him without sacrificing my stature for favors with him."

"Winston, you're a good friend. You've always been a good friend. I cherish the relationship we have. I apologize for any misunderstanding evolving from our earlier get-together. I'm truly sorry."

"Accepted."

Churchill pushed Roosevelt's wheelchair to the door. One of the president's Secret Service agents took over for the prime minister. Churchill walked with Roosevelt to the embassy's diplomatic entrance. They extended their incidental *adieux*. Churchill waited until Roosevelt's limousine exited the embassy grounds.

The EUREKA Conference concluded Wednesday, the 1st of December. The Big Three reaffirmed the unconditional surrender policy with Germany and Japan, although Stalin did raise a bit of a tiff with his perception that the British and Americans have violated that basic principle in their separate peace with Italy. Stalin eventually sloughed it off since the Soviets had not participated in the defeat of Italy. Roosevelt and Churchill both reassured Stalin that planning was progressing well for a May 1944 launch of OVERLORD. Stalin offered his commitment to initiate a major offensive on the Eastern Front in coordination with the Western Allies' landing in France. He also reiterated his pledge to join the Pacific campaign against Japan once Germany is defeated.

As Churchill predicted, Stalin was not particularly eager to discuss post-war arrangements for any liberated countries. Roosevelt mentioned the Morgenthau Plan that proposed to render Germany an agrarian country, devoid of industrial capacity. Stalin supported that plan, but Churchill did not, and Roosevelt remained neutral, not overtly supporting his Treasury secretary's proposal. At a minimum, the leaders agreed to divide up Germany between them for post-war administration.

—

Tuesday, 7.December.1943
USAAF Station 356
Saffron Walden, Essex, England
United Kingdom
16:20 hours

"**D**amn weather guessers really got it wrong today," observed Dusty Langford.

"Got that right," Rolo Stanfield affirmed.

The squadron briefed for another RHUBARB mission into France, but weather observation reports from advance reconnaissance aircraft indicated the local weather was unacceptable for any type of visual operation. They remained at standby all day long, including having sandwiches brought to them for lunch. Very low, solid, overcast clouds replaced the dense fog. The weather aircraft reported multiple layers of broken and complete clouds. None of the pilots liked being restrained, including Brian, but the more experienced pilots just accepted the realities of Mother Nature. The chilly, damp, autumnal air kept the pilots inside with the warmth of the coal heater.

As the afternoon wore on, the less experienced pilots displayed cabin fever signs with tempers flaring and arguments increasing. Pete chose to ignore the disturbances as they invariably worked themselves out. Brian just ignored them, often closing his eyes to feign napping.

The squadron remained at standby until the sky darkened into dusk, made all the darker by the clouds. They eventually secured in time to make it to the Officer's Mess for the evening meal. Brian checked the message board, as he always did. *Sure enough.* There was a message from Charlotte.

Please call
as soon as you are able.
Nothing wrong.
Charlotte

The 4th Fighter Group officers ate meals together in one sitting. They were served more meat and vegetables than the veterans had during the dark days of 1940 and '41. This evening's meal was roast beef, baked potatoes with some of the fixin's, and green beans with carrots. Meals were always loud, raucous affairs with his countrymen. When the meal was done, they moved to the bar, which became quite crowded with the group pilots seeking the evening's libation. Brian enjoyed a couple of beers with his comrades before he quietly bowed out and went to the telephone booths. He had to wait for nearly ten minutes, and two other pilots, one from each of the other group squadrons, joined Brian in the wait.

A middle booth opened up. Brian entered, closed the door, and sat on the small bench. He gave the operator the telephone number he knew by heart. It took the usual four operators to make the final connection.

"Winchester 4-3-7-9," came the voice he loved to hear.

"It's me, Sweetheart."

"Thank you for calling, Brian. Everything is great here, nothing to worry about."

"Good. What's up?"

"The American 9th Infantry Division moved into the Winchester Barracks, and as I hear, they also have units camped in Bushfield, Barton Stacey, Alresford, and Basingstoke." All the sites were located in Hampshire, a county in south central England, and none of them were far from Standing Oak Farm.

These guys were one of the first American infantry units to enter combat in the current war. They had participated in combat operations in TORCH, Algeria, Tunisia, and HUSKY. There is only one reason they are in Winchester—the invasion of Nazi-occupied France. I can't tell her any of that.

"Did you know they were coming?"

"No. Is there a problem?"

"No, no. American soldiers are overrunning the town. They've asked us for everything we can supply."

"That sounds like a good thing."

"Yes, well, except for the people of Hampshire and His Majesty's Government who have been buying up everything we can deliver. To my surprise, they offered to build greenhouses on our land if we would grow vegetables for them. Mabel has operated a greenhouse . . . small, but still, she grew things through winter. She thinks she can handle the scale-up if the Americans build secure buildings, supply the heaters, and grow lamps, and even an electricity generator for each building just in case electrical power is interrupted. The major who visited us said they could do it."

"Are there any strings attached?"

"None that we can ascertain. They just want fresh vegetables for their troops, and they acknowledge that we are already selling everything we can produce. By the way, my darling, we made our first trade with Lord and Lady Selborne. Our team very much appreciates more meat."

"Sounds like you have things well under control."

"Challenges of riches. We're still trying to work out the details. So, you're OK with all this?"

"Sure sounds like good business, Charlotte. Please let me know if there is anything I can do to help."

"You know I will. Until then, everything is going along nicely. Now, there was one other change beyond the greenhouses." Charlotte paused, but Brian listened. "An Interior Ministry man visited the farm this morning. He delivered a paper signed and stamped by the ministry that commandeered a parcel of the Harris property for a training facility of sorts."

"Commandeered?"

"Well, perhaps that was not the best choice of words. I imagine they could just take the land, but they want to lease about ten acres of the 85 we have. Fortunately, only about two acres are usable for farming. They want the farmland for a separate access road. They want to build some specific buildings to train their troops in urban warfare."

"Can we review and adjust plans to support their needs and perhaps be able to save something useful after the war."

"I asked that. The man didn't know but thought an officer from the division's engineer battalion would contact us."

"Can we still use the rest of the land?"

"He seemed to think so, which is why they proposed a lease rather than a buy arrangement and the separate access road."

"Do you see any conflicts with your plans?" Brian asked.

"A lot of American soldiers about. We are still absorbing what all these soldiers mean to the community."

"I imagine there will be problems, but hopefully nothing serious. On the positive side of the ledger, they will not be here very long."

"How long?"

"I don't know. We are not involved in the planning, and I'm fairly certain that it is highly classified and protected whatever they are planning. If I were to venture a guess, I would say six months . . . to springtime. Think about what you want after the war is done, when those units will go home."

Charlotte did not reply straight away. Brian waited patiently for her to cogitate. "Easier said than done, I suspect."

"Sweetheart, all anyone can ask is to do the best you can. I urge you not to fret about things. I suspect events are going to move very fast. If we can keep up, we stand to benefit from helping in these events."

"OK, Brian. Thank you for listening and for your counsel. I'll do the best I can."

Wife and husband completed the call with words of intimacy and affection. Brian glanced outside the booth. Six of his brethren were waiting for an open booth. He quickly hung up the telephone handset and stepped out. Brian went outside to think for a few moments. The fog had returned and thickened substantially. He wanted to be with Charlotte, to help her with these decisions, but war was war, and he was part of it.

———

Tuesday, 7.December.1943
Guest Villa No. 1
Carthage, Tunis
Tunisia
21:35 hours

President Roosevelt had hosted the dinner. The president's guests at supper had been Generals Eisenhower and Spaatz, and newly promoted Brigadier General Charles Loomis Booth, USAAF [USMA 1924], Assistant Chief of Staff for Logistics, 12th Air Force. Also in attendance were Harry Hopkins, Commander Harry Cecil Butcher, USNR, General Eisenhower's naval aide, and the president's middle son, Colonel Elliott Roosevelt, USAAF, Commanding Officer 90th Photographic Wing, 12th Air Force, with a group of nine officers from Elliott's unit. The president had been in a jovial mood, although he had appeared a bit gaunt and noticeably tired—worn out.

By the time of this meeting, General Tooey Spaatz had been promoted to be the commanding general Allied Northwest African Air Force that included the USAAF 12th and 15th Air Forces, and the RAF Northwest Africa of which Sir John Spencer's fighter group was a part.

After dinner, the president excused himself, moved to the library, and asked Eisenhower to join him.

"I'll make this very short, General. I'm quite tired. It's been a very long day. Prime Minister Churchill and I agreed this morning; you'll be the supreme commander, Allied Expeditionary Force, for the OVERLORD invasion. Congratulations."

"Thank you, sir."

"I'll need a few days once I'm back in Washington. I've some 't's to cross and 'i's to dot with the War Department and Congress. By my current schedule, I expect to arrive at the White House on the 17th. Churchill and I agreed that I would broadcast the official, public announcement of our new assignment before Christmas." Roosevelt paused as if to give Eisenhower an opening. Ike tried to remain stoic and attentive, but he did not speak. "We also agreed that your replacement at Allied Forces would be General Wilson, Sir Henry Wilson."

General Sir Henry Maitland 'Jumbo' Wilson, GBE, KCB, DSO, had been Commander-in-Chief of the Middle East since February. He was a respected combat commander. Allied Forces would continue combat operations in Italy and the Mediterranean region, while the Allied Expeditionary Force formed up for the anticipated OVERLORD landing in Normandy, France.

"Good man," Eisenhower added.

"Excellent. You'll have a couple of weeks to tidy things up for the handover of your command without being premature regarding your new assignment.

I'd like you to return to Washington after the announcement for discussions regarding your upcoming duties. You need to take some leave for time with your family. The prime minister and I would like you back in London by mid-January to assume command of the final planning and execution of OVERLORD."

"Yes sir. I think I can manage that."

"I'm certain you can, Ike. You deserve this opportunity. Now, I'm afraid I must call it a night. I need my beauty rest. I'll see you first thing in the morning on our flight to Malta."

"Yes sir. I'll be there."

President Roosevelt with General Eisenhower flew to Malta for ceremonies with Governor Field Marshal Lord Gort. The following day, Roosevelt and Eisenhower conducted an aerial tour with fighter cover of the HUSKY battlefields on Sicily. On the 9th, the president flew to Tunisia and then to Dakar, Senegal, where he boarded the USS *Iowa* for the return voyage to the United States. Roosevelt would arrive at the White House mid-morning on the 17th of December.

———

Wednesday, 8.December.1943
Allied Forces Headquarters Forward
Reggia di Caserta
Viale Douhet
Caserta, Campania, Liberated Italy
14:00 hours

After leaving the presidential party in Sicily, General Eisenhower flew to the Allied Forces forward headquarters. His chief of staff, General Beetle Smith, escorted him from the airfield to the royal palace that had been commandeered as the forward headquarters of Allied Forces and the 15th Army Group.

"The advance team has done an exemplary job, Beetle."

"Yes, they did, especially given the size and expanse of the palace. We're using only a small fraction of this place."

"So, we've room to grow."

Both generals laughed.

"Mark called just before you arrived," Smith said, referring to General Mark Clark, Commanding General, 5th Army. "His reconnaissance patrols indicate the Germans are going to defend a line anchored at Cassino. Monty's 8th Army is meeting increased resistance on the east coast. By the way, I know you've been busy with all the politics and the summit conferences. George is safely ensconced at his headquarters in London. He has publicly been recognized as the commanding general, First U.S. Army Group (FUSAG)."

"How is he handling his new role?" Eisenhower asked.

"I met with him in London a couple of weeks ago while you were tending to the leaders. He was grumbling, but in a nice way for George. He recognizes and accepts his place and duty in this affair. I'm convinced he knows precisely what is at stake. He'll do what we need him to do."

The knock on the door preceded the entry of Eisenhower's *Aide-de-Camp* Captain Julius 'Juli' Calhoun, USA, soon to be promoted to major. "Excuse me, General. A personal courier just arrived with a private message for you." Eisenhower nodded his consent.

An armed Army lieutenant with Intelligence Branch lapel insignia entered, saluted, and immediately opened a large, leather, across-the-shoulder satchel to extract an envelope. He handed the sealed envelope to General Eisenhower.

"Is any response required?" the general asked the courier.

"None was requested, sir."

"Very well. Thank you, Lieutenant. Safe journey."

"Thank you, General. By your leave, sir," he said and saluted. The lieutenant executed a precise about-face and departed.

Eisenhower opened the envelope and removed a single piece of notepaper.

From the President to Marshal Stalin
*   The immediate appointment of General Eisenhower*
to command of Overlord operation has been decided
upon.

Roosevelt

Cairo, Dec.7.43
Dear Eisenhower,
*   I thought you might like to save this as a memento.*
It was written very hurriedly by me as the final meeting
broke up yesterday, the president signing it immediately.
*   G.C.M.*

Eisenhower handed the note to Smith.

"Wow! This is from Marshall and the president. Congratulations, Ike. Justly deserved, I must say."

"Thanks, Beetle, but I'm afraid I must ask you to keep this private until the president's public announcement."

"Who'll replace you?"

"'Jumbo' Wilson."

"He should do nicely."

"My opinion as well. Now, let's go hear what the commanders and staff have to say."

A large, ornately appointed dining room had been transformed into a map room with an oversized conference table. All of the corps commanders and above were present. The gathering of generals would spend the next two hours presenting their status and the plans to break the German defenses.

—

Friday, 10.December.1943
USAAF Station 356
Saffron Walden, Essex, England
United Kingdom
15:35 hours

The 334FS launched a quarter of an hour late to plan but on cue from 8th Bomber Command. They climbed through the overcast by sections and joined up between layers. Pete turned the squadron of fighters to the proper course for their rendezvous point. They saw the bomber formation ahead of them enter another cloud layer. Peterson kept them at maximum range airspeed and entered a climbing left turn until they broke out on top of the intermediate layer. The weather reconnaissance aircraft informed them that the clouds were scattered to broken over the target. The CIRCUS 68 target was an odd-shaped railway-switching yard nestled in the bend of Sambre River just prior to the confluence with the Meuse River at Namur, Belgium.

Surprisingly, no enemy fighters rose to engage them. The squadron of B-17s encountered minimal flak, dropped their payload on their target and turned for home.

The squadron broke with the bombers with the English coast in sight. They landed back at Debden without firing a shot.

"That was an easy enough mission," noted Sweet Sweeny.

"Don't get used to it," Dusty Langford responded. "We've got hard fights ahead."

"We got the mission done," added Brian, "and it looked like the heavy metal covered the whole target and more. We all came home without a scratch. In my book, that's a good day."

"But we didn't do anything," protested Boy Williams.

Brian sat his chair down on all four legs and looked directly at Boy's eyes. "Did any enemy fighters engage our bombers?"

"No sir."

"Then we did our job. You new guys," Brian paused. He always had difficulty referring to them as young since they were still older by age than he was. Brian remained the youngest pilot in the squadron by age, but he also had the most combat experience of all the 4FG pilots. "You new guys will learn to be grateful for the easy missions when they come." For reasons he did not know, Brian felt an urge to be more talkative than usual. "We used to complain about flying shipping protection patrols, but at the height of the Battle of Britain, when we were flying four, five, six combat sorties a day for weeks on end, the shipping patrols did not seem so boring."

"Yeah, but isn't aerial combat what we were intended to do?" Antler Henricks asked.

"No. Our job is to do what our leaders need us to do," Brian responded with a little more hardness than he intended. He consciously softened his tone. "Sometimes we shoot up the ground. Sometimes we engage enemy fighters. Sometimes we just protect others by our presence above those we are assigned to protect. When we accomplish our assigned mission, we've done our job. You should feel good about doing your job."

"So you say," Boy said.

"You've both flown a CIRCUS to the border of Germany. You've seen the Germans waiting for us to bingo. Like the Skipper told us last week, we will transition to the P-51D late next month. From that point on, we will be escorting the bombers into all of Germany. I think it fairly safe to say that the degree of excitement on those missions will go up many times. After a few of those missions, I imagine you will soon be grateful for milk runs like we enjoyed today. We see far fewer enemy fighters these days than we did three years ago. I suspect that reality will change dramatically when we escort the bombers into Germany. Getting shot at by some Gerry bloke intent upon killing you is not so much fun, Boy. Be thankful for the easy ones."

Williams nodded his head in acknowledgment, if not agreement.

Brian looked at each of the other pilots around him. No one spoke. Brian leaned his chair back against the wall and closed his eyes, even though he did not feel a yearning for sleep. *They will learn.*

———

Friday, 24.December.1943
Allied Forces Headquarters Forward
Reggia di Caserta
Viale Douhet
Caserta, Campania, Liberated Italy
19:55 hours

The signal company assigned to Allied Forces Headquarters had set up the High Frequency (HF) radio unit. Generals Eisenhower and Smith sat in two straight back wooden chairs in front of the radio. The large palace room was arranged with chairs and couches along the periphery like a large dance hall. Rows of folding chairs had been prepared for the officers and men of the headquarters staff. Remote speakers had been connected and set on pedestals so that anyone who wanted to listen to the president's Fireside Chat would be able to hear. A broad mixture of uniforms filled the room—British, Canadian, Australian, New Zealander, Italian, French, and American Army and Navy personnel. The entire forward element of the headquarters staff had been invited, although not all of them chose to attend.

A sergeant appeared, switched on the radio, and fine-tuned the receiver. Swing music played, although somewhat scratchy. A few of the younger enlisted men moved to the music. When the song finished, crackling static replaced the music.

"Ladies and gentlemen, the president of the United States," the announcer stated.

After a short pause, the president spoke, "My Friends:

"I have recently returned from extensive journeying in the region of the Mediterranean and as far as the borders of Russia. I have conferred with the leaders of Britain and Russia and China on military matters of the present – especially on plans for stepping up our successful attack on our enemies as quickly as possible and from many different points of the compass."

Numerous muffled conversations broke out. The listeners tolerated the disturbances until a colonel stood and commanded, "Quiet, please! We're here to listen to the president."

"Within three days of intense and consistently amicable discussions, we agreed on every point concerned with the launching of a gigantic attack upon Germany.

"The Russian army will continue its stern offensives on Germany's Eastern front, the allied armies in Italy and Africa will bring relentless pressure on Germany from the south, and now the encirclement will be complete as great American and British forces attack from other points of the compass.

"The commander selected to lead the combined attack from these other points is General Dwight D. Eisenhower. His performances in Africa, in Sicily, and in Italy have been brilliant. He knows by practical and successful experience the way to coordinate air, sea, and land power. All of these will be under his control. Lieutenant General Carl Spaatz will command the entire American strategic bombing force operating against Germany.

"General Eisenhower gives up his command in the Mediterranean to a British officer whose name is being announced by Mister Churchill. We now pledge that new commander that our powerful ground, sea, and air forces in the vital Mediterranean area will stand by his side until every objective in that bitter theatre is attained.

"Both of these new commanders will have American and British subordinate commanders whose names will be announced to the world in a few days.

Several generals rose to pat Eisenhower on the back and offered congratulatory and encouraging words. The president continued to report on his high-level view of the world situation. Colleagues also took the opportunity to convey season's greetings. Eisenhower tried to be attentive to the well-wishes as he sought to absorb the president's words in the distance.

"On behalf of the American people -- your own people - I send this Christmas message to you, to you who are in our armed forces:

"In our hearts are prayers for you and for all your comrades in arms who fight to rid the world of evil.

"We ask God's blessing upon you -- upon your fathers, mothers, and wives and children -- all your loved ones at home.

"We ask that the comfort of God's grace shall be granted to those who are sick and wounded, and to those who are prisoners of war in the hands of the enemy, waiting for the day when they will again be free.

"And we ask that God receive and cherish those who have given their lives and that He keep them in honor and in the grateful memory of their countrymen forever.

"God bless all of you who fight our battles on this Christmas Eve.

"God bless us all. Keep us strong in our faith that we fight for a better day for humankind -- here and everywhere."

"Ladies and gentlemen, you have just heard the president of the United States," the announcer said.

Contemporary music took over the airwaves. The Signal Corps sergeant switched off the radio and departed.

"So, it's now official and out in the open," Smith said, placing his left hand on Ike's right shoulder.

"The president just told the world. No avoiding it now." Both men laughed. Eisenhower's expression instantly returned to seriousness. "Are you sure you won't go back with me . . . as least you could see Nory?"

"Thank you, Ike, but no. Duty calls. I'll close things up here, get you headed west, and then I'm going to London to check on George, and especially to get the headquarters organized."

"I've always admired your dedication, Beetle, but really . . . this next one will likely take us to the end. You really should go see Nory. We'll not likely get another chance for a year or more."

"She knows, Ike. She knows. I need to do this for myself, for you, for God, mother, and country."

"Very well, Beetle. I'll not argue. I'll head back to Algiers in the morning. I've got some personal things to close up as well. I'm going to head to Marrakech. Churchill invited me to spend New Year's Eve with him on my way back to the States. He has a fairly serious case of pneumonia he apparently contracted in Tehran and needs the dry air. I'll see you in mid-January in London. This is the big show, Beetle."

The room had cleared out by the time the two generals finished their chat. The remainder of the evening was devoted to saying good-bye. Some of them would transfer from Allied Forces to the new Allied Expeditionary Force for Operation OVERLORD. Others would remain in their current assignments. A few would be transferred to other assignments in theater and in the States.

—

Saturday, 25.December.1943
Standing Oak Farm
Winchester, Hampshire, England
United Kingdom
04:20 hours

The house in the early morning, pre-dawn hours remained quiet and dark as Charlotte and Brian sought to complete the last of their modest Christmas celebration arrangements with only the fire and candlelight for illumination. Brian brought the crackling fire to a moderate size to provide warmth for the winter chill and the flickering light they felt was sufficient for their task. Charlotte made them a pot of tea. They enjoyed a 'cuppa' by the fire before they got started. Jacob had felled the modest height, perfectly shaped conifer tree from their property a week ago. The crew had helped to festoon the tree with simple decorations. They managed to accumulate a simple present for each household member with a couple of additional gifts for the two boys.

The plan for the day called for a household celebration with Edith and Mabel, but especially for the children Ian and Todd. They allowed the children to stay up a little longer than usual last night to expend some of their excitement. They found sufficient tables and chairs to fill the living room, dining room, and kitchen for the family, and the crew and their families. Charlotte had gone overboard to provide the same food items for the workers who now lived in the converted house on the Brownfield property that served as a dormitory. Charlotte had wanted everyone to be together for what seemed like a hopeful Christmas, but the logistical reality had intervened.

"I forgot to tell you yesterday, Mary called me yesterday morning to inform us that she gave birth to a baby girl on the 14th of last month. They are all doing fine. She and John agreed to name her Charlotte Mary. It made me cry with the honor. I had invited them to join us for Christmas, but they already had plans."

"Is Air Vice Marshal Spencer on leave?"

"No. He apparently has his hands full supporting operations in Italy."

"Hopefully, they both agreed on the name."

Charlotte laughed. "A bit sensitive, are you?" Brian smiled and shook his head in the negative. "Yes, so Mary told me. She waited until they had agreed on the name before calling us. Thus, I must say congratulations to my stud," she raised her cup, "for doing your part." Brian shook his head again, as they both chuckled softly. "I also received the latest summary reports from Kansas. Bobby secured the contract for air support to our primary customer for next year. He felt very positive. He also indicated they were preparing a post-war plan to transition the airline under the presumption that the primary customer will not have a need. That seemed like a really wise project."

"Absolutely. Bobby's pretty sharp."

"I know I was impressed," Charlotte noted, "when we met them in Cornwall last month. I was sad that you had to run off, but meeting Bobby, Gerty, and Mister Hughes was the highlight of the journey."

"Not me?"

Charlotte placed her cup on the end table beside her chair. She went to and knelt in front of him, and then, she leaned forward to kiss her husband. "Are you OK?"

"Sure. Why?"

"You sound rather vulnerable, actually."

"No. I'm just kidding. I'm fine."

"You must never forget that I love you, Brian. It took me a while to develop those feelings, but I love you very much . . . to the deepest recesses of my heart."

Brian smiled. "That is always nice to hear. I have loved you since before you found the light." They both laughed softly, not wanting to wake anyone.

"OK, I'll grant you that much. I was only saying that I'm most grateful for the opportunity to meet Bobby, Gerty, Howard, and the others. Now, I have faces to the names. I love them. They were so nice, and Howard was a genuine charmer."

"I'm glad you got the opportunity." Brian finished his tea. "We'd better get our prep done before the kids start waking up. It's going to become chaos once that happens."

Charlotte finished her tea. "Before we do that, I'm reticent to ask, but how is the war going?"

Brian chuckled. "Pretty good, I'd say, which is why they gave us four days leave for Christmas. We're supposed to transition to a new fighter next month."

"What, no more jugs?"

They both laughed again. "Nope, just yours, darling."

Charlotte looked at Brian with a puzzled expression, not recognizing his euphemism.

Brian cupped his hands in front of his chest.

"Oh, you naughty boy," she said and stood. "Hop to it, my randy bloke."

They added nuts, dried fruit, and a few pieces of candy they could find to each person's mantle stocking, and they retrieved the last few presents from the bedroom closet for the boys and placed them under the tree. They stood back, surveyed the scene, and agreed they had completed what they had planned to do.

"You've done an exceptional job, sweetheart," Brian stated and kissed Charlotte. "Just in case I might not be so quick on the trigger, happy anniversary, two days early." Brian embraced her this time and kissed her again.

Charlotte was not satisfied and took a more intimate kiss with their embrace. She noticed the time and pulled back the blackout curtains. The sky of morning twilight lightened outside. The crew would be here soon for the morning milking and might arrive before the boys rose for Christmas morning. The family's day was about to begin. They were ready.

—

Friday, 31.December.1943
Flower Villa
Route d'ourika
Marrakech
Morocco
16:30 hours

"Welcome to Marrakech, Ike," Prime Minister Churchill said and extended his right hand to Eisenhower.

"Thank you, Mister Prime Minister," Ike replied as the two men shook hands.

"Please, Ike. In these private social settings, we're just two blokes cast into history's cauldron together. I think we can enjoy the familiar."

"Very well, Winston, it shall be."

Churchill led Eisenhower to an interior room looking out on an exquisite lush and colorful garden that occupied the square courtyard. "I thought champagne is in order to celebrate your new assignment."

Eisenhower accepted the flute. "How are you feeling? How is your recovery going?"

"The warm, dry air has worked wonders, as Lord Moran had suggested." Winston raised his glass. "A toast to our new supreme commander, Allied Expeditionary Force." They clinked glasses and took a good sip.

"That was a pretty serious case of pneumonia, I do believe."

"So Lord Moran informed me. I'm just grateful for being done with the incessant coughing. I still have an occasional cough, but at least I can finally sleep. I seem to be on the mend, thanks in no small measure to this lovely climate."

"We're all enormously thankful you're recovering. I can't imagine the upcoming campaign without your wisdom."

"Thank you, Ike. The feelings of respect are mutual. Now, speaking of the upcoming campaign, have you had the opportunity to study the current state of the COSSAC planning?"

"No, not yet. I've been occupied with the transition for the last month. Beetle Smith is in London working on the build-up of the AEF staff. We've discussed absorbing COSSAC and Fred Morgan becoming Beetle's deputy."

"Are you comfortable with that move?"

"Yes, of course. Fred is a very good man and an exceptional planner. As we discussed last month, I share your apprehension regarding the initial assault force's size and the terrain to support their rapid advance. From what I know so far, I think the logistics plan is closer to being settled, which gives me confidence we'll solve the initial assault force size issue."

"I'm glad you feel that way, Ike. I'll confess to you privately and personally that I've a mortal, bone-shaking fear of stalemate. If the Germans can stall our invasion, the advantage immediately shifts to them. Their lines of communication are far shorter and less vulnerable than ours. That reality alone scares the hell out of me."

"We can't avoid the difficulties of seaward transfer and resupply, which makes the air support plan all the more important. I've several concerns about the air plan, and I'm fairly set upon one command change."

"What is that?"

"I'm not satisfied with the aggressiveness of General Eaker. He's too . . . shall we say . . . by-the-book, when we'll need advanced, innovative thinking. The book hasn't been written for what we're about to do. We are and will be writing the book as we go."

"Who do you want instead?"

"General Doolittle."

"You mean the same Doolittle who just took command of the 15th Air Force last month?" Churchill asked.

"Yes."

"Well, we stole Admiral Cunningham from you, so I guess it's only fair we allow you to steal Doolittle from Jumbo Wilson."

"I'm glad you approve, Winston. I still need to convince General Marshall, Secretary Stimson, and perhaps even the president. I also want to bring many of the command and general staff officers with me. I'm comfortable working with them. We work well with each other. They're trusted colleagues."

"Yes, of course. I'll put in a good word with the president if you wish."

"Thank you for that, Winston, but I'd rather open the topic myself first, if he asks you, please, by all means. I'd appreciate your support. Beetle has my list for command and general staff officers. He's already begun working with your chiefs of staff. I intend to work the remaining American assignments while I'm in Washington."

"You should have whomever you believe will best serve our purposes," Churchill responded. "I can assure you that we'll do our part to support you. The staff is important because they'll coordinate the necessary work to achieve the objectives, but it's the plans that you'll execute this coming spring that matter the most. I'm comfortable with the logistics plan so far in our ability to move reinforcing units quickly across the beach and into battle. But the entire logistics plan depends upon a sufficient beachhead depth and expanse to protect the port facilities, and that all hangs upon the combat capacity of the initial assault force. We must solve that critical issue. I think the case for the Normandy beaches has been decided. Do you agree?"

"Yes, all the way around. Admiral Ramsay is working feverishly to improve the shipping and landing craft problem. I think you're well aware of the extraordinary efforts in the States to produce more landing craft in time."

"Yes, I am. President Roosevelt has been most generous with his support, even to the point of diverting replacement landing craft from the Pacific to OVERLORD. I believe we'll have the troops available if we can find the landing craft."

"The initial assault force and plans to secure the beachhead will be my highest priority once I take up my new posting."

"A related question, where do you see the strategic bombing campaign in your OVERLORD thinking?" asked the prime minister.

"To be frank, I think I'll have my hands full with the ground operations. Air and naval support are essential to the furtherance of the ground operations objectives. The strategic bombing effort is more distant but still applicable. For example, POINTBLANK that you and the president sanctioned a year ago at Casablanca is intent upon diminishing or eliminating the enemy's fighter capabilities. That objective supports the ground operations by removing the enemy's air-to-ground threat to our forces. Where there may be a conflict in demand for strategic bombing services, I believe the priority must be with the ground forces demands. I also support the assignment of Tooey Spaatz to lead the U.S. Strategic Air Forces initiative and directing the strategic bombing campaign on Germany. Jimmy Doolittle and Tooey work well together, and I believe I can depend upon them to manage our air support demands in proper balance with the strategic objectives."

"That makes sense, Ike. In more immediate and practical terms, when are you scheduled to depart on your return flight?"

"The pilot wants to take off at 05:30, so I need to leave here before five."

"There should be no problem with that. We'll just celebrate a perhaps not prosperous but successful New Year until you must depart."

Eisenhower laughed and infected Churchill.

Sarah Churchill, who had been with her father since they left England last month, joined them for dinner and the social intercourse of the evening, midnight, and early morning, although she had no reason to stay up all night with her father. They did not have fireworks or noise-generators, but they did have French champagne and Russian caviar as they celebrated what they hoped would be a much better New Year. Once the celebratory words faded, Sarah excused herself and went to bed. Churchill and Eisenhower turned their talking to family, and the days of peace they both hoped lay beyond the years of war.

Friday, 31.December.1943
Hotel Dorchester
No.53 Park Lane
Mayfair, London, England
United Kingdom
23:30 hours

The squadron had been on alert all day without being launched. They were finally released at sunset. By prior agreement, they all made their way into London. Several of the wives and girlfriends were staying at the hotel, including Charlotte, who had already checked into their room. Brian reunited with his wife in the room. The urge to divert their attention from the evening's plan struck them hard, but Charlotte proved the stronger one this time.

They straightened their clothes. They kissed one more time before leaving the room. Brian held Charlotte's shoulder in front of him. He looked deeply into her gorgeous, blue-gray eyes, smiled, and said, "Happy fourth day after our fourth anniversary, my sweet. I'm so blessed to be married to you."

"Oh, you silly man. I love you very much. Now, we need to get downstairs if we are going to celebrate New Year's with your mates."

The hotel-sponsored New Year's Eve party was being held in the ballroom. An array of people filled the ballroom right up to the edge of the dance floor. A small swing band played in the far corner. Most of his mates were present and apparently already well lubricated. Introductions were completed. Charlotte had met some of the pilots but none of the wives and girlfriends. A few of the couples started to dance. Brian was not confident of his dancing skills, and Charlotte did not feel much better. The festive spirit dominated all of them, and they all reveled in the celebratory sensations.

Brian saw Lady Marilyn Morrison first across the room and raised his right arm to wave. She made eye contact, turned her head, and then made her way through the crowd toward Brian and Charlotte.

"Welcome to the Dorchester celebration, Lady Morrison," Brian shouted over the din. "What brings you to the Dorchester."

Marilyn hugged and kissed Charlotte, and then she delivered the same to Brian. "Jeremy ran into Jonathan at Shepherd's yesterday evening, and Harness mentioned your party. So, we thought we would crash the party."

"I'm glad you did. So, Jeremy is here?"

"Yes, somewhere. I've lost him. Linda and Jonathan are here too."

"How is married life treating you?" Charlotte asked.

"Pretty good, when I'm home. My job keeps me in the air far more than Jeremy as the base commander. He will have been in that job for two years next month. He also says there are rumblings of promotion and assignment to Fighter Command."

"Stanmore?"

"Yes. I'm not too keen on the idea. I like having a home—a place to drop anchor. Hamble has been like home to us. Jeremy's never really owned a home. When he needs to get away, he's just been going to his brother's place."

"Nice place to go, I must say," Charlotte added.

"Yes, it sure is, but it's not his . . . not ours."

"Are you two going to put down roots somewhere?" asked Charlotte.

"We're talking about it. We've our eyes on a couple of places near Hamble."

"Not far from us," Charlotte observed. "We should . . ."

"Ladies and gentlemen, and I use that term loosely," Pete Peterson said loudly at the microphone when the band stopped. "You've five minutes to fill your glasses so we can celebrate properly."

Brian flagged a waiter with a bottle. All three of their glasses were not quite filled. As the waiter finished, Brian heard Jeremy.

"There you are," he shouted, "you wily little weasel." Jeremy hit Brian in the shoulder. He kissed Marilyn, and then he looked like he had second thoughts. Jeremy grasped her, bent her back slightly, and kissed her far more intimately and passionately than expected. As he righted her, he looked at Brian and Charlotte. "She is such a gem."

"Oh, stop, Jeremy. That's just the alcohol talking."

"Yes, it is, and I've no shame in my love for you, my gorgeous dolly bird."

"Ah, found you," came Jonathan's familiar voice from behind Brian.

They all turned to see Linda and Jonathan winding through the throng of people. All of them embraced and kissed.

"Looks like we made it just in time," Linda announced.

"The hour has arrived," Pete announced. "Grab your honey and your glass." He paused for the second hand on the clock to catch up. Brian held his champagne glass in his right hand, wrapped his left arm around Charlotte's shoulders, and kissed her forehead. "Here we go," Pete said. "Ten, nine, eight, seven, six, five, four, three, two, one, Happy New Year, everybody." Cheers filled the room. Glasses clinked. They all embraced and kissed again.

"Happy New Year, sweetheart," Brian whispered into Charlotte's left ear as they held each other.

Someone in the crowd began to sing, "Should auld acquaintance be forgot and never brought to mind?" The ballroom quickly picked up the familiar refrain. After several stanzas, the words rapidly began to blur and fade away. A few diehards pressed on with the traditional Scottish song of remembrance and renewal.

As the noise began to dwindle, Brian turned to Jonathan. "I'm glad you and Linda could make it."

"Likewise, my friend. We don't get to see you much these days, certainly not as we did back during the battle."

"Nope, those were hard days, though."

"Yes, they were, but they were good days to have survived."

"You got that right. How's your family?"

"Mum & Dad are doing quite well. Rosemary completed her residency and is now a full-fledged medical doctor. She is practicing at Watlington Hospital, Oxford, if you're ever in the area. She would love to see you."

"I'm usually headed south and east these days."

"As are we."

"Please say hi and send along my best wishes to your family, including Rosemary. I do miss them."

"Maybe when this whole sordid affair is concluded, we can reunite at Carlingon Castle for a weekend."

"That would be delightful."

The crowd began thinning quickly.

Jeremy said, "We've a suite. Why don't we take this little gathering upstairs?"

Brian looked at Charlotte, who shook her head ever so slightly. "We'll pass, Jeremy, but thank you for the invitation. I think we'll call it a night. Perhaps we can all get together for breakfast."

The three couples agreed to meet at nine in the hotel's dining room. Jeremy had another day of leave, but Jonathan and Brian had to be back to their bases by noon. Charlotte would travel with Marilyn and Jeremy. She would get off the train in Winchester while the Morrisons continued to Southampton.

Charlotte and Brian made it to their room. Brian immediately set the nightstand alarm clock since they both were tired and did not want to miss their breakfast date with friends. They shucked their clothes and promptly set about their private celebration. Sleep and their warm embrace claimed the two lovers.

—

Saturday, 1.January.1944
Flower Villa
Route d'ourika
Marrakech
Morocco
04:45 hours

Prime Minister Churchill stood in the villa's gated courtyard with General Eisenhower. The general wore his waistcoat uniform jacket that now bore his name. The prime minister remained attired in his light blue siren suit, the overalls that Churchill often chose for convenience and comfort. The pre-dawn hour was unusual but not unprecedented. Both men were quite accustomed to odd hours. Neither of them had gone to bed after their celebration of the New Year, the first New Year since the war began that the end might be within reach.

"Thank you for spending your last day in theater with me, Ike."

"Thank you for your gracious invitation, Prime Minister, and it was an honor to celebrate the New Year with you, and this is a delightful place to spend a day of hope."

"I eagerly anticipate your return and your assumption of supreme command. You shall lead us on this grand crusade to liberate Europe from this damnable Nawzee scourge."

"Thank you, sir. Like someone once said, I shall return." Both men laughed at the offhand reference to the now-famous proclamation of Ike's one-time boss. The two men shook hands. "See you in two weeks, Winston. Happy New Year. Please pass my good-bye to Sarah. Enjoy the rest of your stay in Marrakech and complete your recovery."

Eisenhower took his seat in the back of the staff car. They departed for the airport a few minutes away.

The C-54 Skymaster in VIP configuration took off as soon as the general, and his small entourage were comfortably aboard and secured. Their baggage had been loaded earlier. The aircraft would take the shortest and quickest route back to Washington, DC, across the South Atlantic to Brazil, and then north across the Caribbean. Eisenhower would spend a couple of days at the Pentagon, a week on leave with his family, and another few days to receive guidance and instructions from the president, the secretary of War, and the chief of staff. Upon returning to England, General Eisenhower would assume command of the Allied Expeditionary Force, as supreme commander for Operation OVERLORD and the final push to defeat Nazi Germany.

—

About the Author

Cap Parlier

—

Cap and his wife, Jeanne, live peacefully in the warmth and safety of Arizona—the Grand Canyon state. Their four children have established their families and are raising their grandchildren. Their grandchildren are growing and maturing nicely with two college graduates so far and another in her sophomore year.

Cap is a proud graduate of the U.S. Naval Academy [USNA 1970], an equally proud retired Marine aviator, Vietnam veteran, and experimental test pilot. He finally retired from the corporate world to devote his time to his passion for writing and telling a good story. Cap uses his love of history to color his novels. He has numerous other projects completed and, in the works, including screenplays, historical novels as well as atypical novels at various stages of the creation process.

—

Interested readers may wish to visit his website at: http://www.parlier. com for his essays and other items or subscribe to his weekly Blog: "*Update from the Sunland.*" Cap can be reached at:

Cap@Parlier.com

—

Saint Gaudens, Saint Gaudens Press and the Winged Liberty colophon are trademarks of Saint Gaudens Press.